# The Magic of Redemption

# Isles of Illusion

Book One: The Promise of Deception
Book Two: The Art of Misdirection
Book Three: The Magic of Redemption

# The Magic of Redemption

## Isles of Illusion

By

## Jessica Sly

MOUNTAIN**BROOK**FIRE

# Dedication

To my sister, Meghan

# Chapter One



*London, 1916*

WISPY TENDRILS OF DARKNESS CURLED OUT from beneath the door before me. Shivering, I braced against the wall of shadows that I sensed opposing me from the other side, knowing that I needed to venture into it if I were to find the answers I sought. The dying evening light and brisk April air exacerbated my trembling as I reached for the knob, and my long wool sleeves barely seemed to block any of the chill.

Eerie creaks halted my hand and drew my attention to the suspended sign above the door. Faded letters spelled out "The Molly Malone," and a rush of adrenaline and memories lit my veins on fire. I hadn't set foot in this establishment since that fateful evening when the alluring Irishman Cornelius Marx—or rather, Ciaran O'Conner—had tried seducing me and almost succeeded.

My then-fiancé Baze had intervened, but that led him to discover that I had been sneaking around behind his back, investigating a series of murders without his knowledge. As I fled the scene, drugged and vulnerable, an anonymous attacker struck, attempting to strangle me and snapping my father's pearl necklace in the process. Fortunately, Baze and his partner at Scotland Yard, Bennett, managed to save my life and preserve the precious heirloom by recovering a single pearl and mounting it into my wedding ring.

Despite the positive outcome, the memory still stung.

I hesitated, tapping my heel on the pavement. Mere months ago, nothing could have ever compelled me to return, to relive that shame—that is, until I learned that the barkeep, Lewis Riordan, harbored a secret related to Cornelius, Shay O'Sullivan, and the mind-bending saga in which we were ensnared.

Metropolitan Police patrols had observed Riordan meeting with known members of the Irish Republican Brotherhood—a nationalist organization under whose name Cornelius carried out his misdeeds—which meant Riordan was likely a member as well. Not only that, but undercover informants had recovered letters between the barkeep and IRB members stationed across the channel in Ireland. One such correspondence alluded to a plan by the IRB-backed Irish Volunteers to launch an attack against the opponents of home rule and self-government.

And that correspondence came from Shay O'Sullivan himself.

Anger curled my hands into fists. Though it had been nearly two years since our confrontation in Bath, the Irishman's steely presence and foreboding words stirred relentless unease and urgency in me. From the moment of Cornelius's and my first encounter at the engagement gala, Shay had been the master puppeteer pulling the strings, the one who had taught Cornelius everything he knew—everything from his proficiency in sleight of hand to his wicked ability to control the wills of others with his mind.

Shay was the reason Bennett, my father, and so many more innocent people were dead. He was the reason I still couldn't achieve a restful night without waking in a cold sweat. He was the reason the world never quite felt safe.

Everything led back to Shay. If I could stop him, then I could stop the torment for good.

A drunken man behind me grunted and shooed me out of the way so he could stumble inside. The lively music and the warm smells of hearty stew and abundant spirits assailed me briefly as the door swung shut. Embers of hope sputtered to life, but I reminded myself that it was impossible for Finn to be the musician behind the feisty uilleann pipe commanding the pub. He had returned to Ireland after Cornelius's death, and I prayed he was leading a full and happy life.

If I were a rational woman, I would wait for the promised police backup—they were far overdue for arrival—but the longer I delayed, the more opportunities Mr. Riordan had to escape. What would it hurt if I simply started the conversation early? I knew how to be discreet. Perhaps I could weaken his guard and prime him for the moment when the real interrogators would arrive.

Mind made up, I stiffened and pushed inside the pub. Energetic music and robust banter just about bowled me over as I weaved through tables and chairs and slid onto one of the rickety stools lining the bar.

Large though not overweight, Riordan barely had space to shuffle about behind the counter. His meaty forearms rippled with firm muscles as he swiped the inside of a mug with a rag. After serving up three frothy beers to a squat man, he turned toward me. His narrowed, beady eyes roved up and down my body, and his mouth twisted.

Alarm nipped at me. Did he recognize me? Surely not. Last time, I had borrowed plain attire from my maid so I could blend in to the crowd, whereas tonight, I donned a full ensemble of expensive jewelry, a tailored blue walking suit, and feathered hat. Besides, three years had passed since we saw each other—more than enough time for memories to cloud.

With a sniff and a twitch of his bulbous nose, Riordan leaned toward me. "I think yer in the wrong place, missy."

"I am quite aware of my surroundings," I said with an even, hopefully authoritative, tone. "I'll have a Guinness, if you please."

He chortled gruffly as he prepared the drink. After he placed it in front of me, I took a few quick gulps, aware that he analyzed my every movement. Beer still wasn't my preferred drink of choice, but I kept my expression pleasant as the bitter liquid coated my tongue.

Leveling a stare, Riordan drummed his fingers on the bar's wooden surface. "So, what be bringin' a pretty young Englishwoman out to mix with our kind?"

I nodded toward the musicians performing in the far corner. "I came to listen. The Irish know no rival in the realm of entertainment."

He snorted. "I would've pegged you as a Bach or Beethoven type."

"You judge too quickly, sir." I placed a hand on my chest in mock incredulity. "I find Irish music far more engaging than the classical composers. In fact, I'm quite inspired by the culture and good-natured people of Ireland, and I have been troubled by the dissent between our two lands, especially with the Great War threatening to make the conflict worse." As I lifted the mug to my mouth, I peered over the top of it and said, "You wouldn't happen to have news from your homeland, would you?"

Riordan flipped another empty cup and wiped the inside, features pensive. "What be you wantin' to know?"

"How are the people?" As the music crescendoed, the fiddle racing against the beat of the bodhrán, I raised my voice. "I know that, for the most part, Ireland has avoided much of the fighting, but they aren't free from threat. I have prayed that with the reintroduction of the Home Bill, the aggression would end and everyone would become more unified. Do you think that's possible?"

"You tell me, missy." He guffawed. "On one side, you've got the Irish Volunteers usin' every lick o' force to push home rule through, and on the other, you've got the Ulster Volunteers tryin' to shoot down any attempt at self-governance—sometimes literally. And the Irish people are caught right in the middle—nothing more than collateral if they get in the way. That sound like unification to you?"

"Surely the passing of the Home Bill would stop that."

Cords of muscle in Riordan's neck flexed. "That's *if* it passes, but we're not gettin' our hopes up. The House of Lords struck it down twice before, so there be no reason to believe this time will be any different. The British have got their boots pressed firmly into our backs, and they want to keep it that way."

"Regardless, I wish the Volunteers wouldn't resort to such violence." I squeezed the course mug between my palms. "These forces claim to be helping the people, but how can they believe that if the battle leads to the suffering of those same people?"

Setting down the mug, Riordan squinted. With outstretched arms, he placed his palms on the bar and leaned forward. "This isn't your fight. Why do you care?"

I tapped a finger against the mug and chose my next words carefully. "My father devoted his life to helping the Irish achieve peace and establish home rule. He died for it. I merely want to know that he didn't die in vain."

Riordan's voice grew low and gravelly. "People die in vain all the time, missy. Can't help it if your father was among them. Such be the way of the world."

My throat tightened as I recognized the same words Cornelius had once uttered. "Well, that's a positively grim view of it. Forgive me if I hold to something a little more hopeful."

Riordan tilted his head and sniffed. "You look a mite familiar. Do I know you from somewhere?"

Prickles of warning niggled at me. I was prodding too far, rubbing his patience too thin. How much longer could I feign innocence before he uncovered my motives?

Remaining on the stool, I managed to keep my voice light. "No, I'm afraid not. This is my first time visiting your fine establishment, Mr. Riordan."

He blinked, then gave an unsettling smile. "How be you knowin' my name if you've never been before?"

The erratic drumming of the bodhrán vibrated in my chest, and the tin whistle shrieked in my ears. *I've ruined it. He recognizes me. I need to get away. Quickly.*

"I'm afraid I have tarried far too long." Summoning a confident smile, I reached into my reticule and tossed some coins onto the bar to compensate for my drink. "Thank you for your hospitality and for answering my prying questions, but I'm afraid I must go."

As I stood and turned, Riordan seized my wrist. "Why're you in such a hurry?" he murmured with raised eyebrows. "I thought you came to enjoy the music. We've quite the program planned for tonight."

Fear compressed my lungs. "Yes, well, I believe I have had my fill. Besides, my husband is outside waiting."

Riordan's firm belly jiggled in a laugh. "You're tellin' me a proper gentleman would allow his pretty defenseless wife to enter a grody dump like this all by her lonesome?" His gaze dragged down my body and back to my face. "I highly doubt it."

Words barely came, but I managed to whisper, "Unhand me."

His grin widened. "Or what?"

Curling my hand into a fist, I spoke louder and clearer. "I said, unhand me."

Riordan stared, rigid and unblinking, but after a pause, he opened his hand to release my wrist.

*That worked? I didn't think that would work.*

Rolling my shoulders back, I nodded, mumbled, "Good night, sir," and spun toward the door. Harried steps carried me outside and around the corner. My heart pounded as the air cooled my flushed cheeks. Nausea overturned my stomach, but through sheer stubbornness, I forced my body to keep itself in check.

That had been close—and foolish—but what was done was done. At least I had gleaned a little more information than before. The two opposing forces in Ireland were growing in strength, and considering the status of the Home Bill and its two previous failures, it seemed their conflict might soon come to a head. What might Shay's role in that be?

Faint but heavy footsteps reached my ears. I spun.

Riordan barreled straight for me.

I cried out and twirled to flee, but he slammed into me, snaked his huge arm around my neck, and wrenched me toward the alley. The hat flew from my head. He swept my feet out from under me, and my neck popped as he used it to keep me upright. I gasped, breathless, as his thick forearm crushed my windpipe.

"Thought I wouldn't recognize you?" His putrid breath beat against my ear. "Thought you could turn up and poke about without consequences?"

I clawed at his arm, twisted my head, pumped my feet—anything to loosen his hold—but he only flexed harder, cutting off my ability to make a single sound. *Don't let me go out like this. I've come too far.*

"You were with Cornelius, weren't you? You were the one I drugged. I heard you bested him in the end." He wheezed in morbid laughter. "Well, you won't be doin' the same to me, missy."

His arm throttled my neck harder, and my spine cracked painfully as black spots danced before my eyes. Numbness needled my legs. I sagged into him. How could I die like this? How—

Something metal clicked. Riordan stiffened.

Then a low, commanding voice set my hopes alight.

"Release my wife. Now."

Chapter Two

Despite the pain, I craned my neck and managed to glimpse my rescuer. Baze held his arm outstretched and pistol pressed against Riordan's temple. The white-hot ferocity in his eyes kindled fear even in me.

None of us moved. Though the barkeep had stopped actively choking me, his arm remained in place and prevented me from speaking. Baze's gaze flicked to me for the briefest moment before his expression darkened and he stepped closer to Riordan, twisting the weapon's barrel farther into the man's flesh.

"I said, release her." His voice sent a chill up my spine. "I won't ask you again."

Ever so slowly, Riordan's muscles loosened, and when he finally let go, my numb legs failed to recover quickly enough. I fell hard on my side. Baze twitched as though wanting to assist me, but he kept his eyes and gun trained on the Irishman. "Rollie, cuff him," he ordered.

Seemingly appearing out of nowhere, Sergeant Rollie Bounds sidestepped Baze and snatched Riordan's arms. Though tiny in comparison to the brutish man, Rollie expertly clacked the cuffs into place and proffered his own weapon to keep Riordan in check.

With the man incapacitated, Baze finally dropped his rigid stance. Stashing his pistol, he knelt by my side and helped me sit up. "Are you all right? Are you hurt?" he said in a rush as he brushed hair from my face. He examined my scraped palms and then tilted my chin upward to look at my throat.

"I'm okay." I pushed his hands away, coughed, and massaged the raw skin of my neck. "If I had a shilling for every time I've been choked in this alley, I'd have two shillings." I grimaced. "Which isn't a lot, I'll grant you, but it's extremely odd that it's happened twice."

Baze shifted his jaw, annoyance sparking in his eyes. "And if I had a shilling for every time I've had to come to your aid after you'd charged headfirst into a place you shouldn't have ventured, I'd have far more than two."

Indignation rose. "Well, I wouldn't have had to go in if you hadn't taken so long to show up."

"Don't pin this on me." He aimed a thumb at his chest. "I told you to wait. He was scheduled to work all night, so he would have stayed put long enough for us to arrive. You *wanted* to go in because you get off on the thrill."

"So what if I do?" I shrugged.

He huffed. "What happens when you get yourself into a situation there's no coming back from, hmm? What happens when I'm not here to bail you out?"

"That won't happen. I have no doubt you'll always find a way to reach me if I'm in trouble."

"Al, you know that's not a realistic—"

"Shut up!" Riordan grumbled. "God Almighty, you're annoying."

I wrinkled my nose at him. "And you're a pig."

Baze rolled his eyes. "Adelynn, you should really try not to aggravate the man who just tried to kill you."

"Aggravation is the *least* he deserves."

With a sigh, Baze shifted and slid his arms beneath my knees and behind my back, but as he braced to rise, I slammed a halting hand on his shoulder. "What are you doing? I can stand perfectly fine."

He looked at me skeptically, but I wriggled out of his hold and used him as support as I wobbled up onto my feet. He rose with me, keeping wary hands outstretched as I took my first step, then two.

The third sent a wave of numbness up my legs and buckled my knees, throwing me straight back into Baze's supportive arms. His eyes twinkled as he pursed his lips.

I clenched my teeth and waved a finger in his face. "Very well. You may carry me, but I forbid you to speak about this again."

"Yes, dear." Baze's smile and single dimple broke through as he swept me up into his arms.

Baze scrubbed his hands down his face and leaned back in his seat. After seeing Adelynn home—where he prayed she would stay or God help him—he had made for New Scotland Yard and prepared for Riordan's interrogation. Try as he might, though, Baze couldn't coax anything out of him. The Irish brute had screwed up his crooked mouth, crossed his bulging arms, and refused to budge. Adelynn's foolhardy stunt had thrust him into high alert and sealed his lips tight.

So much for their lead.

Feeling the full weight of his weariness, Baze heaved himself out from behind his desk, shoved his hands in his pockets, and hobbled down the hall, leaving his cane behind. With every intervention and treatment tried and still no improvement, it was clear his leg would forever remain a husk of what it once was, flaring up every now and again to remind him of the malformation it suffered. Fortunately, he was learning to avoid the movements that aggravated the muscle and could navigate the day-to-day with minimal intrusion.

However, a half-healed injury was still an injury, and even though Baze had thrown himself deep into his work since returning a few months after his honeymoon, he always seemed to get stuck with the simplest of cases. Superintendent Whelan hadn't said anything definitive about it, but Baze could read between the lines. He was all but useless in the field now, especially if it came down to a foot chase. He probably shouldn't have even been tasked to go after Riordan, but he had insisted on being included.

Rollie, God bless him, tried to keep Baze's spirits up, but for some reason, the junior policeman's encouragement was never enough to pacify the negativity Baze harbored within. Though they had been partnered for nearly two years now, they had yet to form a bond that burrowed below the surface. For many years, Bennett had poured into Baze as both a mentor and a friend, but now that Baze was serving as the same to Rollie, he wasn't sure how to balance the two roles. He had barely figured out how to navigate his own trials. How could he possibly speak into the life of a younger man?

Venturing farther into the hallway, Baze came upon a row of large photographs hanging on the wall. He stopped in front of his own unit. The black-and-white image, though many years old, was as familiar to Baze as the day it was taken. He'd been a constable at the time, and he stood dressed in the formal uniform and helmet just like the rest of them.

Next to him stood Bennett, a hint of his familiar cheeky grin creasing his mouth even though they'd been ordered to attention.

Baze's throat clamped shut as a wave of emotion rolled through him. He pounded his fist on the wall beside the photograph. Beckoning memories hauled his thoughts back in time to police training.

The moment he had turned eighteen, his father shipped him off to learn self-defense to atone for a vicious attack and robbery he endured and barely survived when he was sixteen. As Baze had stood in the line of other trainees, trembling and scared out of his skin, that's when Bennett found him. Bennett had joined the Metropolitan Police a few years prior—he always had a heart for helping people and righting injustices in the world—and happened to have volunteered to assist in training new recruits. From that moment forward, Bennett never let Baze out of his sight, walking him through the drills, explaining procedures and terminology, and serving as his defender when more veteran trainees tried to haze him with cruel pranks.

Though Baze's father had been the one to force him into the field, Bennett was the reason Baze had survived police training, and he was the reason Baze had stayed in the profession for as long as he had.

However, now that Bennett was gone and his father no longer dictated his life, what was keeping him with the Met? What more was left for him here? What good could he—a cripple—do as an inspector?

His injury kept him mostly chained to his desk, and the horrors he had seen and the lives he had taken—criminal though they had been—were beginning to wear on him.

But if he wasn't an inspector, what else would he do? It was all he knew. Plus, he had a wife for whom he needed to provide.

Baze sighed as he stared at Bennett's image. "What would you tell me to do?" he whispered.

The low clearing of a throat snapped Baze out of his reverie. He backed away from the photograph and turned. Whelan leaned with his back against the wall and puffed a cigarette to life. Releasing a stream of smoke, he said, "I must not give you enough work if you've got the time to be gallivanting through the halls."

"Sorry, sir." Baze straightened. "I was merely stretching my legs. I'll return to work shortly."

Whelan rolled the cigarette between his fingers and coughed. "What are you doing here, Ford?"

Baze frowned. "Sir?"

"You heard me."

"Well, I finished an interrogation earlier, and then I plan to—"

"No. What are you doing *here*? Your mind is clearly elsewhere. Has been for a while now."

Baze clenched his jaw. Whelan knew the circumstances surrounding Baze's abrupt entry into the Met. That wasn't a secret. But Baze had kept his emotions close to his chest and managed to evade scrutiny—or at least he had thought. How should he answer? If he were truthful and revealed his doubts, would the superintendent hold that against him? Or would the man understand?

Stroking the bridge of his nose, Baze formed and measured his words carefully. "My mind has been in many places of late. The past several years have caused me to reflect upon what life looks like for my wife and I . . . and what I might want it to look like." Baze let his hand fall limp at his side. "I apologize if that has distracted me from my work. I shall be more diligent."

Whelan folded his arms and looked down at the floor. "I've mentored and led dozens of men—men who held no other aspirations outside of working for the Met. They lived and breathed their duties. They faced obstacles, yes, but they were always surefooted, never doubting their decisions to be here." Head bent forward, Whelan eyed Baze from under his low, bushy brows. "I'm considering you for a promotion, Ford. Detective chief inspector."

A promotion. More work. More responsibility. More doubt.

With air draining from his lungs, Baze managed to murmur, "Thank you, sir. I'm honored."

"Are you?" Whelan pushed off the wall and drilled into him with penetrating eyes. "I'm planning to put in the recommendation with the higher-ups in a month, but that's all it is. A recommendation." He glanced toward Bennett's image, then back at Baze. "You've got to decide what you want, Ford. Think long and hard on it. Because I'm not about to put the lives of my men in the hands of someone whose heart's not in it."

Whelan lumbered back down the hall, leaving Baze speechless. The superintendent had struck truth. Baze's heart *wasn't* in it—and hadn't been for some time. Though he couldn't simply flip the switch of his motivations, he felt the pressure to quickly make a decision prodding his conscience. Guilt twisted his stomach. Bennett had been posthumously promoted to detective chief inspector, an aspiration he had long endeavored to achieve. Motivated or not, how could Baze throw away something that Bennett had never been able to do?

# Chapter Three

With the previous night's attack still fresh and niggling at my mind, I set out near midafternoon for my scheduled tea at the Fords' residence, hoping it might distract me from the chaos at hand. To my delight, Emily arrived at the same moment as I, her young but sprouting son, Basil Allan, clinging to her hand yet walking on confident feet. He was a picture of adorable decorum in his brown woolen suit composed of knickerbockers, stockings, waistcoat, and crisp white shirt.

Brightening, I made to call out, but I barely had time to utter a syllable before Basil Allan shouted, "Addy!" He pulled out of his mother's hand, scampered across the pavement with surprising speed, and collapsed toward my legs.

I bent my knees and caught him. "Oh, you're getting so fast."

Emily laughed as she approached. "That is quite the understatement. Last week, the little nipper managed to escape during his bath and race straight out the door, his pink little bottom hanging out for all to see."

Basil Allan giggled and grinned up at me, his bright hazel eyes large and captivating. "Mama couldn't catch me."

"Couldn't she? Well, I'm sure you are the fastest boy in London." With a beaming smile, I swung him up into my arms, then grunted under his weight. "You must be the heaviest too!" I poked his round tummy. He squealed and tucked his head against my shoulder.

I squeezed him tight and leaned my cheek against his soft head, basking in his sweet toddler scent and enjoying the feel of his small, squishy body pressed against my bosom. Over the months leading up to his third birthday, his white-blond hair had begun darkening to a brown hue that more closely resembled his father's, and with Emily's curl contributing mild texture to his locks, it was clear he was going to be quite the handsome charmer when he matured.

Basil Allan shifted and placed a hand on my chest, and his tiny palm sent a pang through my heart as though poking a dormant bruise. Baze and I had already been married two years, but the conversation regarding children had barely begun—and not for a lack of my trying. Basil Allan's rapid growth heightened the urgency within me. He would be a young man before we realized it. With each day that passed, my longing grew, my longing to be a mother, to watch Baze embody the role of a father, and to raise our children alongside Emily and Bennett's son.

"He is growing far too quickly." I sighed and patted his back as the aching knot of yearning in my stomach wound tighter.

Emily's eyes softened, and her voice lowered. "You still have time."

I swallowed hard. "You are kind, Emily, but my hope grows thin."

She nodded and thoughtfully scratched her son's back. "I do not wish to insert myself into your marital issues, so I will merely ask— have you talked to him?"

"Of course! I have brought it up time and time again, but he—"

"Let me rephrase." She smiled faintly. "Have you listened to him? Have you asked him for his thoughts and then simply let him speak?" When I remained silent, biting my lip, she continued. "Marriage is about compromise, though it is not always easy. Bennett and I argued our fair share, and whenever we disagreed, I found that listening solved more problems than any discourse I might add."

Bitterness soured my stomach. "Why should I listen to him when he hasn't taken the time to listen to me?"

"Adelynn." Her voice grew stern. "Relationships are not a place for keeping score. He's your husband. Talk to him."

Before I could respond, the butler opened the door and invited us inside. We followed him into the parlor where my mother and Baze's mother, Frances Ford, were already seated and engaged in polite dialogue.

When we entered, Mrs. Ford leaped to her feet. "Welcome, dears." She gave Emily and me each a small squeeze before stealing Basil Allan from my arms. Though he wasn't her grandson by blood, the older woman doted upon him as though he were her own. "How is my handsome gentleman today?" she cooed and tickled his chin.

Mother greeted me with a light embrace. "It is wonderful to see you, Adelynn," she whispered into my ear.

"You as well," I replied, feeling a tinge of guilt. When had I last come to see her? In the busyness of settling into married life and losing myself in the search for Shay O'Sullivan, I often forgot to carry out the common courtesy of visiting family, my mother included.

She pulled back and smiled as she caressed my face. She looked as pristine as ever, with her fair, graying hair pinned into a genteel updo and a green-and-gold tea dress drawing out the stark emerald color of her eyes. From this close, I could see fine lines etched into her face, though they only served to accentuate her beauty.

After the four of us settled into our chairs, the maids brought trays of tea, cucumber sandwiches, and scones with clotted cream, but my stomach churned, the mix of scents and tender discussion of children banishing my appetite.

We began the pleasant affair with small talk, commenting on the weather, giving updates about our day-to-day activities, and hearing of family happenings, including that Baze's eldest brother, Percy, was due to receive a new grandchild at any moment.

"Children are an incredible gift." Mrs. Ford bounced Basil Allan on her lap and allowed him to nibble on a scone. Despite her age, her hair retained much of its black pigment, though her white streaks had become thicker of late. "I am thrilled Percy is about to bless me with yet another great-grandchild, but I do hope I will not have to wait much longer to meet my next *grand*child. Besides, I am sure Basil Allan would appreciate a close playmate."

Though she said it jovially, her words may as well have been a dagger plunged into my chest. I had braced for the possibility of this topic rearing its condemning head—considering Mrs. Ford's obsession with Basil Allan, how could it not?—but I hadn't anticipated it to arrive this soon. At least my mother was well aware of my feelings on the matter and chose to refrain from adding her own commentary.

"Oh, I think Basil Allan is quite enjoying being the only child around." Emily's interjection doused me in relief. She snorted softly. "He is positively spoiled. I don't know how well he would handle sharing the attention."

"He will simply have to learn." Mrs. Ford tsked and smiled at me. "I merely bring this up for your sake, dear. Some ladies at the auxiliary have started inquiring, and I imagine other tongues have begun wagging. Most young couples of your breeding produce offspring straightaway for social and familial benefits. I should hate for rumors to begin."

Realizing Mrs. Ford wouldn't drop the matter unless I offered an explanation, I straightened my spine, forced a playful smile onto my face, and curated the best neutral response I could muster—after all, I couldn't give her an affirmative timeline when I didn't even have one. "We are making plans, Mrs. Ford, I assure you. It shouldn't be long now, so there is no need to belabor the point." The last sentence came out a tad more clipped than I intended, so I took a sip of tea as though it would soften my words.

Mrs. Ford twisted her lips and brushed her fingers through Basil Allan's hair, but if she had thoughts, she didn't voice them. Rather, she angled toward Emily. "I met an upstanding gentleman at Mr. Ford's house party last week. He is comely but kind, and he is the heir of a large estate. When I inquired, he informed me that he desires to wed and settle down. Perhaps I could introduce you."

Now it was Emily's turn to stiffen, but her tone remained calm and submissive. "I would like that very much, Mrs. Ford. Thank you."

I marveled at how she had delivered a courteous and kind response while simultaneously putting a quick end to my mother-in-law's inappropriate questioning.

Still, Mrs. Ford seemed keen to continue despite the hints dropped. "It is a shame about what happened with that handsome sergeant—oh, what was his name? I think you two would have made a fine couple. Perhaps the future may yet allow you to rekindle what had begun to develop."

Fighting off a wince, I glanced to Emily and was anguished to see her face fall. Sergeant Rees Andrews would likely always harbor affection for her, but a match between Rees and Emily was impossible—not only because Emily didn't reciprocate his feelings but also because he had taken Emily and her son hostage at gunpoint two years ago. Driven to madness by the darkness lingering in his mind from his encounter with Cornelius, Sergeant Andrews had nearly done himself in to escape. Though Emily had been able to talk him down and help free him from the magician's phantom grip, she couldn't erase his transgressions in the eyes of the law.

"I admire your optimism, Frances, but nothing can ever exist between us," Emily said softly. "He was in prison until two months ago. The courts allowed him freedom in exchange for his voluntary enlistment in the war. He was sent to the Western Front."

My throat tightened as I pictured the heavy combat erupting in Germany and imagined Sergeant Andrews engaged in the conflict. Ever since England declared war in August of 1914, it had stolen thousands upon thousands of young men from their families and thrust them into terrible violence. I believed in the cause, that we were trying to strike down true evil, but every time I scanned the daily newspaper and saw the updated casualty count, I couldn't help but simmer with fury and fear. Convict or not, I prayed that Sergeant Andrews would survive to return home.

A frustrated grumble emitted from the back of Mrs. Ford's throat. "This war is such a horrible thing. I'm so very thankful the new conscription law only applies to unmarried men. Even if it does eventually include men who are married, my oldest three are above the stated age, and Basil will be excluded on account of his physical disability." She set her cup down with an angry *clink*. "It is unfortunate, though, that it has already begun to take all of the eligible men, especially when there are so many fine young ladies in need of a husband."

Emily's fake smile struggled to hang on as she attempted to ease Mrs. Ford's concern, and I found my mind wandering to Ireland and to Finn. To my knowledge, Ireland didn't have any conscription laws in place, so unless Finn joined of his own free will, he should be safe from the war—and though I didn't doubt his noble heart, he didn't seem the type to engage in physical warfare in order to fight injustice.

"Speaking of young men"—Mrs. Ford turned to my mother—"Aubrey tells me you have begun meeting. I do hope he has been offering services that are to your satisfaction."

Mother flashed a curt smile. "Yes, he has been excellent."

Alarm fluttered in my stomach. Baze's third-oldest brother, Aubrey, worked as an estate agent. Why would she have need of his expertise?

Swallowing my apprehension, I said, "Are you looking to move?"

Mother finished the sandwich on which she had been nibbling. "No, I shall be living in the home Thomas left me for the foreseeable future." She shifted as though uncomfortable, further stoking my unease. "I have, however, begun to inquire about the possibility of selling his property in Ireland."

I blinked as my mind groped for any sense in her words. While I was content to move on from talk of children and husbands, I neither expected nor wanted to venture into the territory my mother had just entered. "What do you mean sell it?"

"Do not fret. I'm not hurting for money." She folded her hands in her lap. "Now that it has been several years since Thomas's death, I thought it best to ensure my assets are well documented and organized. In light of the war, Aubrey believes it would be wise to consolidate what assets I have left and to keep them within English borders . . . which means selling Thomas's Irish property."

The scar on my heart split open and exposed the pain of my father's death, raw as the day I first lost him. My voice spiked in volume and intensity. "How could you possibly entertain such an idea?"

"I understand how you feel, darling, but you have never been to that estate, and I am paying for its upkeep despite its vacancy." Though sadness flickered in her eyes, she smiled. "I know that it may hurt to give up things that were sentimental to him, but it is merely a house. We still have our memories, and those can never be taken away."

"You can't do this." My muscles tensed, trying to thrust me to my feet, but I managed to steel myself in place. "Sell it to Baze and me. We'll buy it."

"Adelynn, you have only begun learning how to manage your own estate. You don't need to assume the responsibility for another."

"You don't know what we can handle."

"Adelynn—"

"I forbid you to sell it!" I snapped. "I—"

"Adelynn!" Mother matched my tone, her eyes fierce and cheeks flushed. "Do not speak to me in that manner. You are a grown woman and above such blatant disrespect." Her expression softened but remained firm. "I have not yet finalized my decision, but as your father left the property in my name, it is my decision to make, and I shall do what I think is best."

Eyes and nose burning, I bit my lip to keep my next objection from erupting. She was right—I had never ventured to Father's Irish home, but the thought of simply passing it off to a faceless stranger made me sick to my stomach. That home represented an entire era of my father's life, and now that I was confronted with the reality of losing it, I resolved to do all I could to keep it.

Billiard balls clacked and scattered across a carpet of red. Two striped balls sank into the pockets. From their position beside the table, Baze and Frederick sipped from their whisky glasses as they watched Aubrey smirk, raise his cue, and circle around to line up his next shot. Percy,

Aubrey's competition, harrumphed and crossed his arms.

Aubrey shifted his cigar to the side of his mouth and knocked in another ball, leaving him with only three more until victory. "You should know by now not to wager with me, Perce. I'm up to—what—a five-game streak? Just watch this." Clamping down on his cigar, Aubrey bent forward, aimed for an exaggerated moment, and smacked the ball with his cue. It curved to the right, grazing the intended target and careening in the opposite direction.

Percy laughed aloud. "And you should know by now that pride goeth before the fall." He clapped Aubrey on the shoulder and shoved him out of the way.

Intent on Percy's actions, Baze silently rooted for his eldest brother. Aubrey was the most competitive of the bunch, often employing devious means to achieve a win, so it gave Baze unbridled joy when he lost. Not to mention, Aubrey had been a few rungs short of a bully when Baze was young, and though not as strong as it had once been, their rivalry still grated at Baze even though they were grown.

Of course, Percy and Frederick had had their moments of transgression throughout Baze's childhood, hardly going out of their way to defend Baze from Aubrey's cruel treatment, but they had since apologized for turning a blind eye. Reconciliation between the four of them had finally come, and Baze suspected the attitude shift had occurred when he confronted their father and refused to take his manipulation lying down, something the others hadn't had the backbone to do themselves.

Several months after Baze returned from his honeymoon, Percy suggested that they gather for a weekly social affair—just the four of them. Though wary at first, because it gave ample opportunity for three to gang up against one, Baze had come to greatly anticipate their get-togethers. Sometimes, they would uncork the newest whisky and talk for hours. Other times, they would engage in spirited games of billiards or darts. And still others, they would drive to nearby St. James's Park and walk the path round and round.

Despite the forward strides in their relationship, Baze still found it difficult to relate to them fully—after all, they had had decades to form a bond while he watched longingly from afar—but they were making an attempt to include him, and he appreciated the effort.

Grasping the top of his cue, Aubrey leaned his weight onto it and jutted his chin at Percy. "It's been nearly an hour since the last call. Do you suppose you should check on Eleanor?"

A lump crawled into Baze's throat as he pictured Percy's eldest daughter, a mere one summer his junior. She had been admitted to hospital with labor pains early that morning, but fourteen long hours later, the child had yet to arrive. Frederick had suggested canceling tonight's gathering so Percy could be with his family, but considering men were all but useless in matters of birth, he determined that an evening with his brothers would keep Percy's mind occupied.

Brows pinched, Percy cast a glance at the telephone sitting on the corner table. "I imagine if there is an update, they will call." He turned back to the game. "When I last spoke to my son-in-law, he said all was progressing normally—albeit slowly."

"I am sure all is well, but we won't be cross if you choose to go to them." As Percy thrust the cue forward and missed his shot, Aubrey snickered. "Perhaps you should leave anyway to spare yourself further embarrassment." He bumped Percy's shoulder as they traded places, and then Aubrey's stark blue eyes—identical to their mother's—locked on Baze. "And what about Adelynn?"

Mid-swallow, Baze inhaled sharply, and the whisky set fire to his throat and lungs. He bent in painful coughs, and when he recovered, he managed, "What about her?"

"Oh, come now." Aubrey drew from his cigar and released a stream of smoke with a laugh. "We are all waiting with bated breath to hear you finally announce she is in the family way."

Nausea and alcohol burned in Baze's stomach, and he tugged at his collar. "You will be one of the first to know, I assure you," he said, hoping his vagueness would prompt his brother to drop the matter.

Though Aubrey's next turn yielded another missed ball, he barely seemed to care, his attention now fixed on Baze. "You have been saying such for two years. Perce is about to become a grandfather thrice over and you've yet to even sire your first."

Baze scoffed. "Percy is two decades older than I am."

"So? By the time I had reached your twenty-eight summers, I had already brought both of my daughters into this world. You're falling behind."

"I didn't realize this was a competition."

Aubrey's eyes flashed. "Everything's a competition."

"Leave him be," Percy muttered as he knocked a solid-colored ball into a pocket, pulling ahead.

Baze swirled his whisky in the glass and watched the amber liquid swish up the sides. He yearned to down the rest of it to numb the turmoil within, but ever since overcoming his violent addiction to opium—which very nearly killed him—he tried to be more conservative in his consumption of such substances, his favorite drinks included.

"Why the hesitation? Afraid Father will swoop in the moment you announce a new Ford is on the way?" Aubrey continued. "I suppose I don't blame you. He's been salivating over you for years." A new thought dawned on his face. "Or is it something more? Maybe you're unable to—"

"Enough." Percy whacked Aubrey's arm with his cue. "It's your move."

With a careless shrug, Aubrey took his place. As the billiard balls clattered across the carpeted table, Frederick shifted toward Baze. With a quiet voice, he uttered, "Two years *is* a long time. Is everything all right?"

"We're fine," Baze whispered back, still watching the spiraling liquor.

"I realize it is a sensitive subject, but I have read ample literature on the topic. If it *is* something more, there are many successful interventions that can help couples—"

"I said we're fine!" Baze shouted, drawing the wide-eyed stares of all three brothers. "It's none of your blasted business when I choose to start a family." He slammed the glass onto the side of the table, sloshing liquid over the rim.

The three exchanged tense glances before Aubrey cocked a condescending eyebrow. "And you've included your wife in that decision, have you?"

Baze glared, but the truth of the question stilled his tongue.

"Ahh, so it's not that you *can't* have a child." Aubrey laid his cue across the table and ambled into Baze's space. Cigar smoke curled before his accusing eyes. "You merely don't *want* to, and you're imposing your will to force your sweet wife into submission. I hate to say it, Baze, but despite your every effort to avoid it, you have become exactly like Father."

Baze lunged and seized Aubrey's collar. Aubrey grabbed him in return. Their fists came up—but before either of them could land a blow, Percy and Frederick leaped into the fray and wrestled them apart.

With Frederick pinning his arms, Baze fought to free himself and snapped, "I'm nothing like Father."

"Ha," Aubrey barked. "You're the spitting image."

"That's enough." Percy slapped a hand on Aubrey's chest and pressed him back. "I think we should conclude for the night. Separation would serve you two well."

Aubrey resisted the push, then elbowed away and smoothed his waistcoat. "If you gents are too afraid to say it, then I will." As he bent toward Baze, Percy's palm came down on his shoulder. Smoke from his cigar stung Baze's nostrils and aggravated his eyes. "You need to take a good, long look in the mirror, Baze. Father tried to force you and Adelynn together to have children, and now you're forcing her not to. You may try to convince yourself otherwise, but that egotism is precisely what drives Father. Whether intentional or not, you are following directly in his stead."

Baze braced his legs, attempting to lunge at Aubrey once more, but

Frederick anticipated the attack and held him in place. He yanked Baze around, then squeezed the nape of his neck and guided him toward the study door. "Don't pay him any heed," Frederick muttered. "He doesn't know what he's talking about."

But as Frederick ferried Baze from the room, Aubrey's words wreaked havoc in his mind, ravaging the walls he'd constructed to defend and justify his actions. He and Adelynn were compromising on the matter—a far cry from what his father had done to her. Now simply wasn't the time for a child, not with the Great War raging around them and Shay O'Sullivan yet at large.

Still . . . what if it was inevitable? What if Baze was fated to follow in Alistair Ford's footsteps—both as a husband and as a father—no matter what he did to avoid it? The man had raised him after all. What if that wickedness resided in Baze and was merely biding its time, primed and ready to escape?

And what would be the catalyst needed for Baze to finally snap?

# Chapter Four

Still reeling from Mother's revelation, I sought a light dinner of roasted hazelnuts and black tea—all that I could fathom stomaching—and slipped into a warm bath. Though the anxiety coiling in my belly persisted throughout the evening, the bath's soothing waters eased my body aches and calmed my pounding heart. When I finished, I combed out my hair, dressed for bed, and settled under the covers with a book, propping its spine on a pillow laid over my midsection. Try as I might, however, I couldn't concentrate on the words.

Why would Mother sell Father's Ireland estate? How could she let such a thought enter her mind in the first place—and without consulting me? Time was already chipping away at the memories I clung to, and Father's physical effects were all that helped keep him tethered to me.

With a lump in my throat, I focused on my wedding ring. Three diamonds cradled a pearl that Baze had recovered from a necklace my father had gifted me. The ring, and the pearl, symbolized so much more than my marriage. It symbolized the people I loved—both the living and those gone from this world.

Heavy emotion compressed my chest, but before it had time to escalate, Baze's voice filtered in from down the hall. Frowning, I glanced at the clock. What was he doing home at this hour? On the nights when he joined his brothers for their weekly rendezvous, he usually didn't return until I had already fallen asleep.

Baze crept into the room, shoulders bent and expression weary. I peered at him over the top of the book, following him with my gaze as he crossed to the wardrobe, shed his coat, tugged off his waistcoat, and began unbuttoning his shirt.

"You're home early," I said softly, sensing disquiet in his stiff posture.

Keeping his back to me, he replied with an equally soft tone. "Aubrey and I had a bit of a row and concluded it would be best if we all returned home. Besides, Percy's grandchild is due to arrive at any moment, so he needs to be available should they need him."

I tilted my head. "A row about what?"

"Nothing of consequence. Merely a brothers' disagreement." Baze jerked his shirt out of his waistband and ripped off his shoes. Then he padded toward the bed, crawled across it, snatched the pillow away from me, and flopped onto his back, his head cradled on my stomach where the cushion had been. Scrubbing his hands down his face, he heaved a deep sigh and dropped his arms limp at his sides.

"That bad, huh?" I asked, his head bobbing slightly in time with my words.

Rather than answer, he sighed again and closed his eyes. I waited a beat, then another, allowing him time to process the thoughts brewing within—but still he remained silent. If two years of being married to Baze had taught me anything, it was that he didn't always want to discuss the problems that weighed upon his heart, at least not straightaway, and he found the most peace by simply drawing near to me.

Denying the strong urge to interrupt his meditation, I shifted my book to one hand so I could carry on reading and used my other to comb my fingers through his dark hair. The silky strands, nearing the need for a trim, glided across my skin, and I spotted a tiny wink of silver above his ears. My stomach fluttered. When we first said our vows, I didn't believe I could grow any more attracted to him, but that had been entirely and utterly false, for each new day revealed a new detail about him that only heightened his desirability.

Pulses of heat radiated from where his head compressed my abdomen, so I wiggled deeper into the mattress and turned back to reading as a distraction. His head gently rose and fell with each of my breaths. Every so often, his muscles twitched, signaling that sleep was tempting his mind to surrender. Were it not for the absence of snoring, I would have assumed he had already drifted away.

"Whelan said he plans to recommend me for a promotion."

His abrupt statement snatched my attention away from my novel. Though his eyes remained shut, his brow had furrowed into a concentrated crease. I turned down the edge of a page and laid the book aside, then resumed stroking his hair. "When did he tell you that?"

"Yesterday."

"That's wonderful." I smiled, but when his expression didn't change, I sobered. "Isn't it?"

"It feels too soon."

"Rubbish. If anything, it isn't soon enough. You stopped Cornelius, you helped bring Charles Caine to justice, and you have solved several prominent cases since. It's high time they rewarded you for your contributions."

His features hardened further, and his eyes opened and affixed on the ceiling. "I don't know that I even want it."

Understanding dawned, but I remained silent and continued pushing my fingers through his hair until his eyes rolled back and fluttered shut. A new sigh, this one deep and cleansing, rushed from his nose. I rubbed my thumb over his forehead as though to smooth the lines from it and finally whispered, "For what it's worth, you are one of the best inspectors I know—and I'm not merely saying that because I'm your wife. You are every bit deserving of a promotion. I am so very proud of you, and I will remain proud of you no matter what you decide to do."

Baze took up my free hand and kissed my fingers. "Thank you."

With a light smile, I said, "What else did Whelan say?"

His faint dimple emerged as he began massaging and triggering pressure points in my hand, one in my thumb and one in my palm. "I think that's enough interrogation for tonight. It's my turn to question you."

I lifted my chin. "What do you want to know?"

"We should talk about your nightly endeavors."

Defensiveness arose. "What is there to talk about? I'm simply continuing my investigation."

"Not simply." He rolled toward me to make eye contact. "It's consuming you. You barely sleep for fear of missing something, and when you do sleep, your nightmares return, keeping both of us from resting peacefully."

I wrapped my hand around his to halt his movements. "What would you have me do, then? Shay is still out there."

"I realize that, but you have become more and more withdrawn—depressed even—since we returned from Bath. You said you banished Cornelius from your mind, but I believe you have invited O'Sullivan right in to replace him."

"I have done no such thing." I sighed. "I know what I'm doing."

"Do you?"

"Please, where is your faith in me?"

"It's not for a lack of faith but the knowledge of how far you've gone before."

A sickening blend of anxiety and obstinance swirled in the pit of my stomach. After all I had conquered thus far, how could he think so little of me? Did he believe my mind weak enough to allow Shay to take hold of me as Cornelius once had?

Burying my doubts in the depths of my heart, I nodded. "If it would please you, I promise to leave my investigations for waking hours and allow you to get better rest."

He flattened his lips. "I suppose that's a start."

"Don't worry so much, Baze. All will be well." Flicking at his nose, I released a delicate chuckle. When his head bobbed with the flexion of my stomach, the amusing sight of it made me laugh again, but that only served to exacerbate the movement, and soon, I had regressed into a fit of giggles as his head bounced up and down.

Sitting up, he raised an eyebrow. "You think that's funny, do you?"

"I'm sorry," I wheezed through laugher. "You looked so silly. I can't help it."

"How's this for silly?" He flipped onto all fours and poked my side.

I gasped as a sharp *zing* lanced up my torso. I tucked my knees to my chest and swatted his hand away. "You are *not* to tickle me, Basil Ford!"

"Or what?" He laughed and prodded my side again.

Squirming but unable to escape the torment, I reached above my head, clasped the pillow, and flung it at him. It bounced off his face and swept his hair sideways across his forehead in a staticky mess. He halted, eyes wide and mouth agape.

Then his features twisted in a devious grin.

"No!" I squealed, rolling to the side as he snatched up the pillow and swatted me in the back of the head with it. With a yelp, I grabbed for the second cushion and vaulted off the bed as he came swinging at me.

We dashed about the room, pillows slinging and sides heaving in laughter. My petite build gave me an advantage as I ducked and dodged his barrage and landed my own attacks.

"Hold still!" he hollered, lungs heavy with exertion and glee.

Loose hair flying into my face and eyes, I continued to assail him and avoid his return fire. Soon, my body quivered and grew sticky with sweat. Time to put this to an end. I unleashed a frenzy of swipes and seemed to have him cornered—until he released a yell and charged straight for me, cushion outstretched. I squeaked as we tumbled onto the bed. He held me pinned between the pillow and the mattress, my arms trapped beneath.

I wriggled and tried to free my limbs. "Release me, you fiend!"

Breathing hard, he leaned more of his weight onto the pillow, which pushed a grunt from my chest. "You have lost, madam. Surrender."

His triumphant smirk stoked the competitive drive within me, and

I bit back, "Never." Try as I might, however, I couldn't twist free. I huffed. "This is unfair. You're larger than me."

"All's fair in a pillow fight." His boyish smile grew suggestive as he leisurely dragged his gaze over my face. Awakening desire in his eyes kindled a hearty fire in my stomach. With a husky voice, he bent toward me, and his velvety lips whispered against my own. "As the victor, I should like to claim my spoils."

Heat skittered across my limbs and evaporated my breath. "You think that's the proper way to woo a woman, do you?"

He kissed me lightly—enough to give me a taste of what I desired yet leaving me craving more. "You tell me." He kissed me again, slower. "Is it working?"

Pulse racing, I tried not to let it show that his advances were stripping my every defense. "You'll have to let me up if you want an answer to that."

"I quite like you where you are."

The hint of mock danger in his sultry tone sent a new shock of anticipation coursing through me. Just as I parted my lips, his mouth came crashing down upon mine, hungry and forceful. A moan rumbled in my throat as his hand found its way to my thigh. He smoothed his lips down my neck and to my collarbone, tugging at the skirt of my nightgown.

I finally managed to yank one arm free and slid my fingers into his hair. "You just wait. Someday, you shall have a brood of strong sons who will give you a fair fight."

A groan reverberated in his chest. "You can hold your own."

"Even so . . ." I caught my breath, hesitating only a moment before venturing, "I believe it's time."

Baze's body tensed, and his advances slowed before his lips retreated from my skin. As he tilted back, the spark in his eyes dulled. "What do you mean?"

"I think you know." I smiled, then applied pressure to the base of his head, intent to kiss him once more.

Baze angled his face away and resisted my attempt to proceed. The vein in his neck tapped wildly as he sucked air in and out. Then he released a frustrated growl, rocked backward, and came to a stand.

The sudden release of weight forced a gasp into my lungs. Body taut in unfulfilled yearning, I sat up and clutched the pillow to my chest. "Why did you stop?"

He began buttoning his shirt. "Because you and I are expecting to get very different things out of this moment."

I squeezed the pillow to give myself the courage I needed to be forthcoming. "I want what you want."

"No, you want more."

I bristled. "And why shouldn't I? Is it a crime for me to want children with my husband?"

He rubbed the bridge of his nose, then seemed to realize he'd given away his contemplative tell and shoved his hands into his pockets. "It's too soon."

"Too soon? Baze, it's been two years. Most of our peers start within a few months."

"There's no rule that says we must model our lives after our peers." He forced an uneasy smile. "Why can't we enjoy our marriage for a while—just the two of us?"

Though a sweet sentiment, I knew there was more to his reluctance, so I embraced candor. "I want a child, Baze."

His expression hardened. "I said it's too soon."

I hurled the pillow onto the ground and lurched to my feet. "That's complete nonsense, and you know it."

"I'm done discussing this."

As he rotated toward the door, I caught his arm. "Do I not get a say?"

He grasped my wrist and plucked my hand from his arm, then yanked me closer. "I am the head of this household, and as such, I will decide when it is time for us to expand our family."

Pain polluted my hope as I pulled from his hold. I lowered my voice, keeping my calm despite the compulsion to lash out. "This isn't like you, Baze. You've never spoken to me like that before, and I don't believe you truly mean it." Remembering Emily's gentle feedback, I placed my palm on his chest. "Tell me what's wrong. Please. I want to help."

"Drop the matter. *That's* how you can help."

"But—"

He knocked my hand away, then hastened through the door and slammed it shut.

Baze returned to bed several hours later, but I pretended to be asleep until he settled. Long after his snoring commenced, I continued to recline on my back with my hands folded over my stomach and eyes locked upon the darkened ceiling. Though unconscious, Baze's mere presence hardened my muscles and simmered rage in my belly. He had the means to fulfill my heart's desire—could do so this very night—but he refused. And he wouldn't even tell me why.

Frustration mounting, I rolled from the bed and plodded across the room. I yanked on my silk robe and stole out the door. Grit burned behind my heavy eyelids, and my limbs drooped with fatigue, but I ignored my body's cry for rest.

Shadows spread before me as I crept through familiar passages until I reached the door of Baze's study. His crisp pine and citrus scent—usually a scent I delighted in—irritated my nostrils as I negotiated the tight space to my own desk. Though the room had been allocated as Baze's retreat, he had graciously agreed to set up a small area for me as we investigated Shay O'Sullivan. He had reserved skepticism about the arrangement, but it had come to prove as an encouragement to us both, allowing us to draw closer together by exchanging ideas, sharing discoveries, and enjoying the occasional intimate respite.

Plopping into my upholstered but firm chair, I heaved a sigh and surveyed the papers strewn about in haphazard stacks—newspaper clippings, journal entries, official case documents of which Baze had allowed me to make copies. Two years gone and we'd barely scratched the surface of who Shay O'Sullivan was.

A flash of red drew my eye to a full article pinned to the corkboard at the back of the desk. The headline read: "Woman found dead on train in Bath Station." Subhead: "Poison likely the cause of asphyxiation." And directly in the center of the text, the reporters had printed a gruesome image of Katherine Quinn's body. She lay facedown in the train's aisle, her fiery hair fanned out around her head.

My stomach twisted. In the last meeting between Shay and me, he had in his possession Katherine's coveted claddagh, a silver Irish ring representing their union. He had refused to answer my questions about Katherine's welfare and left me to speculate. It wasn't until Detective Chief Inspector Sydney Whitaker, the man who had helped us solve the Bath poisonings and had become a dear friend, called us to confirm Katherine's death and then mailed the article as proof.

The events in Bath were supposed to bring light, healing, and reconciliation to Baze and me. He had emerged with a treatment plan to manage the pain in his leg, and I had finally mustered the courage to banish Cornelius from my mind for good.

But Shay had come barreling into the fray and sent my world spiraling once again.

A quiet, spiteful voice hissed in my ear. ***You cannot escape.***

Breaths coming quick and sporadic, I slammed both fists onto the desk. Shay had been Cornelius's mentor, the one who taught him to use stage magic and harness the real power of manipulation. My nightmares should have stopped with Cornelius. The constant fear of death and terror should have ended with him too, but here we were, three years later, and I was in a more vengeful, sleep-deprived state than ever before. All thanks to Shay.

***You will lose everyone you have ever loved,*** the voice continued. ***He will come for you.***

A feral growl tore from my lips as I launched to my feet and swept the papers off the desk. They scattered and twisted onto the floor. I needed to do something. Anything. The weight of Shay's presence augmented by day-to-day stresses was strangling the life out of me. How much longer could I withstand this burden before suffocating?

*You know exactly what to do.*

Gooseflesh spread across my skin as I considered it. Katherine had taught me how to conjure a vision at will, to extend my mind and voluntarily look through the eyes of our enemies. I had even achieved it once, back in Bath, when Baze had been in danger of losing his life. However, Katherine had cautioned that with the benefits came great danger.

*"If I linger in the vision for too long,"* she had said, *"I run the risk of his mind influencing my own. It's easy to allow the darkness to seep in if you open the door wide."*

I knew her words to be true, for I had faced the pull of darkness when I confronted Cornelius, when he had utilized every ounce of strength to try to break my mental defenses. The Almighty had given me the strength to weather his attacks, but I could only imagine how much stronger they would have been if I had opened my mind willingly.

Yet . . . what other option did I have? Shay was going to persist in using his powers, so why shouldn't I use my own—regardless of risk?

*You must fight fire with fire.*

With my blood roaring in my ears and my heart thundering in warning, I plopped back into the chair and pressed my palms flat on the desk. Every instinct screamed at me to stop as I squeezed my eyes shut.

And thrust out with my mind.

Darkness smothered me. Ice flooded my veins. Paralysis took every muscle captive. My stomach pitched, engulfing me with the sensation of falling, then careening, and finally spiraling into nothingness. A pinprick of light blossomed in the distance.

*Whoosh.*

Brightness exploded. I jerked to an abrupt halt as the light dimmed to a tolerable level. Scenery materialized before me—a cluster of tiny stone cottages nestled in a green hillside, hedgerows containing herds of woolly sheep, lush grass interspersed by well-worn paths. Women milled about, some gathering dried laundry and some corralling exuberant children. I stood on the front step of one of the cottages, peering out at the expanse before me.

"You comin', Shay? We've got to hurry if we want to reach Dublin before nightfall."

My head swiveled toward the voice belonging to a grimy man with scraggly clothes, long beard, and flat cap. As I dropped off the step, a deep masculine voice rumbled in my throat as my lips—or rather, Shay's lips—moved in response. "Aye, I was thinkin' we might—"

He snapped his mouth shut and stilled. His eyes widened and fixed on a distant pasture. My gut hitched with dread as his heart thrashed in my chest.

"Ohhh, Adelynn," he purred long and low. "This be a grave mistake. I told you to leave well enough alone. I told you to forget about me and go back home. You should have listened, for there be no comin' back from what you have just unleashed." His vision blurred. "Whatever happens from this moment forth is on your head."

My mind shot from his body. A dizzying jumble of images flashed before my eyes. Nausea heightened as I lurched through scene after scene. Some pulled me in, holding me there, forcing me to witness the carnage, before propelling me back into nothingness.

*Whoosh.* Soldiers wielding rifles streamed into chaotic, body-ridden streets. *Whoosh.* A young man with a familiar face fired a gun upon his comrade and then himself. *Whoosh.* Basil Allan screamed and thrashed in the arms of a stranger. *Whoosh.* Finn arched and gasped in pain as inky blackness clouded his wide eyes. *Whoosh.* Baze teetered at the edge of a great precipice, hands grasping at empty air, before he toppled and disappeared into the abyss.

*Whoosh.*

The study came crashing back. A strangled cry filled the room. Something hard slammed into my side, knocking the wind out of me.

Gasping, I pawed at whatever I could get my hands on and managed to grasp the desk and clamber to my knees. I'd fallen out of the chair.

Shock pinned me to the spot. My limbs quaked violently, and my stomach twisted into a thousand knots. From deep in the depths of my being, a rolling flame of terror and shame consumed me. That had been wrong. That had been evil. And I had willingly let it in.

***You did the right thing.***

"Adelynn?" Baze's distant voice filtered through the halls. His uneven footfalls declared his approach, but I couldn't move, not even when he came bursting into the study and fell by my side. He set his pistol on the floor and gripped my arms, then touched my head. "Adelynn, are you all right? What happened?"

Still I couldn't move, my eyes glued to the floor and teeth chattering.

Baze's hands came around my jaw and angled my face toward him. "Adelynn, speak to me. What happened?" As he stared into my eyes, comprehension slackened his features. He swallowed and finally whispered, "What have you done?"

# Chapter Five

I HUNKERED QUIETLY ON THE COUCH with my arms curled against my chest and my knees pulled up to make myself as small as possible. Baze loomed before me with his arms crossed, weight shifted onto his healthy leg, and eyes downcast. His jaw muscles pulsed, his silence deafening. The single light from the side table cast hard shadows across his pinched brow.

Dread kept a strong grip on my insides, sending numbness across my limbs. What had I done? How could I have been so foolish?

*You did what was necessary.* The voice from before sounded weightier, more confident. *It is the only way to get what you want.*

Baze expelled a sigh, and the short burst made me jump. As I hugged my arms tighter to my chest, he finally spoke. "What were you thinking?"

*How callus of him to ask you that. Remember what he did to you earlier? What was* **he** *thinking?*

The stark memory of the quarrel we'd had mere hours ago zapped through me, and angry words burst from my lips before I could stop them. "You left me in such a state, I needed something to keep my mind occupied. You all but drove me away."

"Don't blame *me* for this." Spite dripped in his voice as he lowered his arms and clenched his fists at his sides. "You have been wanting to do this for some time now. Our argument was the excuse you needed to defy my warnings and connect yourself to that man."

Rapid tears dripped down my cheeks, and I swiped at them, frustrated by their betrayal of my emotions. "I'm sorry," I whispered, the fight draining from my bones. "I didn't do it to hurt you. I did it because I want this to end . . . I'm so, so weary, Baze."

He sighed again and relaxed his hands. Though his posture remained guarded, his eyes grew soft, a warm chocolate brown in the candlelight. "What did you see?"

As I closed my eyes, my visions erupted just as quickly and as vividly as before, filtering through each terrible scene until they transitioned into the final image—Baze . . . disappearing into a black abyss.

No. I refused to allow that to happen. I didn't yet know how, but I would find a way to stop Shay before he could snatch my loved ones from me.

Fixing my gaze on the elaborate design of the carpet, I slowly recounted my interaction with Shay, deliberately leaving the rapid-fire visions unmentioned. "Shay is in a small village in Ireland somewhere. There were women and children there. Men too. I think it may be his hiding place, where he's planning his next move. He . . . he realized I was there."

"Did he say anything?"

The carpet blurred as I stared harder at it. "That I've made a grave mistake." Chills grazed my skin, and I began trembling.

Baze sank next to me, tugged the quilt off the back of the couch, and draped it over my shoulders. As I pulled the blanket close around me, he leaned forward and stroked the bridge of his nose. Compassion glistened in his eyes, but his bent spine and taut jaw exposed his anger. "I don't disagree with him." He dropped a heavy hand on my knee and squeezed. "But what's done is done. We will face this as we have faced all past opposition."

I nestled against his side and pressed my face into his shoulder, overwhelmed and humbled by his forgiveness and love—a forgiveness and love I didn't deserve.

The vision of Baze's death invaded my thoughts again, searing into my mind's eye the look of shock on his face as he plummeted. Bile burned my throat. For as long as I had been experiencing visions, I still had yet to ascertain exactly how far in advance I witnessed them before they occurred. Perhaps it was different every time. Though, if I had to guess, I would surmise that the scenes that had flashed in quick succession were likely visions of what would come to pass if Shay's plan came to fruition.

"I think we need to go to Ireland," I murmured into Baze's shirt.

A soft exhale wheezed through his nose. "What do you think we'll accomplish there?"

"Two years of investigation have led us to dead ends at every turn, but now I know where he's hiding. I'm sure we could use the landmarks I saw to help us locate him. Besides, he knows I'm watching now. I would rather take the initiative than wait for him to strike first."

Baze stroked his nose and remained silent, eyes brimming with thoughts.

"Before Shay realized I was watching, one of the men he was with mentioned Dublin. If that's where he's been scheming, then that would be the best place to start." I recalled the hard conversation I'd had with Mother the day before. "We could stay at my father's old estate in Dublin. It's near enough to city center and would give us quick access to the Dublin police if we needed them."

After a short pause, Baze's voice rasped. "Okay."

I sat up. "Okay? Just like that?"

He twisted to look back at me. "I'm as weary of this as you, Al. If we must take the fight straight to O'Sullivan, then that's what we'll do."

I swallowed. "It will be dangerous."

"What *hasn't* been dangerous?" A tiny smile drew out his dimple. "Besides, if you confront O'Sullivan with the same ferocity as you did Riordan, then this will be over before he realizes what's hit him."

Chuckling through a new surge of tears, I cradled his face with my hands and kissed him. The tension in his muscles released, and his breath warmed my lips as he whispered, "I shall charter passage to Ireland first thing in the morning."

"I'm coming with you."

It took a moment for Emily's bold declaration to register in my head. We strolled through St. James's Park, arm in arm, breathing deep the fresh spring air. My conversation with Baze seemed to have occurred a lifetime ago, but it had only been this morning. When Baze set out to procure tickets for our voyage, I had raced to tell Emily of our plans. After all, Shay's influence had impacted her life as much as it had mine.

"Emily, it's going to be dangerous."

"I've been in dangerous situations before."

I thought of Bennett, of how Basil Allan would never know him. Emily was all he had left. "But what about your son? If you—"

"What about my son?" Her eyes sparked, and she spoke with a sharp tone I rarely heard escape from her lips. She must have sensed my unease, for she sighed. "I'm sorry. I didn't mean to snap."

"It's all right." I squeezed her arm. "You seem troubled. What's bothering you?"

She went quiet as we turned onto Blue Bridge. When we reached the middle, I tugged her to the railing, faced her, and gripped her hands in mine.

She avoided my gaze as she said, "Finn is in Ireland."

Realization struck. I fought against a smile. "You want to find him."

Her brow furrowed, and she gave a hesitant nod.

Now I let my smile sneak through. Finn's letters to Emily had grown more regular of late, and I imagined her return correspondences were just as frequent. Though I didn't know the exact contents of their messages, I was confident that they had long traded formal pleasantries for more friendly conversation.

"I think he would be delighted to see you." I tilted my head as her expression fell further. "But why should that trouble you?"

Redness crept into her cheeks as she cast her gaze at Buckingham Palace in the distance. "It has been three years since I lost Bennett, and sometimes I believe that I have healed. However, the wounds seem merely callused, for there are times when grief rubs them raw and rips me completely open." Her chin quivered. "What if I am unable to move on?"

Emotion tightened my throat. I didn't know what it was like to lose a husband—God forbid that ever happen—but I did know what it was like to lose someone I loved. Though I believed I had a better handle on my emotions than most people, there were moments, as Emily described, when the overwhelming loss of my father would outright bowl me over—a phenomenon that had only become stronger as the years passed.

I encircled her hands with mine. "Bennett is and will always be a part of you. I don't believe you should move on. You merely need to move forward."

Her glistening blue eyes widened. Tears rimmed her lids as she pulled from my grasp and wrapped her arms around me. I embraced her in return, and we held each other tight for a good long while. "Let's go find Finn," I whispered.

She pulled back and wiped a few stray tears from her cheeks. "Do you know how long we'll be there?"

"No. It may take some time to find Shay, so it could be days, perhaps even weeks."

She nodded. "Then I shall have to find someone to watch Basil Allan. I don't know if Mr. Ford would allow Frances to—"

"We need to bring him with us," I blurted, my mind bursting with the vision of Basil Allan being taken by a stranger. When Emily looked at me quizzically, I rushed to explain. "I don't think it would be smart to leave him in the hands of someone else, even someone we trust. If our enemies were to learn we had left him behind unguarded . . ." I banished the disturbing notion. "I think he would be safest in our company."

Understanding washed over Emily's face, but to her credit, she didn't seem deterred. "It's settled then."

Mother greeted me with a warm hug and directed me into the sitting room. "Two visits in one week? You positively spoil me." She grinned, and I tried not to let her jovial demeanor stir up guilt. Even though we resided in the same city, conducting regular visits was not something I always remembered to do. Perhaps I took her closeness for granted, assuming she would always be there when I needed her.

A maid brought us tea and snacks, and I waited until she'd taken her leave before speaking. "I have been reflecting a great deal about what you plan to do with Father's property. It wasn't fair for me to react in such a hostile manner yesterday. I don't quite know why such a thing affected me so strongly. After all, it's as you said. I have not even been to that home." I twisted my hands in my lap. "I'm sorry."

"Thank you, darling. I know the thought of parting with anything of your father's is difficult." She smiled sadly. "I cannot even bring myself to clear out the clothes in his wardrobe, so it is a wonder how I could ever hope to sell something as large as a home." She sipped contemplatively, and when she swallowed and lowered the cup, her features relaxed into serenity. "Your father brought me to Ireland once, you know."

I straightened, my curiosity piqued. "Really? When?"

"More than two decades ago. You were a mere twinkle in our eyes." She chuckled. "Having just purchased the property there, he wanted me to help him christen it before he began his work. We walked through each room, praying peace and goodwill over it, and we concluded by carving our initials into the mantel."

Bittersweet delight warmed my heart as I pictured my parents together, praying and walking hand in hand. "Why didn't you ever go back?"

"I wanted to. In fact, we had originally planned to travel together whenever business called him there. That was when you came along, and we deemed it too difficult and perhaps too dangerous to bring an infant across the sea, especially with the growing hostility in Ireland at the time." Mother caressed the side of her teacup. "There was a moment when you were young, perhaps eight or nine, when Thomas tried to revisit the matter of our accompanying him, but the hostility between the English and the Irish had only worsened, not improved. So I told him no."

The revelation stole my breath. I could have been traveling with my father all those years? What would my life have looked like if we all stayed together? How much deeper could my relationship with Father have been?

"I didn't know that," I said softly.

Mother's brow furrowed. "I know my decision stole time away from the two of you, and I am sorry for that. To this day, I am unsure whether it was the right decision, but it was all I knew to do to keep you safe at the time."

Quick anger seized me—anger that her decision had cut short the time I could have spent with my father—but I wrestled it away. She had done the best she could with the information she had. How could she have known Father was going to die so young?

I laid a hand on her wrist. "I know that everything you did was out of love. Thank you."

Her smiled warmed, and she took another sip of tea. I tried to drink from my own, but the steaming aroma smelled bitter, almost sour, and curbed my craving. With a grimace, I set it aside and turned to Mother. I could stall no longer.

"I have been thinking about what you said," I ventured. "That I have never visited Father's second home. Baze and I were discussing it last night, and we would like to go there on holiday before you sell—if you would allow us to. Father lived a completely separate life in Ireland, and I would like to experience just a tiny piece of it before it's gone forever."

Mother contemplated a moment before nodding. "I think that sounds like a lovely idea."

Her wistful look awakened remorse, and before I could consider the implications or the impending danger, I found myself asking, "Would you like to accompany us?"

Tears reddened Mother's eyes as she lifted them to the ceiling. Her silence stretched on, and my heartbeat thumped faster with each passing second. Finally, she shook her head. "I am touched by the invitation, but I must decline. I already had the opportunity to live that life with Thomas, and it is now behind me. This is a journey you must take for yourself." Hope brightened her features. "Though, if you remember it, will you check the mantel for me? I would like the assurance that our initials still remain . . . and perhaps you and Baze could add your own."

I leaned into her embrace and kissed her cheek. "I will. Thank you, Mother."

When Superintendent Whelan grunted permission for entry into his office, Baze's heart all but stopped. As he stole into the cramped space, its sticky warmth dampened his skin, and the heavy cigarette odor clogged his nostrils. He struggled to form the right words. The superintendent was well aware of everything Baze had encountered the past several years—including Adelynn's visions, Cornelius Marx's true powers, and even their confrontation with Shay O'Sullivan in Bath. So hopefully, the man would be open to Baze's proposition.

Whelan stared out from under his bushy eyebrows. "Thought through your promotion, Ford?"

"Yes, sir. I mean, no, sir." Baze grappled for a coherent response. "I have given it thought, but that's not why I requested to speak to you."

"Out with it then."

"I need your permission to pursue an investigation in Ireland."

Whelan's eye twitched, and then a boisterous laugh punched from his gut. He slapped his knee and fired up a cigarette. "That's a good one, Ford. You almost had me there."

"It's not a joke, sir." Baze managed to keep his composure, and his solemnity must have registered with Whelan, for the man shut his mouth and stiffened, cigarette mid-puff. "Adelynn may have discovered where Shay O'Sullivan is hiding, and by discovered, I mean she saw a new vision. We believe he's somewhere close to Dublin. This could be our chance to strike."

Whelan sniffed. "He's Ireland's problem now, not ours."

"That may be, sir, but he's the reason why Cornelius Marx terrorized London, and he's the reason Bath suffered those poisonings. While he may be in Ireland now, there's nothing stopping him from bringing murder to our shores again. He's not going to stop until someone stops him."

"And you think you're the one to do it, eh?"

"Yes." Baze firmed his jaw and tried to keep emotion out of his voice—to an unknown degree of success. "He's taken a lot from me, sir. I've been involved with this investigation from the beginning, and I intend to see it through to the very end. For Bennett. For my family. For all those innocent people who may yet stand to get in his way."

Whelan drew long and deep on his cigarette before tucking it in the corner of his mouth. The smoke clouded and dissipated around his face, and its dispersal made Baze's eyes water. Finally, Whelan cleared his throat. "When you make landfall, your first order of business is to seek out Superintendent Darragh Moore with the Dublin Metropolitan Police. He's a good man. Might not be able to help you, but it never hurts to know who your allies are." He heaved himself from his chair, tugged up his trousers, and lumbered around the desk to meet Baze face-to-face. His gravelly voice grew low. "I know you're aware, but I can't send my men to get you out of trouble. The moment your feet leave England, you'll be on your own."

Baze nodded. "I understand, and I accept the risk."

Whelan's jaw twisted as he stroked his mutton chops, then extended a hand. "Take that blighter down."

Baze's stomach squeezed as he accepted the gesture. "Thank you, sir." He hadn't expected the conversation to go so smoothly, but he was grateful for it. He loosened his grip on the superintendent's hand, but Whelan suddenly squeezed hard, sending numbness to the tips of Baze's fingers, and tugged him closer.

Whelan tilted his face mere inches from Baze's. "While you're away, I expect you to give more thought to your promotion." His voice wobbled ever so slightly. "And I expect you to return to inform me of your decision—in person. Am I understood?"

The meaning behind the man's words struck Baze square in the chest. He couldn't rightfully promise such a thing—and Whelan knew it—but he gripped tightly to the superintendent's hand and murmured, "I'll do my best, sir."

## Chapter Six

I CLUNG TO THE RAILING AND angled my face into the wind as crewmen cast off our ship's moorings and set us loose upon the River Thames. With only one smokestack and a handful of passenger cabins, our vessel wasn't as grand as *Titanic* or *Carpathia*, but with a name like *Lady Gwendolen*, she was as grand as she needed to be.

Waves splashed, the ship pitched, and my stomach lurched. I swallowed hard and pressed a fist into my stomach.

Baze's supportive hand found its place at the small of my back. "You're looking a mite green, Al. Perhaps you should go lie down."

I waved him off. "No, I don't want to miss the departure."

"Have it your way." He sighed. "But do try not to embarrass me by getting sick all over the deck."

Emily joined us and hefted Basil Allan up to the railing so he could peer at the city passing us by. With eyes round and sparkling, he giggled and pointed out fleeting landmarks. As the ship picked up speed, she released steam from her smokestack in a loud burst. Basil Allan squealed and burrowed into his mother's chest.

I laughed and clutched at my hat as the increasing wind gusts threatened to tug it off my head. Baze's arm circled my waist and pulled me against his side, and we enjoyed the moment in silence, smiling and basking in the sun's bright rays.

The Thames carried us through London and soon spit us out into the North Sea. A southward turn brought us into the Strait of Dover lined with bright white cliffs that rose high and proud above the water. Sharp and steep, its craggy formations conjured the vision of Baze falling over the edge. I looked away and leaned into him.

When the excitement of the journey eventually waned, Baze cleared his throat. "I don't know about you ladies, but I should like to see to our rooms before the hour becomes too late." He touched Emily's arm. "I booked us adjacent accommodation so that we could stay close by one another."

Emily plopped Basil Allan onto the deck and smiled. "That was very generous. I will pay you back once I—"

"It was a gift, Emily." Baze motioned his hand in dismissal. "I shall hear no more of it."

He offered me his arm and turned us toward the cabins. As we rotated, the deck lifted, my knees weakened, and the contents of my stomach lurched into my throat. I clamped my mouth shut against the force and clung to him for support. He chuckled and held me upright. "I have heard that it takes a few days for people to find their sea legs."

"Really?" I muttered. "You seem to be getting on just fine."

He grinned. "Perhaps my crooked leg evens everything out."

Belowdecks, we discovered our staterooms exactly as Baze had said—right beside one another and joined with a single door in the middle. Baze's and my space was modest but adequately decorated, with a four-poster bed against the right-side wall and a simple fireplace looming across from it. Brimming with our clothes, trunks, and personal effects, it immediately felt like home. The door to Emily's room sat to the left of the fireplace, and another door near the bed opened to a lavatory.

I drew up to the three portholes in the far wall and peered through one of them. Though belowdecks, our room rested above sea level and allowed me to view the drifting landscape as clearly as when I was standing in the open air.

Baze shuffled up behind me, wrapped his arms about my waist, and rested his chin on my shoulder. "No turning back now," he whispered.

I matched his volume. "I wouldn't have wanted to turn back even if we could."

"Are you ready for what we might find?"

"Ready as I'll ever be."

"And you think you'll be able to keep your mind in check?"

I turned slightly in his arms. "What are you insinuating?"

"You know exactly what I'm insinuating." He gripped me tighter. "We don't know what awaits us when we make landfall. I just want to make sure you're not going to go down a path you shouldn't."

***Your mind is all but lost already.***

The small voices of darkness began whispering in my thoughts, raising gooseflesh on my skin. I made to speak, but the moment I opened my mouth, my stomach heaved. I knocked Baze's arms away and managed to make it to the nearest bin just as I vomited.

While my stomach emptied itself entirely, something tugged at my hat, pulling out the pins and tossing it onto the bed. Then Baze's hands came around my face and brushed back the stray hair. "You've got it bad, Al. What can I do?"

Too weak to respond, I spit into the bin and moaned as my insides cramped.

A soft knock came at the adjoining door, followed by Emily's voice. "All right in there?"

"Come in," Baze called, and when she did, he said, "Adelynn's seasick."

Holding Basil Allan in her arms, Emily smiled sympathetically. "Poor dear. Here, let me tend to her." She passed her son off to Baze and then helped me straighten and stagger to the bed. My stomach seemed to flop into my chest as I lay carefully onto the sheets. She rested the back of her hand on my forehead. "There's no fever. It's likely just a mild case of nausea. Nothing a bit of ginger and a warm compress can't fix."

Out of the corner of my eye, I noticed Basil Allan starting to fuss and kick his feet against Baze's hip. Baze wrangled the child into his other arm and said, "I think I'll take this rascal for a walk in the fresh air while you tend to Adelynn. Wear him out a bit, if that's all right."

She nodded. "That's very kind, thank you."

As Baze took his leave, Emily bustled about, finding a clump of ginger and warming a compress. She coaxed me to a stand so she could help me out of my traveling suit and corset before I collapsed back on the bed. Her thin brows drew together as she massaged my sore abdomen and then covered it with the heated pad.

The ginger stung my tongue, but relief soon rolled through me. Looking through my lashes, I studied Emily—her full blonde curls, her petite face, and her deep blue eyes that had already seen so much for a woman so young. Light from the portholes glinted off something on her chest, and I noticed a chain and pendant hanging from her neck. I reached for the jewelry and rubbed its smooth surface in my fingers, quickly realizing what it was. A simple gold band—a man's gold band.

"You don't wear this very often," I said quietly. "I thought you were afraid of losing it."

Emily tugged it from my grasp and wrapped it in her fist. Her eyes brimmed with moisture. "I am . . . but I couldn't bear to leave him behind." She wiped her face with the heel of her free hand, then laid it atop mine and let out a short exhale. "Are you frightened about what we might face?"

I stared at the ceiling, allowing my feelings to shoulder their way to the forefront. What I felt was far more than nausea and fear. Beyond the seasickness, a breathtaking coldness cut into me, like a spike being driven farther and farther into ice—and the voice that had awakened with Shay growled in the deep.

***You know the fate that awaits you . . . you know all their fates. So why haven't you told them? Perhaps it is because you know they'll abandon you the moment you do.***

I wrapped my hand around Emily's and hugged it to my chest, powerless to speak but needing her strength. How could I possibly reveal that I had seen her son captured? Convincing her to bring him with us was my attempt to stop that from happening, so why create panic where there need not be any?

Baze limped leisurely along the deck as Basil Allan ran circles in front, holding his stubby arms straight out horizontally and making exaggerated sounds with his mouth like that of an airplane. Baze smiled as he watched the boy's enthusiasm burst from his small body. Several weeks ago, Emily had taken him to see a motion picture that featured an airplane, and he had been obsessed with the contraption ever since.

The sun above crept closer to midafternoon, and a pleasant breeze cut through its warmth. Clicking his cane in tandem with his steps, Baze took in a deep breath, though the salty air seemed incapable of untangling the knots of anxiety in his gut—for the farther the ship carried them to Ireland, the tighter the knots pulled.

O'Sullivan had to be defeated, but was Baze willing to risk Adelynn's mind, or her very life, to do so? She was already spiraling down a dark path, and it was clear she would throw herself deeper if need be. What if she went too far?

A tug on his trousers snatched his attention to Basil Allan peering up at him with eager hazel eyes. "Can you be the airplane next, Bay-Bay?" he asked in his squeaky voice.

Hard as it was to decline such an innocent request, the aches Baze's leg had been exhibiting of late warned that he mustn't put any undue stress upon it. He grinned, hiding his bruised pride, and mussed the boy's brown curls. "I think you are a much finer airplane than I would be. Come, show me again."

Basil Allan refused to relent and tugged once more. "Please, Bay-Bay? *Please?*"

Realizing that the boy wasn't going to give in without a proper explanation, Baze tapped his calf with his cane. "I'm afraid I can't run, buddy."

"Oh." Basil Allan frowned. "Why?"

Baze sighed. "My leg's injured."

"Why?"

"A bad man hurt it."

"Why?"

Baze stilled his tongue as he pictured Collin Donoghue, the young Irish teenager who had been manipulated and used by Cornelius Marx. With his mind under Marx's control, Collin had inflicted a devastating blow to Baze's leg in the final conflict at the Empress Theatre. Collin was as much a victim as Baze had been, but Basil Allan wouldn't know the difference, so Baze opted for a simple answer. "Because I was trying to stop him."

More confusion crumped the boy's face. "Why?"

Baze chuckled and pointed ahead with his cane. "I think that's enough questions. Why don't you continue playing."

Rather than obey, Basil Allan scrunched his nose and studied Baze's leg, then stuck out his tongue and began favoring his own right leg as he walked. The gesture might have prodded Baze's pride further were it not for the fact that Basil Allan looked equal parts ridiculous and adorable doing so.

Before they could go far, something over the ship's railing stole Basil Allan's attention. Exhibiting incredible speed for an individual with such short limbs, he sprinted away and ascended the rungs.

Fear spiked, and Baze gave chase. Calf muscle spasming, he snagged the back of Basil Allan's coat and then wound a hand around the boy's stomach to foil any attempt to topple overboard. "You've got to be careful, buddy. That's a long way down."

Beside them, Baze noticed a father and young son standing along the railing in the same manner. "Higher, Papa, higher!" the son cried. With a laugh, the father lifted him one more rung, and the boy started gesturing to things in the distance, which the father proceeded to name and explain.

Basil Allan patted Baze's arm, then faced the sea and pointed. "What's that?"

Baze tried to follow the boy's pudgy finger. They were still in the Strait of Dover, and the bright sun had lit the white bluff with a magnificent glow. "That's a cliff."

"What's that?" The child pointed again.

Baze squinted. "A tree."

Another point. "What's that?"

Shuffling feet and loud conversation drew Baze's gaze over his shoulder as a boisterous trio ambled by. Then an insistent yank on his sleeve preceded an exuberant, "What's that? Papa, what's that?"

Baze whipped his head toward Basil Allan. The air surged from his lungs. A punch to the gut would have hurt far less than the words the boy had just uttered.

How much had Emily told him about Bennett? He was far too young to know the full truth, but did he even understand that Bennett was dead? Or had she fashioned a white lie to quell the boy's curiosity whenever the topic came up? Either way, for the sake of Bennett's memory and Baze's conscience, he couldn't hide the truth.

Tucking his hands in Basil Allan's armpits, Baze lifted him off the railing and deposited him on the deck. He lowered to one knee, laid his cane across his lap, and gripped the boy's arms. "Listen, buddy. I know that I spend a lot of time with you, but I'm not your father."

With a frown, Basil Allan looked at the father and son, then back to Baze. The statement clearly didn't make sense in the three-year-old's fledgling mind, so Baze fished in his coat pocket and came out with the scuffed portrait of Bennett that he always kept close. He held up the photograph. "This is your father."

Basil Allan cocked his head, then giggled and poked Baze's cheek. "No, you!"

Baze's heart sank. He prayed for the courage and the words to continue. With a firm grip, he took Basil Allan's hand and showed him the portrait once more. "No, this is your father. His name is Bennett. That's your name too—Basil Allan Bennett."

The child studied the photo a little longer this time, then said, "Where is he?"

Another blow straight to the gut. Baze swallowed and tried to still his quivering voice. He again prayed for the right words to say to appease the child's curiosity but also not hide the truth—or at least the important bits.

"He's in heaven."

Basil Allan absently skimmed his finger over Bennett's face. "Why?"

"Do you remember that I told you I hurt my leg while I was trying to stop a bad man?" At the boy's nod, Baze continued. "Your father used to catch bad men too, but one day, he was gravely hurt. And he— he died."

"Will he come back?"

"No, buddy." Baze's throat threatened to cut off the rest of his words. He placed a hand atop the boy's head. "But he loved you so very much."

Basil Allan's inquisitive eyes widened a touch. Then he smudged his hands over Baze's cheeks, smearing tears Baze hadn't even realized had spilled. "Why are you crying?"

Baze swiped at the remaining tears and grappled for composure. "Because it's sad. It's okay to be sad sometimes."

"When I'm sad, Mama gives me kisses to make me better." The boy squished Baze's face between his tiny hands, rose on his tiptoes, and planted a light kiss to Baze's nose with a gentle "*Mwaa!*" His probing hazel eyes all but melted the remnants of Baze's self-control. "All better?"

Baze forced a smile even as his stomach plummeted. "Yes, buddy. I'm all better."

## Chapter Seven

As the evening waned, my seasickness waned with it. I even managed to keep down a brothy bowl of soup and slice of toast with orange marmalade. The weariness lingered, however, so after dinner, I retreated to our stateroom and recruited my maid, Margaret, to help me change into my nightgown, thankful for its loose, forgiving fabric.

Hardly an hour passed before the others retired as well, and it didn't take long for Basil Allan to discover the conjoining door and initiate a silly game of peekaboo with Baze. From where I sat cross-legged on the bed, I watched the toddler hide behind the door and then pop out with a loud exclamation, drawing a mock cry from Baze. With each of Basil Allan's giggles, Baze tried to keep up the act but couldn't help but laugh in response. Soon, Emily snatched up her son for bedtime, much to his great disdain.

Baze bid them goodnight and then latched the door. As he crossed to the wardrobe, he shook his head with an amused smile.

Gathering the courage to call attention to what I so clearly saw upon Baze's face, I pulled my hair over one shoulder and started plaiting it loosely. I tried to keep my voice light and indifferent. "Basil Allan adores you, you know."

Baze slipped out of his coat and unbuttoned his waistcoat. "He's a mischievous one, but that would be expected for a child of Bennett's."

Lowering my voice, I ventured one more step. "You're so good with him. I dare say you're a natural . . . and I believe you will be just as good with our children someday."

The smile vanished as he shot me a look of annoyance. "We've already talked about this, Adelynn."

"No, *we* haven't talked about anything." I angled toward him, but he turned back to his task, obviously keen to ignore me. "Why don't you want a child?"

"I never said I don't want one. I said it's too soon. Now is not the best time."

"Then when is the best time?"

He tossed his waistcoat into the wardrobe with a sigh. "I don't want to discuss this right now."

Undeterred, I scooted from the bed, padded across the floor, and slid between him and the bureau. "*When?*"

A frustrated exhale whooshed from his nose as he scowled down at me. "I don't know when."

I folded my arms. "That's not an adequate answer."

"What more do you want me to say?"

"I want you to tell me the truth."

"That is the truth."

"But it's not the whole truth," I snapped, tone rising. "I know when you're keeping things from me, Baze, and you've just lied straight to my face."

"Keep your voice down," he whisper-shouted, flicking his eyes toward the conjoining door.

With a strained huff, I wrangled control of my words. "Talk to me. All I want is to understand. Help me understand. Please."

His throat tensed with a swallow before he shook his head. "And all I want is for you to respect my wishes and drop the matter."

Every strand of control within me snapped. "What about my wishes?" I shouted and poked him in the chest. "Why do you get the only say? I'm the other half in this relationship. Do you know what I've given up for you? I left my mother. I changed my name. All for you. The least you can do is fulfill this basic request as my husband."

Baze curled his lip. "You sound just like my father."

I blinked. "Excuse me?"

"You heard me." He angled his face inches from mine. "He once tried to manipulate me for his own gain, and now you're trying to do the same."

I gaped, cheeks flushing and tears flooding. "How dare you."

"Am I wrong?"

With a growl, I shoved him toward the door. "Get out."

"Hey, stop—"

"Get out. Get out!" I advanced and swiped haphazardly until he darted through the door. I slammed it after him and flicked the lock, then whirled and collapsed against it, sinking to the floor and hugging my knees. Long-suppressed sobs finally surfaced.

Baze jiggled the handle. "Open the door." The solid wood muffled his terse words. "What are you going to do? Keep me locked out here all night?"

I ignored him and stayed paralyzed on the floor. Soon, his pleas for reentry ceased, and I was left alone with the agony of wondering why my husband was choosing to deprive me of my deepest desire.

I jerked awake. Numbness prickled across my skin, but as I wiggled my fingers and toes, pain came rushing in. Lying stretched on the hard floor, with my face smashed into the boards, my body positively ached. As I struggled to sit up, I peered about the room. Though the lamp still glowed dimly, the darkness outside the portholes indicated night had fully sprung.

Grit scratched my eyes as I blinked myself further awake. I couldn't recall when I'd stopped crying and fell asleep. Or perhaps I had cried myself to sleep.

*Baze.*

Feet still numb, I scrambled up and unlocked the door, expecting to find him slumbering on the other side, but the hallway was empty.

Concern rising, I grabbed my robe and lashed it around me, then hurried outside. An icy breeze poured over the railing, and I shuddered. How could I have left him out here in this frigid weather? He would surely catch his death.

The ship wasn't that large, so he couldn't have gone far, but the longer I looked—rushing from the lounge to the dining room to the bow—the more my stomach wound into knots. As I approached the stern of the ship, I rounded the corner to the very back and discovered a bench facing out to sea. Baze lay upon it with his arm curled and tucked under his head and his shirt unbuttoned at the neck. His body shivered lightly.

Tiptoeing, I drew closer, and as my feet swished across the deck, his eyes slipped opened and locked on me. Weariness weighed down his eyelids as he stirred and sat up.

Folding my arms around my chest to combat the cold, I crept to the bench and sank beside him.

Wordless, we stared into the black sky. Water foamed atop the large inky wake trailing behind the ship. The whirring engine and churning sea filled our silence.

"I'm sorry." The roaring water nearly snatched away Baze's whisper.

I stiffened against his apology but remained quiet.

"It was wrong of me to treat you the way I did and say the things I said." He scrubbed his hands over his face, then raked his fingers into his hair. "I was a complete git."

My mouth twitched as I resisted a bitter smile. "Yes, you were."

Still shivering slightly, he bent forward, locked his fingers between his knees, and bowed his head. "Everything I said to you earlier, about being like my father—I meant every word for myself." His eyes glistened as he focused on the wooden slats beneath his feet. "I've done all I know to do to heal from his mistreatment, but I fear it's too late. I fear his cruel persona lies dormant within me, ready to awaken the moment we have children." He stroked the bridge of his nose. "You asked for the truth, Al—and the truth is, I'm afraid. I'm afraid I'll become like him. I'm afraid I'll corrupt our children just as he did me."

Understanding radiated across my damaged soul like a salve, and the instinct to contradict his feelings, to assure him that he was nothing like his father and never would be, nearly compelled me to respond in protest. But I held back. It had taken him enough effort to admit this much to me, and he didn't need my overbearing monologues squashing any further vulnerability.

"I'm sorry for keeping it from you." His shoulders contracted. "I wasn't sure you would want to hear it. What kind of a man fears having children and then moans about it to his wife?"

The objections I had quelled a second ago came surging back up. I tilted my head. "Would you ever turn me away or shame me for sharing my fears or my doubts with you?"

He shot me a frown. "Of course not. You can always come to me."

I nearly chuckled at his naïvety. "And you can always come to me. I know I can be assertive, but if you have something intimate to share, I want to be a place of safety and solace for you." I stroked the hair above his ear and then traced his lobe, coaxing his eyes shut. "I'm sorry if I ever made you feel like you couldn't confide in me."

His breath fled his lungs in a deep sigh. "Don't apologize, Al. I'm the one in the wrong."

I slid my hand under his chin and pulled his face toward me. As I stared into his mournful eyes, my hurt gave way to empathy. Knowing the real reason for his hesitation didn't remove my longing for a child, but it lessened the sting of his refusal—at least a little.

"You are incredible with Basil Allan," I said, gentle but adamant. "He looks at you with absolute adoration, and I don't think a man who inspires that kind of esteem in a toddler has a cruel bone in his body." I stroked his cheek with my thumb. "If you treat our children with even a fraction of the care that you do Basil Allan, you will be a brilliant father."

For a moment, he rested the weight of his head in my palm, searching my eyes with his. Then he straightened and nicked my hand from the air. As he massaged the muscle, he rotated his body toward me, pulling his leg up onto the bench and tucking his ankle under his other knee.

"I care deeply about your desires, Al, and I want to give you the opportunity to become a mother." He hesitated, and I saw the coming contradiction in the rolling of his lips. "But there are problems I still have yet to resolve with my father." With a sigh, he met my gaze, his expression pinched in remorse. "I'm asking, not demanding . . . will you allow me just a bit more time?"

Disappointment flooded my bones, but I fought to keep it from appearing on my face. My nose prickled as I forced a slight smile of submission and murmured, "Okay."

## Chapter Eight

*LADY GWENDOLEN* MADE BERTH IN DUBLIN Port at the mouth of the
River Liffey a few days later in the early morning. Our approach to
Dublin had revealed glimpses of the famous green shore, but as we
churned toward the dock, the city's tall buildings and sprawling expanse
blocked any view of the emerald countryside. Structures and ships of
all sizes lined both banks, and with the city rising in the background,
the atmosphere didn't feel much different from London Port—except
for the air. Though tinged with the stench of smoke and petrol and fish,
the air smelled richer somehow, more grounded in earth and antiquity.

Baze and I disembarked first, with Emily and Basil Allan trailing
behind us. I marveled at how Baze maintained solid footing on the
slanted gangplank, especially while balancing on his cane with one
hand and supporting me with the other. I, in contrast, had never fully
developed my sea legs, and now that we were back on solid land, my
body appeared not to have the faintest idea what to do with itself and
chose to press into Baze's side. As we reached the bottom of the ramp,
I extended my leg and touched my toes to Ireland for the first time.

A flash of heat exploded through me. I gasped and clung to Baze
as I endured the fiery sensations rippling through my body. The
phenomenon felt akin to the physical warning I often experienced when
a vision was about to yank me into scenes of unknown—but this
presence was more neutral, more controlled . . . and it left my mind
intact. The longer I stood, the more regulated it became, pulsing through
my veins in time with my heart's natural rhythm.

Katherine, Finn, and others had speculated that Ireland was the
source of our gifts—holy and malevolent alike. During his

performances at the Empress Theatre, Finn had told stories of ancient fairies giving power to his magic. While I didn't believe such pixies existed, I *was* certain that our world harbored many supernatural faculties just below the surface.

Could there be some truth to Finn's tales? Was Ireland the source of our power?

"Al, are you all right?"

Baze's whisper coaxed my mind back to him and diminished the sensations racing through me, but they continued vibrating beneath the soles of my feet.

***You mustn't tell him about what you just felt. He'll be angry if you do.***

The voice gave me pause. Considering how upset Baze had been that night when I opened communication with Shay, perhaps it was best to spare him another eruption and opt for a pacifying answer. "Yes," I breathed, using his strong frame to right myself. "Yes . . . I'm merely nauseous."

"Still?" He shook his head and, supporting my arm, turned me toward the car. "That won't do. The moment we arrive at the estate, we shall give you something to alleviate your symptoms."

As we continued toward the automobile, I glimpsed Samuel at his dutiful post, and my heart swelled. The middle-aged chauffeur was helping several youngsters affix our trunks to the car for transport. He and several of our other staff members had graciously agreed to accompany us for the duration of our stay. In fact, my request that he join us had invited his revelation that Father often brought Samuel to Ireland to serve as his chauffeur while there.

I pulled away from Baze and touched the chauffeur's arm with a smile. "Thank you for coming, Samuel."

"It is my great honor, Miss Adelynn. I was delighted to serve Mr. Spencer, and I am equally as delighted to serve you, if not more so." With a wink, he opened the door of the back seat.

Skillfully navigating Dublin as though he were a native Irishman,

Samuel chose to take us on a scenic route. We motored along the River Liffey straight through the heart of the city before crossing over a bridge. Not far into our journey, Basil Allan clambered onto my lap and pressed his nose against the glass. I wrapped a protective hand around his waist and peered out as well, drinking in the sights—the very same sights my father would have seen.

"If you look to your left, you might be able to glimpse Trinity College," Samuel said as he drove. "It contains a historic library that houses ancient artifacts and manuscripts." He continued weaving through some smaller streets and then pointed. "And there is Dublin Castle. That's where Mr. Spencer conducted the majority of his business."

Through the buildings peeked an ancient castle tower. I pressed my fingers to the window as though to reach through it and touch the structure. My whole life, I had only heard tales of Father's time spent here, soaking up every description of the people he met and the places he went, and now I was looking upon one of them with my own eyes.

Baze leaned around me. "That's been standing since Medieval times, you know."

I raised an eyebrow and tapped his chin. "You *would* know that."

He shrugged, his dimple appearing with a smirk.

As we crossed the river once more and turned west, a great green expanse lined with full trees opened before us, lush and inviting. "This is Phoenix Park," Samuel explained. "It is home to several of Ireland's governing individuals, including the president, and it is also where Mr. Spencer resided. We are mere minutes away now."

I caught my breath. Phoenix Park. The location of the killings in which Cornelius Marx's father had been involved. The man evaded capture for years until he was tracked down, and my father had testified to bring him to justice. With his home tucked inside the park, had Father witnessed the murders firsthand? Is that how he was able to convict the man?

Samuel directed the car through tall stone fences flanking a paved drive and parked in front of a modest but beautiful home. I nudged Basil Allan to return to Emily before we exited the car, and as the doors latched behind me, I twisted my clammy hands against my stomach and faced the house.

Shaped like a basic rectangle and constructed of the same gray stone as the fences, the unassuming building featured two rows of four white-trimmed windows with a red door centered between them. Two flat chimneys jutted toward the sky on both ends of the house. Smoke streamed from the stacks, and lights shone from the windows, signaling that the staff members who had gone ahead to prepare for our arrival were hard at work.

Baze edged up to my side and placed his hand at the small of my back. "Go on," he said softly. "I'll be right behind you."

Squaring my shoulders, I marched to the door and pushed inside. Warm air kissed my cheeks, and the strong aroma nearly bowled me over—a familiar blend of tobacco, leather, and spices. Father's scent. My stomach fluttered, and I almost lost the resolve to continue, but my feet reluctantly carried me forward.

I stroked my pearl ring as I wandered from room to room—the foyer, the sitting room, the bedroom, the kitchen, and then into a second sitting room. His scent followed me, swathing my shoulders as though he himself escorted me. I approached the fireplace and focused on the wooden mantel. Sure enough, as Mother had said, the initials *T* and *C* marked the dark grain. Smiling faintly, I traced the etchings with a delicate finger before turning back to my exploration.

If there had been personal belongings left scattered about after his death, the staff had long since removed them, for the space was too tidy, too pristine. There should have been open books stacked upon the side tables, used ashtrays strategically placed in each room, and coats tossed over the backs of the sofas as Father was prone to do at the end of a long day.

When I slipped into his study, my heartbeat quickened. It was smaller than his study at home, but it felt cozier. Like the rest of the house, the desk had been cleaned, its surface free of the documents, books, and letters that he usually kept strewn about. However, three objects had been left in place—an ornate little box and two framed portraits angled toward the plush leather chair.

As I lifted the lid of the box, a pin popped up and released a chiming melody. "The Parting Glass." Father's favorite song to sing to me before departing.

Soothed by the music, I picked up the first photograph and turned it over to reveal my mother's image. The woman gazing out at me appeared decades younger than the one I knew, with smooth skin, youthful eyes, and a stunning yet playful smile. She had been enchanting, but even though her physical beauty now had faded with time, there came with it a deep wisdom and grace that I so admired.

Setting it down, I moved to the second portrait, this one of a small girl—me.

I gulped in a breath as I stared at my chubby face dotted with freckles. I couldn't have been more than two or three years old, with light, nearly white curls secured away from my face with a huge bow. I'd been sat on a wooden chair in a lacy pinafore and dress and looked absolutely peeved for having to endure it. Though I held my back straight and my legs tucked as someone had likely instructed me to do, I'd managed to cross my arms and pout in time for the camera to capture my displeasure.

A sudden sob seized my lungs. I slammed the photograph onto the desk and clapped a hand over my mouth to keep the emotions contained. Every time Father went away, I had always kept him at the forefront of my thoughts, grasping tightly to his memory and praying desperately that he wouldn't forget about me, that he would return to me.

Now it was clear I needn't ever have worried.

Grief squeezed my chest and bent me forward. I supported myself against the desk with a trembling hand as shallow breaths and weak cries jerked from my lips. The last time sorrow this deep had consumed me had been the day after Father died—and I had resolved never to allow myself to endure that painful feeling again. Yet, despite my every effort to maintain control, my heart chose to betray my mind and permitted the dam to rupture.

"Papa." The single word squeaked through my lips.

Just as my knees weakened and threatened to spill me onto the floor, warm arms came around me from behind and supported me in a strong but tender embrace. Baze's face burrowed against my neck. He remained silent and merely held me as I allowed my long-suppressed emotions the chance to finally release with all of their raw, ugly power.

*Heat scorched my fingers through the crude clay mug. Blowing into the coffee's trickling steam, I wandered through my tiny home—a shack really—and out the door I had propped open to let cool air enliven the space. I planted myself upon the crumbling stone step and sipped from the brew, then winced as it scalded my tongue.*

*Dew clung to the grass, and fog hovered low in the hills. A shepherd guided his small flock of sheep up a nearby slope and through one of the ancient and fracturing stone fences. Two women beside a gentle creek sang softly as they hung damp laundry out to dry. A cluster of children ran by, giggling and kicking a ball between their feet.*

*One of the young girls hobbled after the group on makeshift crutches, and my chest tightened as I recalled the attack she had survived—a scuffle between loyalists and everyday folk that had erupted in violence. Luckily, I'd been close, had been able to pull her from the brawl . . . but the nature of my powers couldn't reverse the damage done to her—it could only deal swift justice to the offenders.*

*Soon, she and our kin wouldn't have to worry about such things. We wouldn't have to quarrel with our brothers and sisters. Though the path I had chosen was one of aggression, one that would paint me as a villain, I was willing to bear that burden if it meant freeing others from the bondage of fear and, ultimately, from Great Britain.*

*An unprompted feeling of unease pinched my stomach. I frowned and fixated on the sensation, trying to determine where—*

*Pain pierced the bottom of my feet. I gasped as it shot up my legs and raked through my body. The mug fell and shattered. Thrusting out a hand, I caught myself against the doorjamb, then bowed my head and ground my teeth as the pain seared through my veins. A deep, heavy pull cemented my feet to the ground as though securing me to something, to the earth, to Ireland, to . . .*

*Adelynn Ford.*

*I swung my head north—toward Dublin. She was here. Why? Why was she here? After she so foolishly connected her mind to mine, I thought I had done enough to scare her away, had made the consequences clear. Obviously, I had misjudged her brazenness, for despite my warnings, despite the darkness she had allowed to penetrate her mind, she chose to enter my domain.*

*I pounded my fist into the doorjamb. My knuckles popped, but the fire simmering in my muscles masked any new pain. I didn't want to go on the attack—after all, my last offensive move of removing Kate from my path had nearly done me in.*

*But Adelynn was forcing my hand. If she persisted, I would have no other choice but to act—and if I could endure the torment of killing the woman who meant more to me than any other soul on this earth, then dealing with Adelynn and her allies would be mere child's play.*

## Chapter Nine

Darkness embraced me as I gradually came to. My eyes stung and my body ached from the emotions I had expelled the night before. I wasn't sure how long I had wept, but after I calmed, Baze had carried me to bed, where he'd held me close until sleep claimed me.

***Your father didn't want you to join him in Ireland, because he wanted to get away from you. This place was his escape.***

I expelled a harsh sigh and turned onto my back, rejecting the intrusive thoughts. *Stop it. That's not true.*

Hunger pains slithered up my torso. Other than the single bowl of soup and slice of toast, I hadn't been able to stomach anything for the entire three-day voyage. Maybe my body would behave now that we were safely on solid ground. My mouth watered as I pictured the staff preparing a delectable morning feast and, unable to settle enough to acquire a couple more hours of sleep, I slipped from bed.

Though I tried to keep my rustling to a minimum, Baze's soft snoring ceased as I dressed for the day. Yet, if he had awakened, he chose to remain silent as I finished and stole from the room.

Padding down the hall, I followed a mixture of warm smells into the formal dining room. There, I found Emily and Basil Allan sitting at the table with a full breakfast of fruit, bacon, eggs, smoked haddock, baked beans, black pudding, grilled tomatoes, and toast. Basil Allan was far too occupied with shoveling the beans into his mouth to notice my approach, but Emily smiled a greeting. "Good morning, Adelynn. You're up earlier than I anticipated."

I shrugged and rubbed my arms against a chill. "You are as well. I'm surprised you didn't sleep longer after such a strenuous voyage."

"If I could have, I would have, but with this little nipper around, I'm afraid leisurely mornings are a thing of the past." Emily lightly pinched Basil Allan's cheek. He tipped his head away with a displeased grunt and continued eating. Emily laughed and gestured to the chair opposite her. "Please, join us."

As I sat, a wave of scents assaulted my nose—some pleasant and some repulsive. My stomach lurched. I swallowed against rising bile and grimaced. This queasiness was supposed to have ended when we made landfall. Why did it linger?

Emily examined me for a tick, then passed me a plate of toast. "So, what is our plan of action for today?"

I lifted a slice and spread it with a negligible serving of strawberry jam, all the while trying not to be sick. "I need to breach Shay's mind again to try to uncover anything more about his location. We need to find him as soon as possible."

Emily wiped a trickle of sauce from Basil Allan's chin before steering her attention back to me. "Do you think that is wise?"

***Tell her off. She doesn't understand what you're going through.***

Annoyance hardened my stomach. "I can't all of a sudden sit on my hands simply because it might be dangerous. Otherwise, we've come all this way for nothing."

Emily's brows pinched together. "I don't believe it will have been for nothing. Keeping your mind safe is of utmost importance. Perhaps there's another way. Perhaps we can find Shay without—"

"There is no other way," I snapped, then muttered a half-baked apology. I rubbed the pearl on my ring. "You don't understand, Emily. This man is not going to stop unless we stop him."

She stroked her son's hair, her eyes compassionate. "Just promise me that if you find yourself beginning to succumb to the darkness, you'll retreat. Even if it means giving up the fight." Her voice wobbled. "Your life is not worth it."

***You can't stop. You'll never stop. And you know it. Your life is already forfeit.***

I stared hard at my ring, a lump in my throat, knowing she was right but refusing to accept any outcome that didn't include Shay O'Sullivan's end. He had taken enough from me, and I refused to let him take any more.

"Our trials thus far have proven that the only way to combat this darkness we face is to walk daily in the light." Expression contemplative, Emily folded her serviette and laid it gently beside her plate. "Adelynn, when was the last time you petitioned the Almighty or sought wisdom in the Scriptures?"

My body shivered as though an icy wind had blown past. The Almighty's voice had grown quiet of late, not that I wanted it to, but with all the burdens I was shouldering, prayer had been the last thing on my mind. Surely God understood that.

***Oh, He'll be fine without you. Trust me.***

With a shrug, I said simply, "I've been busy." I bit off the corner of my toast, but the moment it touched my tongue, my stomach spasmed. Pressing a hand to it, I forced myself to swallow and managed to keep it down. Barely.

I cast Emily an expectant look. "I don't suppose you have any suggestions for resolving lingering seasickness?"

She tilted her head. "Are you still nauseated?"

As if in response, my insides fluttered. "Sometimes it's nausea, and sometimes it's simply a light stirring. The intensity rises and falls. I thought it would have cleared by now."

Emily studied me for a quiet moment, then sighed. "You might try chewing on some ginger again for temporary relief, but there are no remedies for what I believe you are experiencing, not of the medicinal nature anyway. I believe you may be feeling the quickening."

The hair on the back of my neck prickled. "The what?"

"The quickening." Her lips spread in a kind smile. "It's the moment when a mother first feels her child move within her."

Gooseflesh swept across my body. A flicker of hope sputtered to life, but I quickly snuffed it out with denial. I clutched at my stomach and tried to absorb her words—words that I knew couldn't be true, words I didn't *want* to be true. Not now. Not when we had just brought ourselves to the edge of a great conflict with Shay. Not when Baze remained so adamantly against this.

***If it is true, your husband will surely abandon you.***

"You're mistaken," I whispered with a shake of my head. "It's impossible."

Her voice grew gentle. "I know you are taking the recommended precautions to avoid such a thing, but they are not foolproof. Far from it."

"No," I continued to mutter under my breath, beating down any trace of hope that tried to surface. "I'm sorry, Emily. This can't happen right now. It's lingering seasickness. Nothing more. I'll have Margaret bring me some ginger, and that'll be the end of it."

"Perhaps you should seek a doctor merely to be sure. I could go with you if you like."

"I said no." I raised my voice. "I don't need a doctor because I'm not—"

"Who needs a doctor?"

Baze's sudden voice jolted me. I clamped my mouth shut as he pulled out the chair beside me, dropped into it, and cornered me under his anxious gaze.

Emily smiled as though nothing were amiss. "Oh, 'tisn't anything of concern. Adelynn is still experiencing seasickness. I suggested she seek a doctor for a more potent remedy."

I relaxed slightly. *Bless you, Emily.*

"Ah, I see." As though the matter were already forgotten, he began fixing himself a plate of food. "I plan to go into the city today," he said as he scooped a large helping of tomatoes and black pudding onto the China. "Whelan gave me the name of the superintendent of the Dublin Metropolitan Police. If we're to start a war, it's best that I make as many allies as possible."

Emily and I locked eyes, and she gestured for me to respond, but when I kept my mouth shut, she faced him instead. "I think that sounds like a wise idea."

Pausing mid-bite, Baze glanced between us, then narrowed his eyes and swallowed. "Is something the matter? Have I missed something?"

***If you tell him, he'll abandon you.***

I lurched back from the table on screeching chair legs and burst to my feet. As I whirled, Baze caught my arm. "Wait, slow down. What's wrong?"

"Nothing." I yanked from his grasp. "I'm going to lie down."

Tears nipped my eyes as I swept from the room, one hand over my mouth and the other cradling my abdomen. No matter how desperately I longed for it to be true, I couldn't allow myself to entertain even the slightest hope that a seed had taken root in my womb. Not when Baze had made it clear he was against it. Not when it could drive him away.

Adelynn's strange behavior weighed upon Baze as Samuel drove him into the city. Was she truly afflicted by an acute case of nausea? Or perhaps it was something more, something of the womanly nature—in which case, he would gladly allow Adelynn to defer to Emily's expertise.

Still . . . it irked him to think that she was keeping something from him, no matter how delicate a concern it might be.

He didn't have long to think hard about it, as Samuel turned onto Great Brunswick Street and eased up beside a building perched on the corner across from Trinity College—the central barracks of the Dublin Metropolitan Police. Having been christened as the new police station mere months ago, the structure displayed a pristine granite exterior ornamented by four sculpted heads, two constables and two superior officers.

Baze relayed a meeting time to Samuel before the chauffeur sped away to make a return trip to pick up the women. Then Baze faced the building and took the front steps slowly and one at a time, his cane clacking with his ascent. His leg had been bothering him since they docked in Dublin Port—more than usual. Perhaps the constant swaying of the ship's deck had taken its toll.

Rehearsing the words he would say, Baze passed beneath an imposing arch, guarded on either side by the two officers' heads, and entered through a heavy wooden door. *God, guide my tongue. Help me say the right things so I don't make a complete fool of myself.*

A young constable manned the front desk, dressed in a black uniform that matched the style of the London Met. Though the similarities were a stark reminder of Great Britain's grasp on Ireland, the familiar vestments made Baze feel more at home.

"Good day to you, sir." Baze put on a cheery voice and leaned onto his cane as he stopped.

The constable looked up. "Good day, indeed," he said with a light accent. "How may I help you, sir?"

"I'm Detective Inspector Basil Ford with the London Metropolitan Police, and I would like to speak with Superintendent Darragh Moore. Can you take me to him?"

The man regarded Baze a moment, his clean-shaven jaw shifting as his gaze flicked to the cane, before he nodded curtly, rose, and gestured to the long hall. "Right this way, then."

The constable escorted Baze through the corridor, and Baze did his best to keep up with the man's long strides. Along the way, they passed several office doors, and Baze surmised that one end of the building was devoted to the high-ranking officers while the rest housed the barracks for the rank-and-file policemen.

When they came to an open door, the constable swerved inside. Baze followed, stepping around the constable to fully enter the modest office. A man whom Baze assumed was the superintendent sat behind a simple desk, reading through a stack of papers with a pair of spectacles worn low on his nose. His slim build, freckled skin, and band of thinning red hair appeared in complete contrast to Whelan's gruff and bulky physique to which Baze was so accustomed.

The constable knocked on the door frame. "A detective inspector from London's here to see you, sir."

Darragh Moore glanced up. "London, you say?" He snatched off his spectacles and tossed them onto the desk with a light clatter. "You're quite a long way from home, boyo. What's it that brings you to me?"

As the constable took his leave, Baze planted his cane before him and rolled his shoulders to attention. "I arrived in Dublin with my family yesterday. We'll be staying in the area for the foreseeable future, so I thought it would be prudent to stop by and introduce myself. Superintendent Richard Whelan told me to seek you out."

"Ol' Richie? You mean to tell me he hasn't retired yet?" Moore's sky-blue eyes sparkled.

Baze cracked a smile. "No, sir. If he has any say, he'll be with the Met until he dies."

A high-pitched laugh and wide grin stretched Moore's thick red-and-white mustache. He burst to his feet, came around the desk, and took Baze's hand in a firm greeting. "A pleasure to meet you, boyo, a pleasure. What might I be callin' you?"

Usually, Baze thought it best to maintain formality until he could cultivate a deeper relationship with the individual, but something about the man disarmed Baze. Besides, Whelan apparently thought highly of the man, and that was praise not easily won.

"Call me Baze," he said.

"Excellent. You can be callin' me Darragh." The superintendent tapped his toe to the base of Baze's cane. "Why don't you have a sit? No sense keepin' you on your feet while we chitchat." He returned to his seat with nimble steps and said, "What happened?"

"Broke my leg." Baze settled into one of the two chairs facing the desk and planted his cane between his knees. "Had a run-in with a criminal."

"I thought as much. There's no shortage of our boys who be carryin' a deformation in one sense or another." Darragh held up his left hand and wiggled his fingers—or at least, he wiggled two of them, for the fourth and fifth digits were gone. Only the smallest stubs remained. "Got these pinched in a ladder while I was chasin' an escapee in me twenties. Came off so fast I didn't even feel it." He grinned. "But I caught the man, and that's all that matters." He folded his arms over the desktop and leaned forward eagerly. "So, what's brought you to Dublin? It must be more than a holiday if you came out of your way to meet with me."

"Yes, sir." Baze gripped the top of his cane to keep from stroking his nose. "I'm here because of a case I worked in London in the spring of 1913. It involved—"

"A crazy Irishman masquerading as an English magician," Darragh said calmly. "Left a wake of bodies in the name of revenge."

Baze raised his eyebrows. "You've heard of it?"

"Oh, I'm quite sure all of Great Britain knows about that case. I, personally, took special interest in it on account of the ancestry of Cornelius Marx—or whatever he called himself. It's hard enough keepin' the peace in Ireland without gobdaws like him goin' and taintin' our image. He doesn't represent the lot." Darragh stroked his mustache. "I understand you had another brush with death in Bath only a year later, is that right?"

"Yes again, sir."

"Good on you. Faced down evil head on—twice—and came out as the victor. You've got grit, boyo." The superintendent squinted one eye. "So, you're here because of Cornelius Marx?"

"Indirectly, yes." Baze squeezed the cane. "Sir . . . does the name Shay O'Sullivan mean anything to you?"

Shock loosened Darragh's features, and when he responded, his voice had lost its playful tone. "I have not heard that name uttered in many years. How did you hear of him?"

"I haven't merely heard of him, sir. We've crossed paths." Baze tipped forward. "He was behind the killings in Bath—perhaps even the killings in London. Are you aware of his connection to Marx?"

"Aye. Adoptive father." Darragh nodded and rubbed his finger stumps. "First time I heard O'Sullivan's name was early in my career. He was a traveling magician who had married an Englishwoman, adopted two young urchins, and performed throughout the countryside to make a living. I was on holiday near County Clare when an orphan keeper was murdered. There wasn't evidence enough to condemn anyone, sure, but many in the area claimed O'Sullivan had been the culprit."

Darragh expelled a sigh. "Strange happenin's always seemed to follow O'Sullivan wherever he went—and not the good kind. Deaths. Disappearances. Upstandin' men suddenly turnin' violent. But despite the Royal Irish Constabulary's efforts, he always evaded investigation. Last thing I heard, his wife had vanished, and I assumed the boys had, too, until Richie told me what was happenin' in London." He tipped his head at Baze. "So, you've come to Dublin chasing O'Sullivan, is that it? What's he done to pull an English inspector all the way to Ireland?"

Baze hesitated. Should he come right out with the full, untarnished truth—including everything about Adelynn's visions? Her supernatural connection to O'Sullivan was the only way to explain how they knew he was planning something in the first place. Besides, Whelan knew everything and had done nothing but serve as their most staunch ally.

At the encouragement shining deep in Darragh's light-blue eyes, Baze found his lips loosening—and before he could stop himself, the explanation of Adelynn's first vision at their engagement gala popped out of his mouth. So he pressed on. He walked Darragh through the entire sequence of events leading to Marx's death, then explained the incidents in Bath and finished by revealing Adelynn's most recent actions linking her to O'Sullivan.

"Based on what she saw, we believe he has his sights set on Dublin. We don't exactly know what he's planning, but as you said, nothing good ever follows him." Baze wet his lips and composed himself for a moment. "That's why I'm here, and that's why I've come to you. For an ally."

With the tale complete, Baze heaved a sigh and leaned back.

Darragh scrubbed a hand over his balding head, indecision twisting his mouth and mustache. "You realize how barmy you sound, boyo?"

"Yes, sir. I'm sure you think I'm insane, but it's the truth. All of it. Give Whelan a ring if you wish. He's aware of everything."

Darragh set his mouth in a straight line and squinted at Baze, absently rubbing his stubs.

A knock sounded at the door. Then it opened, and a constable stuck his head through. "Sir, you're needed out front."

"One moment." Darragh waved his hand, his eyes never leaving Baze as the constable retreated. Finally, he leaned back and clapped his hands on his knees. "I believe you."

Baze's heart leaped. "Truly?"

"Aye. Richie can sniff out complete eejits from a mile away, so if you've earned his trust, then you have mine." He got up and glanced at his pocket watch, then gestured for Baze to stand.

Baze hurried to rise and collect his cane. "Thank you, sir."

With a gentle smile, Darragh aimed his hand to the door. "I'll see you out."

As they marched into the hall, Darragh spoke low. "You're not under my command, boyo, so you're free to do as you wish, but if you learn anything more of O'Sullivan's schemes, I would like to know about it. Or at least inform me if you plan to act. He's a tricky one, and I don't want you to be goin' in alone. Aye?"

"Of course." Baze's head reeled. He hadn't expected this conversation to go so smoothly, but he was thankful nonetheless.

When they reached the front desk, Baze halted to bid Darragh farewell but was distracted by two young policemen conversing noisily at the other end of the hall near the barracks entrance. They laughed, and one knuckled the other on the shoulder, then spewed a quick string of Irish.

Though Baze couldn't decipher the words, the jovial tone sounded familiar—but only just, as though the truth of it were buried deep in a memory that Baze had long forgotten.

Drawn as though pulled by an invisible string, Baze ambled toward them. The men carried on until they noticed Baze's approach and stopped, faces contorted in annoyance. "Need something, sir?" the one on the left snapped.

The murk of Baze's memories cleared as he stared at the young man. With a crop of short brown hair, sharp green eyes, and the wispy beginnings of a beard, he couldn't have been more than twenty. However, he towered several inches over Baze's head, which was quite the feat considering the last time Baze had seen him, his crown had barely reached Baze's chest.

Jaw slack, Baze shook his head and whispered, "Collin."

## Chapter Ten

COLLIN'S FACE—NO LONGER THE ROUND face of a boy but the angled face of a man—melted into shock. He blinked and gave Baze a quick once-over. "Mr. Ford? Wha . . . what are you doin' here?"

"I could ask you the same question." Baze's mouth went dry as he took in Collin's garb, the black uniform of a Dublin constable. Collin joined the police? Why? After reuniting Collin with his brother, Liam, Baze had sent them back to Ireland with the prayer that Collin would live a quiet, peaceful life—and especially that he would stay far away from danger. Why would he throw himself straight into a profession that guaranteed it?

Darragh came up beside them and chuckled. "It appears you two be knowin' each other, aye?"

Baze stepped back to allow the superintendent room. "Yes, sir. We met in London three years ago."

"Well, what's got you tongue tied then?" Darragh knuckled Collin's shoulder. "You know, you're not due on patrol for another few hours. Why don't you take ol' Baze out for a pint."

Collin shifted from foot to foot. "Are you sure that's appropriate, Mr. Moore?"

"One or two beers isn't going to get you fluthered, Donoghue." Darragh snorted and poked Collin in the gut. "I've witnessed the stomach you've got in you."

With a shaky inhale, Collin peered at Baze as though looking for approval, and when Baze nodded, Collin whispered something in Irish to his companion and then jerked his head at Baze. "Come on then. I know a place."

Marching on long, lanky legs, Collin immediately outpaced Baze, but it took the young man only a few strides to realize Baze had fallen behind and slow his gait. After a quick look at Baze's leg, Collin cast his gaze at the ground and jammed his hands into his pockets. Even with Collin's measured pace, however, Baze struggled to keep up, but he clenched his teeth against any complaints that surfaced.

Just down the street, they passed into the area called Temple Bar and shoved into one of the corner pubs with a bright-red exterior, tinted windows, and boisterous music. All it took was one nod of Collin's head at the barkeep for two Guinnesses to appear at their table. By the time Baze took in the rowdy atmosphere—including a small stage featuring exuberant musicians surrounded by cheery, drunk patrons—Collin had already downed half of his beer.

Following suit, Baze swallowed a few swigs of the stout and licked froth from his lips. Then he leaned forward as though to escape the noise around him. "When I sent you away on that ship, I thought that would be the last time I saw you." Baze smiled. "You look good, Collin."

Body shaking slightly as he bobbed his leg up and down, Collin tapped his fingernails on the side of his glass. "Thank you, Mr. Ford. You as well."

"What's happened since you left? I want to know everything."

Cords of muscle popped in Collin's jaw—his face much squarer and thinner than when Baze knew him. "There's not a lot to tell. When I got to Dublin, I found shelter at an industrial school. I hadn't been wantin' to stay there long, but circumstances bein' what they were, there was nowhere else for me to go. The work was really hard, but I managed." He shrugged and took another gulp of beer. "Once I turned seventeen, I applied to the DMP. I started part time and only just became a constable. I've been livin' in the barracks ever since."

The longer Collin talked, the more aware Baze became of a glaring omission to his tale.

"What about Liam?" Baze tilted his head. "Where was he?"

A slow swallow rippled down Collin's neck. "He was around."

"What does that mean?" Baze attempted to draw his gaze, but he kept his eyes averted.

"He was tryin' to help us survive, that's all. Good jobs were hard to come by. He had to go outside Dublin to find work, but he always sent me money." Collin's leg bobbed faster. "It's fine. I didn't really care." Despite the attempted apathy, his forehead gleamed with sweat, and his brows twitched together.

After the months of effort Baze had put in to track Liam down and reunite them, he couldn't believe Liam had turned right back around and abandoned Collin at the first sign of misfortune. Hard to find work? Baze doubted the claim was true, betting that Liam had only used it as an excuse to soften the blow of his negligence. What kind of brother deserted his family? Especially after the horrors Collin had endured. He had been all alone in England—worse than that, he'd been manipulated and mistreated—only to return to Ireland and be alone once more.

"Where's your brother now?" Baze asked through his teeth.

Collin shrugged. "I'm not his keeper."

Not the response Baze had hoped to hear. He drank from his Guinness to avoid spouting something too hostile. Managing to swig away the impulse to rake Liam across the coals in front of his brother, Baze set the beer down, cocked his head, and opted for a change in subject. "Your English sounds excellent, by the way."

Collin's leg came to a halt. He grasped his glass and sat a bit straighter. "One of the other constables has been teachin' me. I've been tryin' to practice as much as I can."

"Well, I'd say it's paid off." As Collin's cheeks turned pink, Baze fought back an amused smile. He tugged Collin's uniform sleeve. "Tell me about this. What in the blazes made you want to become a policeman?"

Pink turned to red as Collin coughed and ran a finger around the lip of his glass. "You did," he muttered.

Unsure he'd heard correctly, Baze tilted his ear closer. "Pardon?"

"You did," Collin said louder, his leg bobbing again. "When Cornelius was . . . when we were at the theater . . . you took care of me. You made me feel safe. Even after what I did to you, you still protected me. You got me home. I decided I wanted to do that. I wanted to protect others and make them feel as safe as I did with you. I hope to become a detective someday so I can stop men like Mr. Marx from hurting others too."

Deep within Collin's wet green eyes, Baze caught a glimpse of the young boy who had once fallen prey to Cornelius's control. But that boy had escaped, and in his freedom, he now burned with confidence and purpose. The desire to help others had led him to the Dublin Met, and it was clear that was exactly where he needed to be.

*"You've got to decide what you want, Ford."* Whelan's voice echoed in Baze's memories. *"Think long and hard on it. Because I'm not about to put the lives of my men in the hands of someone whose heart's not in it."*

Baze's chest tightened. Collin had pursued his career because he looked up to Baze and because of a purpose higher than himself. How could Baze sit there and accept such praise when, deep down, he felt like a fraud?

"Thank you." Baze slowly tipped his head. "That was a kind thing for you to say."

"I meant all of it, Mr. Ford."

Awkwardness ensued, with Baze unsure what to say next and Collin squirming in his seat. An icy breeze cut through the thick, warm air of the pub. It numbed Baze's fingertips and the skin of his arms. Hackles raised, he darted a wary gaze about the space, taking in the rowdy dancing, the lively band, and the clustered patrons. Nothing seemed amiss.

Collin cleared his throat and jutted his chin. "So, what happened to Miss Adelynn?"

Shaking off the uneasy feeling, Baze returned his attention to Collin and chuckled. "I married her."

"Really?" An awed smile lit Collin's face. "I was hopin' you would. Got any kids?"

"No," Baze said a little too quickly. "No, I'm afraid not."

"Are you plannin' to? I think you'd be a deadly pa."

Now it was Baze's turn to shift uncomfortably. "I'm sure that's somewhere in our future." Not too keen on delving further into the topic, Baze steered the conversation another direction. "What about you? Is there a woman in your life?"

A visible line of red rose from Collin's neck all the way up to his temples. He coughed and tilted his head side to side. "No . . . not really."

"Not really?" Baze raised his eyebrows suggestively.

"Well, there's a *cailín* who lives on my patrol route who . . . I mean, she . . ."

"You fancy her?"

Collin dropped his gaze and tapped furiously against the side of his glass, but a smile tugged at his mouth.

The icy wind from before returned, skittering up Baze's neck and sending a chill down his spine. This time when he turned to survey the pub, a man stepped into view and lumbered toward their table. For a moment, shock rendered Baze immobile. Though it had been several years, the telltale red hair and familiar green eyes gave away the man's identity.

Liam Donoghue.

Apprehension dragged the happiness from Collin's features as his brother's shadow covered him. Liam scraped a disgusted stare over Baze before targeting Collin. "I need a word," he said, voice low and tense.

Baze shoved up from his chair and forced his way between Collin and his brother. Heat built under Baze's collar as he spoke steadily and glared down at the Irishman. "Collin was just telling me about you— about how you abandoned him after I sent you home. You were supposed to watch over him. How could you do that to him?"

"Shut up. You hardly know the half of it." Liam rammed his shoulder into Baze's chest, swiping a foot behind his ankle and collapsing him back into his seat. Before Baze had a chance to recover, Liam gripped the scruff of Collin's neck, yanked him from the chair, and towed him out of the pub.

After Baze departed for the police station, I had been in such a state that

Emily convinced me to accompany her on a walk to soothe my nerves. We left Basil Allan in my maid's care and took to the city to enjoy the pleasant weather and explore. Though Emily clearly wanted to ask about what had occurred at breakfast, she was kind enough to refrain— for now anyway.

I distracted myself by taking in the sights of Dublin. The pavement ahead guided us along the River Liffey. Trimmed trees growing along the sparkling river, augmented by a plain stone fence, added a taste of nature. Though the day was still young, crowds of people already filled the streets, many of whom tipped their hats with polite greetings of "Mornin' ladies" or "What's the *craic*?"

Ahead, a grand pedestrian bridge stretched across the waterway, connecting the two sides of the city. We turned onto the white cast iron structure, trekking up the steps and making our way over its gentle slope. When we reached the other side, we paused a moment at the stone fence to gaze back at the place from where we had just come.

A wave of tingles skittered down my spine. I tensed, the sensations alerting me to possible danger—but as the feeling rolled across my limbs and swirled in my stomach, I frowned. This wasn't anything like what I experienced before a vision. It felt almost . . . warm.

Touching my fingers to the stone railing, I scanned the other side of the river to try to locate the cause of this disturbance—and then I saw her.

Siobhan.

The Irishwoman who had assisted Finn onstage at the Empress Theatre. The woman who had warned me that Cornelius—not Finn— was the cause of the London murders. And the woman who had helped Baze locate me in the final confrontation before finally freeing herself from Cornelius's control.

Hardly breathing, I watched her stroll along the river walk. While employed at the Empress Theatre, she had dressed in a more masculine style, masking her exotic beauty, but now, it seemed, she embraced it. She had grown her hair out, and its dark tresses spilled over her shoulders in a loose half-up, half-down style. Her flowing green dress accentuated her curves and enhanced her porcelain skin.

She wasn't alone either. A rugged man strode beside her, escorting her with one arm and carrying a young child in the other.

Siobhan said something and looked at the man with an easy smile and shining eyes. He laughed. The child in his arms appeared younger than Basil Allan but not by much. A ray of sun glinted off the boy's eyes—a striking glacial blue. A familiar blue.

My breath caught. Surely not . . .

Siobhan stopped then, pulling the man to a stop beside her. Her smile faded as she peered across the river. It didn't take long for her to notice me. We locked gazes, and what seemed like a lifetime of shared experience and understanding flowed between us. Despite everything Cornelius had put her through, nothing but contentment shone in her eyes.

Night upon night, I had lain awake, worrying and praying that she and Cornelius's other victims would find peace. Her presence here was a declaration of perseverance and of answered prayer. She had risen above her circumstances and prevailed.

If she could do it, perhaps I could as well.

I nodded reverently. My gesture sparked a genuine smile as Siobhan nodded back. The man leaned down and said something to her. She acknowledged him, clinging tighter to his arm, and allowed him to lead her back onto their path—but not before she cast me one final glance.

One final goodbye.

Emily squinted and leaned forward. "Isn't that the woman from the Empress Theatre?"

"Yes." I followed Siobhan with my eyes until she and her beau turned up a side street and passed out of sight.

"Praise God," Emily whispered. "What a testament to His faithfulness."

After lingering several moments longer, Emily wound her arm through mine, and we crossed the street and continued our promenade. Stacked storefronts drew our attention—some with bold lettering on large windows and some boasting vibrantly colored exteriors.

We didn't get far before Emily leaned into me and tensed, her eyes directed ahead. I followed her gaze to see a swinging plaque above one of the plain doors several paces ahead—a plaque that read, "Dr. John O'Malley."

Gritting my teeth, I ripped from her grasp. "I said no, Emily."

"There are no consequences to seeking the opinion of a practiced physician," she said in exasperation. "I truly think it would help ease the torment you feel . . . no matter the result."

My stomach flipped as though trying to agree with her, but I ignored it. "I don't need to visit a physician, because I am certain of what I feel."

"I am sure you believe that, but our hearts and minds can be deceitful. You of all people know that." Her voice grew soft. "I didn't realize I was carrying my first child until I was nearly twelve weeks along. I was completely oblivious. It wasn't until Bennett pointed out my strange behavior and changes in my physique that I chose to get an exam. And lo and behold . . ."

**You can't be with child. Baze will abandon you if it is true.**

I inhaled through my nose and fought to keep my composure. "That may have been true for you, but this is different. I will say it one more time, Emily. I don't need to see a physician."

"Adelynn," she said with a rare edge to her tone. "Sometimes I wish you wouldn't be so—"

Her eyes fixed on something over my shoulder, and the blood drained from her face.

Senses on alert, I spun, expecting an enemy to jump out at us. But there was no one in proximity. Rather, Emily had focused on a tented wooden sign near the road with a colorful advertisement emblazoned upon it. A magician in a top hat and tailcoat held his hand outstretched amid a flurry of white feathers. A dove flew near the top corner. The words "The Dubliner" stretched beneath the magician.

Emily's fingers covered her lips as she breathed, "It's Finn."

## Chapter Eleven

The theater loomed before Emily through the darkness. Holding Basil Allan, she stood on the pavement just outside the single door with Adelynn and Baze at her flank and patrons dodging them to get inside.

After she and Adelynn discovered the sign advertising Finn's show, they had promptly secured tickets, but now that the time for the evening performance had arrived, hesitation began to prod Emily's stomach. Her turning up without warning—and after these two long years—would likely be a shock to Finn. Would her presence cause him joy or strife?

She stared at the dual posters of Finn plastered to the windows. His slightly polished yet dressed-down appearance—combined with his roguish smile and dark curls—made her heart flutter. Had his eyes always been that blue or had the illustration enhanced their color?

Adelynn gently bumped her shoulder. "Are you all right?"

Emily nodded, but her words wobbled. "Yes, I'm fine. It has merely been a long time."

Baze cleared his throat. "We'd best go inside before all of the good seats are taken."

Arm in arm, Adelynn and Baze went ahead as Emily hoisted Basil Allan onto her hip and followed. Warm air infused with the faint smell of musk and old wood greeted Emily as she waited for her eyes to adjust to the dark interior. After passing through a small foyer, they entered a moderately sized auditorium filled with a dozen rows of chairs formed into two columns. At the end of the space stretched a stage that rose to about knee height, upon which sat a table holding various magical props, including a vase of white primrose flowers. The image tugged at a string of memories—Emily and Finn's first meeting, Finn's tender trick with a bouquet, their sentimental parting, and the hundreds of letters they had exchanged in the time since.

Emily's cheeks grew hot, and the quickening pulse in her neck seemed to steal her breath. Several letters in, Emily had known with certainty that he was beginning to take her heart captive—piece by piece—and she had cautiously allowed it. Their relations, growing more and more familiar with each letter, were why she wanted to accompany Baze and Adelynn to Ireland. She needed to know for sure whether there was truly something there—something more.

After finding a seat near the middle on the left side, Emily settled Basil Allan on her lap and bobbed her leg, both to keep her son entertained and to calm her nerves.

Adelynn leaned over and covered Emily's hand with hers. "You have nothing to fear. He will be delighted to see you."

Given that were true, Emily yet felt another layer of doubt. Though she no longer displayed an outward expression of mourning for her husband, inside her heart, the mourning was just as visceral as the day she lost him. The two emotions—grief for Bennett and attraction for Finn—were constantly at odds. What if she couldn't reconcile them?

The lights dimmed, and the crowd applauded. Before she could prepare her heart any further, Finn emerged.

He spread his arms wide, stepped to the front of the stage, and flashed a dazzling smile. Despite the grand depiction on the poster, he presented a more casual air, with a crisp white shirt, green wool waistcoat, and tan trousers. He seemed at ease in this garb, the informal appearance complementing his rugged complexion and unruly curls.

Finn clapped his palms together and bowed. When he straightened, his eyes scanned the crowd. They passed briefly over Emily but didn't stop. She stiffened. Had he noticed her?

"Thank you for joinin' me this evenin', good folks," he announced with an exuberant tone. "I thank you especially for allowin' me to commandeer the stage of me great friend Séamus. You're all in excellent hands so. But if, by chance, you disagree with that statement in the end, you have my permission to chase me off the stage."

Emily's eyes slid shut as she absorbed the sound of his sweet voice and alluring accent.

"Let's begin with a classic, shall we?" Finn proffered his index finger. A flurry of wings sounded backstage and preceded a pure white dove darting into the air. She roosted on Finn's finger and gave a contented coo. He smiled and stroked her head. "This is my beloved Maeve. We've been through thick and thin, she and I. We've witnessed many things. Terrible things. Incredible things."

Taking Maeve in his right hand and squishing her wings to her plush body, Finn spun toward the table. "As a result, we have developed a deep level of trust now." He flipped Maeve onto her back and pressed her lightly onto the table. Her head protruded over the edge closest to the audience. "'A dove?' some might ask. 'Wouldn't a dog or even a cat be a more suitable animal companion?' Perhaps, but I was bitten by a dog in my youth, and I've never met a cat that doesn't have claws."

Finn used his left hand to grasp Maeve's beak with his thumb and forefinger. Ever so gently, he tilted her head backward. He went still. In that moment, he caught his breath—and the audience along with him. Then he peeled his fingers away and held up both hands. Maeve remained in position, not a feather twitching out of place.

Claps began rippling through the audience, but Finn nipped an upright finger to his lips, quickly shushing the applause.

"I don't know how many of you have been in love before," he whispered, and Emily's heart squeezed, "but it's a feelin' I find difficult to describe. I felt it once—some time ago. Her name was also Maeve."

Wiggling his fingers, Finn circled his hands over the dove. "Whenever Maeve and I were together, I felt as though nothing outside of us existed." He pinched one of the bird's upturned feet and lifted her. Again, she stayed still as though frozen. "In fact"—he grasped her body securely again with his free hand—"there were times when I thought I might soar straight into the sky."

Dropping his arm, he wound up and then thrust Maeve into the air. Emily lifted her eyes to follow the dove's trajectory . . .

But there was no longer a dove.

Finn turned toward the audience, empty palms exposed. Mumbles swept through the crowd, followed by rolling applause.

As Emily tried to applaud with them, Basil Allan squirmed and slipped off of her lap. He occupied himself at her feet with her ticket stub and his toy airplane.

After a humble bow, Finn turned to the table and lifted the primrose bouquet. "I've courted me fair share of maidens outside of Maeve, and one thing I've learned is they have a fondness for flowers." He stepped to the front of his stage. "Are there any *cailíns* out there who might like to be joinin' me as a volunteer? No need to be wary. Some of us men can be brutes, but I promise I'm nothin' short of a gentleman."

The rush of Emily's blood in her ears became deafening. Before she could stop herself, she vaulted to her feet and blurted, "I would like to volunteer, Mr. O'Brien."

Finn beamed. "Excellent. Thank you, madam. Now, if you would—"

Their eyes locked. Finn went still. His smile melted away, leaving his jaw slack. Emily bit her lip as they stared long and hard as though they were the only two souls in the room.

Recovering with impressive speed, Finn averted his eyes and cleared his throat. He gestured to the stage. "If you would be so kind as to join me." His voice had gone rigid, unsure—a far cry from the confident, mischievous voice from moments ago.

Legs numb, Emily scooted through the row and seemingly floated to the front. She barely breathed until she stood directly before Finn, and even then, her lungs refused to cooperate. His soothing earthy scent enveloped her—unchanged after all these years.

"I, um, need you to hold this for me." He thrust out the bouquet.

Emily grasped the stems above his hands. His warm fingers

brushed hers—and lingered. His bright, curious eyes searched her face. "Emily," he said under his breath.

"You'll need to let go," she whispered back, and when he frowned, she flicked her gaze to the audience and back.

As though snapping out of a trance, Finn blinked, released the bouquet, and retreated a few paces. He pressed his hands together and finally resumed his cheery performer's tone. "Be the flowers to your likin', ma'am?"

Emily inhaled the luscious scent and smiled. "Yes, they're beautiful."

"Glad to hear it. You don't mind helpin' me with a wee trick now?"

Holding the bouquet to her chest, she tilted her head. "I'm not going anywhere."

Finn's ears turned red, but he managed to keep his expression exuberant as he snatched a deck of cards off the table. "Those flowers you're holdin' were picked near a ringfort said to be a dwelling place for the *aos sí*. We often use these flowers to ask the fairies to keep our homes safe." He shuffled with practiced hands, then splayed the cards toward Emily. "If you please."

She pulled out a card and looked at its face—an ace of hearts.

"Once you've memorized it, return it to me." He extended a hand.

She nodded and placed it in his palm.

With a smirk, he glanced at the card and twirled it around. "Now, when they're not protectin' us, these fairies can be quite mischievous. They so enjoy a savage prank every now and again." He smacked the card between his palms before sweeping his hands apart, the card now gone.

Anticipating the secret of the familiar trick, Emily fought against a smile as the crowd gasped.

Finn rolled his eyes in mock exasperation. "There they are. As expected." With a contemplative stroke of his chin, he turned toward Emily and gestured to the blossoms. "They're quite taken with flowers, I hear. May I have a look?"

Emily acquiesced and extended the bouquet.

Fluttering his fingers, Finn circled his hands above the primroses. Beads of perspiration dotted his forehead. After a few moments, a thin white object emerged through the petals. When it had risen halfway, he snatched it up and flashed it toward the audience. The crowd erupted in applause.

Arms spread wide, Finn clipped to the front of the stage, bowed, and then backtracked. He took Emily's hand and lifted it high. "Please show me beautiful volunteer your appreciation."

Emily's cheeks warmed as she endured the audience's praise.

"Your assistance was invaluable." He lowered her hand, but before letting go, he tugged it to his lips and kissed her knuckles, sending gooseflesh skittering up her arm. His eyes locked on hers. "Keep the flowers as me thanks."

Mouth dry, Emily nodded and, reluctantly, slipped from his touch. However, as she turned, he bent toward her ear and whispered, "Stay behind after I'm done. Wait for everyone to leave. We need to talk."

Patronizing applause chased Finn as he stumbled through the curtains into the chilled darkness of backstage—into safety. He sucked in air and stripped out of his suffocating waistcoat. Sweat soaked the shirt underneath. He planted his palms upon a nearby table, bent forward, and bowed his head. Drops of perspiration fell onto his hands and the furniture's wooden surface.

Why were they here? They shouldn't be here. Any of them—Baze, Adelynn . . . and especially Emily. When Finn left England, he did so with the hope and the fervent prayer that he was taking with him any darkness that might linger. That they wouldn't have to endure anymore heartache on account of his actions. That he could protect them.

But he couldn't do any of that if they were *here*.

***Stay away from them. You'll only cause them pain.***

How *could* he stay away? More specifically, how could he stay away from Emily?

He'd made a grave mistake—corresponding with her, developing feelings for her, giving her false hope that they might foster something more. He should never have written that first letter, but his selfish desires had corrupted all judgment, had convinced him that the chances of their reuniting in person were slim. After all, he was in Ireland and she was in England. But now she was here—in the same city, in the same building—and every sinew and muscle fiber within him quivered hungrily with the knowledge that, should he choose to, he could march out there and take her as his own.

*If you pursue her, you will hurt her. You can't be trusted.*

Finn straightened and smeared his sleeve across his forehead to absorb the sweat. He would rue the day he inflicted pain upon her, but he couldn't simply turn tail and flee. She had deliberately sought him out. She *wanted* to see him. So if he abandoned her now, if he disappeared into the hills, never to return, would that not wound her more?

*So, either you act upon your affections and rain destruction upon her friends and family or you make her believe that your affections are a lie and desert her. Whatever will you do?*

"Shut up," he muttered through his teeth. Hot air thickened in his lungs, and he wrenched at the top buttons of his shirt if only to give himself a fresh breath. Yet, despite the warmth, icy air swirled at his feet, numbing his toes and sending gooseflesh sweeping up his legs.

The war of two selves continued—the war he thought he had won—but it had been a false victory. Damaged, but not defeated, the enemy had simply retreated into the shadows, sitting back on its haunches until the moment it could attack again. For a time, Finn had been able to live in the light, clinging to his tiny seed of faith. No matter what he did to cultivate it, however, he couldn't seem to make it sprout. And in a moment of vulnerability—wrapped in loneliness and depression—the enemy had struck straight at the heart of his weakness.

This time, he feared it would drive him to his end.

## Chapter Twelve

After the last trick concluded and Finn retreated backstage, Emily relayed his message to us. Obeying his request, we stayed in our seats, and as I watched the crowd pour from the auditorium, I leaned toward Emily and whispered, "Could you believe Finn's face when he saw you? He was utterly enraptured."

She whisked a loose curl behind her ear. "He was merely surprised. That's all."

"Oh, I think he was far more than that."

"Well, perhaps a little." Her cheeks flushed to the color of rouge.

The boisterous noise level dropped with each guest who shuffled out the doors, and soon, the space fell quiet. With the silence came a chill that raised the hairs on my arms. A tingle at the base of my head prompted me to glance about the room, then focus on the stage curtains. From so far away, it was hard to be sure of what I saw, but I thought I glimpsed small dark tendrils flailing at the base of the fabric.

Before I could rise to investigate, Finn emerged, sweeping aside the curtains and the mist with them. He clomped across the stage and dropped down to the floor, his shoes emitting a sharp *clap* as he landed. "Is this real?" He shook his head at us. "You're not ghosts sent to haunt me?"

Grinning, I lurched from my seat, traversed down the aisle, and threw my arms around his neck in a tight embrace. When I pulled back, I squeezed his shoulders. "Do I feel like a ghost?"

Finn looked between us as Baze and Emily approached—though, for some reason, he appeared to ignore Emily. Thankfully, she didn't seem to notice as she struggled to hold Basil Allan still. The child squirmed and kicked and whined, so she lifted him to the stage and turned him loose. Now free of her son's distraction, she turned her wide blue eyes upon Finn.

His voice grew low, almost accusatory. "What are you all doin' here?"

I lifted my chin. "It's a long story, but in a word, we're here to stop Shay."

Alarm sparked in Finn's eyes. "That's not smart. You shouldn't be here. It's not safe."

"We're aware of the dangers." I tried to sound confident to dispel his concerns. "But we had to come. I . . . I used what Katherine taught me to reach out to Shay's mind. He's hiding somewhere close, and we have to find him before he does to Dublin what Cornelius did to London."

Finn exhaled heavily and ran his fingers through his curls, and I took his hesitation as an opportunity to give him a quick once-over. How old was he now? Mid-thirties perhaps? Fine creases seemed permanently etched into his brow and beside his mouth, and a few silver strands caught the light amidst his otherwise dark hair. Faded purplish bags underlined his eyes, and his irises weren't the bright blue I remembered. Rather, they appeared a dull granite, like a sea overwhelmed by a storm. They weren't the eyes of the liberated man whom I'd sent off with blessings almost three years ago. Why did he seem nearly as troubled as the time we first crossed paths? What had happened to him?

As though sensing my scrutiny and speculation, Finn caught me in a deep stare. His emotionless gaze penetrated my soul and threatened to unearth all that I'd buried. I couldn't blink. Couldn't breathe.

***He knows. He knows of the darkness that plagues you . . . because it plagues him too.***

My insides twisted. Determined to keep my inner struggles confidential—especially from Baze—I blinked to break our connection and said softly, "What happened when you returned to Ireland?"

Finn glanced to Emily—finally—then back to me. "I'm not sure how much Emily shared from our letters, but I suppose I can tell you a brief summary." He folded his arms and relaxed his shoulders. "Soon as I got to Dublin, I made straight for Liscannor and found me parents' home as I left it. 'Twas a complete mess. I spent several months fixin' it up. In the meantime, I found work as a carpenter while entertainin' the local children with street magic."

A shadow fell over his features. "All was well until I felt a shudder of darkness race through the land. It awakened something in me . . . something I thought I had destroyed. I can't quite explain how, but I knew then that Shay had returned to Ireland." He looked between Baze and I, his eyes gleaming with remorse. "Emily told me everythin' that occurred in Bath. I'm sorry you were dragged further into this. I prayed hard as I could that that wouldn't be the case."

Retreating within and pushing out slightly with my mind, I felt the touch of darkness to which Finn referred. It hovered around him like a dense cloud. The further I probed, trying to break through, the louder my own dark whispers became.

"*Vroom!*"

I jumped, Basil Allan's cheerful exclamation yanking my mind back to safety before I could delve too far. The child dashed in circles about the stage, his airplane held high, as exuberant *whooshes* flowed from his mouth. We all watched him for a time, soaking in his blissful ignorance.

Finally, though I didn't want to, I broke the silence. "I'm sorry about Katherine, Finn. Were you close?"

He stiffened. "We were, I suppose. She was like a mother to me, but I hadn't seen her in nearly a decade, not since Ciaran and I sailed to England. I barely knew her in the end."

"I'm sure it still hurts though, losing someone you loved."

He smiled bitterly. "Are you *tryin'* to make me remember the pain?"

"No, of course not. I just . . ." I thought back to the long days and weeks following Father's death, tried to remember what had helped me the most. "I just want to acknowledge that loss is hard, and I'm sorry you are having to endure it."

Taking in a deep inhale, he offered a single hesitant nod.

For the first time since we began our dialogue, Emily took one step toward Finn, then clutched her hands to her chest and halted, a blush tinting her cheeks. "We missed you . . . and are pleased to see you now."

Though she spoke in the plural, I surmised she spoke only for herself—as did Finn, apparently, for his ears flushed a bright red. As his softening gaze roamed her face, he dropped his arms to his sides and allowed the rigidity to sag from his shoulders.

Emily eased closer. "We should like to see more of Ireland while we're here. Perhaps even your home, if you would allow it. You could—"

"No." Finn's eyes and body hardened—the walls had come back up. His voice rose as he jutted a hand toward Emily. "Why did you come here in the first place? You should have stayed in England. You should have forgotten about me and moved on with your life." His lip curled. "You were a fool for comin' and especially for bringin' *him*." He jabbed an accusing finger toward Basil Allan, who still scampered about the stage—carefree and oblivious.

Emily quivered, and I pulled her tight to my side as Finn continued his tirade. "Do you realize how dangerous it is in Dublin right now? Forget about Shay—there's civil unrest you have to be worryin' about. Riots. Beatin's. Shootin's. None of you are safe so long as you stay here. You're already after losin' your husband. Do you really want to lose your son too?"

A cry escaped Emily's lips, and I opened my mouth to shout back, but Baze stepped between us. "That's enough." He shoved Finn backward. "How dare you speak to Emily that way. We're your friends. We did everything in our power to help you, and this is how you thank us?"

"I appreciate all that you did for me, but that's far behind us."

Finn's nostrils flared. "You need to leave. Shay is dangerous. It's only a matter of time before he comes after you."

"You seem pretty certain of that," Baze said with surprising composure despite his braced posture. "Are you working for him?"

Fire lit in Finn's eyes. He flinched toward Baze, his chest heaving, his fists clenching, and I thought he was about to throw discretion to the wind and attack.

To my relief, he relaxed his hands and shook his head. "I'm not—"

"Leave him be. If he were workin' for me, he wouldn't have entertained your annoying inquiries for so long."

The smooth, familiar voice resounded throughout the auditorium and sent an icy shock racing through me. I whirled toward the stage in time to see Shay emerge from the curtains. Garbed in a tweed vest, frayed trousers, and flat cap, he ambled to the middle of the stage.

Baze shoved Emily and I behind him. He reached to his waist and drew his gun, but before he could aim, Basil Allan passed in front of the Irishman.

Emily's cry echoed as Shay intercepted the child. He swept Basil Allan into his arms as though he weighed nothing and speared Baze with a calm but intense stare. "Put the weapon away, Inspector. I'm not here to hurt anyone." He brushed a light hand over Basil Allan's head and smiled. "You said you were wantin' to find me. Well, ask and ye shall receive."

## Chapter Thirteen

"L ET HIM GO!" E MILY SCREAMED, PUSHED me aside, and made a dash for the stage.

"No!" Baze caught her about the waist. He heaved her backward and held her against his chest. "Stop, Emily. There's nothing we can do. We can't risk it."

"Let me go," she growled. She kicked her legs and pried at Baze's arm, but he proved too strong.

"You needn't worry, Mrs. Bennett," Shay said calmly. "I've no intention of hurtin' your son. He's merely here as insurance to keep the good inspector from firing upon me."

Keeping one arm wound around Emily's struggling form, Baze aimed his gun at the floor and bit out, "What do you want?"

"I came to tell you to leave, but it appears Finn has beat me to it." He took Basil Allan's toy airplane from him and flew it around as though trying to play. "So I'm goin' to tell you everythin' I'm plannin'. Down to the last detail."

I frowned, tensing. "Why would you do that?"

He swept his firm gaze across us. "Because when I do, you will see that this is no place for you—for women and children especially. In return for my transparency, you will leave Ireland."

"And if we don't?"

"Then you will not like what happens next."

I risked a glance at Finn. He stood rigid and alert, arms limp at his sides, eyes trained on Shay—but he didn't appear as rattled as I might have expected. In fact, there was something almost submissive about his posture. Had he been aware Shay was here this whole time?

Basil Allan wrestled his toy back and scrunched his nose. "Who are you? Mama says not to talk to strangers."

Shay chuckled. "Oh, I'm not a stranger. Far from it. I am merely here to talk to your mam and her friends for a bit. Are you okay with that?"

"I suppose." Basil Allan shrugged. "I want down."

"I'll let you down in a moment, Little Baze. I promise."

"No, I want down." Basil Allan kicked into Shay's stomach and pushed against his face.

Emily jerked forward, but Baze held her in place.

Rather than try to subdue the child, Shay murmured, "All right, all right," and squatted. He allowed Basil Allan to slide from his arms and tumble to his knees so he could continue playing. Shay shifted into a cross-legged position, all the while keeping Basil Allan's body between him and Baze. I caught a glimmer of tenderness in Shay's eyes as he studied the boy, but that quickly faded as he shifted his focus to us. "I'm not goin' anywhere, so I suggest you make yourselves comfortable."

Baze delivered Emily into my arms, and I helped her quivering form lower into one of the front seats. Holding tight to her shoulders, I sank onto the armrest. Baze and Finn, however, remained standing. Baze readjusted his grip on the gun, keeping the barrel pointed at the floor but poising his thumb over the hammer.

Shay knuckled the bill of his hat and tipped it higher on his forehead. "I won't bore you with a long backstory, but I do believe it is important for you to know why I do what I do. Perhaps that will make you think differently of me. Perhaps you'll even join me." His mouth curled in a smirk, and then he focused on Basil Allan.

"Kate and I had always wanted children, a whole swarm of them, but we couldn't . . ." He cleared his throat and stroked Basil Allan's cheek with gentle fingers. "We were visitin' an orphanage, thinkin' maybe we'd be givin' one of the *weans* a home, but that's when I witnessed the vilest side of man. Late that evening, the keeper of the orphanage beat a young boy to death." Shay's face appeared etched in stone. "That's when me power appeared, as though by magic, as it were—and I knew exactly what I had to do. I took control of that monster's weak mind and made him turn the weapon upon himself. I forced him to beat his own skull in until the floor was soaked with his blood."

I closed my eyes, trying not to picture the gruesome scene, but it flared to life against my will, bright and vivid. The worst part of all was that I didn't disagree that the man's death had been just.

"That's all I'm wantin'," Shay continued. "To protect the innocent. And right now, the innocent are the neutral people of Ireland."

"Protect the innocent? I've never heard a more bold-faced lie," I snapped. "What about Katherine? She was innocent, but you killed her in cold blood."

Shay's eyes shot daggers. "She was standin' in me way, and as such, she made an enemy out of herself. I offered her the chance to join me, but she refused. Her death is on her own hands, not mine." He inhaled long and deep, then released it. "I've been given an extremely valuable gift, one that allows me to find evil men exactly like that orphan keeper and put an end to them."

"That's not your job," Baze said softly. "There are hundreds of good men across Great Britain who are devoted to keeping the peace and enforcing justice so the citizens don't have to."

"You've an honorable call," Shay acknowledged, "but you and your comrades can't be everywhere, and there are corrupt men even among the police. The system is slow and broken. Just look at the Phoenix Park murders. Ciaran's birth father evaded capture for years before finally swingin' by the neck. How many more people do you think he hurt in that time? Sorry, but I refuse to sit idly by."

I squeezed Emily's shoulders if only to bring myself comfort. Why did I feel such a war within me? Shay was the enemy. He was the reason we were in this position, the reason Basil Allan and I were without our fathers. *They* were innocent. How could that possibly be justice?

"Provided everything you say is true, why are you in Dublin?"

Baze asked. "Why does Adelynn seem to believe you have greater plans ahead?"

"Because I do," Shay retorted. "I'm not a political person, now, but the political strife in Ireland is turnin' brother against brother. That'll only lead to civil war and the deaths of hundreds, perhaps even thousands." His throat muscles tightened, and his eyes glinted harsh in the dim light. "I love this land, and I love her people. Were it up to me, I would live out the rest of my days peacefully in the countryside, but I can't ignore what's happenin'."

"What does that mean?" Baze shifted onto his healthy leg. "What are you going to do?"

Basil Allan flipped onto all fours, waving his airplane around as he began to crawl away—leaving Shay's body unguarded.

Baze caught his breath. He clicked the gun's hammer.

Before he could aim, Shay snatched Basil Allan and pulled him into his lap. "Nooo," Basil Allan moaned and squirmed. "I want to *play*. Let me play!"

"Hang on, Little Baze. I'm almost done." Shay wound a firm arm around the child's torso and turned his attention back to us. "I've been hearin' whispers of a plan to mount a rebellion in Dublin to fight back against British rule."

I caught my breath. A rebellion? So it was true—just as the barkeep Riordan's letters had indicated.

Shay grimaced. "I have no desire to be joinin' such a rebellion, but it will provide a much-needed diversion. With the police and British Army distracted by the uprisin', I shall slip into Dublin Castle where the Lord Lieutenant resides. He's a lackey for the British monarchy. If I can take control of him, I can make me way into the other heads of state. And if I can achieve that, hopefully, I can force them to finally come to an agreement over home rule and end the civil war before it has had a chance to begin."

Silence overtook the auditorium. Even Basil Allan stopped whimpering. Cold air enveloped me as I considered Shay's words. He was going to break the minds of Ireland's lawmakers to shove the bill through—but once that was complete, what then? Who was to say he would stop there? He would hold control over the entire administration and, thus, the country. This was far larger than local affairs. He would control the laws, he would control the justice system—who lived or died—and he would control the people.

Shay propped an arm under Basil Allan's legs as he shifted to his knees and then stood. Emily and I mirrored his actions, coming to our feet and inching close to Baze.

"There. You know everythin' now." Shay sighed. "It's time you honored my wishes and held up your end of the bargain. You have twenty-four hours to depart Ireland. I don't care how you leave, but you must never return." He tilted his head. "I have eyes and ears everywhere to make sure you obey, for if you defy me, you will face dire consequences."

Baze released a mirthless laugh. "You think we're going to allow you to waltz into Dublin Castle and take control of its dignitaries?"

"You will if you truly care about those you love." Shay squeezed Basil Allan's cheeks with his large fingers. "I have been more than generous now, tellin' you what I'm plannin', allowin' you the time you need to make a wise decision. I simply ask that you extend the same generosity to me and stay out of matters that don't concern you."

"These matters *do* concern us," I shouted, drawing all attention my way. "The moment I lost my father to the IRB, it became my concern. We won't be going anywhere."

"Don't be foolish, Adelynn." Shay tsked. "You should consult the others in your party before speaking for them. Take this time to truly consider what you're willing to sacrifice." He narrowed his eyes. "I do believe I have taken up too much of your time now." He leaned his face against Basil Allan's ear and murmured, "When I put you down, Little Baze, I want you to run to your mam as fast as you can."

Emily sucked in a breath, and Baze tensed.

With his eyes trained on Baze, Shay bent and set Basil Allan's feet gently on the floor, but he kept his arm wound around the boy's stomach. "You've been such a good lad," he whispered. "Be sure to ask your mam for some sweets now. Go on." Shay gave him a gentle tap on the bottom and nudged him forward.

Basil Allan squealed with glee and ran toward us. Emily lurched to intercept her son, but I managed to grab her wrist and stop her. "Stay back!" I shouted as Baze took aim.

Shay reached into his pocket.

*Crack!*

Fire and smoke exploded around Shay's body. My vision flashed white, and the sound rang in my ears. I clung to Emily, my heart roaring, until the sensations faded. Squinting through the dissipating haze, I looked for Shay—but he was gone.

He had disappeared into thin air.

## Chapter Fourteen

BASIL ALLAN LET OUT A CRY. His airplane went skittering across the stage as he scrambled for the edge, away from the dissolving mist where Shay had once stood. He half-fell, half-leaped into Baze's awaiting arms. "That was l-loud," Basil Allan stammered through large tears. "I'm s-scared."

"I know, buddy. I know." Baze hugged the child tight. "It's over now. You don't have to be scared."

Emily tore from my arms and tried to take her son from my husband, but Basil Allan rebuffed his mother's attempts and clung harder to Baze's neck. "My ears h-hurt," he whined, rubbing the side of his head against Baze's shoulder.

Indeed, my own ears had yet to cease ringing, irritated by the loud crack of Shay's exit. How much more was Basil Allan suffering for having been right next to the blast?

"You'll be all right. Here, let me help." Baze nuzzled the side of the child's head and kissed his ear. "Will you show me the other one?" Hiccupping sobs, Basil Allan turned his face and allowed Baze to peck his other ear. "There now," Baze whispered. "All better?"

With quieting cries, Basil Allan nodded and dropped his head back against Baze's shoulder. He lay there for a moment and then finally twisted and reached for his mother. Baze stooped and delivered him safely into her arms.

"He went through the trap door."

Finn's statement spun me toward him. I'd almost forgotten he was there for how quiet he had been. His neutral expression kept his thoughts hidden, but when he finally looked at us, his eyes betrayed his fear. "You have to do as he says. You have to leave."

"We shall do no such thing," I blurted.

"Adelynn," Baze warned.

But the challenge only stoked the fire within me. "I refuse to let him blackmail us. I've had enough of that." I slashed a hand through the air. "He claims to have eyes and ears throughout the city, but I think he's bluffing. He can't possibly control that many people at once. Every power has a limit."

Baze placed his hand between my shoulder blades and sent Finn a grave look. "What do you think? Was he was telling the truth?"

"Shay was always far stronger than Ciaran, so I see no reason to doubt him." Finn's expression crumpled. "I don't want to be seein' any of you harmed. Please leave."

I shook my head and peered up at Baze. "We can't. You know we can't."

"You're not listenin'!" Finn smacked a hand flat on the stage. "If you stay, you'll die. Or worse . . . the people you love will die." His eyes briefly flicked to Emily. "Ireland isn't your responsibility. If she falls, it's not for a lack of anythin' you did."

"This is bigger than Ireland." I allowed my tone to drop as the fire in me began to peter out.

Apparently weary of sparring with me, Finn targeted Baze. "You're just goin' to stand there and let your wife throw herself into danger, are you?"

Baze tilted his head side to side and sighed. "It wouldn't be the first time." His light, exasperated tone appeared at odds with the crease of worry in his brow. He bowed his head a moment, grazing his finger over his nose, before releasing an even deeper sigh and acknowledging me. "I think we should send the staff home. All of them. I don't want them in the crossfire." He gestured toward Emily. "You and Basil Allan should leave as well."

Emily clutched her son to her chest, and apprehension awoke in her eyes. "What about you and Adelynn?"

Baze's eyes slid to mine, and I could tell he was fighting every impulse to include me in the evacuation—but he knew the truth as well as I.

"Because our minds are linked," I answered for him. "Mine and Shay's. I'm the only one who can find him."

Baze's shoulders fell a touch, as though hearing the words said aloud affirmed his decision. "We'll tell the staff tonight and prepare for their departure, and in the morning, I'll let Darragh know what O'Sullivan said about the rebellion. I doubt he can help much, as it's no more than hearsay, but it can't hurt to put him on alert."

I rubbed his arm. "Good idea."

"You're all mad!" Finn's shout punched through the air. "You've no idea what Shay is capable of. I don't understand how—you know what? Fine." He shoved his hands into his trouser pockets and trekked up the aisle toward the auditorium door. "Do what you wish, but I won't be havin' any part in it."

I spun to follow, but Emily stepped in my path. "Let me talk to him." She smiled faintly. "I may be able to get through to him."

The door slammed as Finn disappeared through it, and I fought the compulsion to dodge her and scramble after him. There was too much hope pouring from her eyes—affection even—so I backed down and took Basil Allan from her. "Good luck."

On light, hurried feet, Emily stole into the foyer and searched the space for Finn. She spotted him about to shove backward through the door into the night—perhaps never to be seen again—and her heart lurched. "Wait!" she called.

He halted, fixing her with an irritated look as cold air gusted through the gaping door. The wind seeped straight through Emily's dress, and she grasped her hands to her chest with a shiver. Heaving a sigh, Finn pushed away from the door, let it swing shut, and wandered toward her. He kept his hands slotted in his pockets, his mouth a straight line.

Emily noticed his blushing ears peeking through his curly hair and fought off a smile. No matter how hard he tried to maintain a steely front, his body couldn't help but betray him.

"I never got the chance to say it, but it's good to see you, Finn," she said calmly, trying to keep her emotions from spiking.

His mouth opened, then closed. With a slight shake of his head, he said, "You shouldn't have come here."

The words struck a blow to her confidence, but she kept her expression neutral. "In your last letter, you said that you wished to see me, that you hoped we might reunite in person." She twisted her fingers against her stomach. "Do you no longer feel that way?"

He yanked his hands from his pockets but seemed to think better of whatever he had planned to do and let them fall to his sides. "Me feelin's haven't changed, but the circumstances have. When I wrote that letter, I wasn't aware of all that was about to occur, and I certainly didn't want you involved." Scuffing his shoe on the floor, he lowered his voice. "But I did want to see you."

At a loss for words, Emily clutched Bennett's ring dangling around her neck and squeezed it tight. Her yearning for her husband went to war against her growing desire toward Finn. That desire, though vastly different than the love she had felt for Bennett, was just as strong—and that frightened her a little.

Finn took a step closer. His earthy scent enshrouded her as he tucked a gentle finger under her chin and lifted. "Listen," he said softly. "I know Adelynn can be stubborn, but you must convince her and her husband this is a fool's errand. Then you must take your son and get out of here."

Bennett's ring grew warm and slick in her palm. Now that she was here, now that she had found Finn and had begun uncovering the true depth of her feelings, she didn't want to leave him—but, first and foremost, her responsibility was to her son. Was there a way to see to Basil Allan's safety while pulling tighter on the cord that connected her to Finn?

Moisture clouded her vision as she stared into Finn's troubled blue eyes. "Come with me."

He sucked in a breath. "I can't."

"Why not?"

"I just . . . I can't."

"Now who's being stubborn?" She allowed an amused smile to tease her lips, then tilted her chin away from Finn's touch. "When we return to our lodging, I imagine we shall further discuss what transpired here tonight, but I know deep down that Baze and Adelynn have already made up their minds. Nothing you or I say could change that."

Finn raked a hand through his hair and paced in a small circle, indistinct mutterings following in his wake. Eventually, he came about and headed behind the counter of the ticketing booth and scrounged around for a slip of paper and a pen. After scrawling something on the note, he stomped out of the booth, picked up one of Emily's hands, and tucked the folded page into her palm. "If you need anything during the remainder of your stay—however long that may be—call this number. I shall come immediately. No questions asked."

She shook her head. "I know you don't like it, Finn, so you don't have to—"

"I mean it, Emily." He squeezed his fingers around hers, crumpling the paper securely within. "Anythin' at all, no matter how large or small, I will come."

Finn slipped through the side door into the shroud of night and locked it. Slinging his light sack over his shoulder and dropping the key in his pocket, he set off down the street toward his flat. He passed through Temple Bar, dodging cheery drunkards stumbling outside of raucous pubs blaring music of the fiddle and uilleann pipe. Temple Bar spit him out onto the main thoroughfare running parallel to the Liffey. Moonbeams and city lights blinked on the water's ripples.

***You should have fought harder. Their deaths will be on your head.***

The internal hisses sent prickles down his spine. He clenched the strap of his pack and tried to buck against the sobering statement—but how could he deny it? Emily had said it herself. She came here to see him, and though Adelynn and Baze might have known the danger they were about to face, the fight never should have been theirs in the first place.

Finn wished he had never gone to London. He wished he had never allowed Ciaran to manipulate him. He wished that he and Ciaran had never even . . .

Pleasant memories whispered through his mind, memories of his dysfunctional but devoted family. Shay, Kate, Ciaran, and himself. Though not bound by blood, they had been his whole world. He'd spent some of the richest moments of his life with them—gaping in awe as Shay took them to yet another castle ruin, competing with Ciaran over who could master a complicated card trick first, staying up well into the night asking Kate life's most puzzling questions.

Then, in a flash, it was gone.

At least, it felt like a flash. In reality, their implosion had been a slow burn. Shay had nurtured Ciaran's powers, stoking his simmering flame of revenge. As Ciaran surrendered to the dark pull, Finn withdrew and met his needs of connection elsewhere—with Maeve. They had planned to leave, to marry, to start a new life. Until she disappeared and Shay attacked . . .

"Peaceful night, isn't it?"

Shay's voice sliced through the night air.

Finn whipped his head up. Twenty paces ahead, Shay leaned with his arms crossed atop the stone railing. He gazed out across the river.

"*Athair.*" The word leaped from Finn's lips on its own accord. A word he despised. *Father.*

Shay looked at him askance. "I'm surprised you still see me as such."

"Force of habit." Finn bristled as he joined Shay against the rail. "I'll try not to repeat it."

If the comment ruffled Shay, he didn't show it. He simply continued to skim his gaze across the tranquil water. Movement in his hands drew Finn's gaze. The fingers of Shay's left hand rippled absently, flipping a plain silver ring between the tips with the adeptness of a magician trained in ring tricks. But Finn recognized the trinket immediately—Kate's claddagh.

The sting of her loss struck him full in the chest.

"Why did you kill her?" Finn asked under his breath.

Shay glanced out of the corner of his eye. "Who might you be talkin' ab—"

"Kate!" Finn snatched Shay's wrist and wrestled his hand into the air, then gestured to the claddagh. His voice cracked as he repeated, "Why did you kill her?"

Shay ripped from Finn's grasp and fixed the ring protectively onto his little finger. "I gave her a choice. She chose death. You can't blame me for her actions."

A morose laugh punched from Finn's mouth. "So you'd kill the people you love to help strangers."

Brows drawn, Shay spoke in a monotone. "I've come too far to turn back."

Not long after Finn's deliverance in the cell of Pentonville Prison, he had prayed for the redemption of his family. Kate had demonstrated a glimmer of faith before they parted, but Ciaran and Shay had clearly been lost—and Ciaran would remain such for eternity now. Finn wrestled with the fact that his prayer had gone unanswered. Maybe his soul had been too broken, his faith too small for a being as powerful as the Almighty to consider his prayers.

If that were the case, why should he continue petitioning for Shay? Why even bother hoping?

"I have nothin' more to say to you." Finn shoved off the rail and bumped Shay's shoulder as he passed.

With a quick turn, the man lashed out and caught Finn's arm. He tugged him close, warm breath buffeting Finn's ear as he spoke low. "Help me."

Hope poked through the dismay, but as Finn scoured Shay's face for the true meaning behind his words, he realized he was asking for help to carry out his plan—not to turn from his ways.

Finn gritted his teeth. "No."

"You think you're all high and mighty now that you've had a taste of the light? Well, I know what's really going on inside your head." Shay tapped Finn's temple with a stiff finger. "You believe you are redeemed, but the sins of your past say otherwise, and now your conscience is in chaos. You don't know who you are anymore."

Finn seized Shay's collar and lifted his fist—but then he froze, unsure what to do next and unable to conjure any words to refute the statements.

"I think"—Shay wrapped his hand around Finn's upraised fist—"you know exactly who you are. You simply don't want to accept it." He applied pressure, attempting to lower Finn's arm. Finn resisted for a moment, then relaxed his muscles and allowed Shay to twist it against his side. Something akin to genuine concern crawled into Shay's expression. "It's only you and I left. We must band together to honor Kate's and Ciaran's memories."

"They would both still be here if it weren't for you," Finn bit out.

Unfazed, Shay tilted his cap down so that it shadowed his eyes. "Be careful how you proceed, Finn. If you choose to oppose me, as Kate did, there will be consequences. Because remember"—he dug his fingernail into Finn's temple—"you're always carryin' a piece of me wherever you go. I have allowed you to walk free because of what you mean to me, but all it would take is one gentle tug on your mind to regain control. And that's when people get hurt . . . like that Englishwoman of yours. You wouldn't want that now."

Fear trapped the air in Finn's lungs. He winced at the nail cutting into his skin and weakened beneath the darkness strengthening within him. *God, what am I doing wrong? I don't know what to do. Why do you feel so far away?*

***Because you were never worthy of being saved in the first place.***

The biting pressure finally abated as Shay dropped his hand and slipped his fingertips into his pockets. "It was good to see you, *a mhic*. You may not believe me, but I have missed you." He ambled backward and inclined his head. "May God never weaken you."

# Chapter Fifteen

My nightmares returned with a vengeance. This time, Shay took center stage. He lurked in the blurred fringe of my periphery, watching and waiting. "You must leave," he whispered, "or the consequences will be swift."

Images flashed before me, the same visions that continued to torment me. Soldiers marched across bloody streets. A man fired upon his comrade. Finn screamed as his eyes turned black. Basil Allan thrashed in the arms of a stranger. And Baze toppled over the edge of a chasm.

Then I jerked awake.

Bolting upright, I heaved and tried to catch my breath as I darted my gaze about the darkened room as though expecting Shay to jump out and attack. Sweat plastered my nightgown to my chest, and my hair stuck to my neck.

Something gentle massaged the soft tissue of my hand, and I twisted to find Baze sitting cross-legged beside me, hair messy and nightshirt wrinkled from sleep. He worked my palm silently as his eyes probed for answers.

I gulped in a breath before I could speak. "How long have you been sitting there?"

He stole a look at the wall clock. "Not too long," he murmured. "Perhaps fifteen minutes." His thumb triggered a sore spot. "I heard you mumbling. I tried to rouse you, but you were deep asleep." He gave my hand one final squeeze before covering it with both of his. "It's been some time since you experienced a nightmare that severe."

"Yes, it has," I matched his low tone.

"Was it about O'Sullivan?"

With a faint nod, I swiped sweat from my forehead with the wrist of my free hand. "I'm sure his appearance yesterday triggered it." I swallowed. "I know it will be dangerous, Baze. I know he said some frightening things, but I believe we are supposed to stay."

Baze inhaled slow and deep. "I agree, but Emily and Basil Allan need to go home."

Though I didn't doubt Emily would do whatever she had to in order to keep her son safe, would she be willing to leave Finn so readily? With each day that passed, a new piece of her heart took root in the soil of this green land, and if she returned to England, those pieces would be left behind—with Finn.

"She won't like that," I whispered.

"I don't particularly care. It's not open for discussion." He went back to massaging my hand, rougher this time.

Baze's firm strokes on my palm coaxed my eyes shut and dragged my mind into a calmer state. Considering Shay's direct threat, I had expected more of a heated discussion, more counterarguments lobbed back and forth, but Baze and I were aligned in nearly every way. I wasn't sure if that made things better or worse.

"We'll need to let everyone know," I said. "Shay gave us only twenty-four hours to decide, so we need to make sure the staff and Emily are out of harm's way before time runs out."

"We have time enough for breakfast." Baze released my hand, grasped my face, and kissed my forehead. "Better to break the news on a full stomach."

The cords of nausea tightened in my belly, but I didn't breathe a word as we crawled from the bed and began readying for the day. The daily routine played out as though nothing were amiss—with Margaret styling my hair and lacing me into my corset and gown and Baze's butler whisking out the wrinkles in his tailored coat and gray trousers. With that completed, we followed the savory scents to the dining room.

Outside of the scraping of cutlery on the plates and Basil Allan's contented humming, we broke our fast in silence. Emily fussed over her son, ensuring he ate the proper portions, and I pushed around the food on my plate. Every part of me wanted to tell Emily our plan at once, but a new emotion doused my fire.

Doubt.

Was staying truly the right thing to do? Thus far, none of my visions had come to pass, but that merely heightened my unease. Were they a consequence of taking action to stop Shay . . . or of choosing inaction?

***Choose wrong and people will suffer.***

"Emily," Baze said before I had a chance to ponder further. He kept his tone matter-of-fact as he aligned his cutlery on his empty plate. "I've come to a decision regarding Shay's entreaty."

Lowering her fork, Emily flicked her gaze to me, then back to Baze. "Oh?"

"I think it best that you and Basil Allan return home to get as far away from here as possible. I plan to visit the Dublin police station today, before which I shall purchase two tickets for your return trip."

Emily's neck muscles tightened as obstinance glinted in her eyes. "What about you and Adelynn?"

"We are going to stay. You know as well as I that Adelynn is linked to that man, and I won't rest until that connection has been severed—however we have to do it." As Emily's glistening eyes shifted to me, Baze cleared his throat to reclaim her attention. "The decision is mine. My top priority is to keep you and your son safe, so I won't entertain any objections. My promise to Bennett is stronger than any argument you could lobby."

Nostrils flaring, Emily stroked her son's hair. "What about Finn?"

"I'm sure Finn will yet play a role in this fight." Baze's expression softened. "Once it has resolved, you may choose to return . . . if you wish."

Emily stared at her empty plate, chewing her bottom lip and fluttering her lashes. She sucked in a breath. "Very well. I will comply."

Baze relaxed in his seat with a sigh. "It is for your sake, Emily, and that of your son's. You must hear my heart in that." He waited a moment as she prodded her eggs with her fork, rosiness coloring her cheeks. Then he nodded at her silence and shoved back his chair. "I'm off to the police station, then. I suggest you begin packing your things."

When he'd gone, Emily spoke bitterly. "Why am I the only one being sent away?"

I stabbed at a tomato slice on my plate. "It's not just you. We also plan to send the staff home as well. The fewer people who remain, the better."

"But what if Shay hurts you? What if—"

"We knew the risks when we first chose to come here. His threats don't change a thing. It merely increases our urgency." I gave her a sympathetic look. "You know Bennett wouldn't have wanted you anywhere near this place."

"Bennett's not here, now, is he?" she muttered.

"All right then." I tossed my fork down with a sharp clatter. "What would you contribute if you stayed? What value would you provide? If it's enough, perhaps you could convince Baze to let you stay."

Her head shook slowly, tears gathering in her eyes. "No, I know I'm useless."

My scalp prickled. "Emily, that's not what I meant."

"It's all right." She pressed on a sad smile. "I know I'm being difficult. Of course I must leave to protect Basil Allan, but . . . ." A tear streaked down her cheek. "When Bennett walked out our door for what became the last time, I had no idea he would never come back. I fear the same will happen now."

My heart ripped as I watched her face wilt. I pushed from the table and came around to her, then dropped into the chair beside her. "I can't say for certain that all will play out exactly as we plan, but we can't stand by and do nothing." I scooped up her hand. "And you are not useless. Not even in the slightest. Your faith gives us the strength to keep going and helps us not to lose our own. When you intercede with the Almighty on our behalf, I know He listens—and that is more valuable than anything any of us can bring to this fight."

Hope blossomed on her delicate features. She wound our hands together and squeezed. "Then allow me to pray right now."

After purchasing tickets for Emily, her son, and the staff through the British and Irish Steam Packet Company, Baze headed to the police station. While winding his way to Darragh's office, Baze noticed Collin and Liam conversing in hushed tones at the end of a secluded corridor. He would have approached were it not for the urgency beating in his chest, so he made a mental note to check on Collin once he was through with the superintendent.

Just before entering the office, a sharp chill raced up Baze's spine. He shuddered, hesitating slightly before shouldering through door. Upon his entrance, Darragh brightened and offered a hearty handshake in greeting. "Isn't this quite the surprise. Good to see you, boyo."

As their hands parted, Baze noticed a plain-clothed man sitting in one of the two chairs set before Darragh's desk. Peering from under a flat cap, the man quirked an eyebrow as he made a slow examination of Baze. Likewise, Baze took in the man—ruddy complexion, slight build, and dark, droopy eyes.

"This is Sergeant Art Fitzgerald. He's one of my undercover men." Darragh stroked the two nubs of his missing fingers, sat backward on his desk, and wiggled his bushy brows the man's way. "I've got him deep in a group of potential rebels. Some would say you're close to enterin' the upper echelon, eh, Arty?"

"Indeed, sir." Fitzgerald's voice sounded younger than Baze had anticipated.

Darragh angled toward Baze. "What's brought you all this way so soon after our first meetin'? Already found somethin' on O'Sullivan, have you?

"Yes, sir."

"Well, go on then. Spit it out."

Casting Fitzgerald a hesitant glance, Baze leaned on his cane and debated whether to relay the sensitive information in the presence of a man he didn't know.

"Oh, it's all right, now. Arty's clean as they come." Darragh motioned his hand dismissively.

Another chill skittered across Baze's skin, but he chose to trust the superintendent. He walked them through the events at the theater, starting with Finn's performance. To their credit, Darragh and Fitzgerald sat stoic and silent as Baze explained O'Sullivan's plans to leverage a rebellion to infiltrate Dublin Castle, then detailed the threat he had lobbed at them.

"My wife and I are going to stay for the time being, but we've decided to send the rest of our party back to England," Baze said as he concluded the account.

Darragh twisted his lips, stroking his beard. "This isn't the first I've heard of a rebellion," he said pensively. "There's been whisperin' for months now. I've got a few men undercover, Arty included, but they haven't been able to unearth anythin' conclusive. Such info must be above their stations. Considering what you're tellin' me now, however, it appears we haven't got much time to lollygag." He glanced at Fitzgerald, and before he'd even spoken a word, the man nodded.

"I understand, sir."

Darragh returned the nod. "Good." A ripple of thought crossed his pale wrinkled features as he eyed Baze. "We can handle things from here if you would like to return to London. I'm not questionin' your bravery, now, but O'Sullivan threatened your wife. I would think you'd want her as far from here as you could get her."

"Trust me, if I could send her away, I would." Baze fought to keep the exasperation from his tone. "However, she's adamant upon staying, and I learned long ago not to stand in her way when she sets her mind to something. Besides, we work as a team." Confident though his words had been, deep in his conscience, he was still trying to convince himself that Adelynn's staying was a good idea. Because he didn't think so. He wanted her gone. He wanted her safe. But he needed her to locate O'Sullivan—and thus, his dilemma.

"You're a rare find, boyo." Darragh smiled. "Not many men of your breeding hold their wives in such high esteem. She must be a special *cailín*."

Baze's chest tightened. "She is."

"Got any wee ones at home?"

"No." Baze almost added "Not yet" to the end of his statement, but he bit his tongue.

"I see." Darragh twisted toward his desk and snatched up a paper and a pen. "Where are you and the missus stayin'? I'll put a man on patrol in case O'Sullivan decides to make good on his threat."

"Thank you, sir," Baze said and recounted the address.

"Right then." Slapping the note down upon the desk, Darragh crossed behind it and glanced between Baze and Fitzgerald. "Our immediate course of action is to discover the details of this so-called rebellion so we can intercept O'Sullivan and take him down." He nodded once. "Let's go get him, lads."

Dismissed, Baze and Fitzgerald vacated the office. Baze opened his mouth to engage the sergeant, but the man had already put several feet between them. Near the entrance, Fitzgerald approached a man leaning backward against the wall—Liam Donoghue. They hunkered close and began a hushed exchange.

Suspicions heightened, Baze watched until the men parted ways, Fitzgerald disappearing into the adjacent hall and Liam turning Baze's way. Baze scrutinized the Irishman—he had his hands tucked into his pockets, but there was something taut in his demeanor. As he drew nearer, Baze lifted his voice and said, "After your quick departure yesterday, I didn't think I'd see you so soon. What brings you here?"

Liam's expression turned to stone, but his pace didn't slow. "Me brother's here. I came to see him."

Before Liam could pass, Baze thrust out a hand and caught it against Liam's chest. "We both know that's not true," Baze murmured.

"Collin said you abandoned him after returning to Ireland, but after searching for him as long as you did, I can't for the life of me figure out why."

Liam knocked Baze's hand away. "Money was tight, and I fell on hard times. I did what I could for him with the resources I had."

"By leaving him on his own?" Baze growled. "Why didn't you send for me? I would have helped."

Liam sneered. "I don't be meanin' offense, Inspector Ford, but I've got more dignity than to be acceptin' handouts from a rich aristocrat." His voice dripped with hostility as he tapped a knuckle on Baze's chest. "You helped enough, anyway. Got your claws sunk into him, you have. Just look at him, struttin' around in that uniform. Your spittin' image. If anythin', he was the one who abandoned me."

Gooseflesh prickled on Baze's skin as Liam's harsh, hazy eyes pierced him. He shivered. "If you're not here for your brother, then what are you truly doing?"

"Back off, Inspector. I am not your enemy."

Baze gripped the tip of his cane so hard that his fingers ached. "For Collin's sake, I truly hope not."

Liam grimaced. "Good day to you." He sidestepped and checked Baze's shoulder.

As Liam's heavy footsteps stomped down the hall, Baze stared at the wood slats between his shoes. What had prompted Liam's aggression? Baze had tracked him all across Ireland in order to reunite him with Collin. At the time, Liam had been overjoyed and expressed immense gratitude—but the man from three years ago seemed completely different from the man who had just stormed off, and not in a good way.

Could Liam be trusted? And if not, what did that mean for Collin?

# Chapter Sixteen

*A CHILD SCREECHED AS HIS MOTHER spun him around in time with my fiddle. I sawed my bow across the strings in a hearty reel and laughed. Most of the village, young and old alike, had gathered around a roaring fire as the sun set behind the hills. Some danced, some sat, some ate— but we carried on as though our troubles were mere fables. If only it were a reflection of reality.*

*Well, a few days from now, I could start creating that reality.*

*I filtered through song after song until my fingers ached and people began leaning on one another in exhaustion and drunkenness. Our faces stretched in undying delight. As the fire simmered low, parents carted their children off to bed while some of the more mature crowd poured another drink and formed circles of conversation.*

*Holding a final note with a slow vibrato, I let the music hang in the air—then finally released. The sounds of the night filled the absence—singing sedge warblers, chirping bush crickets, barking red foxes. I pulled in a deep breath. Soon . . . soon I would have the power to make all of my people's burdens light.*

*Squeaky hinges drew my gaze to a nearby gate. Two figures stole through and marched straight for me, their mouths arranged in straight lines. I shifted my instrument and bow into one hand and touched lightly on their minds. They were yet at the mercy of my control—so why were they here? I hadn't called them back.*

*Panting, they stopped several paces away, but I spoke first. "What are you doin' here? You're supposed to be keepin' watch in Dublin."*

*They exchanged a glance, and then Fitzgerald said, "The Fords are choosin' to stay."*

*His voice sliced through the chilled air like a knife slicing into my gut. Anger rose, but I maintained control of my voice. "Are you sure?"*

*"Yes, sir. I was there at the police station when the inspector arrived to tell the superintendent what their plans are. Apparently, they're putting the mother and her child on a ship tomorrow morning, but yer man and his wife are stayin'."*

*I mashed my lips together to keep fury from escaping in a jumble of profanities. Foolish. They were so foolish! Adelynn most of all. She had seen what would happen if they stood in my way. Never had she been given reason to doubt her visions were real, so why did she choose now to tempt fate and play games with her loved ones' lives? Did she not realize she was about to set in motion all of her forewarnings?*

*Strangling the neck of my violin, I spoke low and even. "Clearly, I underestimated their recklessness. That was my error, and I won't be makin' it again. If they aren't going to respond to my generosity, then we must make them endure the consequences."*

*Fitzgerald pondered a moment. "What about a hostage? The kid maybe?"*

*My throat tightened at the idea of putting that child through such a strenuous ordeal—but it might be the only way we could see this through to the end.*

*"Does the inspector suspect you?" I asked.*

*"I don't think so. He started to come onto me, but the superintendent spoke on my behalf and diverted his suspicions."*

*"Good." I glanced at Donoghue, noting the deep crease in his brow and his dazed eyes. The man had once possessed a strong will, resisting my influences in the name of his younger brother, but I had long squashed that drive. He liked to test my limits in moments he thought I wasn't paying attention, nearly clawing his way out of the pit before I booted him back down. For now, at least, he appeared fully compliant.*

*"Go find the boy," I instructed, voice taut. "Both of you. You shouldn't have much trouble. The inspector won't be hard for you to*

*subdue, not with his leg in its current condition, and the women shouldn't pose a threat. Don't kill anyone. This must be done tonight."*

*"Yes, sir." The men nodded and clomped back the way they had come.*

*Staring into the crackling fire, I tucked the violin under my chin and eased into a somber melody. "You brought this upon yourself, Adelynn," I whispered and let the music consume me.*

The creak of a distant floorboard jerked Baze from sleep. He lifted his head, alert, listening. Faint rustling from down the hall reached his ears and prickled the hair on the back of his neck. With the staff already sent away, the house should have been silent at this hour. By all rights, Emily should have been gone too, but she had insisted upon remaining until morning so she could say farewell to Finn, and Baze didn't want to add to her emotional turmoil further by refusing.

He sat up and inched his fingers over the gun on the bedside table. He quickly checked that Adelynn still slept—she breathed deeply in the throes of the unconscious—before slipping to his feet.

Weapon poised, Baze crept into the hall, enduring calf pain in exchange for a quiet and even gait. A dim light and several more creaks emitting from the sitting room drew him forward. He pressed his back against the wall and edged toward the corner. Craning his neck, he shifted a little farther until he could peek into the room.

Clad in her nightgown with her hair a tangled mess of curls, Emily stood in the middle of the space. Basil Allan lay completely comatose in her arms, his pudgy cheek smashed into her shoulder. With her eyes shut and feet slightly apart, she rocked slowly from side to side. She hummed something indistinguishable.

Baze blew out a breath and lowered his pistol, but as he shifted backward, his foot pushed a groan from the floorboards. He winced as Emily's eyes drifted open and found him. "Sorry, I didn't mean to disturb you," he said with a hushed tone—though, he was sure even a normal volume wouldn't wake Adelynn with how deep she slept.

Emily smiled faintly and patted her son's back. "Come out for a midnight snack, have you?"

"No, I heard a sound and wanted to ensure it wasn't an intruder."

"Oh. I'm sorry for waking you."

"Don't be." He ventured into the room. "What are you doing up at this hour?"

"I couldn't get this little nipper to settle down. I think he's having nightmares." She sighed. "Rocking seems to be the only thing that calms him at the moment."

Baze chuckled. "I don't know how you do it, Emily."

With a grin, she shifted Basil Allan's weight onto her other arm. "You would be amazed at the things of which you are capable when you become a parent."

The mantel clock's ticking reminded Baze just how late it was—or rather, early, for it was half-past two in the morning. He set the gun on the side table and crossed to her with hands outstretched. "Why don't you to give him to me? I'll rock him for a while so you can get some sleep. You have a long day ahead of you."

"Oh, no, I couldn't ask you to do that."

He smiled and raised insistent eyebrows. "I want to."

Emily tilted her head and studied him for a long moment. Finally, she nodded and passed Basil Allan to him. The toddler moaned and squirmed a little, but once they got him settled, his head supported on Baze's shoulder like a pillow, he quieted and melted into dead weight again. Heat seeped from his little body into Baze's chest and straight to his heart. Sudden emotion squeezed his throat.

"Thank you," Emily whispered.

"Of course."

Rather than take her leave, she lingered and watched her son for a time. Then she turned her kind eyes upon Baze. "He sees you as a father, you know."

The emotion surged up from his heart and prickled his nose. He sniffed and managed to murmur, "I know."

"I don't mind that he does. After all, you have filled the role so naturally, and I am thankful you are willing to do it. I'm sure Bennett would be humbled to know his son would be so well loved."

Baze shrugged lightly. "I'm happy to do it."

She laid a gentle hand on his upper arm. "You may think your actions no more than a kind gesture, but they are far more significant. When you hold your own child one day, you will experience a love that completely shatters everything you once knew of it, and then you will understand exactly why this mean so much to me."

A boulder settled in the pit of Baze's stomach. He rocked gently and fixed his gaze on the distant floor. "Did Adelynn tell you to say that?"

"No, I mean every word of it." She smiled sympathetically. "But . . . I suppose, if we're talking about Adelynn and the decisions you face together, I think fear can hold us back from pursuing the things that truly matter in life. I would simply hate for you to miss out on these sweet joys because of a fear that I know you have the strength to overcome—especially if you face it with the Almighty at your side." With a comforting squeeze of his arm, she kissed him tenderly on the cheek before shuffling from the room.

With the concentrated warmth from Basil's Allan body mixing with the heat of Baze's conviction, Baze was sure he was about to combust right where he stood. Still, he only tightened his embrace, and though the child was dead asleep, his soft little hand came up and wrapped around Baze's neck. The boulder in Baze's stomach sank further as he ventured toward the window overlooking the front lawn and stared into the darkness.

Basil Allan was a handful—a right little nipper as Emily so endearingly called him. He had moments of fussiness, tantrums, and full meltdowns, but they were offset with moments like this one—sweet peace. No matter how much Basil Allan frustrated him, Baze would never wish the child out of his life. In fact, he was certain he would willingly *give up* his life to keep him safe.

Still, those feelings didn't banish the fear he held toward having his own child—and the fear of turning out like his own father. Cold. Manipulative. And heartless.

His fingers twitched with the urge to stroke the bridge of his nose, his constant reminder that he carried the weight of Alistair's everlasting disapproval. How could Baze have any hope of becoming a good father when a man like *that* had raised him? Besides, the moment Alistair learned a new Ford heir was on the way, he would immediately try to weasel his way back into Baze's life. Could Baze protect his child from Alistair's expectations?

Could he protect his child from himself?

Basil Allan heaved a contented sigh, smacking his lips with sleep, and nuzzled his face farther into Baze's chest.

And Baze's heart nearly exploded.

Emily had alluded to a much stronger love than what Baze felt right now—a much stronger love than he even felt for Adelynn. He couldn't imagine how that was possible.

But maybe, if he could confront his fears *and* his father, he would be ready for a taste of it. Perhaps when this conflict was over and they returned home, he would talk to Adelynn about—

Headlights flashed in the darkness. A sleek black car slipped into the drive and crawled toward the house.

Alarm flared. Baze ducked and crept behind the drapes, then peeked out. The car stopped about twenty feet from the front of the drive, and the headlights dimmed. Two men stepped out, urgency and wariness in their postures. Baze caught a flash of red hair and felt a swirl of confusion. Liam Donoghue? What was he doing here?

Trying not to make sudden movements, Baze spun and hunkered toward the sofa. He laid the child on the cushion—which thankfully didn't wake him—and snatched his gun from the side table. He checked the bullets, then disengaged the safety.

With his stomach in his throat, Baze hastened to the front door and stole outside. He descended the steps just as the men came within reach.

Surprise slacked Liam's features upon seeing Baze, but he recovered quickly. He marched toward Baze—until he noticed the gun. Liam drew up and lifted his hands slightly. "Thank God you're awake. It's Collin. He's in trouble."

Baze squinted at the other man and recognized Fitzgerald—Darragh's undercover man? Why were he and Liam here together? His fingers tightened around the weapon. "What's happened?"

"Collin was on patrol earlier in the night and ran into a rogue band of nationalists. He was shot." Liam spoke as though out of breath, and terror flickered on his face, which seemed sincere on the surface at least. "They've taken him to hospital, but it's not lookin' good." His eyes darkened. "He's askin' for you."

Baze's muscles quivered as he pictured the young man in such peril, and he felt a strong urge to rush to Collin's side . . . but Baze couldn't leave the women alone, not when O'Sullivan's threats still stood. That was, of course, assuming Liam was telling the truth. Baze needed to probe for more. The two Irishmen were acting too suspicious for him to—

"Bay-Bay? Who are they?"

Baze sucked in a breath and spun. Basil Allan wavered sleepily in the open doorway, one hand clutching the knob and the other rubbing at his droopy eyes. Baze held out an assuring hand and spoke lightly. "Everything's all right, buddy. Go back in—"

An arm locked around Baze's throat from behind and yanked him backward.

"Get the kid!" Liam barked.

Baze twisted and rammed his elbow into Liam's ribs. As the Irishman gasped, Baze grabbed his arm, bent forward, and pulled. The momentum threw Liam over his head and onto the ground. Now free, Baze straightened, aimed his gun, and looked frantically for Fitzgerald.

The man was sprinting for the doorway, Basil Allan nearly in his reach. There was enough room. Baze had an opening. But what if—no time!

A split-second decision flexed Baze's fingers.

*Bang!*

The bullet hit its mark. With a grunt, Fitzgerald stutter-stepped but didn't stop. He ducked and snatched Basil Allan from the step, then reeled back toward the car. The toddler began wailing.

Baze swore, but as he lined up a new shot, Liam's arm crashed down on his wrist. The gun flew from his grip.

The flash of a knife hurtled toward Baze's chest. He whipped up his forearm to stop the blow, but Liam rotated the weapon and jerked it backward against Baze's arm. Fire engulfed his limb as Liam came charging back at him, blade poised and dripping blood. Baze waited one extra second, then sidestepped. He struck at Liam's wrist to remove the knife and simultaneously thrust out a foot to catch Liam's shin. The man spilled face-first onto the ground.

Baze pounced. He flipped Liam onto his back, drew back his fist—

Basil Allan screeched.

Baze whirled toward Fitzgerald. Basil Allan kicked and struggled as Fitzgerald wrenched open the boot of the car. Tears streamed down the child's red face. "Bay-Bay! Help! Bay—" The man clamped his hand over the toddler's mouth and shoved him inside.

"Stop!" Baze shouted. "Let him—"

A foot plunged into Baze's stomach. He folded, gasping.

Liam lunged upward, grabbed Baze's head, and drove his knee straight into Baze's face.

Bone popped. Light flashed.

Baze collapsed. Sounds faded in and out as dizziness swirled. With his nose and mouth pressed into the ground, he inhaled dirt and dust with each ragged breath. He coughed and, wrestling against the sensation of blacking out, lifted his head.

Liam and Fitzgerald hopped into the automobile. The doors slammed.

"No," Baze croaked. Somehow, some way, his muscles found the strength to move and heaved him to his feet. His face throbbed.

Something warm and smelling of iron trickled between his eyes. The world spun, but he stumbled forward and started to run with his hand outstretched as if to pull Basil Allan back to himself by sheer willpower.

Half a dozen strides in, his scarred calf muscle seized and brought him slamming back to the ground. He cursed and grappled at the pavement with his fingernails.

With a screech of spinning tires, the assailants careened out of sight—Basil Allan with them.

Silence followed. Air wheezed in Baze's chest as he gaped at the empty drive. Numbness and vertigo consumed his body, and just before he slipped unconscious, he heard a woman's anguished wail in the distance.

# Chapter Seventeen

Basil Allan was gone.

As I tried to absorb everything that had happened a mere hour ago, I finished steeping the tea and prepared cups for the three of us. Adrenaline chased away any lingering traces of sleep. This was my fault. I had witnessed his kidnapping. I had told Emily to bring him.

I had all but ensured this would happen.

Somehow, I forced my quivering fingers to pour the brew, arrange a tray, and carry it to the sitting room where Baze and Emily rested in chilling quiet, Emily curled up in the large chair and Baze seated on one end of the sofa.

I delivered the first cup into Emily's hands. Her stony expression didn't change as she accepted the drink and held it loosely in her lap. With her hair in disarray and nightgown hanging slightly off one shoulder, her unblinking gaze remained fixed on something across the room. Though her sobbing had tapered off a while ago, her cheeks remained flushed and raw, and her eyes drooped under swollen lids.

Unsure what to say, I opted for silence and carried the tray to the sofa. I placed it on the side table and sank next to Baze. He sat bent forward, elbows on his knees, holding a cold compress over his nose and eyes with both hands.

Ever so gently, I touched his shoulder. "Show me your face. I want to see if the swelling's come down."

"It's fine," he rasped with a slightly nasal tone.

Clenching my teeth, I pulled one of his arms away—the one that had a bloody slice in the fabric—and worked to wrench the sleeve up. "Let me at least bandage your other wound."

I used the liquid carbolic acid I'd retrieved for his face and began cleaning the cut. It started at his wrist and sliced horizontally into the pale flesh of his inner forearm. Though it didn't appear deep enough to warrant stitches, it had bled a fair bit, so I dabbed at the skin, disinfected the wound, and wrapped it in a bandage.

When I had finished and relinquished control of his arm, he straightened his spine and finally removed the compress from his face, squeezing it until his knuckles turned white.

I leaned forward to glimpse the damage. The skin above his nose, just between his eyes, had been split open and looked inflamed and painful. Swelling had inflated the bridge of his nose, and a faint bruise had already begun to color the corners of his eyes. His nose was likely broken—again. Though, if I wasn't imagining things, it appeared straighter than it had before.

His bloodshot gaze turned on me. "Can you see where they've taken him?" His voice teetered on the precipice between anger and grief.

I risked a quick glance at Emily—still emotionless, she had fixed her eyes on me—and looked back to Baze. "I'm not sure now is the right time. They've only just gone."

His voice spiked. "I said, can you see—" He clamped his lips shut and closed his eyes, the muscles in his face shuddering. Finally, he repeated in a whisper, "Can you see where they've taken him? Please."

I swallowed slowly and nodded. "I can try."

Determination hardened my stomach as I faced forward on the sofa and laid my hands flat on my thighs. Oh, how quickly the tide could turn. Several meager hours earlier, we had gone to bed with a plan, confident we could defy Shay without repercussions, flush him out of hiding, and prevent his plot from unfurling. We thought we had him cornered, but he had been in control all along.

I closed my eyes and focused all of my willpower on one thing— finding Shay. The more I practiced the skill, the easier it became to detach my mind from my body and invade the mind of another.

This time was no different.

My consciousness slipped effortlessly from my material form. Darkness shrouded me as I careened through the metaphysical realm in search of Shay. Then, with a burst of light, I burrowed into his mind. A small home with stone walls and primitive wooden furniture surrounded him. He collected a worn quilt from a chest, approached a single bed, and tossed the blanket so it spread across the mattress. When it settled, the lone individual lying beneath it came into view.

Basil Allan.

The toddler's cheeks were red and stained with tears, but for the moment, he seemed calm. "Where's Mama?" His little voice sounded pinched.

Shay tucked the quilt around him. "She will be collectin' you before you know it, but she was tellin' me you must sleep before you can see her."

Basil Allan puckered his bottom lip. "I want to go home."

"I know. You will soon. But as I said, you need to sleep first." Shay glanced about and then leaned closer with a whisper. "How about this—if you obey and go to sleep without anymore fussin', I shall let you have a peppermint stick in the morning, and then we'll go see your mam. How does that sound?"

Basil Allan nodded and wriggled farther beneath the quilt.

"Good lad." Shay ruffled the toddler's hair, then heaved to a stand, one of his knees protesting with a crack. "It shall be mornin' before you know it."

Shay wandered to the window across the room, settled his hands in his pockets, and peered out. Darkness blanketed the rustic village that encircled his home, and the waning crescent moon illuminated a loose cluster of thatched cottages with wisps of smoke blowing from their chimneys.

"Are you pleased by what your actions have reaped, Adelynn?" Shay whispered, voice oozing with condescension. "I warned that you'd be payin' the price if you chose to ignore my request. I didn't want it to come to this, but you forced my hand. So here's what is goin' to happen now."

He cast a glance over his shoulder at Basil Allan's sleeping form. "I shall remain in Dublin, but my men are goin' to take the boy far away from here, and if you want him back, you'll have to track him down and take him back. With all that you've learned of touchin' the minds of those I control, I have no doubt you'll be able to do it." He placed one hand on the wall beside the window and leaned upon it. His voice grew severe. "If, for some disturbin' reason, you choose to abandon your young ward and continue to pursue me, he *will* get hurt. That I can promise you."

Fear flooded my system and nearly made me lose my grip on Shay's mind.

"They'll be leavin' at first light, so you'd best be ready to go by then if you don't want to lose much ground." He closed his eyes, and I felt a strong shove against my mind. "Now get out."

A sharp jolt thrust me backward. Light and dark flashed in my vision until my father's sitting room materialized into view. With a gasp, I sank into the sofa and gaped at the ceiling.

Rage churned in my gut like a cyclone and swirled up my throat. Shay had us trapped. He had targeted the most innocent one among us because he knew we would drop everything to rescue him, no questions asked.

"What did you see?" Baze's curious, concerned voice snapped the frenzy within me. He and Emily held me intently in anxious stares.

I popped to my feet and paced in the center of the room. Words tumbled from my mouth, nearly all in one breath, as I explained everything I had witnessed. As I spoke, Emily's skin paled, and a heavy cloud darkened Baze's features.

"Shay knew exactly where to strike." I folded my arms tight to my chest. "He knows I'm the only one who can find him. He knows we won't abandon Basil Allan—and I would never suggest we do, but . . . it means we must let him win."

"We did what we could," Baze said, his voice calm and resigned. "Ireland will have to take care of itself. This family comes first."

My heart squeezed, and those dreaded tears finally bubbled to the surface. I'd managed to stay fairly disengaged, if only to be the reassuring presence that Baze and Emily needed while they lamented Basil Allan's abduction, but it seemed my emotional barrier had weakened.

Baze set the compress aside, came to my side, and rubbed my arms. "You should get as much rest as you can. Both of you. I would like to set out at daybreak."

He crossed to Emily and dropped a comforting hand on her shoulder. She bit her lip, her eyes flooding once again. When he angled toward the hallway leading to our room, I plodded forward to follow, but as I reached Emily, I bent and kissed her head. "We'll get him back," I whispered. "I promise I shall do everything in my power to make it happen."

Emily's tears plopped softly into her tea, and she nodded—silent.

Inside our room, I found Baze rummaging through his wardrobe. He peeled off his nightshirt and began to dress as though preparing for the day.

I frowned. "What are you doing? You said we have to get some sleep."

"I said *you* have to get some sleep." He threaded an arm through his shirt. "I'm going to go to the police station to let Darragh know what's happening . . . and to find Collin."

My heart fractured. *Oh, Collin.* He had been rescued from Cornelius's control only for his brother to fall prey to the same manipulation. If Shay had managed to take Liam's mind captive, was it possible he had seized Collin's too? The boy hadn't experienced the same redemptive transformation that freed Finn, so it was possible Cornelius's power still lurked in his mind, primed and waiting to strike.

I trailed light fingers down Baze's spine. "Be careful. You don't know if Collin is—"

"I know."

I tilted my head. "How's your nose?"

"It doesn't matter." He shrugged and buttoned his shirt.

"Of course it matters." I tugged his arm to turn him slightly my way.

He pressed his lips flat and looked everywhere but at me, moisture gleaming in his eyes.

Protectiveness rose up as I suddenly realized the deceitful thoughts he entertained. "This isn't your fault." I gripped his face with both hands. "Baze, look at me." He pulled in a long breath before finally acquiescing. "This isn't your fault," I repeated. "Those men would have taken Basil Allan regardless of who was watching him. They took you by surprise. You did all you could to stop them, and I know you'll do all you can to get him back."

Tumultuous thoughts churned behind Baze's eyes. Then, he slid his warm hands around my neck, dipped his head, and kissed me. He moved slowly, intentionally, as though to draw out the sweet moment as long as he could. I surrendered to him, grasping the fabric between his shoulder blades and allowing him to take what he needed. When his lips eventually broke from mine, he enfolded me in his steady arms and tucked me against him.

"I love you, Al," he whispered.

"I love you too," I whispered back, my voice muffled in his chest.

He kissed my head and squeezed just a little tighter. "Please get some sleep. I'll return as soon as I can."

## Chapter Eighteen

BAZE BURST THROUGH THE BARRACKS DOOR of the Dublin Metropolitan Police station. Day had begun to break, rousing several policemen for their morning patrol, and Baze prayed Darragh was here. In his haste to leave, he had forgotten his cane and was forced to limp from room to room. Whether by extreme luck or divine intervention, he discovered Collin slumbering in the second chamber. He seized Collin's nightshirt with both fists and hauled him from the bed, ripping a groggy yell of protest from him.

Collin pried at Baze's hand, but he held fast and marched into the front hall as fast as his leg would allow. They passed the constable manning the desk, drawing him to his feet with a shout of alarm. "Sir, what are you doin'? Stop!"

Not breaking stride, Baze towed Collin farther down the hall until he came to the superintendent's office. He barreled his way inside, heaved Collin around, and threw him to the floor in front of the desk.

Eyes wide, Darragh surged to his feet. "What's the meanin' of this?"

The constable stumbled into the doorway, out of breath. "Sorry, sir. He came up too fast. I couldn't stop him."

Darragh's startled but studious gaze jumped from Baze to Collin scrambling on the floor and back to the constable. "It's all right." He waved his hand. "Go back to your post. I'll sort this out."

"Yes, sir." The constable nodded hesitantly, then closed the door behind him.

Darragh smacked his hands on the desk's surface as he examined Baze's face. "What happened, boyo? You look terrible."

"Liam Donoghue and Sergeant Arthur Fitzgerald happened, sir," Baze growled, doing all he could to keep his reactions under control. "They came to our home last night, they assaulted me, and they abducted my . . . my nephew."

Collin stilled, and Darragh's spine went rigid.

"Didn't know you had traitors working for you, did you?" Baze continued, frustration mounting as restraint slipped away. "How many others are hiding right beneath your nose? Hmm? Are you so complacent that you—"

"All right, that's enough," Darragh snapped. "Take a seat. The both of you."

Collin dragged himself up and onto one of the chairs, but Baze remained on his feet, body tense and trembling as though preparing for an attack.

Darragh sighed. "Take a breather, boyo."

Pain throbbed in Baze's nose and in the cut between his eyes as he gulped in one breath, then a second. His pulse began to decelerate as he released an exhale in a steady stream.

"Good." Darragh nodded and sank into his chair. "Tell me what happened now. Slowly. From the beginnin'."

Baze walked through the entire series of events, from when Liam and Fitzgerald first approached under the guise of Collin's attack to when they screeched away. By the time he finished, his calf muscle screamed for a reprieve, so he dropped onto the seat beside Collin.

"You sure it was Fitzgerald?" Darragh asked, voice aggravatingly composed. "You said it was dark out. Perhaps you were mistaken."

"I'm positive."

Darragh pointed at Collin. "What about you? Can you shed any light on your brother's comin's and goin's, particularly last night?"

His face awash with conflicting emotion, Collin wagged his head. "*Níl*, sir. I don't even know where he's livin' at the moment."

Sympathy twinged Baze's chest, but his anger for Liam's actions overpowered it.

Rubbing the scarred flesh of his deformed hand, Darragh pursed his lips and swiveled to the side in his chair. Then he looked at Baze out of the corner of his eye. "Well, I can send some men to your house to gather evidence and start buildin' a case against them, but I've a feelin' you're not here to ask for my help, aye?"

"No, sir." Baze squeezed his kneecaps. "I have a lead on where they're taking Basil Allan, and it's far out of your jurisdiction. I merely came to inform you of Fitzgerald's betrayal, for if he's been compromised, there may be others."

Darragh's freckled skin flushed. "Fitzgerald was a good man. I can't imagine what turned him."

"I believe Shay's power turned him—both him and Liam," Baze said quietly, drawing a short gasp from Collin. "He is capable of manipulating men to do horrible things, things they would never do of their own accord. That makes him incredibly dangerous—because we have no idea who is under his influence or not." Baze hesitated, already regretting the next words he was about to say. "Which is why I can't trust your men anymore. I don't even know if I should trust you. Not with my family's lives on the line. I'm sorry, sir."

Disappointment filled Darragh's eyes, but he nodded slowly. "I understand. Were I in your shoes, I'd be concludin' the same." He folded his arms and placed them atop the desk. "I realize I can't convince you my mind is clear, but if you find yourself in dire straits, my door is always open. In the meantime, I'll try to flush out any corrupted ones who might be tryin' to infiltrate our ranks."

"Be careful, sir," Baze warned. "Once he's in your mind, it's hard to escape without aid from the Almighty." He thought back to the moment Cornelius Marx had violated his own mind, cringing at how helpless he had been, completely at the mercy of that maniac.

"Understood." Darragh tipped his chin. "Best get out of here then. The longer you lollygag, the farther away they get with your wee chiseler."

"Thank you, sir."

"Godspeed."

Baze limped from the office, heaving a deep sigh and allowing the weight of it all to drag his shoulders down.

"Mr. Ford, wait."

Collin's hesitant voice pulled Baze to a halt. He approached, hands wringing and eyes downcast. "*Tá brón orm*," he muttered. "I-I'm sorry . . . for what Liam did to you. I'll try to make it right. I promise you, I will."

Instinctive anger primed Baze's tongue to lash out, but he forced himself to take a calming breath and spoke quietly. "This isn't your fault. It may not even be Liam's fault. You know what it's like to be under that control." Baze shifted to his healthy leg and caught the boy's wince.

Collin continued twisting his hands and finally met Baze's eyes. "When you find the child . . . if Liam's there, can you . . . help him?"

Still reeling from the events of that morning, Baze wanted Liam to experience only the harshest punishment, but he couldn't take Collin's hopes and dash them into dust—not especially if Liam was a victim himself.

"If he's there," Baze managed to murmur as he gripped Collin's shoulder, "I'll do everything I can to help him. You have my word."

Sleep eluded me. Myriad thoughts swirled in my mind. After a couple of hours, I rolled from bed and picked out my wardrobe for the day— something comfortable yet unassuming—and planted myself in front of the mirror. With our staff members, fortunately, on their way back to England, I was left to dress myself, not that I wasn't capable, but on a day like this, I wasn't sure how I would find the energy.

My stomach shifted and protested as I tightened the corset. Annoyed, I pressed on, ignoring my body's pleas to free it from the garment. I'd been wearing a corset nearly every day of my life since I was an adolescent. Why should it bother me now?

Yet, as it squeezed my chest, my bosom ached and my midsection resisted. Puffing out a frustrated sigh, I loosened the laces, popped open the busk, and tossed it at my feet. With my hands on my hips, I glared at myself in the mirror. Yes, I had gained some weight since the wedding—domestic life tended to have the effect, or so I'd been told by many meddlesome women—but surely that wasn't enough to warrant a new change of clothes, unless . . .

Little by little, I turned to the side so that I could view my profile. My bust and hips had filled out—a fact that Baze had been delighted to notice several weeks ago—but could there be more to it? I pressed my hand just below my bosom, then slowly dragged it down my torso. It slid freely until my fingers encountered a slight rise in my abdomen. My breath hitched as I cupped the swell in my palm. A faint flutter tickled me from within.

Surely this wasn't anything more than bloating. Surely . . .

Emily's faraway words invaded my thoughts. *"I believe you may be feeling the quickening . . . It's the moment when a mother first feels her child move within her."*

I closed my eyes, nausea rising. This couldn't happen now—not when Baze still clung adamantly to his resolve, not when Emily's own child had just been kidnapped. Still, maybe Emily was right. Maybe calling upon a doctor to give me a definitive no was the wisest path forward, especially if we were about to venture further into danger.

Tossing on a robe, I marched resolutely from the room. First, I checked on Emily. She dozed on the sofa, her body's small tics and twitches indicating that sleep held her firmly in its grasp. Then I sought out the telephone in father's study and booked the services of a traveling physician.

With the appointment made, I paced by the front door in the hopes that I could intercept him before he could knock. No sense waking Emily for this. Though she had been the first to point out my odd behavior and had offered to join me should I choose to visit a doctor, I didn't want her to know that I had changed my mind. Not that she would snitch to Baze—she would never betray my trust like that—but the fewer people who knew, the better I could guard this secret . . . if there was even a secret to be found.

*What do you think your friend will think when she learns you're lying to her? Especially with her in such distress over the loss of her child? How utterly selfish of you.*

My stomach soured as I endured the internal barrage, knowing I couldn't say a word to refute its claims.

Within a half hour, a car pulled into the drive, and a short middle-aged man in a long trench coat and carrying a medical bag exited the vehicle. He ambled toward the house. I gauged his approach through the window and then darted to the door and swung it open.

He stood with wide eyes and hand poised to knock. His mustache twisted as he pursed his lips and took in my garb—I'm sure I looked affright. "Good day to you, ma'am." He tipped the brim of his hat in greeting. "I'm Dr. O'Malley. I understand I am here for a house call."

"Yes, you're here for me. I'm Mrs. Ford." I beckoned him inside and exchanged a quick handshake. "If you would please follow me."

I led him into my bedchamber and closed the door. My heart thudded. Sweat pressed my nightgown to my skin. I rubbed my palms together as I faced him. "I need a physical examination."

His bushy brows rose as he gripped his medical bag before him with both hands. "May I inquire as to the reason?"

I hesitated, thankful I hadn't yet eaten for the burst of nausea that turned my stomach. The moment I spoke life to this notion, I couldn't take it back. It would become real.

With a mouse-quiet voice, I finally said, "I believe I may be with child."

A light smile relaxed Dr. O'Malley's features. "I see." He set his bag on the corner chair, followed by his hat and then his coat. As he scrubbed his hands in the washstand, he said, "Could you please describe the symptoms that have led you to that conclusion?"

My wobbly knees threatened to spill me onto the floor, so I sank onto the end of the bed. "I've been gaining weight. I've been nauseous of late. I'm emotional. I'm achy."

"When was your last menses?"

I scoured my memory. There had been spotting—enough to make

both Baze and me believe all was normal—but nothing of the intensity to which I was accustomed. Realization struck as I said, "I don't remember."

Those final words stole the breath from my lungs. All the signs were there, staring me in the face—practically screaming at me—and had been doing so for months. How had I been so blind?

No, I hadn't been blind. I had chosen not to see it.

Hooking a stethoscope around his neck, Dr. O'Malley came to my side and squatted, but rather than speak, he studied me a moment. "Are you carryin' this alone, *a leanbh?*"

Heart in my throat, I looked into his eyes—deep brown pools of concern and compassion. They were the eyes of a person I could trust. So I nodded weakly.

His weathered hand slipped over my trembling fingers. "Then I shall carry it with you, if you would allow it, for I believe no one should ever have to walk through troubled times alone." His gentle Irish accent soothed my tension. "There is nothin' to fear about the examination. I have guided hundreds of women through what you are about to experience, and I have walked beside enough mothers to see many a wee babe grow into upstandin' adults." He stroked my cheek with his callused thumb, then tipped my nose. "We'll get you the answers you seek and see to it that you're looked after. Aye?"

I nodded, sniffling. "Thank you."

Dr. O'Malley instructed me how to position myself and began by pressing the cool stethoscope to my stomach. He would listen, then slide it over a few inches and listen again. When he progressed to the physical examination, I squeezed my eyes shut and clutched the linens beneath me. It was only when I heard the splashing of water that I realized it was over. He dried his hands, helped me tug my garments into a decent state, and sank before me again.

"It is as you surmised, Mrs. Ford," he said gently. "You are expecting."

Air punched from my lungs and took all my words with it.

"The child's heartbeat is strong and steady," he continued, "and though it is hard to be completely accurate, I can estimate based on your measurements that you are perhaps fourteen to sixteen weeks along, which would put your delivery date at about mid-October."

Sixteen weeks. Four months. I had been pregnant for four months. I thought through all of the arguments Baze and I had engaged in, all of the resentment and heated emotions we had directed at one another. As we fought over the decision whether to have a child or not, I had already been carrying that very child.

Dr. O'Malley took my hand and squeezed. "I can see this is not the news you had hoped to hear, but I wish to put your mind at ease by assurin' you that feelings of doubt and nervousness are normal. In fact, many of the mothers under my care find themselves confronted by fear in one way or another." He tilted his head, his kind eyes boring into me. "Is there no one you can tell to help you through this? Not even your husband?"

*You can't tell Baze. He told you he didn't want this. He will leave you if he finds out.*

I managed to swallow back enough emotion to rasp, "It's complicated."

Dr. O'Malley brushed his thumb over my fingers a moment, then nodded. "What I said earlier stands. I don't wish to see you carry this alone. You have my number. I realize you may return to England soon, but so long as you are here, you may call me at any time, day or night. I will answer." His mouth eased into a kindhearted smile. "You have been blessed, Mrs. Ford."

*No, you have been cursed.*

Clashing emotions tumbled through me. Having a child had been my heart's deepest longing when Baze and I entered into marriage, but it had gone unmet for so long that apathy had begun to whittle my hope down into a bitter ache. Until now . . . now, the doctor's words had revived that hope and transformed it into reality.

But now that my greatest desire had been fulfilled, I wanted God to take it away.

## Chapter Nineteen

GRAY CLOUDS CREPT ACROSS THE SKY and dumped rain upon the land as Emily stared out the front window at the lawn and the park beyond. She had already tossed all of her belongings in her trunk, but Baze and Adelynn still silently bustled about, hardly uttering a word except to ensure they had everything they would need.

Emily picked at the skin by her thumbnail until it bled. Her weary eyes burned as she watched cars go by. She thought she had experienced as much pain as she could fathom when she lost Bennett, but this cut far deeper. It felt like she had been ripped open and was watching her lifeblood siphon slowly from her body.

A loud *bang* in the front hall made Emily jump. Adelynn had dropped her bag beside Baze's.

Emily turned back to the window. Another car sped into view, but this one slowed at the end of the drive. It stopped just long enough to allow a man to jump out and then raced away. Emily's heart throbbed. Even after knowing one another for only a short time, she would recognize that swaggering gait and those dark curls anywhere.

Propping a hand over his head—as though that would protect him from the rain—Finn jogged toward the house and soon disappeared from Emily's sight. Then a knock sounded at the door.

Baze burst from the other room and pressed a finger to his lips to signal their silence as he slunk to the window. Adelynn came hot on his tail, and Emily didn't miss the protective hand she held over her abdomen, solidifying Emily's suspicions. Baze leaned slightly to peek at the newcomer. After a short beat, he relaxed his shoulders, stalked to the door, and swung it wide.

"What are you doing here?" Baze growled, low and direct.

Adelynn nudged Baze out of the way. "Don't make him stand in the rain," she muttered. "Please, come in."

With a quiet "Thank you," Finn passed between them and stormed into the sitting room where Emily hid. His frantic blue eyes darted about the room, then finally found her and locked on tight.

She fought against new tears as they exchanged shared sorrow.

Baze dropped a hand on Finn's shoulder and yanked him around. "You didn't answer me. What are you doing here?"

Finn knocked Baze's arm away. "I came because—"

"Because of Basil Allan?"

The accusation in Baze's words soured Emily's stomach. Why was he acting so hostile? Did he truly suspect Finn of wrongdoing, after all they had been through?

Finn squared his chest with Baze's. "What are you insinuatin'?"

"I'm not insinuating anything." Baze took a step closer. "You seemed quite unsurprised earlier when O'Sullivan showed his face at your performance, and now you've turned up mere hours after Basil Allan's kidnapping. How else could you have known unless you're one of his pawns?"

Emily opened her mouth, but Finn hurled his rebuttal before she could interject.

"Why are you accusin' me of sinister motives when Adelynn's the one who willingly linked minds with your man?" Finn aimed a condemning finger toward her. "How do you know she hasn't been compromised?"

Baze seized Finn's shirt and shook him. "Don't you dare speak about my wife like that."

"I'm only speakin' the truth." Finn wrenched Baze's hands away. "You can't deny it. She's opened herself to—"

"Please don't fight," Emily whispered, her voice cracking. Everyone halted and turned her way, tension suspended in the air. Anger clamped down on her throat. "This won't help me find my son."

Ever so slowly, the posture of the two men relaxed, and they cast one another a final glance, one resigned and the other acquiescent.

Eyes grating like sandpaper, she targeted Baze with a fierce glare. "He's here because I called him. This land is his home. He knows it better than any of us, and if we're to find my son, we need as much help as we can muster. So stop fighting. We have enough enemies to worry about without turning on each other."

She held Baze in her reproachful stare until he folded his arms and nodded. "Of course. I apologize, Emily."

Satisfied, she slid her eyes to Finn. He gulped in a breath as he held her gaze, eager yet hesitant.

As though sensing a shift in the room, Adelynn tugged Baze's sleeve and coaxed him toward the adjacent room. "A word please."

When they'd gone, Finn crossed to Emily and sat gingerly on the cushion beside her, his knees angled her way. She found herself leaning toward him impulsively but stopped short of sinking into him. A painful zing laced up her finger as she tore further into the skin, and she winced.

Finn straightened, alert, searching for the source of her pain. When he noticed her hands, he balked. "What are you doin'?" He snatched up her left hand and grimaced at the blood on her index finger. "Just look at the state of you. We need you well if you're to be getting' your little man back." He reached into his waistcoat pocket and pulled out a handkerchief. Gently, he wrapped it about her finger, then bent his neck and kissed it.

Despite all of the heavy emotions flooding her system, bashfulness still managed to plow through and heat her cheeks.

He squeezed her hand in both of his and softened his tone. "Shay won't hurt the lad, Emily. He is capable of many things, but hurtin' children is not one of them."

"Are you sure?"

"I would never lie to you. I swear it upon me mam's grave."

Though he'd said the words to comfort her, she couldn't lower her guard. Not yet—not until she held Basil Allan safe in her arms.

She focused on their intertwined hands. "Thank you for coming."

"Of course." His thumb caressed her throbbing finger. "Why wouldn't I have come?"

"Because it will be dangerous." She met his eyes, searching for any hint of regret. "You could have said no."

"I wanted to come."

"But why?"

A small incredulous laugh puffed from his lips. "If you want me to say it plainly, then I'll say it. I care about you, Emily." Her heart fluttered as she sucked in a breath. She tried to pull her hand out of his, suddenly self-conscious, but he held fast, her action triggering an amused quirk of his eyebrow. "Though we have only been distant correspondents to one another, I have come to care for you deeply." He swallowed. "And I want to see if we can be something more."

Warm sensations skittered across Emily's skin, and for a brief moment, she forgot about the pressing danger. She allowed her lips to spread into the slightest smile, which, after having sustained a knotted expression for several hours now, brought blessed relief. "I want that too."

Finn's returned smile creased the skin beside his mouth, but it didn't quite reach his eyes—for deep within those sapphire pools lurked a dark shadow. He had experienced an incredible conversion, snapping the last strand of Cornelius's influence, but that didn't take away the tempting pull of a life of darkness. Faith was still a novelty to him—new and unknown. It was so easy for new converts to backslide and become tempted by the same sins that had trapped them before, especially when not surrounded by people who could hold them accountable.

Gently, Emily lifted her free hand and pressed it flat to his chest. His muscles seized, and his breath hitched. Heartbeats pattered wildly against her palm. "You have been alone since you left us, and loneliness can pull us into the darkest of places. How are you *really*?"

Her hand rose as he inhaled deeply and held it. Brows twitching together, he shook his head. "Why are you askin' about me? You should be focusin' on yourself."

This smile came easy. "Because I care about you too." She removed her hand and brushed her fingertips against the scratchy stubble of his jaw. "But more than that, I care about your soul."

He leaned forward a touch, then must have remembered himself, for he straightened and tilted away from her contact. "Things have not been as easy as I'd been anticipatin', but I am well."

"Are you sure?" She maintained intent eye contact, not letting him look away. "Remember, you said you would never lie to me."

The corner of his mouth twitched upward. "I did say that, didn't I? Well, evasion isn't lyin', now, is it?" Just as Emily frowned and opened her mouth, he squeezed her hand and said, "I'm only coddin' you. I appreciate your concern, Emily. I really do. Me soul is managin'. It can hang on a while longer until we get your little man back." He released her hand and scooted away, signaling their conversation over.

Emily bristled, wanting to press for more, but she supposed he wasn't under any obligation to share his deepest sentiments with her. They weren't married—weren't even courting. So she swallowed her remonstrations and backed off.

Still, she resolved to bring it up again—soon. For she couldn't escape the feeling that something was moving within him. Something dark.

Ever since the doctor confirmed my delicate condition, I constantly battled the fierce urge to cup my abdomen in my hands, but as I paced near the dining table in front of Baze, I managed to fold my arms tight to my chest to keep them from incriminating me.

Baze leaned backward against the hutch. "What did you wish to speak to me about?"

I tilted my head side to side. "Nothing. I merely wanted to give them a moment alone."

He grimaced. "Do you really think we should encourage that?"

"Encourage what?"

"*That.*" He gestured in the direction of the sitting room. "Finn and Emily. Surely there are more eligible men out there who would be a better match for her."

Coming to a halt, I narrowed my eyes at him. "What's wrong with Finn?"

He paused, furrowing his brow. "You know exactly what's wrong."

"Enlighten me."

With a scowl, he lowered his voice. "He was involved in the plot that killed Emily's husband."

"Only because Cornelius was controlling him." I relaxed my expression in understanding. "Is that why you're acting so hostile toward him? You blame him for Bennett's death?"

"No. I'm acting hostile because I don't trust him."

"But why?" I began pacing again. "Finn broke free of Cornelius and surrendered his life to the Almighty. He's a different man now."

Baze sighed. "He surrendered, yes, but do you think it's that easy? Marx wreaked havoc in Finn's mind for *years*. I don't think you can experience something like that and not suffer lasting effects. Just look at you. You had nightmares for a solid year until you told Marx to get out, and even then, you've constantly felt O'Sullivan's pull." He pushed off the hutch and stepped in my path. "You've always been attuned to the darkness around you. Tell me the truth. Do you sense darkness in Finn?"

I snapped my mouth shut. Recollections of our reunion with Finn filtered through my mind and made me shiver. His once clear eyes had clouded, hinting at the turmoil within. Despite tasting freedom in that prison cell, he had allowed the alluring whispers of temptation to drag his mind back into the trenches . . . he and I both.

"I'll take that as a yes," Baze whispered harshly, his warm breath tickling my face.

Mouth suddenly dry, I swallowed hard and met Baze's dark eyes.

"You were patient with me when I struggled to battle the demons left behind after Cornelius died. The least we can do is be equally as patient with Finn. He's like a child learning to walk, and to make matters worse, he hasn't had anyone to show him how. He's been all alone. I was fortunate enough to have you."

Baze released a long exhale through his nose. "If he has stumbled, then we shall help him get back up, but until that happens, I don't want Emily to entertain his advances."

"Emily is a grown woman." I couldn't keep the growl from my voice. "She is not yours to command."

"But she is mine to protect," he said in a rush. His face reddened as he cast his eyes to the floor and fiddled with his wedding band. "I promised Bennett I would protect her if anything happened to him. Back when he was first promoted to sergeant." His tone fell to a whisper. "In return, he promised to protect you . . . should anything happen to me."

Stunned, I placed a gentle hand on his arm. "I didn't know that."

"Yes, well, we didn't think we'd ever have to make good on our promises." Clearing his throat, he stepped away from me. "We're wasting time."

When Baze and I returned to the sitting room, we discovered Finn and Emily perched upon the sofa—closer together than mere acquaintances—and when they saw us enter, they shifted apart. Baze kept Finn locked under a relentless stare that eventually prompted him to rise and cross to the fireplace.

Baze relaxed slightly, then escorted me to the corner chair. He squatted beside me as I sat and firmly grasped my hand. "She's going to find out where they took him." Though he spoke to the room, he focused only on me. His brows rose a touch. "Are you ready?"

I squeezed his hand in confirmation. The weight of everyone's anticipation compressed me as I closed my eyes and centered my mind. Breathe in. Breathe out. Over and over as I tried to concentrate and home in on my target. This wasn't a straightforward task, for it wasn't

Shay I sought but someone whose mind he had touched. There could be dozens. Hundreds even.

*Careful. The deeper you go, the harder it shall be for you to withstand the lure of darkness.*

Dismissing the warnings hissing in my ear, I loosened my muscles and took one more deep breath—then fired my subconscious out of me like a bullet.

Light sparked and scenes flashed. My stomach lurched as tainted minds wandering Dublin jerked me toward them. No, not Dublin. The target hid somewhere in the countryside. That was where I would find Basil Allan.

I managed to break from the pull and forced my thoughts away from the city, soon discovering a faint thread of shadows winding south. I followed it, careening through the hills. Blurred ground rushed up to meet me.

My eyes ripped open. Ancient stone buildings dotted the lush green hills sprawling before me. A little rectangular church stood a mere stone's throw away, with a steep pointed roof, a single arched entrance, a belfry near the back, and an even smaller structure attached near the door. Behind the church, the points of cross-shaped monuments poked up over a stone wall, and a huge round tower loomed above the gravestones.

I turned to look over my shoulder and focused on a man behind me. He wore a scowl and ragged waistcoat, his red hair sticking out beneath a flat cap, but it was the boy clinging to his leg that stole my attention.

Basil Allan.

*Whoosh!*

Something thrust my mind back into the atmosphere, but this time, it took great effort to cling to the physical world and drag myself back to the current place and time. The sitting room appeared around me, dropping me heavily into my body and collapsing me into the chair.

"He's all right," I gasped as I elbowed myself upright, Baze's hand still gripping mine. "Liam and Sergeant Fitzgerald have him, but he's all right."

Emily released her breath in a deep exhale.

"Where were they?" Finn asked, kneeling next to me. As I described what I'd seen, his gaze darted about in thought. Finally, he nodded. "That's soundin' like the monastery at Glendalough. It's close. An hour's drive, maybe."

Nausea turned my stomach. Discovering the location was only the first step. What would happen when we arrived at the destination? Would someone be there to ambush us? Or were they planning to stay just long enough for me to track them down before fleeing to the next place, stringing us all across Ireland to keep us distracted as Shay had wanted?

*Knock-knock-knock.*

Three sharp raps on the front door broke my reverie and echoed through the room. Finn, Emily, and I froze, but Baze sprang to action, creeping to the window and peering outside. He squinted, then did a double take and murmured, "What the . . . ?" He dashed to the foyer as fast as his leg would allow. A squeak of the front door preceded a long bout of silence.

I twisted in the chair and was about to bolt up to investigate, but a woman's sharp, amused voice stopped me in my tracks.

"Are you going to gawk at me all day, brown eyes, or are you going to let me in?"

Chapter Twenty



Katherine Quinn was alive.

Even as I sat across from her in the sitting room and took in her pale face, emerald eyes, and fiery red hair, I couldn't believe my own eyes. She had died. Shay had all but confirmed it, and the newspapers had reported it. There had even been a picture!

"How?" was all I managed to say, the single word laced with fury.

Leaning against the armrest of my chair, Baze slid a reassuring hand onto my shoulder. Emily had curled up on the opposite end of the sofa, and Finn stood with his back to us, arms folded as he stared out the window.

Katherine smiled that cheeky smile of hers, then allowed it to wilt. "I am sorry for deceiving you, angel, but it was imperative that Sully didn't know I was alive. Not that I don't trust you, but it was safer this way."

"How?" I repeated, tears stinging my eyes. "You were poisoned. The newspapers said so."

"The newspapers were correct." One shoulder came up as she sighed. "I tried to flee Bath, but Sully found me before I could. I was cornered and had no choice but to take the poison he offered me." Pain rippled across her face. "It was effective, I'll give him that. Took mere minutes for it to start killing me from the inside out." A little spark twinkled in her eyes. "That was where the fun began. Well, I say 'fun,' but it was harrowing to say the least."

Anger boiled in my belly as I said, "Go on."

"There was a doctor on the train. I saw him when I first boarded." She reached into her reticule and pulled out her signature deck of cards.

She cut them in half, then shuffled them over her lap. "Sully left just as the poison took hold—a critical mistake. I had enough of my wits about me to call for help. As I hoped, the good doctor responded immediately and administered ipecac, and I vomited that vile poison all across the train floor." Her shuffling grew quicker. "I couldn't walk in my weakened state, so the doctor and a posse of men helped to carry me from the train and transport me to hospital."

Silence interrupted only by the *whissh* of her cards filled the room as we processed the information. I shook my head. "But the newspapers took photos. They reported your death."

"Do you not remember, angel?" She tilted her head. "I was a journalist in a past life, and my web of connections is wide and tangled. I staged the photo, drafted the article reporting my death, and used my contacts in Bath to publish the story for all to see, Sully especially."

"Why didn't you tell me?" I pressed, attempting to scoot to the edge of my chair, but Baze's gentle hand restrained me. "I lived for two years believing you were dead. I grieved for you. Many people did. Do you not care about us?"

"It had nothing to do with how much I care for you." Her eyes flicked to Finn, then back to me. "I couldn't tell you because of how closely you and Sully are linked. I knew it was only a matter of time before you tried to see into his mind, and I couldn't have you giving away my greatest secret—because if he knew I yet lived, he surely would have come for me. His ignorance in this matter is what will help us prevail." Her expression perked as she stacked the deck and held it flat between her palms. "We now have him exactly where we want him."

"How so?" Baze spoke up.

"Because, brown eyes"—she tipped her head in my direction—"Sully believes that Adelynn is the only one left who can disrupt his plans. But there are two of us now, and we can use that to strike back at him."

"You've thought of a plan, then," Finn said. A statement, not a question. He finally turned from the window, his expression rigid.

"You know me so well, little dove." Katherine stashed her deck and vaulted to her feet. She planted herself in the center of the room and faced us, hands draped on her hips. "Here's what we're going to do." She nodded toward Emily. "Your son is the priority, and we need to get him back as quickly as possible. You, Finn, and I are going to go after him, for I can track down his kidnappers as well as Adelynn could." She aimed her index fingers at Baze and I. "You two are going to stay here in Dublin. Keep after Shay. Discover the details of the rebellion."

Her eyes locked on me. "Now, angel, you need to take care to only target those whom Sully has taken under his control, not Sully himself. If he learns that you stayed here and didn't pursue Basil Allan, I fear the repercussions." Her eyes glazed slightly. "Once we have retrieved the child, we will rejoin you in Dublin. At that point, provided you've learned when the rebellion is to occur, we shall send Finn, Emily, and Basil Allan to a safe location while we hunt Sully and stop him once and for all.

"So . . ." Katherine returned her hands to her hips and surveyed us. "Any questions?"

No one moved. No one spoke. The ticking of the mantle clock declared the passing of precious seconds.

Finally, Baze swiped his palms on his thighs and stood. "I have no objections." His brows raised in question as he looked at each of us in turn, then stopped on me. "What do you think?"

I bit my lip and looked into the cold fireplace. My head buzzed. I'd just begun to absorb the news that she was alive, and now she was proposing we split ways once again—and for something that could endanger our lives. But if we didn't take different paths, if we all went after Basil Allan, then Shay would succeed, because with Basil Allan as bait, he could string us along indefinitely until he had bought enough time to carry out his objective.

Yet, Shay had warned of dire consequences should we desert Basil Allan and continue to pursue him, so if I made a mistake—if I alerted him to my presence in Dublin—what might he do to the child? What might he do to Baze? And to me and my . . .

Before I realized it, I had tucked a hand against my stomach. Sucking in a breath, I quickly folded both arms against my chest, risking a glance at Baze. Thankfully, he appeared oblivious.

I focused on Katherine, bolstered by the embers of determination burning in her eyes, and finally nodded. "I think your proposal is the best course of action."

"It's settled then." Katherine clapped her hands resolutely, then sighed. "I won't mislead you. This will be dangerous for both parties. Sully has grown more hostile in the years since we last crossed paths. I once believed he could be reasoned with—if done properly—but all reason has left him. He's like a rabid animal, one that must be destroyed." Her eyes clouded.

Emotion squeezed my throat as the scene of Cornelius's death flashed bright and vivid in my memory. "Are you planning to kill him?" I asked softly.

Something like pain skittered across Katherine's face, but she drew her brows taut and managed to maintain a façade of confidence. "That remains to be seen." She cleared her throat. "We shouldn't tarry much longer, but before we depart, I want a word." She crossed to the door and beckoned me with her index finger. "Come, angel."

A ball of dread wound in my stomach, as though I were a schoolgirl who'd been called out by a teacher for misbehaving. Keeping my arms folded tight, I slid from the chair and trailed her into the dining room across the hall. Before she had a chance to engage, I blurted, "What?"

She faced me, stroking her chin and supporting her elbow with her other arm. Her eyes roamed across my body and then my face. "I can sense him all over you," she said, voice low and solemn. "I warned you what could happen if you willingly opened your mind to a power like Sully's."

I lifted my chin. "You've done it, and you're all right."

"I've had years of practice." She narrowed her eyes. "Be wary, angel. I can feel the opposing forces swirling within you, and if you go out there and continue inviting in this darkness without fortifying your defenses, you could be overwhelmed."

Her words stoked a fire of opposition in me. "I'll be fine. I know what I'm doing."

Chewing her fingernail, Katherine closed the distance between us. Then she placed a motherly hand over my cheek. "I'm not questioning your ability but rather your motive. Remember, I've warned you of that pride before." Her voice held a mix of gentleness and sadness. "If you charge headfirst into the fray without a spirit of humility, believing only in your own power, then you will surely be overwhelmed. The allure of darkness is easy and sweet, and there is only One who can help us resist and ultimately banish it."

I stiffened, my skin burning beneath her palm. My defenses came up, trying to deflect her words, until I realized that I was clinging to the pride she had just called out. Melting under her compassionate touch, I released the tension in my muscles and drooped my shoulders. "Thank you for your wisdom, Katherine. I shall take your words to heart."

"I have no doubt that you will." Fine lines deepened beside her lips as she smiled. She removed her hand and pinched my chin lightly. "It is good to see you, angel. I have missed our candid talks." Her smile fell a tick. "I am truly sorry for allowing you to believe I was dead."

As much as I wanted to let my resentment fester—I had mourned for her, after all—her explanation and her sincere apology soothed my incensed emotions and allowed me to see reason. I tossed my arms about her shoulders and locked her in an embrace. "I understand why you did it, and I forgive you."

Her arms came around me in return and squeezed. We clung to one another for a good while until she finally loosened her hold and held me at arm's length. Tears glittered in her eyes, hopeful and resolute. "Let's go stop Sully."

## Chapter Twenty-One

Finn's chest clenched as he stepped into the bright morning sun and headed toward the car, about to lead the two women he loved most in this world down a path sure to be fraught with danger and the unknown.

He opened the front passenger-side door and offered Emily his hand.

Taking it, she ducked her head and slid into the seat. Her deep blue gaze found his, and she squeezed his fingers before letting go.

Then he crossed to the driver's side and stopped before Katherine. She arched her brows, then eyed the automobile. "You sure you know how to drive this contraption? I don't remember ever teaching you how."

"I've had to learn many things you never taught me." He meant the statement to be lighthearted, but bitterness coated his tone.

"Ah, well. You were always resourceful. I am pleased to see you remain so." She nodded curtly and opened the back door.

"Wait, I . . ." A lump in his throat choked out his words, and his ears burned.

Why was he so emotional about this? It had been almost fifteen years since he had seen her, since she had sat back and done nothing as Ciaran turned Finn into his personal puppet. Finn had trudged through every stage of grief when he realized she was never going to come looking for him, that she had abandoned him, and news of her death had only deepened the feelings of apathy.

Yet, even after all that time and the numbing of his emotions, it had only taken one word from her lyrical, motherly voice to plunge deep into his heart and yank everything back to the surface with ease.

Katherine stared up into his eyes—there had been a time when she towered over him—and then gently touched his face with both hands. Her freckled skin reddened as her caresses grew firmer. Her hands trailed to his shoulders. "Oh, little dove. I'm sorry." Her eyelashes fluttered as tears trickled down her cheeks. She slipped her arms around him and drew his body snugly to hers, burying her nose in his chest. "I'm so, so sorry."

***Don't let her back in. She betrayed you. She didn't stop Ciaran. And she didn't stop Shay. She's the reason your mind is shrouded in darkness.***

Finn stiffened, hands trembling at his sides. She had indeed betrayed him, not by anything she had done—but for what she *hadn't* done. She had been an impassive bystander as Shay had poked holes in Finn's mind and allowed Ciaran to take hold. How could he trust that she wouldn't abandon him again when the situation suited her?

But as her quiet cries echoed through his chest, his heart softened slightly, and his body moved despite his mind's protests. He returned her embrace, wrapping her so tight in his arms that a tiny gasp puffed from her lips. Despite everything she had—or hadn't—done, he couldn't seem to suppress the young boy inside of him who still yearned for a mother.

Sporadic divots in the narrow dirt road jostled Emily as they rumbled through the countryside. Sounds of crunching gravel beneath the tires and soft exchanges between Finn and Katherine grew muffled by the ringing in her ears. She stared out the windscreen in a daze, Bennett's wedding band clutched in her fist against her chest as though she could draw strength from it.

If only he were here. He would have taken charge and known exactly what to do. He likely wouldn't have let them take Basil Allan in the first place. Not like she had. Not like Baze—

She shook her head and blocked her thoughts from following that toxic path. This wasn't Baze's fault. Those men had arrived in the dead of night and ambushed him. It was a miracle he hadn't been killed while trying to stop the abduction.

With her lips numb and her mind hazy, she allowed her soul to cry out. *God Almighty, purge my heart of resentment and guilt, and do the same for Baze. He did all that he could, just as I did. Neither of us could have known what the enemy had in store. We need not carry this burden.*

Her eyes slid shut as the prayer soothed her aching heart. *Also, quell the turmoil within Finn. Quiet the voices of temptation. His faith is so new and so fragile, and the evil one does all he can to capitalize on our weaknesses. Don't let that happen. Don't let him be overcome. Lead him away from darkness—for good.*

Amusement tipped Emily's lips. *Be with Adelynn as well. She can be stubborn. She prefers to do things her way, and I am sure you and she often go head-to-head, but she has drifted, and I fear she is walking down a dangerous path, the very path Finn once walked. Keep her from stumbling. Protect her . . . and the new life she carries.*

Tears slipped through her lashes. *And lead us to my son. Take him in your arms and keep him safe from harm. We live in such a broken world, but I know your love for us abounds beyond measure, for our precious children especially. Just . . . let your will be done.*

Emily opened her eyes and her hand to gaze at Bennett's ring. Simple and unadorned, it was all that they could afford at the time. Its circular border had left an indent in her palm, almost as though it were trying to remind her that Bennett's love was forever impressed upon her heart—and that the Father's love ran even deeper.

"We're here," Finn's quiet, monotone voice pulled Emily from her meditation. He cut the engine. Before them stood a grove of oak trees, through which tilted grave markers, stone fences, and a towering spire were visible. Flattening his mouth, Finn lifted Baze's pistol resting between him and Emily and ran his fingers along all of its parts, checking the safety, counting the bullets.

*"Do not fire unless you are willing to accept the consequences of*

*the bullet's path,"* Baze had instructed when he bequeathed Finn the extra weapon and provided brief instruction on its operation. *"Use it only for defense and only if you are certain the shot is clear."*

Emily's throat squeezed as she curled her fingers around Bennett's ring again and asked quietly, "Have you ever shot a gun before?"

"No." Finn stroked the hammer. "But I will if I have to."

Amber light from the sinking sun filtered through the trees as they exited the car and picked their way along a crude path leading to the round tower. They emerged from the grove and stepped into the ancient cemetery, its many headstones worn, toppled, and encrusted with lichen. The tower kept watch on the right side of the plot, with what looked like a dilapidated cathedral farther ahead to the left and a smaller church at the base of a gentle slope.

"Let's check the cathedral first." Finn stepped around the gravestones, followed first by Emily and then Katherine.

Nature's ambience surrounded them—birds chittering, leaves rustling, and gravel crunching. The fresh scent of wood and wind invigorated Emily's steps. They passed wordlessly through the arched entrance and into the center of the long rectangular space. The roof had long been destroyed, leaving the space open to the elements.

Despite the pressing danger, a small sense of calm settled within Emily. This was a holy place, a place where people had once worshipped the Almighty. His fingerprints were all over it, both in the structure itself and the surrounding scenery. The kidnappers had likely chosen this location because of its seclusion, but it only served to reassure her. She would get her son back. Of that, she was certain.

The *how* was another matter.

Contemplative, she folded her arms and wandered away from the group, through the cathedral's side door, and onto the dirt path leading down to the more intact, albeit smaller, church. The steep roof loomed over her, and as she crossed the threshold, its shadows swallowed her. She shivered. The room stood empty and plain, but up above, a complicated network of beams held the ceiling aloft. Such height must boast incredible acoustics. Back in its heyday, when congregants would gather to hear a message, she imagined that the singing went unrivaled.

"Hello?" she asked quietly. The space took her voice and amplified it, pulling the word to the very tip-top of the roof. "Hello?" she said louder, bolder. Once again, her voice stretched and grew and lingered on. After a long while with no response, she sighed and lowered her arms to her sides. It appeared the kidnappers had moved on from the site.

Worry pinched her insides, worry for Basil Allan and for what he might be suffering. Did he know she was coming for him? Or was he in despair, believing she had abandoned him?

As she stared up into the lofted beams, she felt that overwhelming peace again. Unable to keep it contained, she opened her mouth and allowed a low, melancholy melody to pour forth.

"Amazing grace, how sweet the sound. That saved a wretch like me. I once was lost but now am found. Was blind, but now I see."

Emily wasn't a singer by any stretch, but she couldn't ignore the prodding to lift her voice high, to let it rise and echo in this old church and extend higher into the heavens. Her eyes slid shut as the music transported her to a realm of worship and petition.

"Through many dangers, toils, and snares, I have already come. 'Tis grace has brought me safe thus far, and grace will lead me home."

When the last verse slipped from her lips and the final word faded into the air, she stilled to absorb the serenity—to bury it deep within her heart.

"I didn't realize you could sing." Finn's voice whispered through the space.

Emily whirled.

Arms folded, he leaned against the open entrance, his eyes intent upon her.

"I-I'm sorry. I didn't realize you were watching." Heat rushed to her face. "I realize it's silly, singing like this, considering the circumstances."

"Don't be apologizin'." Finn pushed off the jamb and sauntered toward her, halting a few paces away. His slow gaze roamed her face. "That was beautiful." He leaned forward slightly, then steeled his muscles to keep himself steady. His breath grew shallow. "You're beautiful."

Blood rushed in Emily's ears, and the tight space suddenly warmed.

"S-sorry." He scuffed his foot on the ground and turned. "There are more urgent matters we need to focus on."

"No, it's all right." She bounded after him, slotted her hand into his, and tugged him back to her—mere inches now separating them. "I am flattered, Finn. Thank you. You needn't ever apologize for speaking your true feelings." Before she could stop herself, she flattened her hand over his chest and felt the driving beat of his heart against her palm.

The tips of his ears reddened as he covered her hand with his and pressed it tighter to him. "How do you have the strength to move forward, Emily?" he asked softly, almost sadly. "In a time when you should be at your wit's end, I have never seen you calmer. How do you have such confidence . . . such faith?"

Nose prickling with tears, she chewed her bottom lip, then managed to say, "I have walked through incredible hardships, but God has never forsaken me. Whenever I have fallen and believed I would never rise again, He has lifted me up. So, if He has carried me before, who am I to doubt that He would continue to carry me through whatever I face?"

He sighed. "You're a much stronger person than I."

"Rubbish."

"No, it's true. Like your song was sayin', I'm a wretch."

"Without the Almighty, we are all wretches. That's the point. It is what makes His mercy and grace so sweet."

Turmoil drew out the wrinkles in his forehead and deepened the lines near his mouth. "Mercy is wasted on me. I broke free from Ciaran years ago, but I've made a mockery of it. Me mind is still in a fog. I've been tryin' to do the right thing, but I feel like my conscience has been ripped in half. If grace delivered me, why do I still struggle so?"

Pity squeezed her chest. "Because the enemy knows our desires and uses them to tempt us away from the light." She wet her dry lips with a swipe of her tongue, and her action drew Finn's gaze. Beneath her palm, his heart increased from a canter to a gallop.

Steeling herself, she waited with bated breath. She trusted Finn, trusted that he wouldn't do anything untoward, but if his mind was truly enshrouded in chaos, if Cornelius's influence yet lingered in his subconscious, what might it tempt him to do—and would he surrender to its appeal?

"Every person saved by grace will come under the attack of the enemy and will face temptations," she said under her breath. "But God doesn't let us struggle on our own. He gives us the Spirit so that we might have the power to conquer our demons. *You* have that same Spirit, Finn. If you wish to banish the darkness, you need only call upon it."

Eyes hazy and body frozen, Finn remained intent on her mouth. The beats of his heart tapped furiously like the wild beating of a drum. His hand cemented around hers, cutting off the circulation in her fingers—and for the first time, her trust in him flickered.

"*Ahem.*" Katherine's exaggerated interjection shot from the entrance, and the amplification made it sound as though she stood directly beside them. "I realize you two are having a moment, but we've nearly lost the light."

Emily yanked her hands free and stepped back several paces. Painful prickles swept to the tips of her fingers as feeling returned.

Finn lingered, stiff and silent.

"There's clearly no one here, so we ought to decide what to do next." The dying light spilled around Katherine from behind and shadowed her face, but her hands-on-hips posture indicated her restlessness.

"Sorry to have kept you waiting." Emily sidestepped Finn and made to join Katherine, but a tiny flash of white in the wall just to

Katherine's right captured her attention. Curiosity piqued, she approached and plucked it from between two loose stones—a crude scrap of paper. She pried it open and read the words aloud. "'You shall have to be quicker than that. We are already well on our way to the next site. You'd best hurry. The boy misses his mother.'"

Ice glazed Emily's veins as Finn snatched it from her hands and read it to himself. He growled and crumpled it in his fist. "So that's their play then. They're plannin' to lure us from one place to the next to give Shay time to act—just as we thought they might." He jutted his chin at Katherine. "Can you see where they've gone now?"

"Yes. Give me a moment." Dragging a hand along the rough wall, Katherine swung inside the building and leaned her back against it. She planted her feet hip-width apart, bowed her head, and closed her eyes. To an outside observer, she appeared only to be praying, but Emily knew a war waged inside her mind—something Emily would never fully comprehend even after all these years of hearing Adelynn explain the sensation.

Muscles across Katherine's face twitched every so often, and as seconds dragged by, her thin brows drew ever closer together. The spasms traveled to her fingers, then her arms. She bared her teeth and clacked them together as she trembled. A moan emitted from her throat, then a breath sucked through her lips, and her eyes flew wide. Her body released a final shudder before buckling her knees.

Finn lunged and caught her fall. As he helped her straighten, he asked, "What did you see?"

She pushed away from him and swept her hands down her bodice. "The Rock of Cashel."

"That's only about two hours from here." He marched toward the door. "Let's—"

"Wait." She thrust out an arm to bar him from exiting. "We shouldn't go out there after nightfall. We're already at a disadvantage. We don't need darkness adding another."

"Then what do you think we should do?"

"Find a place to lay low. Get our rest. Then we can set out in the morning." She glanced at Emily, eyes empathetic. "They already have a head start, so I don't think we would catch them even if we rushed straight for Cashel. We shall have to outsmart them another way. Besides"—she shrugged—"even kidnappers have to sleep."

Finn regarded Katherine, then turned to Emily. "It's your decision. He's your son. If you want us to keep goin', then we will."

As much as Emily wanted Basil Allan delivered safely into her arms as soon as possible, she knew Katherine spoke the truth. Furthermore, she trusted what Finn had promised—that they wouldn't harm her son.

"I think we should find a place to stay as Katherine suggested," she said resolutely.

"Very well." Finn nodded, though his set jaw and flared nostrils suggested he disagreed with her conclusion. "The village of Laragh isn't too far. We should be able to find safe lodgin' there."

Stars sparkled in the dark blue sky as they made their way into the local Laragh pub. Finn negotiated for a room upstairs while Katherine and Emily waited near the door. Studying her nails, Katherine appeared unbothered by the rowdy patrons and the ripe smell of sweat and spirits, but Emily grimaced and hunkered close to the older woman's side.

Finn's sharp whistle from across the room and a wave of his hand signaled that he had struck a deal. Emily couldn't contain her relief as she bounded to his side and strode on his heels while he led them up a rickety staircase and into one of the many rooms lining the dank hall at the top. The accommodations were mediocre at best—with a single bed pushed against the wall in the center, a cobwebbed rocking chair in the far corner, the smallest of fireplaces across from the bed, and a lonely side table.

Katherine tsked and planted her hands on her hips. "One bed. Really?"

"I'll sleep on the floor," Finn said wearily. "It's safer if we stay together."

She tilted her head side to side. "Fair point."

"Try to get settled now. I'll fetch our trunk and see if I can have some food brought up." Just as soon as he had said the words, he slipped through the door and left them alone.

Emily shivered. Now that she was becoming more acquainted with Adelynn's legendary Katherine Quinn, she understood how Adelynn had met her match. It wasn't that Emily feared Katherine, but the woman had a commanding presence—stronger even than Adelynn's— and Emily decided it best to embrace an agreeable attitude.

Unsure what to do in the silence, Emily crossed to the bed and fluffed one of the pillows, but a sudden disconcerting thought stilled her fingers—she was an unmarried woman about to share a room with an unmarried man. By default, Katherine would serve the role of chaperone to prevent any wayward actions from occurring, but what should Emily do about her attire? She had brought her nightgown, but she deemed the garb far too risqué for wear in the presence of a man who wasn't her husband. Should she sleep in her daytime ensemble— corset and shoes included—simply for decency's sake?

"All right there, poppet?" Katherine asked, voice light. She drifted to the opposite side of the bed, unfastening her earrings. "You've gone all red."

Emily swallowed and tugged at her dress's tight neckline. "I've only just noticed that there's not much by way of privacy in here."

Katherine narrowed her eyes a touch, then grinned and plunked her earrings on the side table. "Finn and I are quite used to close quarters. When we were traveling Ireland with Sully and Ciaran, we often stayed in places much smaller and more intimate than this one. I did not have the privilege of privacy, so out of pure necessity, I chose to educate both of the boys about the customs of women." A soft snort rattled in her nose. "Besides, he was once a *cailín*-crazed teenager. Trust me—he has seen a woman's unmentionables before."

Fire building in Emily's chest nearly made her tear out of her dress right then and there if only to ease the heat. Finn had always struck her as being more naïve when it came to women, but the notion that he was, in fact, well informed and even proficient in understanding her most private behaviors magnified her embarrassment.

Katherine laughed. "If it would make you feel better, we can insist that he keep his back turned to us at all times."

"It would certainly help," Emily said under her breath.

Katherine yanked back the top cover—a plain, threadbare quilt. "While we're on the topic, I would like to know what your intentions are with Finn." She puffed a strand of hair out of her eyes and straightened. "I haven't seen him this infatuated since he was nineteen and engaged to that bonnie lass Maeve." Solemnity faded the amusement from her features. "But the way he looks at you is different than how he looked at her. Far different. When Maeve disappeared, he was utterly crestfallen. Call it a mother's love, but I wish to protect him from experiencing such heartache again." Her hands came back to rest on her hips. "So tell me. What are your intentions?"

Emily closed her eyes. How could she answer with certainty when she didn't even know herself? "I understand what it's like to lose the person who means everything to you," she found herself saying. "After my husband died, it felt as though my whole world had burned down around me, and I thought I would never love again." She smiled sadly. "When Finn and I started exchanging letters, I did so with frail hope. Over time, we found solace in one another. We had both lost people we loved. We had both lived through Cornelius's reign of terror. Finn began to coax my heart out of the shadows, and he showed me it was possible to love again."

Drawing in a sharp breath, Emily clasped her quivering hands to her chest, the clouds breaking and revealing the truth she had known for some time. Her voice fell to a whisper. "I love him."

Katherine shook her head and sighed. "I thought as much." Concern darkened her eyes. "I realize I cannot command your actions, so I would only ask that you ensure your feelings are true before you pursue him. I know your heart's been broken into a thousand shards, but so has his. Handle it carefully."

## Chapter Twenty-Two

HAZY SCENES SWIRLED AROUND ME. AS though embodying a bird, I soared through the streets of Dublin, homing in on an oblivious individual only to jerk away and race to the next one. We didn't have any time to waste. We didn't know how long it would take Shay to realize Baze and I had stayed, and we also didn't know when the rebellion was set to begin. It could be tomorrow for all we knew.

*Rebellion . . .*

The word percolated. Echoed. Almost as though it originated nearby. I refocused my mind and pushed toward it like a dog following a waning scent.

*"Adelynn."*

The new whisper jarred my concentration and nearly made me lose the vision. I mouthed "No" and continued extending my mind.

*Rebellion . . .*

Now it sounded closer, more distinct. I swept into Temple Bar and toward a row of pubs. Loud music droned from behind the doors and blackened windows.

*"Adelynn, this is too much for you."* As though part of a dream, light hands on my arms threatened to tug me back to the present, but I raged against them. The answer was right here. I simply had to grasp it.

In one last-ditch attempt, I catapulted my consciousness toward the nearest pub.

My eyes flew open, and my lips finished saying, ". . . for the rebellion."

I sat hunched at a two-person table with smoldering cigarettes and half-empty mugs of beer littering the surface. A squat, scruffy man opposite me leaned across the table with his arms folded, likely to hear the words of my host over the shrieking music of the uilleann pipe and penny whistle.

"'s almost poetic, really. Launchin' an uprisin' the day after the Good Lord's own risin'," he said without emotion. Shadows of Shay's control sagged his eyes. "How many d'you think'll die?"

"Hard to tell," I said. "The Volunteers will have the element of surprise, but once the British Army and the police get involved, it'll be a bloodbath."

"Doesn't matter I suppose. So long as O'Sullivan can get in and out of Dublin Castle, it will have been a success."

"You know, last I saw him, he mentioned Dublin's not the only target of the rebellion. He said there'd be forces throughout—"

A sharp pain in my hand—my real hand—jolted me.

Just like that, my mind snapped back to the present, back to the room, back to where I had settled cross-legged on the sofa. I gasped. My body shuddered and wilted against Baze.

"Easy," he murmured, supporting me until I'd regained enough awareness to sit up on my own again—though he kept one hand firmly on my shoulder. "Are you all right?"

Eyes still flickering in dizziness, I nodded and swallowed a dry, scratchy lump. Sweat dampened my skin, and my muscles quivered in exhaustion.

With his free hand, he grasped mine and massaged my palm. "You shouldn't push yourself like that. I don't think your body is taking the exertion well. I can only imagine what it's doing to your mind."

"I've no other choice."

Guilt fluttered in my stomach. I could handle the strain, but what would it do to our child?

Dull pain laced up the muscles in my arm from where his thumb dug into my palm. "Did you at least learn anything new?"

Wanting so badly to succumb to the weariness in my bones, I merely nodded.

Surprise slackened his features. "And?"

"The day after Easter Sunday. That's when the rebellion will occur."

His eyes darted about in thought. "That's only a few days away," he said under his breath.

"That's not all." Dread clenched my chest. "I merely heard snippets of a conversation, but it sounds as though Dublin isn't the only target. The rebels are likely spread throughout Ireland." My breathing quickened. "What if the others stumble into a battle? What if they—"

Cursed tears charged to my eyes. Of all the symptoms and sensations that emerged from being in the family way, the random bouts of crying were the worst by far.

"Shh, it's all right." He released my shoulder and swiped the tears from my cheeks. "We're going to get through this."

***He's wrong. The enemy is stronger. You stand no chance of winning.***

"What if this time is different?" I whimpered. "What if we're not strong enough?"

"Where's this coming from?" His tone softened. "This isn't the Al I know. The Al I know is headstrong and confident. She would never surrender without a fight."

"The Al you know has changed." Bitterness crackled in my voice.

His throat tightened in a slow swallow. "Because of O'Sullivan?"

Shame hung my head. I couldn't look at him.

Baze nipped a finger under my chin to raise my face toward his, but I averted my eyes. "Look at me." When I didn't comply, he wiggled my chin gently. "Adelynn, look at me."

Reluctantly, I slid my gaze to his and lost myself in the calm assurance pouring from his russet eyes.

"O'Sullivan's touch on your mind has sent you down a lonely path, but you *are* strong enough to overcome him. You have to fight, and if you stumble, I'll be there to lend you my strength." Firm but tender, his voice soothed my tension. "We're going to stop O'Sullivan. We're going to get Basil Allan back. And then we're all going to go home."

"How do you know that?" I flexed my neck to turn away, but his hand held me in place.

"Because we've been through this before, and God hasn't forsaken us yet."

***Oh, but He will. You just watch.***

The inner voice soured my insides, but I pushed past it and clung to Baze's hope-filled declaration. A flame of determination sparked to life—not raging, but it was there.

I relaxed my head into his supportive hand and nodded. "I will fight."

"That's the Al I know." A relieved smile brightened Baze's features. He kissed my forehead and pulled me into a crushing embrace. I melted into him and nestled my face into his chest, trying to absorb every ounce of strength that I could.

We remained wrapped together until my stomach gave an insistent growl.

Chuckling, Baze pulled back. "Sounds like we should scrounge together some food." He raised his eyebrows, expectant.

I pointed at myself and frowned. "Why are you looking at me like that? I don't know how to cook."

He sighed and massaged the back of his neck. "Well, I suppose the two of us should be able to figure something out."

Nothing had ever made me feel more inadequate as a wife than entering the vacant kitchen and not having the foggiest idea of where to start. Fortunately, we discovered a basket of day-old scones upon the table, but we couldn't survive on pastries alone.

I located a pile of strawberries as Baze stuck his head in the refrigerator cabinet. He extracted a platter of raw bacon and set about coaxing the stove to life. I watched him from the corner of my eye while I rinsed the fruit and readied a knife.

"Don't hurt yourself with that." Baze grinned my way and spun a cast iron skillet in his hands.

I lifted my chin. "You just worry about yourself." Yet, as I poised the blade over the plump berry, I hesitated, stuck my tongue out in concentration, and then sliced. Red juices spilled over my fingers.

Sizzling bacon soon released a delectable aroma into the air and turned my stomach in on itself, ravenous. I finished chopping and assembled the fruit, then searched about for a little something more and unearthed clotted cream in the refrigerator. When Baze added his cooked protein to the spread, we stepped back and giggled at the haphazard feast.

I exhaled in a puff. "To the dining room then?"

He grimaced and tilted his head. "This is hardly a meal fit for a formal dining room. Come. I have a better idea."

We gathered the food onto a tray and entered the sitting room. Baze spread a blanket before the cold fireplace, helped me settle onto it, and arranged the food like a picnic. He watched me expectantly as I bit into the first piece of bacon.

"How does it taste?" His voice lightened in anticipation.

The crispy meat crumbled in my mouth, the fat melting on my tongue. I purred in satisfaction as I finished the piece and tore into the second. "It's delicious." I grinned. "I didn't realize you possessed such a skill."

With a half-smirk, he turned to his own meal, but his amusement soon faded, and he stroked his nose gingerly with a wince. The swelling on the bridge had begun to deflate, the cut scabbing over, but the bruises fanning into the corners of his eyes had darkened to a deep aubergine.

As I studied the injury, I realized that my earlier observation had been correct—the bone in his nose was straighter now. After Baze broke it as a sixteen-year-old, Frederick had tried to set it as best as he could but wound up leaving Baze with a minor bend. However, it appeared that this second break had miraculously snapped it back into its proper place.

Nibbling on a scone, I lifted my free hand and whispered the gentlest of fingers down his nose. "Does it hurt?"

He tipped his head away from my touch and dipped a strawberry in the cream. "No." But the wobble in his nasally voice and the twinge in his eyes told me otherwise.

As the evening wore on, the air in the house grew cold. I cleaned up our plates before retreating to our bedchamber to change from my dress and corset into a nightgown and robe, then joined Baze back in the sitting room where he stoked a hearty fire to life. I snatched a blanket from the sofa, wrapped it about myself, and sank onto the carpet in front of the hearth, watching Baze prod at the wood to stir up the flames. Pleasant *crackles* and *snaps* filled the room.

Once he replaced the brass poker and turned to me, I opened the quilt and extended one side. My unspoken prompt drew him to the floor. He clambered inside the quilt, tugged it tight around the both of us, and wound a protective arm around my shoulders. Heat generated from our bodies and from the external fire soon chased away my chill.

Leaning my head against Baze's shoulder, I trailed my gaze over the lively flames and up to the mantle, to my parents' initials carved deep into the wood. My heart constricted in gratitude. They had etched the letters as a symbol of their love and devotion to one another, but little had they known how meaningful the gesture would be. The markings had endured when hundreds of miles stood between them— and they endured even now that death separated them.

Tears prickled my nose. Propelled by sudden urgency, I wriggled out of Baze's hold and popped to my feet. Gooseflesh swept across my skin as I ripped from the warmth of our plush cocoon into the chill of the empty room. I tried rubbing heat back into my arms as I trotted toward the door.

Baze craned his head, perplexity twisting his features. "Where are you going?"

"Hold on. I'll only be a moment."

Light but firm footsteps carried me to the kitchen. Shadowed lumps emerged though the darkness—the smattering of skillets, cutlery, and food scraps we had left behind from our cooking endeavor. Picking my way through the preparation tables, I dug through drawers and crocks until I found what I was looking for—a small knife.

Triumphantly holding it aloft, I hustled to the sitting room, and when Baze saw the weapon I wielded, his expression twisted further into mild fright. "Um, Al, what are you doing?"

"You'll see in a moment." Standing before the mantle, I traced my index finger over my parents' carved initials in the far left of the molding—*T* and *C*. Then I moved slightly to the right, grasped the hilt of the knife firmly in my fist, and scraped the first stroke into the wood. The blade cut more easily than I anticipated, and within moments, I had added a new set of initials to the mantle. *B* and *A*. I rubbed the new carving with care as my heart expanded.

Satisfied, I twirled and dropped beside Baze. I laid the knife aside, dove back under the quilt and Baze's arm, and snuggled into him, keeping my face angled to admire my handiwork. His eyes, too, were fixed upon it, and though he didn't speak, his arms hardened around me.

We sat like that for a long moment until he broke the silence. "You know, I don't think I've seen anything more terrifying than you emerging from the darkness with a knife in your hands."

"*Really?* I do something romantic and *that's* how you respond?" I jabbed his ribs with two outstretched fingers.

With a grunt, he curved his torso away from my attack and then snickered. "I'm merely trying to lighten the mood." He nodded toward the mantle. "It's a nice gesture. Really."

"I simply wanted to leave our mark . . . just in case." Weariness sapped the fight from my bones. "Anything could happen out there." A heavy sigh drained from my lungs as I pressed closer to him, already mourning the ending of our reprieve—for once it drew to a close, once we ventured into battle, we weren't guaranteed another sunrise.

Baze nuzzled his face into my hair and brushed the tip of my ear with his lips, sending a shiver skittering through me. His breath heated my skin as he whispered, "Then we should make the most of this moment." His lips ventured to the junction between my jaw and my neck, fire igniting beneath each tender caress.

Releasing a low groan, I tilted my head back and exposed my throat to his advances. When his mouth grazed the hollow between my collarbones, I shivered once more, then cupped his jaw and guided his lips to mine. He skimmed his hand over my ribs and down my waist, slowly, delicately, easing me onto my back.

But as he pressed against my curved abdomen, I stiffened. In my haste to act, I had neglected discretion. Surely he could feel the change in my figure.

Baze's body responded in kind, tensing. He angled to look into my eyes, worry written on his flushed face. "Are you all right? Did I hurt you?"

A gasp caught in my throat. Not the words I had expected to hear. As I studied his anxious expression, he appeared truly oblivious. Perhaps the building anticipation kept his mind transfixed enough to blind him to anything that might have otherwise commanded his attention.

Forcing myself to relax, I shook my head. "No," I murmured. "I'm all right. Don't stop." I pulled him back to me, engaging him with passionate kisses to keep his thoughts arrested and away from my secret. As he tugged my nightgown up over my knee, I wrapped both arms about him and let a tight exhale siphon through my parted lips. "I love you, Baze . . . so much."

His warm breath trickled over my neck with his reply. "I love you too, Al."

But would he still love me if he knew the truth of what I hid from him?

## Chapter Twenty-Three

WITH THE RED HUE OF DAWN fading into the pale blue of morning, Finn directed the car to the base of the Rock of Cashel, parked, and got out. His spine popped and protested as they labored up the incline toward the grand structure—a near complete cruciform cathedral and chapel surrounded by time-worn graves, high crosses, and a huge round tower. In his youth, slumbering on a solid wooden floor would have barely fazed him, but now, it nearly did him in. However, if doing so meant Emily was comfortable, he would sleep on a thousand floors.

Cashel sat at the crown of an imposing hill of limestone. The ground leveled out as they reached the summit, much to the relief of Finn's aching calves and lower back. At such a high vantage point, they could see for miles, gazing out across the sprawling fields of trees, hedgerows, and flocks of sheep. The path they followed deposited them at the front of the cathedral—the top of the cross shape—and led them along its right side. Unspoken reverence settled over them.

Finn eyed a majestic high cross up ahead. Unlike the other high crosses of Ireland, this one featured a vertical pillar on one side to hold up the crossbar. Finn assumed there used to be a matching pillar on the other side, but time had stolen that feature. If one looked closely enough, he could make out a faint sculpture of Jesus Christ standing tall against the main part of the cross. Though prolonged exposure to nature's fury had long erased the fine details of the Messiah's face, Finn shuddered with conviction and bowed his head as he passed by.

They rounded the side of the transept and came upon a chapel—its stone whiter in color than the cathedral. Katherine plunged into the gaping entrance, trailed closely by Emily. However, Finn slowed his gait, a sensation of familiarity crawling through him. Pebbles crunched beneath his feet as he slid under the shadow of the doorway and halted.

Lips parted, Finn gazed up into the depths of the ceiling, its flying buttress style sweeping upward and meeting in a rounded point in the center. Memories washed over him. He and Katherine had been here before—with Ciaran and Shay—many years ago. They had taken shelter from a storm within the intimate chapel since it was one of the only structures at the site that retained its roof.

As lightning and rain raged overhead, they had coaxed a fire to life. Shay kept them entertained by creating whimsical finger shadows on the wall and captivating them with fantastical stories—stories of playing tricks with the fairies of legend and tempting fate by slumbering inside mystical ringforts. They had laughed. They had gasped. They had huddled together against the cold. Though their patchwork family of four had been together several years by that point, it had been the first time since his parents' death that Finn felt he truly belonged.

"There's another scrap of paper here."

Katherine's matter-of-fact statement snapped Finn's reverie. He blinked to clear the last of the melancholy memory. She and Emily had drawn near to the cracked sarcophagus sitting on a plinth against the far wall. Intricate carved details resembling the knotted style of the Celts marked the sandstone. Its right side had been damaged, with a good chunk taken out of the front panel. On top of the uneven crack, the corner of a note stuck out from beneath a small flat rock.

Katherine lifted the rock and retrieved the paper. She peeked at the writing. Her face whitened a shade. Her eyes snapped to Finn, screaming unspoken alarm.

Fear slithered up his spine as she handed him the note. He said a quick internal prayer before unfolding it and reading the words silently. *"You were so close and yet so far. Off you go to the next site, but you had best pick up your pace. Tarry too long and we'll start carving him up. Piece by piece."*

It had to be a bluff. Shay wouldn't hurt a child. Finn would bet his life on that. Unless . . . unless the men Shay had compelled to kidnap Basil Allan were acting on their own accord. With Shay's focus on Dublin, his control may have weakened, allowing them to regain some of their free will—and if that was the case, there was no telling what they might do.

"What does it say?" Emily asked, expression eager.

Finn fought to keep the paper from quivering in his hands and wet his cracked lips. "It says, 'You were so close and yet so far. Off you go to the next site, but you had best pick up your pace.'" When he cut off his words, he and Katherine exchanged a knowing glance. He folded the sheet and stashed it in his pocket, hoping Emily wouldn't ask to see it herself.

Katherine cleared her throat. "Well, as they said, we'd best not tarry." She twirled and dropped onto the edge of the sarcophagus before assuming the same posture as she had back at Glendalough. Tiny muscles spasmed across her face as her mind traveled far away.

Emily drew close to Finn's side, close enough that he caught a whiff of her lavender scent—potent and far too enticing. His skin grew clammy despite the wind cutting through the chapel. When she touched his arm with her soft fingers, his knees nearly buckled.

"Do you think we'll be able to catch up?" she asked quietly. "Be honest."

It took every bit of willpower to wrestle his mind away from Emily's alluring presence and focus on her question. Did he truly believe they would catch up? Before they reached Cashel, he had maintained a dash of optimism, but now . . .

"I don't know," he finally said, honoring her request for honesty.

Before Emily could respond, Katherine lurched to her feet with an excited gasp, her eyes sparking with determination. She smoothed her skirt and pinned up a loose portion of her red hair before wedging between Finn and Emily and marching toward the door. "Come. We must hurry. They're at Clonmacnoise."

## Chapter Twenty-Four

"I THOUGHT YOU DIDN'T TRUST ME, boyo."

Baze fisted his hands at his sides as he endured Darragh's suspicious stare. Adelynn moved into his peripheral view as he nodded at the superintendent. "I don't, sir, but we've come into some information that we think you should know." He gestured toward Adelynn. "My wife will be able to tell whether you're compromised or clean. You do remember what I told you about her, yes?"

Darragh's gaze tracked her up and down. "Aye. I do." He knitted his fingers together and leaned back in his chair, amusement crinkling the skin by his eyes. "Do what you must, me dear."

Adelynn lowered her head and narrowed her eyes. On the surface, nothing appeared to be happening, but Baze knew from the subtle flutter of her lashes and the furrow of her brow that her mind was wild at work. He risked at glance at Darragh—the man seemed composed.

Finally, Adelynn exhaled in a rush, and her lips tipped in a relieved smile as she nodded at Baze. "He's all right. We can trust him."

Darragh's chest rumbled with a warm chuckle. "That means a lot comin' from you. I appreciate it." He stroked his mustache. "Now what's this information you were thinkin' I should know?"

As they sat, Baze got right to it. "The rebels will strike Dublin on April the twenty-fourth. The day after Easter. Shay O'Sullivan plans to use the rebellion as cover to slip into Dublin Castle and take the Irish heads of state under his control so he can influence future laws—the Home Bill specifically."

Darragh's eyes widened a touch. "How did you come by this information?"

Adelynn twisted her hands in her lap. "I saw it in a vision, sir,"

Drumming his fingers on his desk, Darragh sighed. "I take it you're not in possession of any physical evidence then?"

Baze sent a wary look at Adelynn, but the unease on her face said she didn't know how better to answer, so Baze simply shook his head. "No, sir."

Darragh thumped a light fist on the desk before leaning forward and folding his arms upon it. "I want to help you, boyo, but you understand how barmy I would sound tryin' to muster our men because of an Englishwoman's outlandish dream?" He eyed Adelynn. "It's hard enough believin' you myself."

"You don't need to tell them," Baze suggested—a long shot, but he had to try. "Just post extra men at Dublin Castle. There are British barracks nearby as well. Perhaps you could request that they double the forces they have on patrol."

Darragh twisted his mouth in compassion and spoke softly. "If you were to be riskin' your life for somethin', would you not be entitled to know what that somethin' was? I can't lie to them."

Baze firmed his jaw as he wrestled against building frustration. "We're going after O'Sullivan whether you help or not, but I would much prefer to do it with your help. Can you not do anything?"

"Unless you come back to me with physical evidence, my hands are tied, I'm afraid."

"Then this was a waste of time." Baze surged to his feet. "I'm sorry to have bothered you."

"Hold on, boyo, hold on. Don't do anything reckless." Darragh growled out an exhale, rubbed his hands over his balding head, mussing the thin red hair, and then sat back in his chair with a thoughtful pucker of his lips. He studied Adelynn, then moved his scrutiny to Baze. "Why don't you go on home for now and let me think on it. I'll ask around, see if I can drum up any ideas."

Anger buzzed in Baze's chest, but he took a deep breath in and out to calm himself. "I suppose that's better than nothing."

Darragh stroked his finger stubs. "I'm sorry, son."

"I understand. As you said, your hands are tied. Good day, sir."

Baze stormed from the room with Adelynn in tow, trying to mitigate his annoyance, but the sharp ache in his leg and the clack of his cane threatened to send him over the edge. When they exited the police station and descended the front steps, the chilled air seeped straight through Baze's coat.

"He's doing what he can," Adelynn said, sliding her arm into his.

"Which is a load of nothing," Baze muttered.

"Give him time."

"We're nearly out of time." Aggravation strained Baze's voice. "We can't afford to—"

"Mr. Ford!"

Collin's yell stopped Baze mid-stride. He and Adelynn spun as the boy scurried up to them, clicked his feet together, and tucked his helmet under his right arm. "Permission to speak, sir."

Baze allowed a slight grin to tip his mouth as Collin's adherence to formality brought the moment a dash of levity. "At ease, Collin. I'm not your supervisor."

A blush colored Collin's cheeks as he relaxed his stance. "Of course, sir. *Gabh mo leithscéal*, sir. I mean, Mr. Ford. I mean—"

"What is it, Collin?" Adelynn interjected, amusement glimmering in her eyes.

"I want to join you." Collin hardened his expression into one of resolve. "Whatever it is you're plannin', I want to help."

Baze tightened his fist around his cane. He'd found Liam Donoghue and sent Collin back to Ireland for the sole purpose of keeping the boy out of harm's way. He was worried enough that Collin had gone on to join the Dublin Met, but if Collin threw himself into the conflict against O'Sullivan, the threat to Collin's life would increase tenfold.

Baze shook his head. "I understand your desire to help, but I can't let you—"

"He's corrupted me brother, Mr. Ford." The moisture in Collin's eyes and the crack in his voice stopped Baze short. "Just like Mr. Marx did to me. How can I abandon him?"

"Collin—"

"Please, Mr. Ford. You risked your life to save me from Mr. Marx. Without your intervention, I would still be lost, so I must do the same for *mo deartháir*."

To that, Baze didn't have a rebuttal. Who was he to keep Collin from trying to free his brother? The young man had a right to fight for those he loved no matter the circumstances. Besides, with Darragh's inaction nearly guaranteed, they could benefit from another ally.

"All right," Baze said, and Collin brightened. "But you'll do exactly as I say. This will be extremely dangerous, and I don't want you going rogue. Am I understood?"

"Yes, Mr. Ford. Of course." Collin bounced on his toes, and his hands quivered in excitement.

"Good. Now, my first order is that you start calling me Baze. Mr. Ford is my father."

"Yes, Mr. Ford . . . erm, Baze." Collin scrunched up his nose.

Baze chuckled and smacked the side of Collin's helmet. "You'll get used to it."

Rather than proceed to the car, we opted to continue down the street, away from the police station, giving Baze the opportunity to explain to Collin what had occurred thus far. I slowed my steps and allowed the men to wander farther out ahead. A cool mist flurried on the wind, catching in my hair and dampening my skin.

I hated the idea of Collin's involvement. He'd been just a boy when Cornelius had taken control of his mind and forced him to attack Baze, and even now, he was barely a man. Though he hadn't admitted it, I surmised from the way he occasionally glanced at Baze's leg that he still bore guilt for what had happened.

Maybe this was the way he would finally achieve healing—by

taking up arms and helping to defeat the very force that took him captive.

Foreboding slithered across my limbs and brought me to a halt. Breath stuck in my lungs as I watched Baze and Collin continue forward, oblivious. The sensation heightened, dizzying my thoughts. I'd become so accustomed to consciously using my gift to conjure visions that I had forgotten what it was like to experience one involuntarily—abrupt, forceful, frightening. Even after all I had learned, I couldn't stop it from seizing control and ripping my consciousness out of my body and into someone else's.

Shay. He stood in the middle of a rustic village of stone cottages and pastures of sheep, the same settlement I'd seen him occupy before. His gaze passed briefly over two men, too quick for me to identify them, and then he knelt, bringing himself to the eye level of a young child standing before him.

Basil Allan.

Shay took hold of the child's wrist and examined a bloodied bandage compressing his hand. Fury boiled so strong in his chest that even I felt it. He lifted his head and pierced the two men with a glare. Now I recognized one of them as Liam Donoghue, his face awash in turmoil. Why was he with Shay? Hadn't he been tasked to flee across Ireland, using Basil Allan as bait to keep us sidetracked? What had prompted him to—

Shay's mind exploded. Pain tore through my head as his dark energy shot toward the men.

Liam's eyes darkened. His hand plunged to his belt and jerked out a gun. He aimed straight at the other man's face and fired. As the man crumpled, Liam jammed the gun under his own jaw. He opened his mouth—*Bang!*

My mind burst from Shay's head with a shock, then crashed back into my own body. A gasp yanked from my lips as the Dublin street faded into view. Pulse pounding, I tried to make sense of what I'd just seen. Liam was dead. Basil Allan was injured. Had it already occurred, or was there still time to intervene? Even if there was time, we didn't know where Shay's village was located.

Then a new thought occurred to me. I had experienced five visions in quick succession when I first touched Shay's mind—and now two of them had happened exactly as I'd seen. Did that mean the others were all but guaranteed to transpire—soldiers fighting in the street, Finn's mind succumbing to darkness, and Baze falling to his death? Was there any way to stop it?

Finally regaining some semblance of control over my body, I propelled my legs forward. Baze and Collin had passed out of earshot, unaware of my internal struggle. I quickened my steps and extended a hand as though to draw them back to me.

Another jab of pain rattled my head. With a yelp, I stumbled and skidded to a stop. Another vision? No, this was different. Closer. Intentional. Realization curled my toes.

Strong scents of citrus and spice enshrouded me from behind. I snapped my eyes to the back of Baze's head, opened my mouth, and—

"Scream and I'll drop you right here."

## Chapter Twenty-Five

MY CRY FOR HELP FELL DEAD in my throat. A hand slipped over my waist as something extremely sharp sliced into the skin of my lower back, cutting straight through the fabric of my dress and corset. I winced and arched away from the weapon, but it only bit deeper.

Shay's low voice hissed in my ear with a blunt, "Walk." He applied pressure to my hip, directing me around and nudging me forward—in the opposite direction of Baze and Collin.

"Where are we going?" I murmured through clenched teeth.

"Somewhere discreet. Where there will be no witnesses."

Obstinance fueled my words. "I thought you said you would drop me right here. Why take me somewhere discreet?"

"Because I would rather not cause a scene, but I will if I have to."

With his arm holding me tight against him, I was sure it appeared to onlookers as though we were merely a couple out for a pleasant stroll. Every sinew and fiber of my body quivered with the desire to fight against him, but the knife pricking my back kept me in submission.

There had to be something I could do, if not to escape, then perhaps to alert Baze and Collin to my abduction. I started ripping at the beads of my dress. One popped free, and I let it fall noiselessly to the pavement. Then I worked on another.

"You have gall, Adelynn. Unbridled gall." Husky anger colored his tone. "You chose to remain in Dublin despite the threat to your friend's child. Your selfishness astounds me."

The truth danced on the tip of my tongue, but I bit it down. As we had hoped, he was unaware that Katherine, Finn, and Emily were in pursuit of Basil Allan at this very moment. If Shay was here right now, completely in the dark, perhaps Liam yet lived. Perhaps the injury to Basil Allan could still be prevented.

"That's because I believe you won't hurt him." I kept my voice calm and sensitive. "As you told me once, you don't hurt the innocent."

Shay twisted the knife point a little deeper.

I gasped at the lance of pain as he whirled me around a corner. Somehow, I managed to pop another bead free and toss it on the ground.

Shadows doused us as we dove deep into an alley lined on both sides with tall buildings, each with a door opening into the narrow passageway. The stench of rotting food and waste stung my nose. When we reached the wall at the end, Shay grasped a fistful of hair at the back of my head and used it to jerk me around. He repositioned the knife at my throat. Its blade bit into my skin, and I kept my chin lifted just enough to avoid its touch.

His gaze roamed my face, and disgust curled his lip. "Ciaran once wrote to me of you. He described your insufferable obstinance. You may think it bravery, but it is your fatal flaw."

***You see? You are broken. Nothing you do is right.***

Like every time before, the internal taunt soured my stomach and confirmed that God had drawn even farther away. After all, why would He stay near to someone as despicable as I? Yet, despite my isolation, my fear drove me to prayer, if only to bring myself comfort. I prayed that Baze would discover the trail I had left behind, that he would reach me in time.

Now, to give him a chance to act, I had to keep Shay talking.

"What about your fatal flaw?" I bit out. "You care so much for those who are persecuted and downtrodden that you would sacrifice your own humanity to save them." I didn't entirely believe my words—for I didn't believe a righteous motive justified a wicked act—but something sensitive flickered in Shay's eyes, so I pressed harder on that bruise.

"You didn't want this power, did you?" Softening my voice, I slipped a hand over his wrist. "It sought you out in a moment of vulnerability and exploited your compassion, and after all the awful things you witnessed but were unable to rectify, you opened your heart to it."

Ever so slightly, his painful grasp on my hair loosened—but he left the knife in place. Uncertainty shrouded his features. "When Kate and I discovered that boy beaten to death in the dead of night, that's when I first felt the power risin' in me," he murmured as though to himself. "It offered me the chance to strike back at the monster who killed that boy, so I let it in." His expression hardened to stone. "All at once, I was consumed. It allowed me to control that orphan keeper. I made him turn the weapon upon himself. Over and over. Until he was dead."

"What happened after that?" I asked under my breath.

"My power grew stronger." His hand ensnared in my hair trembled. "Kate tried to help. She begged me to seek redemption. Threatened to leave me if I didn't. But if I did what she suggested, then so many others like that child murderer would escape judgment." Moisture gathered in his eyes. "So I pledged myself to the darkness."

Understanding began to chip away at the apathy I had directed toward him. With the knife still nipping at my chin, I channeled sympathy through my expression. "Do you not see the deceit in that? Your power has twisted your mind. Where once you fought against true enemies, the darkness has now made you believe that anyone who stands in your way is an enemy." Sorrow gripped my throat. "It made you kill the woman who loved you."

"Shut up," he growled. "She chose to oppose me. I had to do it."

"No." I managed to shake my head gingerly. Warmth flowed across my limbs as words came gentle and easy. "That's another lie told by the evil you're allowing to fester within you. I think the real Shay is still in there. I think he weeps for what you have done."

Neck muscles bulging, Shay's fingers jerked my hair. "You're wrong."

I winced against the pain but managed to meet his eyes with a challenging stare. "If I'm wrong, then why haven't you killed me yet?"

Shay stared back, jaw clenching and unclenching. A lone sweat drop trickled down his temple. For a split second, his walls appeared to come down, his muscles loosening—but then in the same breath, he wrenched my head back, and I yelped. His hot breath beat against my face as he hissed, "That's a problem I'll be solvin' right now."

The knife scraped across my throat.

## Chapter Twenty-Six

"Where's Miss Adelynn gone?" Collin's hand clamped onto Baze's arm and pulled him to a dead stop as the young constable looked over his shoulder, confusion etched on his face and eyes darting across the crowd.

Baze ground his cane into the pavement and followed Collin's stare. Swaths of people poured around them—but none of them were Adelynn. With a prickle of panic, Baze rose slightly onto his toes to see over the bobbing heads, hoping to glimpse the sparkling adornments in her hair, but a torrent of dull earthen tones passed by.

"Adelynn?" he called, backtracking several paces. "Adelynn?" Louder. "Adelynn, where are you? This isn't funny." Even as he said the words, his gut told him this wasn't a prank.

"Do you think she went back to the police station?" Collin asked, his head on a swivel.

Throat tightening, Baze scanned the sea of faces. They had concluded their business with Darragh, so there was no pressing reason for her to return—unless she had somehow gotten it into her head that she could convince the superintendent to give them more assistance than he had first offered. Baze wouldn't put it past her, but if that were the case, why hadn't she informed them of her decision to leave?

Baze nudged Collin's arm and murmured, "Come on." With urgency in his steps and Collin on his tail, he wended back the way they had come, bumping shoulders, shoving people out of the way. "Adelynn!" His voice cracked as it spiked in volume. "Where are you?"

Ahead several feet, a tiny object on the pavement glinted in the sunlight. Baze stooped and retrieved it. A pearlescent bead. He pictured the gown Adelynn had donned that morning—a beautiful ivory ensemble embellished with elaborate embroidery and punctuated with hundreds of beads. A dress of that quality wouldn't fall to bits without help. This bead was intentional.

"I have something," Baze barked, drawing Collin to his side. He proffered the bead.

As Collin examined it, his brow crinkled. "This matches what Miss Adelynn was wearin'. Do you think it fell off?"

Baze straightened. "I think it's more likely she dropped it."

Collin's mouth bent in contemplation. "Could she be leavin' a trail?"

"It appears that way."

"Why would she need to do that, unless . . ." His skin paled.

At the spark of fear in Collin's eyes, Baze tried to keep himself calm though he felt anything but. "Let's not speculate. Look for more. Hurry."

With the command given, Collin set out at a good clip, Baze close on his heels. About twenty paces from the first, Collin discovered another bead, solidifying Baze's suspicion.

She'd been taken.

Anger scrambled his insides. He had noticed her trailing farther and farther behind, but rather than slow for her to catch up, he had welcomed the chance to speak to Collin man to man. He had let his guard down—had been careless—and Adelynn was bearing the consequences.

*God, I don't know what's happened to her, but keep her safe. Allow me to arrive in time to stop any harm that might befall her. Don't let her suffer for my foolishness. Please. I beg you.*

Two more beads led them to the darkened entrance of an alley. One final bead sparkled directly inside—beckoning, foreboding. Intuition screamed at Baze. Adelynn was in there, but they couldn't just rush in. He snatched Collin's arm and tugged him against the wall beside the opening. Cementing his shoulder blades to the bricks, Baze craned his neck and poked his head out just far enough so he could see inside.

Figures moved in the shadows. Baze's vision adjusted slowly, painstakingly. Then their features became clear, and it took every ounce of willpower to steel himself and not charge in.

Adelynn stood rigid at the very end of the alley—and O'Sullivan stood with her.

He had her trapped, with one hand buried in her hair and the other pushing a knife to her throat. Restrained fear contorted her face as she jerked her chin away from the blade. They exchanged inaudible words, and for the time being, O'Sullivan seemed pacified.

Muscles quivering, Baze took quick stock of their surroundings. Several bins of waste littered the narrow space. Both of the establishments bordering the alley had doors leading into it, each situated behind Adelynn and O'Sullivan.

Baze smacked Collin's chest and jabbed a thumb toward the pub at their backs. "The door. Quick. Go inside and see if you can sneak around them. I'll try to draw O'Sullivan's focus."

"Yes, sir." Collin nodded and loped away.

A strangled yelp yanked Baze around. Apparently done talking, Shay had wrenched Adelynn's head to expose her neck. His forearm flexed, and the knife bit into her skin.

All self-control evaporated. Baze surged into the alley, dropped his cane, and snatched up his gun. "Stop!"

O'Sullivan wrangled Adelynn around by her hair, the knife still depressing her throat, and Baze drew up a mere ten paces away, his pistol elevated and clenched in both hands.

When Adelynn saw him, her face relaxed in relief despite her dire situation.

"You're too late, Inspector." O'Sullivan sneered. He jerked the knife. Blood spurted.

Baze seized and opened his mouth, but before he could get a word out, Adelynn arched her neck and screamed, "Stop, I'm with child!"

O'Sullivan froze, the blade mid-slice.

High-pitched ringing cut out all other sounds. A sharp pain blossomed in Baze's gut as though someone had taken that knife and stabbed *him*. He stared hard at Adelynn. *That can't be right. She couldn't be . . . It must be a ruse.*

"Don't hurt me." Desperation laced her voice. A single drop of blood slithered down the blade and dripped off the end. She trembled. "Spare me if only to spare my child. I beg you."

O'Sullivan's lip curled, but he didn't lower the weapon. "You're lyin'."

"I'm not." A groan of effort ripped her throat as she struggled to keep her neck arched. "I give you my word, I'm not."

O'Sullivan's accusatory eyes latched onto Baze, lingered there, until the flicker of a grin twitched the corner of his mouth. "Do you see your husband's face? He looks about ready to swoon. And I'm to be believin' you're carryin' his child and he doesn't know?"

"Yes." She hesitated, then allowed her eyes to wander to Baze, and the truth of what he saw in those pale blue windows thrust the invisible knife deeper into his gut. Her cheeks flushed as tears began to spill. "I hadn't told him yet. I was keeping it from him until the right moment."

A rolling wave of dread followed by prickling numbness swept across Baze's body.

One of the alley doors creaked open in Baze's periphery, but he couldn't tear his eyes away from his wife . . . his pregnant wife.

O'Sullivan tugged his fingers from her hair and circled it around her waist, covering her stomach with his large hand. He stilled, waiting a beat, then two. His nostrils flared, and realization slacked his features. "Well, aren't you a lucky *cailín*," he growled in her ear before finally lowering the weapon. "I'll spare your life for the sake of your child, but I can't be lettin' you—"

The door burst open. Collin barreled through, swinging his baton. The weapon smacked the back of O'Sullivan's head with a fleshy *crack*.

The Irishman went down. Adelynn stumbled forward. Collin caught her fall, swept her up into his arms, and sprinted for Baze.

Every muscle in Baze yearned to take her from Collin, but considering the state of Baze's leg—and his stunned state of mind—Collin was in much better condition to carry her safely away. Instead, he readied his gun and whirled to where O'Sullivan had collapsed.

But the second door now hung ajar, and the Irishman was gone.

# Chapter Twenty-Seven

Urgency pressed Finn's foot heavily onto the pedal as he steered through the narrow and winding country roads. His pulse rushed, and he squeezed the steering wheel until his fingers cramped. Would they really do it? Would they harm a child?

"Look out!" Katherine hissed from the backseat.

Finn focused his attention in time to see a wide stone fence careening toward them. He wrenched the wheel. The tires screeched as they swerved in time to avoid a collision.

Thrown against Finn's side, Emily gasped and grabbed his arm.

"Sorry," he mumbled—but he kept his foot engaged on the pedal.

Rising in the distance, a round tower, dispersal of stone crosses, and crumbling cathedral signaled their arrival to Clonmacnoise. The site was nestled in the bend of the River Shannon, surrounded by green land stretching as far as the eye could see. Like Cashel, it had served as one of the stops on his adopted family's final tour across Ireland— before Finn was to leave for his marriage to Maeve.

Finn took them as far as the road would allow, where it ended abruptly and faded into green grass leading up into the eerie cemetery. He cranked the automobile into a parked position.

"I'll go out ahead in case someone's here." Keeping his eyes from meeting Emily's, he slotted the gun into his waistband. He didn't really think the ancient stones concealed an enemy. He merely wanted to find the kidnappers' note—or anything else—before she could.

Finn marched up the gentle slope and hurdled the low stone fence surrounding the entire perimeter. As he dodged headstones and high crosses, his mind raced. Clonmacnoise housed a cathedral and a smattering of several smaller chapels, far more than Cashel. So where might the enemy have left a note this time? Searching every building would take all afternoon, and the more time they wasted, the more the danger to Basil Allan rose.

*Think, Finn. Think!*

The sound of Emily's lyrical but unintelligible voice quickened Finn's steps. As he approached the chapel, he cycled through the names of the structures—Temple Dowling, Temple Hurpan, Temple Kelly, Temple Ciaran . . .

Finn stopped in his tracks. *Ciaran.* It was a stretch, but if these men were acting under Shay's influence, then there was a chance they were choosing things with meaning. And there was nothing more on the nose than hiding their next note in Temple Ciaran.

Taut with trepidation, he set off east, skirting around the cathedral and toward the smaller, more destroyed building near the back. Temple Ciaran was a sorry sight—with a missing roof, barely upright walls, and leaning doorway. The front end sloped slightly left, and the back end sloped right, almost as though the earth beneath it had grabbed ahold and twisted the church's foundation.

Finn ducked through the arched doorway and took in the space. A vertical stone slab depicting a cross sat upright against the center of the far wall, and a second slab had been wedged diagonally across the corner to the left of the cross. Finn's eyes locked on the crooked slab, his pulse roaring in his ears. Rather than delay the inevitable, he approached and peered inside.

A wooden box rested atop dead leaves and dirt.

Finn closed his eyes and tried to form a prayer, but the only thing his jumbled thoughts could conjure was a weak, *Please no.*

He lifted the box and scraped his fingers along the intricate carvings in the sides. It felt hollow, but he knew better than to assume it was empty. When he cracked open the top, its hinges creaked and a white linen of some sort puffed up, now free of its prison. A red streak marred the cloth.

Repeating *no, please, no* over and over in his mind, he tugged at the cloth to get to its contents. Finally, he uncovered the article within—a thin flesh-colored object no bigger than a house key. Dark, congealed blood stained one end of it . . . and the other displayed a tiny fingernail.

Horror struck him in the chest. He slammed the box shut and clamped his hand over his mouth as stinging vomit surged up his throat.

"What did you find?"

Emily's sweet, oblivious voice chirped from the doorway.

He whirled toward her, fighting to swallow the bile and trying to wipe the alarm from his face—but when she frowned, he realized his attempt had been unsuccessful.

"What is it?" Emily clasped her hands to her chest. "What's wrong?"

"It's . . ." He couldn't get the words out. Lying to her wasn't an option, but how was he supposed to tell her that he was holding a box that contained one of her beloved son's fingers?

Katherine nudged her way past Emily and snatched the box from Finn's frozen hands. As she cracked it open, Emily drew to her side and peeked in. Finn stared at her, watching every twitch of her features as she absorbed what she saw.

Color slowly siphoned from her face, leaving her pale as whitethorn. Her reddening eyes dragged to Finn and pinned him down. "You said they wouldn't hurt him." Her rasping voice barely carried over the rushing wind.

"I know," he managed. "I'm sorry."

"You lied to me!" She shouted this time and threw herself at him. "You said you would never lie to me!" Thick tears spilled from her eyes as she pounded his chest with her fists, the intensity slowly weakening with each strike. Though the blows landed soft, they may as well have been killing blows for the daggers they struck through his heart.

When the fight eventually drained from her limbs, she threw her arms around his torso and buried her face into his breastbone. Her muffled sobs shuddered through him.

He squeezed her tight, tucking her head beneath his chin. *I've been distant, Lord. I know I have.* Anguish brought the bile back to his throat. *Don't be punishin' her because of me. I beg you. If this is me doin', let me make it right. Punish me. Break my body. Take my life. But spare Emily and the boy.*

As painful petitions continued to run through his head, he found himself whispering, "You haven't been believin' in your son's well-being because of anythin' me foolish mouth's been sayin'. You've been believin' because of your faith." Her sobs lessened ever so slightly, so he kept going. "The Almighty's gotten you this far, sure. Do you think He would carry you through the death of your husband only to abandon you now? That doesn't sound like the God you've been tellin' me about all these years."

After several long minutes, Emily stilled and quieted. She loosened her embrace and leaned back in his arms. The hopeful spark that he'd grown so accustomed to seeing—that he'd been relying on—reignited in her eyes. Her gaze softened as it roamed his face, and he felt her heartbeat slowing, tapping in time with his.

"You're right," she whispered. "I shouldn't despair. Not now."

"No." He shook his head. "Not ever." The words seemed to appear out of thin air. He wasn't even sure he believed them, because surely there was a proper time for despair, but so long as he was alive, he never wanted to see Emily despair again.

She sniffed and straightened, then stepped back, and he reluctantly let her go. Wiping her eyes with the inside of her wrist, she turned toward Katherine. "We need to get one step ahead of them," she said, her voice remarkably commanding. "Do you think it's possible?"

Katherine allowed a small grin. "That's the girl." She tucked one arm under the other and tapped her chin. "As for whether it's possible, I don't know. I have never been able to control from when in the future I draw my visions."

Emily's brows drew together. "But you could try?"

"For you, I would do anything."

Finn nearly echoed the sentiment, but he bit his tongue. As Katherine discussed a few ideas with Emily, he stared at the ground and ran back through the locations they'd visited. Glendalough, Cashel, and Clonmacnoise. All places he and his family had stayed on their final excursion—and in the same order.

The pieces clicked into place.

"They're following the pattern of our last tour across Ireland," he said, believing it even stronger now that he'd said it aloud.

Katherine frowned at him, but as the thoughts raced behind her eyes, realization loosened her features. "You're right."

"What do you mean?" Emily asked.

"After Shay taught Ciaran and me the trade of a magician, we often traveled together, performin' to make a livin'. With Kate, too, of course. I got engaged soon after turnin' nineteen"—his face flushed as he bolstered the courage to continue—"and to honor the changin' of the seasons, as it were, we embarked upon a final journey. It was the last time we were happy . . . if you could be callin' it that."

Emily touched a comforting hand to his arm—as if *he* was the one who needed comforting right now. She tilted her head. "So then do you know where they're going to go next?"

"The fairy fort on the way to Galway, wasn't it?" Katherine said.

"Yes, but if we're to be catchin' up to them, we have to go to the place after that." Finn's body tensed as a bitter memory ruptured. "Poulnabrone."

Katherine's eyes widened. "But that's where—"

"It doesn't matter." Before the violent memory could fully develop, he shook his head and made for the church's exit. "If we're to have any hope of gettin' the lad back before they can do more harm, we have to beat them there."

## Chapter Twenty-Eight

THE BARBED WIRE OF DREAD WOUND itself into a tight, painful ball in Emily's stomach. She tried not to imagine what those men were doing to her precious son. She would unravel if she did . . .

This wasn't Finn's fault. She knew that. But that didn't mean she didn't want to scream at the top of her lungs and then unleash her wrath upon him if only to release the tension building in her heart. After all, he was the closest and easiest target.

Somehow, she managed to suppress the hurtful, profane words that congregated on her tongue and forced herself to pray instead. Well, it was less like a prayer and more like a silent outburst—though she was positive her Creator could handle her even at her most enraged.

For the first half of the drive, she stared only at the scenery passing by—the fields, the ruins, the villages. Though the day stretched into early afternoon, when the sun should have been at its zenith, fog hung over the knolls and darkened the landscape. Misty rain clouded the air.

Then she risked a glance at Finn.

He gripped the steering wheel with one hand and absently massaged his temple with the other. Similar to the dreary atmosphere outside, a thick haze veiled his features.

Perhaps an hour into the drive, Finn broke the silence. "The area around Poulnabrone is completely flat and stretches for miles." He spoke quietly and kept his focus fixed ahead. "There won't be many places for us to hide and surprise them." His knuckles whitened as he clenched the wheel. "I think we should park off the main road and stay far enough away that the kidnappers couldn't easily see us from the tomb." He wagged a thumb between Emily and Katherine. "You two will remain in the car while I walk the rest of the way and hide in the tomb."

"That's preposterous." Katherine chimed in. "You can't go alone. We know there are at least two men, and that's already an unfair fight, especially considering they have Basil Allan and would, I'm sure, threaten to harm him further if need be."

"I'm aware of what we're up against." Finn sighed. "But you know how small the tomb is. It'll be easier for me to hide alone. It's important that we maintain the element of surprise. If we can do that, I think I can stun them long enough to get the upper hand." His voice grew cold and resolute. "I've made up me mind."

The truth in Finn's words placated Emily's welling protests, but that didn't stop the fear from scrambling up her throat. That Finn was willing to put his life on the line to save her son both heartened and tormented her. She wanted nothing more than to see Basil Allan recovered safely, but the thought of losing another man she loved was almost too much to bear.

"Just come back to me," she murmured, fully intending to say "us," but the word slipped out.

Something akin to sorrow flickered on his face as the haze in his eyes deepened. "I will try."

When they reached the flat, rocky ground surrounding Poulnabrone, Finn parked the car behind a stone fence a modest distance from the structure, perhaps just enough to conceal them from the enemy. Bolstered by Emily's meaningful request, Finn uttered a quick goodbye before setting his sights upon the imposing Stone Age tomb and plodding over the uneven earth.

Tendrils of darkness shrouded his mind and chilled the air at his feet as he closed the distance to Poulnabrone—a feat of engineering with four crude slabs, two on each side, that supported a slanted roof of the same material. The ancient burial grounds had been the last place he had truly been free—and he had vowed never to return. Not without provocation anyway. For Basil Allan, he would have marched into the fires of hell. What was a little relived trauma in comparison?

Shadows settled heavily upon his shoulders when he stepped into the shade of the tomb's sloped roof, threatening to crush his bones into dust. Wind whistled through the structure and tossed light pricks of rain into his face. Flowers poked through the limestone—everything from the bright yellow lady's bedstraw to the dark blue spring gentian—a welcome pop of color among the gray. Priming the gun for use, Finn leaned against one of the rough walls.

All that remained to do now was wait.

Memories flooded him, battering his mind and forcing images to flash before his eyes. Suppressing them proved impossible. For every defense he tossed up, they had an attack to break it, so he gave in.

Poulnabrone was to be their last stop before Doolin, where Finn and his betrothed would depart, leaving his frayed family to create one of his own. Maeve had joined them there as they took shelter for the night. With clear skies and tame weather, they'd started a fire and told stories beneath the stars. Shay used sleight of hand to enhance his tales, and Kate added her own fantastical flair, but as the night waned, Finn had noticed growing hostility oozing from Ciaran. He should have paid attention to it, should have confronted him—but Finn had brushed it off and bedded down without a care, Maeve tucked snugly in his arms.

Nightmares had kept him locked in the unconscious realm. He had thrashed against the suffocating darkness for hours, and when he finally jerked free, he realized why.

Maeve was gone, and he didn't have to guess what happened.

In a blind fury, Finn had attacked. He hurled Ciaran to the ground and smacked his brother's head against the rocks over and over, cracking bone and spraying blood.

Then Shay intervened.

Finn winced as he felt the stab to his mind as viscerally as he had that day. Like a knife jammed into his skull. Shay had plunged deeper and deeper, shattering thoughts and destroying memories as he went. He forced his way to the last trembling strand of Finn's free will.

And snapped it.

The attack left Finn nearly catatonic. He forgot why he had attacked Ciaran. He forgot about their time spent traveling Ireland. He forgot Maeve—her memory fading, warping, and becoming no more than a distant dream. From that moment on, he had been a soulless puppet until Adelynn had helped deliver him in that dank cell in Pentonville Prison.

*If I was set free that day, why don't I feel free?*

**Because once a prisoner, you are always a prisoner.**

Finn struck the side of the tomb with a fist. When he had opened his heart to the light, he did so with the belief that his life would be different, but the battle for his mind raged on. A weaker battle, perhaps, but it affected him every moment of every day. Maybe it was true. Maybe his infant faith wasn't strong enough to combat this power. Maybe the Almighty had been mistaken in choosing to call someone *that* broken to the light.

Scraping pebbles startled Finn out of his trance. Ducking his head, he fell to one knee and readied his weapon. Footsteps crunched closer— one individual by the sound of it. He held his breath as the person rounded the wall. He aimed. A head poked into the opening, red hair flashing.

Kate held up her hands. "Easy, little dove. It's me."

Finn expelled a strained sigh. Remaining crouched, he clicked the gun's safety on and rocked back against the wall. "What are you doin' here? I told you to stay in the car."

"I think they found us." She hunkered against the opposite slab to catch her breath. "We saw an automobile approaching from the east. They turned toward Poulnabrone but then suddenly wheeled around and sped back the other way. I'm sure they saw us. I think they're running."

Curses flooded his chest, but he kept them contained beneath a frustrated exhale. "I was afraid that might happen." He rubbed his forehead and sent her a grim look. "Where do you think they'll go? There aren't any locations left. We split up after Poulnabrone."

"I don't know." Her thin brows met in worry. "But I'm sure I can find out."

Finn burst to his feet and marched for the entrance. "Let's hurry, then."

"Wait." She grabbed his arm and halted him. Her penetrating deep green eyes searched his face. "You look shaken, little dove," she whispered, then grimaced. "It's little wonder, I suppose. The last time we were here, I watched Sully break you like a wild horse right before my very eyes." Her lips pinched in sadness. "If there's anything you wish to talk about—"

"There's not. We have to keep movin'." He pressed past her, but as her fingers slipped from his arm, buried pain and unanswered questions came barreling to the surface—and one question in particular thrust itself to the forefront.

Finn rotated back, and Kate drew up to avoid a collision. "Actually, I do have somethin'," he murmured, his face inches from hers. "Do you know what happened to Maeve?"

Kate's expression remained stoic, but the laborious ripple of her throat and the wet gleam in her eyes told him the answer.

She shook her head slowly. "Are you sure you want to know?"

He didn't hesitate. "Yes."

"Very well." With a nod, she squared her jaw and looked him right in the eyes as she spoke. "Ciaran believed Maeve had bewitched you, but I think he was merely jealous of your happiness. That night, he placed a heavy presence over Poulnabrone to keep us asleep and then took Maeve. He stole one of the horses and carried her to the Cliffs." Her lashes fluttered against gathering moisture. "Then he compelled her to walk over the edge."

Finn's eyes winced shut as he pictured Maeve falling, her body dashed and broken on the rocks—and then he tore his eyes open before the images could worsen. "How do you know this?" he asked, voice rasping.

"Sully told me."

Emotion clamped Finn's throat shut. He had pulled Ciaran from those cliffs so many years ago only for Ciaran to turn around and sacrifice Maeve to them. Perhaps she would still be here if he had simply allowed Ciaran to fall.

A lot of people would still be here.

Finn cleared his throat. "Thank you." Face burning hot, he turned away from Kate, drew in a shuddering breath, and staggered toward the car. "Let's go find Basil Allan."

*The sharp crackle of gravel punctuated the pleasant evening air. Normally, a car coming into the village wouldn't have roused my suspicions, but the speed at which it was traveling and the abruptness of its halt raised the hair on my arms.*

*From where I sat at my table, studying a detailed blueprint of Dublin Castle, I craned my neck toward the window, then winced as the bruised lump at the back of my head throbbed. The young constable's strike had landed true and allowed Adelynn to slip through my fingers once more.*

*Planting both hands on the table, I rose. With the slightest reach of my mind, I knew instantly who it was—Donoghue and Fitzgerald had returned. But why? I hadn't given such an order. They were meant to tote the lad from place to place to keep Adelynn and her friends occupied. Though, if Adelynn yet remained in Dublin, perhaps they had realized they weren't being pursued and opted to give up the directive.*

*I stormed down the front steps toward the automobile parked on the dirt road.*

*Donoghue slammed the door and spun toward me. He pushed the lad out front, a guiding hand on his skinny shoulder.*

*The moment the lad's eyes found me, he took off, arms outstretched. He collapsed against my leg and hugged it tight, burrowing his face into my thigh. Thick tears soaked through the fabric.*

*I caressed his hair, shushing him gently, and targeted the two men with a glare. I didn't know what they had done to upset him so, but I felt a pinch of pride that he had sought me for comfort.*

*Anger boiled beneath my even tone as I said, "Why are you here?"*

*"They found us." Donoghue growled as he approached.*

*"Who did?"*

*Fitzgerald came up to Donoghue's side, one of his arms bandaged and resting in a sling. "O'Brien and the boy's mother."*

*My thoughts whirled. So Adelynn and her husband had stayed in Dublin while Finn and Emily went after the boy—a risky endeavor, to be sure. It may have even worked had I not discovered Adelynn and the inspector so foolishly returning to the police station.*

*But then . . . how had Finn been able to catch up to the lad without Adelynn's foresight?*

*I jutted my chin. "How did they find you?"*

*Fitzgerald shrugged. "Don't rightly know. There was another—"*

*"Look." Little Baze tugged my trousers and stretched up his left hand. He sucked in quick, trembling sobs. "It hurts. Can you make it better?"*

*"What is it, now?" I crouched before him and grabbed his wrist so I could twist it to get a better view. A linen bandage encircled his swollen hand. Dark spots stained the cloth where his little finger should have been.*

*Something feral lit within me.*

*"What did you do to him?" I asked—calm and quivering.*

*"Don't worry. He was unconscious. Didn't feel a thing." Fitzgerald sniffed and rolled his eyes. "You told us to keep 'em busy. Besides"—he gestured to his wounded arm—"they struck first."*

*Rage seized control. I clutched Little Baze to myself and stabbed at Donoghue's mind.*

*His hand whipped down and snatched his gun. The weapon aimed. Shot Fitzgerald between the eyes. Then it rammed under Donoghue's jaw and—mid-cry—fired.*

*Blood splattered my face. The men crumpled.*

# Chapter Twenty-Nine

REMORSE SEALED MY LIPS SHUT AS we rushed home. Baze drove in unnerving silence as Collin held his handkerchief to the cut in my neck. The silence stretched on as Baze parked, pulled me from the automobile, and swung me into his arms. I clung to him and repressed every argument against his brash action as his leg quivered and threatened to buckle with each irregular step.

Inside our bedchamber, he deposited me in a chair and set about lighting a few of the lamps. Then he stomped from the room. He barked an order at Collin, and in a few minutes, he returned with two rags and a bottle of carbolic acid. He jerked another chair over, sat before me, and grasped my chin. Brusque swipes forced the stinging liquid into my wound.

I inhaled sharply and angled away, but Baze clamped his hand around the back of my head and held me in place. Tears spurted as I endured the procedure.

Soon, his movements slowed, and the swipes grew gentle. Then he took the clean rag and pressed it against my throat, holding it there, motionless. His eyes slid shut as his breathing calmed—and mine along with it.

Sensing the dissipating storm within him, I whispered, "What's the damage?"

With a short exhale through his nose, he straightened and pulled the rag away. "It's superficial." His voice sounded weary. "The bleeding has stopped. It should heal quickly."

My muscles steeled in apprehension. "Thank you."

Without so much of a nod of acknowledgement, he folded the rags, corked the bottle, and set them aside, then stood. He dragged the extra chair away and strode to the opposite end of the room. His fists clenched, then unclenched at his sides, and when he came veering back around, he planted himself before me and looked straight into my eyes. "Is it true?"

Shame lurched in my stomach, followed by a gentle flutter. I pushed both hands against it and fought to clear my throat of an expanding lump. My secret had been exposed in the most callous way, stripping me defenseless and laying all of my lies out for him to see. Now I could do nothing more than offer the raw, hurtful truth.

I sniffled and managed to maintain eye contact as I whispered, "Yes, it's true."

He stood speechless for a strained beat. "How long have you known?"

"Only a few days."

He flinched. "How far along are you?"

"The doctor estimates fourteen to sixteen weeks."

"Sixteen weeks." Calculations flashed behind his eyes. He breathed a bitter laugh. "When were you planning to tell me?"

"I don't know." Making myself smaller in the chair, I lowered my voice. "I was afraid to."

Wincing, he closed his eyes. Tension built in his limbs and in his jaw.

**He doesn't want this. He's going to leave you.**

Humiliation transformed to desperation, and I burst to my feet. "I'm sorry to have to deliver such devastating news. I am. I really am." I began pacing in the center of the room, one hand absently cradling my stomach. "I know it's not what you wanted. I tried to respect your wishes. I did everything I knew to do to keep this from happening, but I failed you."

*I can't lose him. I can't. I have to make this right.*

Words streamed from my mouth, growing more frantic with each step. "I'll shoulder this burden myself. Emily can help me—and our mothers. I won't ask anything of you. I promise. It will be like this child doesn't exist. Just don't leave. Please don't leave—"

"Is that the kind of man you think I am?"

His whisper halted me in my path. I gaped at him through swollen tears. "What?"

Expression a mixture of hurt and confusion, he shook his head slowly. "You think I would abandon you and our child so hastily at the first sign of adversity?"

*Our child. He called it our child.*

Trembling, I swiped at my sodden cheeks and tried to level my tone. "But . . . but you told me you didn't want a child. You told me you weren't ready . . . that you were afraid."

His jaw muscles pulsed as he crossed the distance between us and grasped my shoulders tightly—almost too tightly. "I'm scared out of my wits, Al." His voice barely croaked out. "Were it up to me, we would have waited several more years at least." A rim of moisture glistened over his lower lids. "But it appears God had other plans. Who am I to argue with that?"

He looked down, and with measured, hesitant movements, he lowered one hand and pressed it to my stomach. Though minimized by my corset, the gentle bump fit perfectly under his palm. He sucked in a small breath and met my eyes again, awe glimmering behind his building tears.

I covered his hand with mine, still awash in guilt. "I'm sorry I kept this from you. I wanted so badly to tell you, but I . . . I thought . . ."

"You thought I would leave you." He cringed, and his other hand came up to cradle my cheek. "I'm so sorry if I made you believe that." He locked his gaze to mine. "I don't think I'll ever be ready for this, Al, but I'm not going anywhere. It would take an act of God or death itself to keep me from raising this child with you."

A sob ripped from my lips as I threw my arms around his torso. He returned the embrace and clutched me tight to him, bending his face against my neck and holding me as I cried. His words and his touch mended my heart, healing the resentment that had been devouring me from the inside.

After I finally quieted, he pushed me back slightly, grasped my hips with both hands, and dropped to one knee. "I love you already, little one," he whispered and pressed a delicate kiss to my abdomen.

The fluttering sensations within me intensified and sent elation spiraling through me. I beamed, blinking through a fresh round of tears—those blasted tears—and combed my fingers through his hair. "I think she heard you."

"She?" He raised an eyebrow. "What happened to the strong sons you wanted?"

"Sons will come in due time." I rocked my head side to side. "I think a daughter is what your heart needs right now."

"Oh, is that so?"

"I'm sure of it." Snagging a gentle fistful of his hair, I tilted his head back. "What about a kiss for her mother?"

He grinned and popped to his feet. Then his arms came around me again and his mouth covered mine. His kiss now was different than all his kisses before—transformed into something bold and commanding and determined. Warmth bloomed from my core as I weakened in his hold and shivered at the increasing pressure of his lips. His hands fastened at the small of my back and pulled us together, holding our bodies against one another and tucking our child in the safest place she could ever be—right between us.

"You know," he murmured against my lips, "I also hope for a girl."

"Oh?"

"Mm-hmm." He drew back, and his grin widened. "Because if it *is* a girl, then you're about to get a taste of everything I've endured all these years, and I wouldn't miss that head-to-head for the world."

My mouth dropped open. "You cad!" I knocked his hands away and swatted his chest. "Take that back right now."

Laughing, he dodged my barrage. "It's true and you know it. Any daughter we have is going to reflect you inside and out." He managed to steal behind me and capture me in his arms, pinning mine to my chest.

I craned my neck to shoot him a defiant look. "If that's true, then you're about to become outmatched—two against one. How do you like that?"

He planted a firm kiss to my lips. "I welcome the challenge."

Smirking, I twisted in his arms and nuzzled deep into his embrace. His heart tapped confidently against my ear. With how adamantly he fought against the idea of a child, I never thought I'd ever see him change his mind. So, for the first time since discovering I was expecting, I allowed joy to douse me entirely, and the matching joy I felt radiating from Baze made my own all the more complete. I wasn't alone. We would do this together.

Trepidation tainted my joy a touch. Before we could bring a child into this world, we needed to ensure the world she was about to enter was safe—which meant stopping Shay.

I stiffened. "Baze?"

"I know." His arms tightened, nearly crushing my lungs. "We'll get through this, Al. So long as I draw breath, I will make sure we get through this."

# Chapter Thirty

AFTER THE SETBACK AT POULNABRONE, KATE had conjured a vision that led them to the tree-dotted knolls of Ticknock Forest at the base of the mountains just south of Dublin. Finn sat still with his hands on the wheel of the car, his gaze fixed on the crude thatched roofs jutting between the rocky hills straight ahead. Smoke writhed from the chimneys and signaled people were home, but he had parked far enough away—and partially beyond a bend in the road—so the inhabitants wouldn't notice them.

Though Finn couldn't see him, the shadows thrashing at the gated entrance all but shouted Shay's presence. If the kidnappers had retreated here with their tails between their legs, then that meant Basil Allan was with Shay now, which complicated the matter of his recovery.

Numbness prickled Finn's fingers as he throttled the wheel. Could he really go through with this? Could he risk his own life to save Basil Allan's? The boy wasn't even his, yet he was about to walk willingly into the enemy's lair—an enemy who had once stamped out Finn's free will and was salivating for the chance to do so again.

*If you go to him, he will break you.*

"Finn?" Emily whispered. "Are you all right?"

The sweet sound of her voice sent his fear scrambling away. He rotated toward her and cast a glance at Katherine leaning forward from the back seat. "Listen close. I'm only goin' to say this once, and you're not allowed to argue. I'm goin' in alone."

Emily stiffened. "But—"

"No." He lifted a finger to silence her, hating his forceful tone. "I'm the only one who can convince Shay to let your little man go."

Kate bristled. "What about me? I can be quite convincing."

Finn shook his head. "It wouldn't be wise to reveal yourself to him. Not yet anyway. He still thinks you're dead, and I want him to keep thinkin' that. His ignorance could give us the upper hand in the comin' battle in Dublin."

Her shoulder came up with a sniff, but her set expression and distant gaze suggested she saw the sense in his proposition.

Firming his jaw, Finn glanced at Emily, noting the worried curve of her brow. He let his bravado fall slightly and scooped up one of her hands. "I can get through to him," he said, low and direct. "He broke me once, but I escaped. I'm free now, so I've got the power to resist him, as you said, and maybe even to turn him." The words tasted bitter on his tongue. He wasn't sure he truly believed them—but he knew the effect they would have on Emily.

As expected, her face brightened in timid hope, so he continued threading the needle of persuasion. "There's not a bone in Shay's body that would condone the hurtin' of a child. I promised you that, and I hold to it. So if he's seen what those men did to the lad, his resolve may be falterin'. I can use that to appeal to whatever humanity he's got left, and as his son in everything but blood, I believe he'll listen to me and let your boy go."

Emily tilted her head, lashes fluttering with retained tears as she cupped her free hand against the side of his face. His skin prickled beneath her touch, sending heat through his neck and spilling into his chest. Were Katherine not sitting there watching, he would have responded to Emily's affection, would have brushed a thumb over her soft, parted lips, perhaps would have leaned in—

"If you walk with the Almighty at your side, you are capable of that and more." Those beautiful lips lit a spark of renewal in his soul and then stretched into an encouraging smile. She stroked his cheekbone, leaving a trail of embers on his skin. "I know you have doubts," she whispered. "I know you believe your faith too small for the trials we face, but hear me when I say, even the tiniest seed of faith can move mountains." Her eyes sparkled, so dazzling and so hopeful. "You'll bring my son back to me. I believe it with all my heart, and you should too."

Conviction hammered his chest. In the face of such great danger, how was her faith so strong? So sure? Did she not suffer from the same tormenting voices of doubt as he did? Her son could die—her husband already had. Yet, she didn't waver, her confidence in this unseen Creator so steadfast that she was willing to entrust her son's life to a broken Irishman plagued by despair. How had she achieved such faith?

And was it possible for Finn to ever achieve the same?

With gratitude clenching his muscles, he lifted her hand and kissed her silky skin. "You're a true blessin', Emily Bennett," he murmured against her knuckles, keeping his gaze locked with hers. He slotted two fingers into his sleeve and yanked out a single flower, identical to the one he had gifted her so many years ago when they parted in England.

A delighted chirp sounded in her throat as she grasped it and buried her nose into its red petals, inhaling deeply. Her eyes twinkled. "Do you always keep flowers tucked away in your sleeves for moments such as this?"

He allowed a grin to tug the corner of his mouth. "You've found me out, it seems."

Katherine's head came poking over the front seat, one brow raised. "What about the woman who fed you as a wee babe? What do I get?"

Finn exhaled an awkward chuckle. "I was far from a babe."

"Teenager. Babe. It makes no difference to a mother." She reached over the seat, pulled his head toward her, and planted a solid kiss to his cheek. Then she angled her face toward his ear and whispered, "Just do what your woman has said, now, and keep Sully out of your mind, because if you don't come back, I shall have to retrieve you myself."

As she pulled away, he sent her a stern look, but her eyes sparked with the same intensity, so he let his arguments die on his tongue. Then, with the goodbyes fully exchanged, Finn left the car—and the two women he loved—behind.

Frigid air tingled the tips of his fingers and sent numbness lacing up his arms as he marched around the bend and toward the cluster of homes. A sagging stone fence surrounded the perimeter, weaving in and out of the hills but keeping the houses tucked safely inside. Near the middle of the fence, a rickety wooden gate was latched—but not locked. Finn lifted the bolt and passed through with ease.

There were families here. Women and children. They bustled about as though serving as part of a fully functioning village—hauling the wash, herding sheep, chopping wood. To his right, a door swung open, and a man stomped out. He paused near a younger woman with a baby swaddled against her back, then stroked the infant's head and gave the woman a kiss.

Finn narrowed his eyes but kept walking. These must be the families of the men under Shay's control. Were the minds of their wives trapped as well, or had Shay simply fooled them into believing this harmony was real?

Following the trail of ice weaving through the village, Finn set his sights on the home directly in the center of the settlement—a suitable location for an egocentric man who liked to rule over lesser folk.

His calves aching from the climb, Finn crested the hill and mounted the crumbled stone step leading up to the home's worn wooden door. His consciousness bucked in warning, squeezing his stomach and heightening his blood pressure, but it couldn't prevent him from raising his hand and knocking.

*God, if you're listenin', be with me.*

The lock clicked. The door shuddered and swung back.

Shay stood framed by a soft glow of candlelight. His relaxed features yielded barely a tinge of surprise—he had likely predicted Finn would seek him out. Raising expectant eyebrows, he stepped back and held the door wide. "Good to see you again, *a mhic.*"

Finn held his breath as he passed into the one-room cottage. Shay kept a tidy, austere home, with only the cooking essentials stacked neatly on the countertops lining the back wall. A tattered quilt topped the single bed against the left-hand wall, and a small round table framed by two chairs occupied the middle of the space with the candle flickering on top.

But it was the boy sitting in one of those chairs who arrested Finn's attention.

Basil Allan swung his legs as he drew on a piece of paper and sucked on a peppermint stick. The lad looked Finn's way, and his little eyes brightened. He popped the peppermint out of his mouth and lifted a bandaged hand. "Look."

Keeping Shay in his periphery, Finn edged to the child's side and squatted. "What's happened to you now?" But even as he asked the question, his stomach soured.

"Owie," Basil Allan said and wiggled his hand. Though, from the lightness in his voice and calm expression on his face, he didn't appear to be in pain.

Finn forced a cheery smile and ruffled the boy's hair. "You're a brave lad, you know that?"

Basil Allan bobbed his head, stuck the peppermint back in his mouth, and returned to his drawing, what looked to be a crude sketch of a woman and young child.

"For a lad of his age, he's incredibly well behaved." Shay's quiet voice oozed through the stillness. "His mother has done a fine job with him."

"Until you interfered, that is." Finn curled his lip as he stood and faced the older man.

Shay lingered near the now-closed door, his flat cap casting shadows over his eyes, his hands hanging jadedly in his trouser pockets. He tilted his head. "Why have you come?"

"I came to take the lad back to his mother." Every ounce of strength within Finn went to keeping his legs steeled, stopping him from lunging straight for the man's neck.

Shay's mouth pursed with the hint of a grin. "He'll not be goin' anywhere."

"If he stays with you, he's in danger of further injury." Finn jabbed an accusing finger at the lad. "Just look at what you've done to him already."

"'Twasn't me who did it." Shay's voice sounded taut, but he maintained a look of indifference.

"But it was your men. Actin' under your influence. So that makes you guilty of inflictin' the blow. And they could have done much worse." Finn bared his teeth. "What if they had killed him? If we hadn't caught up to them, they might have done it. Is that what you're wantin'? The blood of children on your—"

"I see what you're doin', Finn, and it's not goin' to work."

"It's already workin'." Finn studied the man he had once loved as a father, the man he had once aspired to emulate. That man used to keep his emotions tight to his chest, but hesitancy weighed visibly on him now. Finn lowered his voice. "I can see it in your eyes. I can see it in your posture. Guilt is eatin' you alive. If you keep the boy, it's goin' to consume you."

"Very well. If you desire to take him so badly, then I'm willin' to strike a deal."

The shift from defensiveness to compliance occurred so quickly that Finn stood staring for a long moment. A chill gripped his spine as Shay's words sank in. He swallowed, apprehensive. "What kind of deal?"

Shay ambled toward Finn, his soles clicking on the wooden floor. "I asked you to join me when we met in Dublin, but now I raise my offer." He stopped a hair's breadth away and angled his face toward Finn's. "Surrender your mind to me. Fully. Do that, and I'll let the lad go."

An invisible fist clenched Finn's chest. He gasped as wicked whispers shrouded his mind, poking and digging and sending jolts of pain through him.

The first time Shay overwhelmed him at Poulnabrone, Finn had felt only one emotion within the emptiness—grief. That Shay was willing to abuse his son so mercilessly had taken everything Finn knew about love and fractured it. Did Shay ever care for him, or had that been an empty smokescreen like one of his blasted magic tricks?

***He never loved you. Because you are unlovable. So you may as well give in.***

Despite the barrage of attacks and tormenting voices, Finn managed to keep his defenses intact. "How do I know you're not lyin'?" he said through gritted teeth. "How do I know you won't just keep the lad once I'm at your mercy?"

"I've done many things, but breakin' me word is not one of them." Shay's shoulders stiffened. "I swear it upon Kate's grave. If you give yourself to me, I'll let him go."

***You'll never be able to convince him otherwise. It's the only way.***

Pain lanced Finn's head as the stabs sharpened and multiplied. Still, he held on.

What if this *was* the only way to save Basil Allan? Shay clearly wasn't going to be swayed by his guilty conscience, so what else was Finn to do? Emily believed in him. He couldn't let her down, couldn't let her faith be tainted, even if it meant giving himself over to the enemy.

*God, I don't see another way. If you're there, show me what to do.*

***It's too late. God can't save you. Your faith is too weak.***

Trembling, Finn tried to cling to the light, but the pain nearly blinded him, the dissenting voices now deafening. A shaky groan siphoned through his lips as the voices battered him, beat him, and—if only to make the torment stop—he loosened his grip on hope.

An opening in his fortifications formed.

Shay sniffed it out and attacked.

Bright light exploded. Then all-consuming darkness. Ice-cold drenched him. Paralysis cemented every muscle and bone in place. The attack ripped and wrenched at the remaining barriers of his mind, seeking to grind it all into dust.

*I'm sorry, God. My faith was too weak . . . so weak.*

The last remnant of his free will quivered on its knees. The demons descended.

Then a gentle voice hushed the noise.

*"Your faith is more than enough, for with faith as small as a mustard seed, you can tell mountains to move, and they'll move. You can tell darkness to flee, and it will flee. Nothing is impossible for you, Finn. Not through me."*

Warmth bloomed across his body, breathing life into his petrified limbs and forcing air into his tremoring lungs.

Shay's blow came down, intent, ferocious—ready to kill.

*Stop, you can't have me!*

A shield sprang into place. The darkness struck, but the barrier resisted. Light bled through.

*Click.*

The faint sound came from somewhere far in the distance. Or maybe it was close. Finn tried to pinpoint the origin, but the unyielding darkness kept his attention rapt. Just as his curiosity peaked, a soft but firm voice sliced through his supernatural battle.

"Let him go, Sully."

Finn gasped. *Kate. No . . . you were supposed to stay hidden.*

The pressure on Finn's mind snapped like the cutting of a taut cord. Sensations flooded back, and the floor rushed up to meet him. He struck. His hip and elbow smarted as he struggled to his hands and knees. Then he lifted his head and gaped at Kate's form in the doorway.

"This is a trick," Shay snarled. He grasped Finn's shirt with a shaky hand and yanked him to his feet, then jostled him. "You did somethin' to me. You're makin' me see this. When did you learn that power? When—"

"It's not a trick." Kate glided into the room and speared Finn with her emerald eyes. "Take Basil Allan and return him to Emily. Then go back to Dublin as quickly as you can. Baze and Adelynn will need you."

Finn shoved away from Shay, glancing warily between his parents as his chest heaved. "But what about—"

"Do as I say."

Still unconvinced, Finn studied Shay. For the moment, the man seemed restrained, his legs rooted to the spot and his stunned gaze locked on Kate.

She smiled faintly. "Everything will be all right, little dove." Tense reassurance coated her tone. "Trust me."

A fire lit in Finn's belly. He twisted and lunged toward Basil Allan. The boy protested as he snatched him up and clasped him tight to his chest. With his heart in his throat, Finn darted past Shay and Kate. Out the door. Across the village. Through the gate.

When the car holding Emily came into view at the base of the hill, Finn allowed every last drop of fear to drain from his bones as he finally surrendered to hope.

From the moment Emily lost sight of Finn over the peak of the hill to when Katherine said she felt Shay's power heightening and decided to intervene, Emily never stopped praying. She sat with her head bowed and hands folded, bending forward as far as her corset would allow. Unintelligible whispers streamed from her lips. She didn't know what exactly she was saying. Not that she needed to. The Almighty knew everything that poured from her heart, and that was all that mattered.

*Lift your eyes, child.*

Emily wiggled her toes, then her fingers, coaxing sensation back into her limbs, before emerging from her tranquil meditation. She lifted her head, slid her eyelids open, and peered through the windscreen.

In the distance, a figure careened down the hill. As it drew closer, shaggy curls gave Finn away. He held something in his arms.

Emily squinted, trying to identify it. Then she cried out.

She thrust the door open and leaped through. Scrambling for balance, she sprinted toward them. Tears came swift and strong. When they were twenty paces away, the protesting bundle kicked and squirmed in Finn's arms. He stuttered to a stop and placed the child's feet upon the ground.

"Mama!" Basil Allan's pudgy face flushed as he scampered toward her, arms outstretched.

Not breaking stride, Emily stooped low, swept him up, and squeezed. She spun them, and he clung to her with unbreakable strength. Laughs punctuated her sobs as she nuzzled his head, rubbed his back, inhaled his smell. He was here. He was alive. Gratitude inflated her chest. A mighty river of *thank you, thank you, thank you* gushed through her mind.

Blinking tears from her eyes, she searched for Finn. He had collapsed to his knees, back hunched and hands covering his face. A posture of submission. A posture of faith. She staggered over to him and knelt. With Basil Allan clutched to one side, she secured a comforting hand around Finn's neck, pulled him into her shoulder, and leaned her cheek against his soft curls. She soaked up every bit of the love and warmth and relief flowing from Finn and Basil Allan.

They were safe. Her boys were safe. Both in body and in soul.

# Chapter Thirty-One

*K*ATE WAS DEAD. *S*HE HAD GULPED *the entire cup of poison down her gullet all in one go. I'd tasted it coating her lips. So how was it that she stood before me now? How did that fire in her eyes burn so much brighter than before?*

*Hand inching toward a knife on the table beside me, I locked my gaze on her. "You're a phantom," I breathed. "A trick of me mind."*

*"Oh, Sully." Her voice—sultry whether she tried to make it so or not—sent tingles down my spine and raised the hair on my forearms. "If anyone can tell a vision from reality, it's you."*

*"Then how is this possible?"*

*Her right shoulder came up in a lopsided shrug—simply another mannerism that confirmed her identity. "You fled the scene before I had expired, assuming I was already beaten. Or perhaps you simply couldn't bear to watch me die." Her mouth tightened in sympathy. "That allowed me to seek help. A swig of ipecac did the trick to rid my body of your poison."*

*Throat tightening, I wrapped my fingers around the hilt of the knife, maneuvered my arm, and concealed it at the small of my back. "Why did you return then? You were free. I believed you dead. You could have slipped away to live the rest of your days in peace."*

*Kate's steely exterior shed a layer of its shell to reveal the empathy underneath. She shortened the distance between us, her alluring hips swaying as she stepped around a chair. She stopped close enough for her floral fragrance to tickle my nose and arrest my senses. 'Twould only take one reach and then I would have her in my arms again, but I resisted the impulse and gripped the knife harder.*

*"I came back for you," she whispered, and my gaze dragged from her soft green eyes to her equally soft lips.*

*"Not for the people, eh?" I snorted and wrestled against a smirk. "How selfish of you."*

*Her grave expression remained steady. "What you did to that boy . . . That's not who you are. You've allowed this power to warp you into something evil."*

*"This is who I am, Kate. It is who I've always been."*

*"No. I don't believe that for a moment." She slipped her hand over my chest, and my heart hammered against my ribs as though trying to kiss her palm. Heat thickened between us. "You used to be kind. Courageous. Sarcastic." Her eyes lightened as she flashed a brief, sad smile. "You fought honorably for those in need, and the love you held for our boys rivaled no other. The great enemy of this world is cunning and deceptive. He has convinced you that manipulation and violence is your only path forward, but just like those you control, you are nothing more than a pawn."*

*I scowled. "Everythin' I do is by my will and my will alone."*

*"The darkness has infected your soul to the point that you cannot discern truth from falsehood." Shaking her head, she stepped closer, her scent dizzying my mind. "Will you do something for me, Sully?" she murmured. "Will you open your heart? Allow the light to stream through. Perhaps if you let God peel the scales from your eyes—if only a little bit—you may yet have a chance to escape. Before you are completely consumed."*

*At the Almighty's name, a painful shock burst from her fingers and sent a jolt through my body. I nearly recoiled, her hand burning against my chest as though on fire, but my longing for her touch forced me to endure the agony.*

*"It's too late." Slick with sweat, the knife hilt shifted in my hand. "Truth or no truth, my plan is already in motion. I can't stop it."*

*"Can't?" Sparkling in the candlelight, her deep green eyes searched mine. "Or won't?"*

*Now it was my turn to shake my head, if only to deflect her words and keep them from altering my thoughts, from penetrating my soul. I didn't fear that she would break through the iron defenses I had formed through years of honing my gift . . . but something didn't feel right. Something prickled deep in my chest—gentle, insistent, and warm.*

*Hope?*

*No, it was pointless. I was beyond redemption.*

*"Don't waste your energy on me, Kate," I whispered through my teeth. "The man you knew is gone, and he won't be comin' back."*

*"I believe that man can be saved." Her eyes hardened with tenacity. "And I am going to drag him out piece by piece or, God help me, I'll die trying."*

*Kate's fingers grappled for my shirt and jerked me toward her. Caught off guard, I stumbled straight into her kiss. Her other hand came up around my neck, and her silky lips took mine under their command.*

*After a mere flicker of hesitation, I relented and molded my mouth to hers. I reclaimed control, working her jaw, sinking deeper into her. A moan rumbled in her throat as I pulled her body flush with mine. I dragged my hand up her spine and cradled her neck, smooth and completely at my mercy.*

*Hunger awakened in me—a hunger rivaling the one that consumed me after we reunited in Bath. I desired her with my entire being, and it was a desire that nearly overpowered my resolve. If I opened my heart as she asked, then I could have her. We could renew our marriage vows and retire into the countryside, perhaps even establish an orphanage of our own. Why shouldn't I allow her to pull me from the depths and set me on the straight path? Maybe there really was another way to achieve my goal. Maybe there was hope.*

**Stop! She is the enemy. She is poisoning your mind. You must stop her!**

*A shock lanced through my limbs, and a gasp jerked from my mouth and wrested our lips apart. As though moving of its own accord, my hand leaped from her neck to her hair, snagging in her flaming tresses and yanking her head back to expose her throat. I whipped out the knife and thrust it against her soft flesh.*

*Nary an ounce of fear distorted her face as she clamped her mouth shut and peered at me through her thick lashes. "Very well," she bit out. "If you won't change for me, then change for Ezekiel."*

*Images of blood and green rushed to mind as the name awakened a memory I'd long tried to kill. Ezekiel. The optimistic young urchin we'd stumbled upon at that orphanage near Doolin. He'd been so bright. Just a few years younger than Finn. The boys had gotten on well. Enough that Kate and I had planned to make him our third adoptee. Until he was slain.*

*Witnesses had said they saw the orphan keeper beating another boy when Ezekiel jumped between them to defend his friend—and the noble act had claimed his life. I'd carried his broken body out of the town and buried him under a fairy tree in hopes that the* aos sí *would watch over him in the afterlife—then I returned to dispose of his murderer.*

*"You want me to die like Ezekiel?" I yanked harder on Kate's hair.*

*She grunted. "I want you to live like Ezekiel."*

*The blow landed right in my gut. I let go of her, my hands hovering in midair as she backed out of my reach. My insides churned. "Get out," I growled. "Leave me."*

*She gingerly massaged her throat. "You pursued me once, back when we were so young and naïve and in love. You traveled all the way to England merely to ask for my hand, remember?" Her inner flame burned white-hot, sizzling against the ice in my heart. "Now it's my turn to pursue you."*

## Chapter Thirty-Two

With the sun setting on Easter Sunday, the tension grew with every passing second. I felt it emanating from Baze as he and Collin studied a map of Dublin Castle together in the sitting room and I paced nearby. They circled points of interest and outlined potential paths of entry, speaking in hushed tones but not so quiet as to exclude me from the discussion.

"That's all well and good," I said as they drew yet another route, "but what if the fighting starts before you get there? What then?"

Rather than answer, Baze brightened and stood. "That reminds me," he muttered and rushed from the room, then returned quickly with a pistol in his hand. He grabbed the barrel and extended the hand grip to Collin. "Here. You'll need this. Do you know how to use it?"

Collin stared at it, then shook his head. "I have my baton."

"Your baton won't be enough. You'll need this for long-distance protection."

Collin's bottom lip worked in thought, but then he shook his head again. "All due respect, but I don't want to be responsible for killin' anyone."

Baze scowled. "There are going to be hundreds of men out there with guns who won't hesitate to kill *you*. You need some way to defend yourself."

"No. I can manage."

My mouth grew dry. I commended Collin's resolve and commitment to his morals, but Baze was right. What could a baton do against a gun? Could Baze defend them both if the situation turned violent?

A knock at the front door arrested Baze's attention. With a frustrated huff, he tucked the pistol in his belt and trudged to the foyer. I followed silently and peeked around the corner as he cracked the door, then swung it wide. The darkened new moon bathed the front steps in shadows, but I could just make out Darragh's frizzed red-and-white hair.

The superintendent flashed a pinched smile as Baze invited him inside. "I don't have much news to report, boyo, but I wanted to give you a touch of encouragement before you charge in." He tipped his head my way. "Good to see you, Mrs. Ford."

When we entered the sitting room, Darragh greeted Collin and swept his gaze over the open map with a nod. Then he targeted all of us in turn with a ponderous stare. "I raised the tip to me superiors, but it seems without sufficient evidence, the Lord Lieutenant is keen to remain where he is. You won't, however, be alone." He pointed to the map, tapping a finger over a gate in the perimeter around Dublin Castle. "I'll have a man guarding Cork Hill Gate. He's been informed of your arrival—and the potential of a skirmish. He'll be waitin' to allow you passage inside." Darragh dragged his finger across the courtyard to a formal entrance. "Make your way here. It's the way into the state apartments where the Lord Lieutenant lives. If you run into the British Army, tell them I sent you. They'll be able to take you to the Lord Lieutenant." His eyes twinkled. "You don't work for me, so if you must use . . . *creative* methods to get him to leave, I can't stop you." He released a rumbling sigh. "I'm sorry I can't do more, boyo, but me hands are tied."

"No, this is enough. Thank you," Baze said, voice optimistic but weary.

I traced the route, mulling over the situation. The addition of direct access to the castle exponentially increased their odds of success, especially if they could rise early enough to reach the castle before any fighting broke out.

Darragh suddenly straightened, head cocked, and gaze targeted on the wall in the direction of the front drive. "Do you hear that?"

We stilled and quieted, listening. Indeed, faint shuffling echoed through the halls of the house, and sounded to be originating from the drive outside.

Metal clinked and shoes clipped as Baze, Darragh, and Collin sprang to attention, hunkering and waving each other through the doors like a well-oiled machine.

"Al, stay here," Baze murmured as he skirted by, hand on the gun at his belt.

I nodded as curiosity gnawed at me. The shuffling sounds continued, followed by the click of a door. Then a familiar sound reached my ears.

A toddler's babbling.

I let out a gasp and sprang forward. Baze shouted my name as I shouldered through them and skidded to a halt in the foyer—just as Finn and Emily emerged through the door, Basil Allan cradled protectively in Emily's arms.

Tears came easy as I hugged her, flattening the child between us. We laughed. We cried. Basil Allan protested and tried to push me away, but I just smiled and sprinkled his little face with kisses.

When I'd effectively peppered every inch of him with affection, I subjected Finn to a crushing embrace, and he returned its intensity tenfold. As he pulled back and accepted a hearty handshake from Baze, I clamped onto Emily again.

Basil Allan suddenly spotted Baze. Bloated tears pooled in his eyes as he thrust out his arms. "Bay-Bay!"

Fatherly pride flushed Baze's face as he took the child from his mother and held him tight, the muscles in his arms flexing rigid and resolute.

As I absorbed the chaos—the smiles of delight, the exchanged handshakes, the comments of relief—I noticed a glaring absence. My stomach dropped. "Where's Katherine?"

Finn's smile faded. "She chose to stay with Shay."

Exasperation, not worry, barreled through me. I suppressed a groan. Katherine—always bullheaded. Always rash. Much like me, I supposed. Were I in her position, I likely would have done the same.

"That's not all," Finn said quietly. "We tried to reach Basil Allan as quickly as we could, but those men—"

"Bay-Bay, look." Basil Allan's squeaky voice drew our attention as he waved a bandaged hand in Baze's face.

Baze took hold of it, turning it slightly to get a better view and allowing me a glimpse of red staining the white dressing. His shoulders stiffened, and his gaze snapped to Finn.

Finn nodded. "They removed his little finger."

Eerie calm befell Baze's features, but a fire ignited in his eyes as he clutched the child tighter.

Darragh clapped Baze on the shoulder as he leaned toward Basil Allan. "Don't be worryin'. The shock'll wear off. So long as he's alive, a wee bit o' damage is manageable. A man can live quite productively without his digits." He held up his hand, revealing his finger stubs to the child. "Lookie here, little man. Not so bad, is it?"

Eyes wide, Basil Allan poked and pinched the twisted, scarred tissue.

Collin peeked around Darragh, his brow crinkled as he stared at Basil Allan's injury. "Did my brother do that?"

Finn shook his head. "Your brother was one of the men who took him, aye, but it's impossible to know who inflicted the wound."

"Wait, so . . . if the child is here, that means you had to've seen Liam." Collin's tone rose with hope. "What happened? You didn't hurt him, did you? Did he return to Mr. O'Sullivan?"

Remorse flickered across Finn's face, but his mouth stayed pinned shut.

I grappled for words so that I might interject—the vision of Liam Donoghue's abrupt death vivid in my mind—but what could I say? Liam had been the only family Collin had left.

"Finn," Baze spoke low and calm, an undercurrent of anger in his voice. "I'd like to have a word in private please. We can go to the study." He handed the toddler back to his mother, then squeezed Collin's shoulder. "Give us a moment. I have some other details to inquire about. Then we'll talk about your brother."

Collin tensed, but Darragh prodded his arm. "Come on, boyo. Let 'em have a chance to breathe. They've had a rough day of it."

As Finn trailed Baze into the hall and the others retreated through the opposite passageway, I ushered Emily into the sitting room and pulled her down onto the sofa. Now away from the commotion, Emily heaved a large sigh and sank into the cushion, and Basil Allan snuggled against her chest. Tension drained from her features, and with it, she let loose the harrowing account of his rescue.

I sat quietly, rapt, as she explained every detail—the notes, the ancient sites, the threats, the confrontation at Shay's village.

And when she reached the end, a faint smiled teased her lips as she stroked her son's hair. "I know this may sound odd, but I never doubted that we would get him back," she said. "I was afraid, of course, but I always believed that God would keep him safe and deliver him to us."

My insides churned as I looked at Basil Allan's bandaged hand, trying to understand how allowing him to lose a finger was God's way of keeping him safe. If God had willed it, He could have kept him whole.

As though seeing my thoughts written on my face, Emily knit her brow. "What's on your mind, love?"

I huffed and folded my arms. "I admire your faith, Emily, but how do you not have doubts? After all that you have been through, you would be right to question God."

She laughed softly. "I question Him every day, but He's big enough to handle me. I only question Him because I'm not capable of fully understanding the plans He has for this world." Her brow crinkled further. "What I *do* know is that He desires to see us well, and when evil and injustice invade our lives, He grieves right along with us."

"Then why doesn't He stop it?"

Pensive, Emily patted Basil Allan's back. "He has already promised to take away our pain and cure our diseases and vanquish evil. But that time is not yet here. Until it comes, we must reside in this broken world, clinging to the knowledge that He is just and that He keeps every promise He makes."

Vision blurring, I blinked rapidly and tore my eyes away from Emily's kind but convicting gaze. A soft snore called my focus to Basil Allan, now asleep. Somehow, he had gotten his hand wrapped in the chain around her neck and now clutched his father's wedding band securely in his round fist. Evil had taken Bennett. Evil had taken Basil Allan's finger. Evil had taken my father. How much more would it take before the end . . . and would God intervene in any of it?

As I listened to Basil Allan's cute groans, I found my hand drifting to my stomach. I caught the slight raise of Emily's eyebrows and bristled, hesitating only a moment before realizing there was no more sense in maintaining my façade.

"I saw a doctor as you suggested," I mumbled, committing fully to the reveal and pressing both hands to my abdomen. "I'm with child."

Emily laughed, then clapped a hand over her mouth. Giggling quieter, she slid her fingers into my palm and squeezed. "Oh, Adelynn, of course you are."

I rolled my eyes. "If you wish to say, 'I told you so,' do it quickly."

"I would never tell you such a thing." Her mouth pulled into a cheeky grin. "Though, I *did* inform you of my suspicions quite some time ago."

Gaping, I yanked my hand from hers. "You scamp!"

She scrunched her nose and stuck out her tongue, then mellowed. "I'm delighted for you, my friend." She tilted her head, frowning slightly. "How did Baze take the news?"

Memories of our heated row followed by his sweet acceptance—eagerness even—lifted my spirits. "He was apprehensive, as would be expected, but his heart has softened." I chuckled, my stomach fluttering. "He may even be more excited than I am."

"I knew he would be." With a contented smile, Emily wound one of her son's feathery curls around her fingers. "To think, Basil Allan will soon have a close companion with whom to grow. Bennett always desired to raise his children next to Baze's." Mischievousness gleamed in her eyes. "And if you have a girl . . . well, just think of the possibilities."

I raised an eyebrow. "Planning your son's future already?"

She winked. "One can dream."

After closing the door to the study, Baze settled behind the desk, and Finn dropped into the seat opposite him. Swallowing, Baze tossed a glance at the whisky decanter beckoning him from the cabinet against the far wall. What he wouldn't give for a glass to take the edge off the emotions he was about to confront—but he knew himself. If he gave in to such a temptation in his current state, it would be too difficult to stop.

Redirecting his attention to Finn, Baze straightened his spine and took a deep breath. "Liam Donoghue and Arthur Fitzgerald are dead, aren't they?"

Finn's eyes widened a touch, then wilted in resignation. "They are. Adelynn saw it?"

"Yes."

"What happened to them? There were no bodies when we got there."

"O'Sullivan discovered what they did to Basil Allan and made Liam shoot Fitzgerald and then himself."

Color faded from Finn's skin. "The poor lads."

"Indeed." Baze forced the implications of Liam's death to roll off him—for now. "And you left Katherine behind?"

"She wanted to stay. She's determined to get through to him." Finn's shoulders sagged. "If she can't, I fear he'll actually kill her."

Baze clenched his jaw. When Finn and the others returned, he had hoped to add Katherine to their plan. She had the same abilities as Adelynn and could give the advantage of foresight to their strategy.

However, the fact she wasn't here didn't change Baze's original plan.

He leaned forward and folded his hands over the desk. "Finn, I need you to do something for me. I believe it's the most important task of this whole operation."

Curiosity lit Finn's face as he matched Baze's posture. "Name it."

"I need you to take Adelynn and Emily and flee. I don't care where you go. Just transport them as far away from Dublin as you can."

"I thought you'd have wanted Adelynn's help, considerin' her gift and all."

"Adelynn can't stay. She's with child." Emotion tightened Baze's throat as understanding stretched Finn's expression. "I realize it's late, but you should leave tonight. The rebels may erect barricades, and I don't want you trapped within the city." He cleared his throat, managing to choke out the rest of his words. "Can you do that for me?"

Finn sat in silence for a moment, grasping his hands between his kneecaps. Then he nodded. "I'll do it. I would lay down me very life to keep them from harm." His posture relaxed, but his eyes grew submissive as he searched Baze's gaze. "I'm in love with Emily, Baze. I was hopin', when all this is over, that I might court her . . . if you would allow it."

Baze stiffened but maintained his composure. The revelation wasn't unexpected, but hearing Finn say it aloud amassed every weapon of resistance in Baze. He didn't want to believe that it was possible for Emily to love anyone other than Bennett, not especially the man who was partially responsible for his death. How was this any different than when Israel's King David sent a man to his death on a battlefield in order to marry that man's wife?

Trying to tamp down his unease, Baze lifted his chin slightly. "I'm certain Bennett would have encouraged Emily to pursue that which brought her happiness, and if such a pursuit leads her to you, then I pray only for God's blessings upon you." He locked his gaze on Finn's, serious and unblinking. "However, if you hurt her, you will answer to me. Is that understood?"

Finn swallowed as the shine in his eyes hardened. "Emily is the most precious thing to me on this earth. If I hurt her, you may do with me what you will."

Baze nodded. "Then you have my blessing to proceed."

Finn's mouth tipped in a relieved smile. "Thank you, Baze."

"I don't want to hear another word of it." Baze gestured his chin toward the door. "You should go. Prepare for departure. And could you send Collin in, please?"

With a final nod of thanks, Finn quit the room.

Doused in silence, Baze wondered how best to break the news of Liam's demise to Collin and began preparing an explanation in his head. He stood and came around the desk, figuring it less intimidating to face the young man without an obstacle. If he could, he would have simply told Collin that Liam had fled, never to return, but that would be dishonest and unfair.

Collin arrived far quicker than Baze expected. He hurried up to Baze and stood at attention, one hand gripping the baton at his belt. His eyes sparked with anticipation. "Did Mr. Finn tell you about Liam? Does Mr. O'Sullivan still have him? I know we have the battle tomorrow, but after that, do you think we can go after him?"

Every rehearsed line abandoned Baze's brain, leaving only the cold, blunt truth.

"Liam's dead, Collin."

Somehow, a mere flicker of emotion transformed Collin's face from a confident constable into a timid teenager. Blood rushed across his face as his shoulders stiffened and his spine grew more erect. He opened his mouth, then closed it.

Finally, he asked, "How?"

"He was shot. O'Sullivan learned what he and Fitzgerald did to Basil Allan and killed them." It wasn't the whole truth, but Baze couldn't bring himself to reveal that Liam had inflicted his own fatal wound. "I'm sorry, Collin." Baze grabbed his shoulder with a firm, comforting hand. "I know what it's like to lose—"

"Don't." Collin jerked away and took two steps back. His chest heaved with mounting emotion, and Baze silently urged him to give in to it, knowing all too well the damaging nature of ignored pain.

"If we succeed tomorrow," Collin said, slow and methodical, "we'll kill O'Sullivan?" His eyes glistened—harsh, forlorn, and vengeful.

Baze lifted a pacifying hand. "Our objective is to stop him," he said, keeping his voice calm. "Whether we kill him or not will be determined by his actions."

Collin shifted his baton in its holster, his knuckles white. "Then we need to get back to work." He spun on his heel and marched toward the door.

Baze made to follow, reaching out his hand. "Wait, Collin—"

The door slammed.

## Chapter Thirty-Three

Evening faded into night as everyone gathered around the formal dining table, chairs pushed out toward the walls. Map upon map lay strewn across the surface, covered in pencil markings. Baze moved to each section of the city, highlighting the route they would take to get to the castle. From there, using Darragh's information, he explained how they would ferry the Lord Lieutenant from the hall, hopefully before Shay arrived.

I stood directly opposite Baze, listening and marveling at his confident authority as he took charge, but when he reached the end and hadn't yet mentioned my specific role, I spoke up. "What about me? Where am I to go?"

Wary eyes turned to Baze as he regarded me. "Finn is going to take you, Emily, and Basil Allan away from here. Somewhere you'll be safe."

I blinked. "What are you talking about? You need me."

"It's already been decided," Baze said, voice firm.

I glanced at the other men, silently petitioning for their support, but they averted their gazes. Jaw slack, I shook my head. "This is ridiculous. I can help you."

Baze pulled his shoulders back. "You're not staying, Adelynn. That's the end of it."

I flared my nostrils, biting my tongue to keep harsh words from spewing from my lips. Then I spun on my heel and stomped down the hall. Baze's uneven gait followed, gaining. I burst into our bedchamber and swung the door shut in his face. He grunted, caught it before it could latch, and pushed his way in.

Fury raced through me as I paced. "I can't believe you're thinking of sending me away."

"It's too dangerous."

"Then you shouldn't go either."

"Adelynn," he said, softer.

"How dare you do this to me." Hot tears spurted. "How dare you think separating us is the best course of action. I thought we were in this together. We vowed to remain by each other's side when we married. We promised."

"Al, this has nothing to do with our marriage vows."

I slashed a hand through the air. "I don't care what you say. I'm coming, and you can't—"

"Adelynn!"

Baze's sharp shout drew me up short. He closed his eyes and took a breath, hands pulsing into fists before finally relaxing. Then he approached and spoke gently. "I know you don't care about the risks. You're fearless. You're willing to rush into danger to protect others. That's one of the reasons I love you so much. But the decisions you make don't affect just you anymore." He pressed a hand over my stomach and lowered his tone. "Where you go, our baby goes."

A barrage of arguments filtered through me, but as I considered each one, I realized he was right. *I* could take the risk, but I couldn't put that risk on our child.

Blinking away tears, I fashioned a new appeal. "Then come with me. Don't go out there."

"Someone needs to lead them."

"But it doesn't have to be you."

He smiled faintly. "It's my duty to keep you and our child safe, and you won't be safe until O'Sullivan is gone." His voice cracked. "I have to do this, Al."

Anguish bubbled up, and the words I had been holding back from him for so long finally burst forth. "I saw you die." Sobs racked my body. "I saw you die in a vision. Back before all this started. I was afraid to tell you . . . because I didn't want it to happen. Please don't let it happen."

Expression calm despite my confession, Baze pulled me into his arms and cradled my head against his chest, shushing me gently.

I struck him with a weak fist, hiccupping cries. "If you go out there, you might never come back. Just like Bennett. I've seen the pain Emily carries every day having to live without him. I don't want to do that. I couldn't live without you."

"Oh, yes you could. You're a spitfire. Sometimes I wonder why you even keep me around." With a strained chuckle, Baze pushed me back, took a firm hold of my face, and brushed away my tears with his thumbs. "If you needed to . . . you could find someone else." His eyes reddened, glistened, and he paused a moment before continuing, quieter. "You've made me a father, Al, and if I have to die to ensure you can safely bring our child into this world, then so be it."

I grasped his wrists if only to keep my knees from buckling. Through my heartbreak, I managed to whisper, "I love you, Baze."

He bowed his forehead against mine. "I love you too."

The time for Adelynn's departure came far too quickly. Baze wished he could have held her tightly through the night, memorizing her, loving her, but their current situation robbed them of the opportunity. Now they stood in the drive with Finn, Emily, and Basil Allan, loading the car under the black, moonless sky. Every emotion tormented him as he thrust Adelynn's trunk into the boot.

As Finn and Emily settled into the front of the car, with Basil Allan curled up in his mother's lap, Baze opened the back door for Adelynn. "Be safe," he whispered. "Don't give Finn too much trouble."

With her mouth twisted into the defiant pout that he had come to know and love—and sometimes disdain—Adelynn took his face in her hands. "Come back to me, Basil Ford."

He couldn't help but crack a small smile. "Yes, dear."

She wiggled his head. "I mean it."

"I know you do." He pecked her lightly on the lips. "Go on."

She dropped her hands, turned to the car, and bent—then paused. Just as he was about to inquire what was wrong, she whirled back to him and lunged. He didn't hesitate, catching her in his embrace and returning her eager kiss. He glided a hand over her beautiful life-bearing hips and gave one final caress to their child growing within her.

And then she was gone.

Heart aching, he trekked inside the house. Collin bustled about silently, preparing to bunk down and await the onslaught of the morning. Darragh had already returned to the police station, unable to assist any further in their plot.

Baze threaded through the hall, choosing to retreat to the study rather than the bedchamber.

*"Come back to me."* Adelynn's words reverberated in his mind.

She knew he couldn't promise such a thing, especially considering it seemed the writing had finally been written on the wall for him. After all they'd endured, he was actually rather surprised she hadn't seen a vision of his death sooner.

A fall from a great height—not how he had pictured he would go. Dublin Castle was several stories high, so as long as he could avoid windows, he might make it out. After all, Katherine had once survived in defiance of Adelynn's visions. Why couldn't he?

Still, if his end was nigh, he wanted to leave nothing unfinished.

Baze sank into the plush chair behind the desk—Thomas Spencer hadn't spared on the comfort—and pulled the telephone to him. He grasped the receiver, positioned the mouthpiece close, and waited, hearing his pulse as loudly as though it were standing in front of him screaming.

Finally, wrangling the last obstinate strand of his bravery, he forced the receiver against his ear. "Alistair Ford, please."

It was late. Was his father even up at this hour? The man used to retire early in the evenings, intentionally removing himself from family conversation or games. Even on nights when Baze desired so strongly to engage in deep conversation—son to father—Alistair had chosen to retreat. His father hadn't been there for him then, so why did Baze suddenly believe he would be there for him now?

"Good evening. To whom am I speaking?"

Alistair's sharp voice came through so abruptly and so clearly that it rendered Baze speechless for a moment.

"Hello? Is anyone there?"

Baze swallowed, his fingers tightening around the receiver. "It's me."

Alistair sighed. "Ah. Basil. Do you realize the hour?"

"I do. I'm sorry if I woke you."

"No, it's all right. I was reading actually." A pause. "Is something the matter?"

A humorous smile tugged Baze's mouth. What *wasn't* the matter? He didn't have the time or the energy to explain everything, so he defaulted to small talk. "I'm in Ireland, you know."

"Yes, your mother mentioned that. Something about Thomas Spencer's old residence."

"Mrs. Spencer is planning to sell it, so we wanted to enjoy it before she does. The thought of losing it has been very hard on Adelynn."

"I imagine it would be."

The conversation lulled. By now, Baze could barely hear his father's voice above the thundering pulse in his ears. Heat rolled across his body as he wound the telephone cord around his finger, then unwound it, then wound it again. If he didn't speak now, he would likely never find the courage to do so.

"Listen, I have some things I need to say to you."

The single statement pulled the trigger. Now he only needed to follow through.

"They're things I've been wanting to say for a long time now."

Silence reigned on the other end.

"You weren't a good father." Baze's voice hitched, and he braced, expecting Alistair to erupt with a rebuttal, but the silence stretched on.

So he forged ahead. "You put all of the responsibility of carrying this family's name on me. From the moment I was born, that was all you saw me as, and it only grew worse as I aged." He stroked the bridge of his nose, still tender and slightly swollen. "When I was assaulted, rather than console me, you all but punished me, exiling me to the police as soon as you could. And . . . I resent you for that."

Nostrils flaring, Baze hooked his fingers under the mouthpiece and lurched from the chair. Sweat plastered his shirt to his back as he paced before the desk. Words that had once been difficult to form now came fast and strong. He almost forgot that Alistair listened on the other line and simply let it all out. "I know you grew up in poverty. I know you didn't have all the luxuries you've given my brothers and me. But what you don't understand is that none of that mattered to me. All I wanted was a relationship with you, but you were so focused on the next generation that you failed to consider the sons right in front of you." Baze rested his forearm atop the chair back, bowing his head. "I've been so terrified to become a father because I'm terrified that I would do to my children what you did to me."

The sound of a terse sigh buffeted the receiver on the other end, and when Alistair spoke, his voice was quiet. "I presume, then, that Adelynn is expecting?"

"Yes, and I want you to be in my child's life." The admission punched from Baze's lips before he had time to ponder it. Frustration clenched his jaw, and he fought with every ounce of self-control to keep his feelings in check. "I'm done letting you try to use me for your own gain. I'm your blasted son, and I want you in my life and in *my* son's life. I don't know what that looks like, but I do know that if we continue as we are, we'll drift further and further apart until we become strangers. That's why I'm calling . . . because I wanted to tell you—"

Baze bit down on the inside on his cheek, wrestling against the phrase he had refused to say—or rather, didn't have the humility to say. Blood tinged his tongue, and finally, he let go.

"I forgive you."

With those three simple words, all the tension he'd been holding dissipated. The ache in his temples lifted. The tight cord of resentment in his belly loosened.

Eyes and nose burning, Baze dropped is forehead against his arm, letting the mouthpiece dangle but keeping the receiver poised for him to hear a response. He waited. With each second that ticked by, his pulse slowed, his heart calmed, and peace overtook him. The hatred that had burned inside him tapered into embers, transforming deep hurt into a weak ache.

What seemed like minutes dragged by without a reply. Baze sighed. He had lobbed incredibly critical statements at Alistair, but he had hoped for at least *some* kind of response.

Baze pushed away from the chair and limped back to the front of it, trying not to let disappointment taint the healing that forgiveness had barely begun to work in him.

Just as he lowered the receiver, Alistair's voice trickled from it.

"Thank you."

Baze froze.

"I appreciate your sharing that with me. All of it." Alistair paused a few beats. "Please give Adelynn my congratulations. Despite your reservations, you have always been a nurturing soul, even when you were very little." A lightness bled into his tone. "You used to catch frogs to care for in the garden and nurse birds back to health after they'd flown into a window." He cleared his throat. "You will be a capable father. That, I have no doubt."

Baze gaped, stunned to silence.

"Thank you again for your candidness. I have . . . much to ponder it seems." Weariness weakened his tone. "I hope the remainder of your holiday is safe and enjoyable. Good night."

When the line clicked dead, Baze dropped the telephone onto the desk and sank into the chair, dazed. He had expected to bear the brunt of his father's wrath. Or at least denial. Anything but this. For so long, he had clung to a sliver of hope that he and his father might reconcile, but years of disappointment had ground it into dust. Yet, as Baze reminisced on his father's words, the cold ashes of hope in his soul began to warm.

Trembling, Baze bent forward and dropped his face into his hands, then shoved his fingers up into his hair. A rogue tear escaped and spilled down his cheek. On its way, it inflicted a fatal crack to the dam holding back years of Baze's neglected emotions.

The crack widened, splintered—and finally broke open.

# Chapter Thirty-Four

A PERSISTENT TANGLE OF TREPIDATION WRITHED within me as we fled the city. For the entire three-hour drive, I kept my hands folded over my stomach, my forehead tilted against the window, and my unfocused gaze lost in the shadowed landscape rushing by.

When we arrived in Liscannor—or at least Finn said it was Liscannor, but it was far too dark outside to see much of anything—Emily coaxed me from the car and into a small thatched cottage. Finn stoked a warm fire to life in a plain hearth as Emily ushered me into the bedroom, out of my dress, and into the bed. She soon joined and tucked Basil Allan between us.

Sleep claimed me the moment my head sank into the pillow, but rather than offer temporary relief from my worry, the realm of the unconscious grabbed ahold of my fears and amplified them. Nightmares pursued me, paralyzed me, and forced me to endure the vision of Baze's death over and over again.

***You can't save him. Give in to despair.***

I watched Baze disappear over the edge once more and opened my mouth to scream—but no sound came out. Anguish crushed my chest, and I loosened my grasp on hope. For if Baze's death was inevitable, why hold on?

***That's it. Come deeper.***

I gasped. My eyes flew open and fixed upon the ceiling above. Though I was awake in mind, my body remained dormant. I tried to wiggle my fingers, tried to sit up—anything—but something held me immobile. A suffocating weight compressed my chest, pushing me deep into the mattress, trapping my breath. From the corner of my eye, I glimpsed a figure with a top hat and oily raven hair hovering in the open doorway. His grin flashed white through the darkness, his glacial eyes trapping me in their alluring snare. Then his echoing laugh chilled my bones.

Panic set in. Sweat pooled between my collarbones. A strangled scream pushed its way up my throat. Despair closed in.

Then a hand, cool and gentle to the touch, grasped my own. *Jesus.* Whispered prayer caressed my ears and spoke peace into my soul. *Jesus.* The dark figure vanished in a swirl of haze. *In the name of Jesus.*

The force upon my chest lifted, and I sat bolt upright. Hair stuck to my face and my neck as I heaved and darted my gaze about the room, searching for Cornelius, looking for an escape. But the room lay bare aside from a single chest of drawers and the bed upon which I sat.

Pressure on my palm snapped my eyes to Emily kneeling beside me. She cradled my hand against her bosom, her mouth still moving in silent prayer. With starlight illuminating her tousled golden curls and light blue eyes, she appeared like an angel sent from heaven to cast out my demons.

Like so many times before, tears fell swift and easy. I quivered, bowing forward in shame. Ratted clumps of hair fell about my face. "Why am I so weak, Emily?" I asked, barely strong enough to force the words out. "I've defeated darkness before, but now . . . I feel so powerless to resist it. I'm completely at its mercy. How? How did it come to this?"

"Oh, dear one. Sometimes the darkness of this world feels too great to bear." Emily continued softly stroking the heel of my hand, sending tremors up my arm and drawing my eyes to a fluttering close. "The enemy is cunning. He prowls this earth in search of people to devour and destroy. He tries to crush us with lies and overwhelm us with temptations. If we're not vigilant, his tricks can lead us astray, but we can stand firm knowing we have been given the power to reject him."

Emptiness expanded within me, cold and painful. "Then I've lost that power."

"No." Emily knuckled my chin and directed my face toward her. "The Holy Spirit lives in you, and nothing you do can ever take it away." Her empathetic eyes glistened. "My heart breaks for the burden you and Finn have carried. You have been walking such a dark and lonely road, but hear me when I say, you don't have to follow that path anymore. You can turn from it."

"It's too late." My sobs heightened. "I've strayed too far."

"You have strayed far, yes, but do you know what?" Her lips tipped in the tiniest smile. "God can keep up with you, and He has been walking right by your side with His hand outstretched. Now all you need to do is take it—and hold on tight. He's got you."

Emily's image blurred and distorted through my tears while her words seeped through me, saturating the dried and dead pieces of my soul with new life. With hope. How could I have forgotten the great power I had wielded when banishing Cornelius? How could I have allowed myself to be deceived—again?

*Because you are weak. You are only capable of failure.*

"Enough," Emily said gently. "I see those lies swimming in your eyes. Don't believe them. Don't allow them to have power over you anymore."

I stilled and focused on drowning out the malicious voices that had been screaming deception in my ears for far too long. It was time I stopped flirting with the devil and turned back to the truth. Despite my flaws, despite my failures, I was a child of the Most-High God, and I need no longer despair.

*Stop it. Don't listen to her.*

*No, you must stop. I've banished you before, and it seems I must do it again. I'm done. You no longer hold any authority over me. Get out.*

Warmth burst from my chest. The weight lifted from my shoulders. The pestering voice at the back of my skull fell quiet, and peace infused every muscle and bone. My body released a cleansing shudder as my cries transformed into joyous laughter.

"Amen," Emily whispered, her laughs joining mine.

I drew against her side, and we held tight to one another for what seemed like hours. How long had I been entertaining evil without realizing it? When had I last felt this serene? This alive? I sighed and caressed my dense abdomen swelling with life.

Straightening with mild alarm, I patted at the bedsheets. "Where's Basil Allan?" I murmured. "Wasn't he here when we went to bed?"

Emily smiled and nodded toward the door. "Look."

Hanging partially ajar, it allowed enough space to see into the next room lit by smoldering embers in the hearth. Finn slumbered on a tattered sofa, one arm bent and tucked under his head, but he draped his other arm protectively over Basil Allan, who had curled up against his chest. Both slept soundly, and a soft snore trickled from one of them.

Chuckling, I leaned my head against Emily's and faced the window. A speck of gold glimmered in the cobalt sky above an emerald horizon. Bright. Renewing. My heart soared across Ireland, back to Dublin.

Back to Baze.

*Protect him. Oh, God, protect him.*

# Chapter Thirty-Five

BEFORE THE BREAK OF DAWN, BAZE rose quietly and donned the plain garb of a common Irishman—complete with a tweed jacket and flat cap. Lacking the time for a proper shave, he scratched at the thickening growth on his jaw and set out to rouse Collin, but the young man was already dressed and ready and had discovered some smoked meat to gnaw on.

Baze wondered how much Collin had actually slept—if at all. Functioning on only a few hours of sleep himself, Baze did what he could to awaken his senses, both mentally and physically. He needed to be on alert. There was no telling what kind of resistance they would face in the hours to come.

Neither of them spoke as Baze drove. He followed the memorized route, strangling the steering wheel and keeping his gaze plastered to the road, which sat eerily empty under a dark sky.

As they approached the bridge spanning the River Liffey, Baze noticed a messy cluster of objects stretching in front of it. He slowed the car, his calf aching with the effort, and squinted. Haphazard piles of wagons, carts, barrels, and other miscellaneous items had been thrown together and blocked the way forward. Uniformed men clambered about and stacked more debris on top.

Collin muttered a harsh word in Irish and then said, "They're putting up barricades."

Baze angled the car against the pavement and parked. This wasn't a good sign. Barricades meant the rebels had already infiltrated the city, and Baze surmised they had fortifications at every major passage into Dublin. Thank God he had gotten Adelynn out of there.

But how were they supposed to get to Dublin Castle if the roads were blocked? Would his leg carry him all that way without collapsing on him? That was assuming, of course, that they could even sneak past the barricade without being spotted and detained—or shot.

A low growl rumbled in Collin's throat as he glared at the obstruction. He wrenched the door handle and dropped a leg out.

Baze caught Collin's arm. "Where do you think you're going?"

"To talk to them."

"No, you're not. That's a good way to get killed."

"*Is cuma liom*," Collin snapped and ripped from Baze's grasp. "I speak their language. I understand why they're fightin'. Maybe I can convince them we're allies."

Another retort leaped to Baze's tongue, but before he had a chance to voice it, Collin surged outside. "No!" Baze swiped but just missed his sleeve.

Collin slammed the door and advanced toward the scurrying hoard of soldiers. Baze's heart clambered into his throat as he watched Collin expose his hands in a gesture of surrender. Several soldiers stopped and circled him. One of them jammed a rifle into his spine. Collin's hands waved with exuberance as he talked quickly, likely in his mother tongue, then gestured to the car.

Baze held his breath and prayed.

Finally, one of the men nodded and slapped Collin's shoulder. The man with the rifle relaxed, and they subjected Collin to a few more good-natured shoves before turning back to their blockade.

Collin swiveled in the car's direction and signaled urgently for Baze to join him.

Baze killed the engine and waited a beat. *This is it. God, go with us.* Then he abandoned the car and made for Collin. Tense air quivered around him as though the city was holding its breath, waiting for the first strike to fall.

"They're letting us pass," Collin said flatly as he approached.

Baze studied the soldiers, and a few studied him back. He tipped his cap to appease the men while hissing under his breath, "What did you say to them?"

"That we were brothers just come in from Galway wantin' to join the fight. I told them we had family beyond the barricade and asked if we could pass to get them to safety."

Baze detected a slight wobble when Collin said the word *brothers*, but he chose to brush past it and focus on the fabricated story. "I didn't think reasoning with them would work, but I stand corrected. You did well."

Collin knotted his lips, then eyed Baze's leg. "We have to walk from here. Are you able?"

"Yes." Baze nodded. "Don't worry about me." In truth, he wasn't sure if he would have the strength or stamina for it, but he refused to be the weak link in this plan.

"Good." Collin spun on his heel and took off at a fast clip.

Massaging his pinched pride, Baze hurried after him. Aches bloomed in his muscle and wrapped over his kneecap, but he forced his mind away from the pain and onto Collin. He wasn't thinking, wasn't considering the risks before plowing ahead. Baze recognized the blind emotion fueling the young constable's impulsive actions—because Baze had once been driven by the same.

They crossed the river and continued southward past another barricade before easing east, observing scattered troupes of soldiers marching in unison with rifles tilted over their shoulders.

"Dublin Castle isn't much farther," Baze said, words taut with exertion. "Just one more—"

Rapid gunfire exploded in the distance.

Baze leaped toward Collin, fisted the back of his coat, and dragged him behind a cylindrical post box. Another round of shots rang out from the opposite direction. Shouts erupted. Soldiers sprinted through the street.

The uprising had started.

Collin sank to his knees, eyes wide. "We've failed."

"No, we haven't. Not yet." Determination heated Baze's veins even as he suppressed a curse. He yanked Collin back to his feet. "It'll take time for them to breach the castle. We have to hurry. Move."

Baze whirled Collin around and forced him forward, hunkering them against the buildings for cover as they hastened along the pavement. His pulse roared and his calf screamed. What if the soldiers had infiltrated the castle? What if the Lord Lieutenant had been exposed, leaving him at the mercy of O'Sullivan's attack?

"That sign says it's this way." Collin pulled from Baze's grasp and darted toward the end of the street.

A cacophony of yells and scuffles, punctuated with gunfire, sounded around the corner just as Collin swung out of view.

Baze sucked in a breath. "Collin, wait! Don't—"

Gunfire exploded. Collin cried out.

Fear spiked, and Baze surged around the corner to find Collin huddled against a wall, bullet holes smoking in the bricks above his head. A cluster of soldiers—what looked to be Irish Volunteers and the British Army—clashed in bloody warfare a mere two hundred feet down the street.

Directly before them sat the locked gate to Dublin Castle.

Baze seized Collin's arm and hauled him back around the corner out of range. He pawed at Collin's limbs and his face, looking for blood. "Are you hurt?"

"No, it missed." Collin gave Baze a little shove and lurched toward the castle.

"Stop." Baze snatched Collin's arm again. "Slow down. You're not thinking."

An angry string of Irish burst from Collin's mouth as he whirled and threw a fist.

Baze dodged and caught the attempted blow, then grabbed Collin's shirt with both fists and threw his back against the wall, punching a grunt from his chest.

"Let me go." Collin squirmed and tugged at Baze's hands—to no avail. Though Collin had grown larger, Baze was still stronger. He'd taken the boy down once, and he would do it again if necessary.

"Acting rashly will only get you killed, Collin," Baze snapped. "Stop and think. You're smarter than this. Use your training." He tried to catch the boy's gaze. "I understand it's difficult. Your brother just died. But you're letting your emotions cloud your judgment."

Collin yanked at Baze's wrists, but his effort was beginning to weaken. His voice pitched higher as he said, "I'm sorry, Mr. Ford. I'm doin' my best not to feel anythin'. I'll try harder. I promise."

Urgency pumped the blood hot through Baze's body, but he couldn't leave Collin in such a state, not when his preoccupation could get them both shot. Baze relaxed his shoulders slightly. "Collin, no one said you shouldn't feel anything."

Collin's eyes grew red with moisture, but he fluttered his lashes, reinforcing the dam. "Liam told me I shouldn't. When Ma and Pa died, he . . . he told me I was weak for cryin' for them."

Anger and empathy clashed inside Baze. He didn't like cursing a dead man, but for all Liam had put Collin through, a piece of Baze was glad he had perished.

Baze risked loosening his hold. "Listen to me. Crying doesn't make you weak. It makes you human. Liam was wrong to tell you that." Mournful memories sprang to life, memories of all the times Baze had suppressed his own emotions only for them to rip him apart from the inside and finally erupt. He moved a hand to the side of Collin's cheek. "You don't have to hold it in. It's *okay* to feel."

The boy shook his head, chest pumping rapid and heavy. "I can't. I don't . . . what if—"

"Collin." Baze touched Collin's face with his other hand, then spread his fingers until he held the boy's head in a warm and secure cradle. "It's okay." Tilting slightly to capture Collin's erratic gaze, Baze softened his voice. "It's okay."

As Collin stared deep into Baze's eyes, sorrow broke across his face. A single tear skittered down his cheek, and that was enough to release the flood. He collapsed forward and threw his arms around Baze, crashing his forehead against Baze's chest.

Gritting his teeth, Baze steeled his legs to keep Collin upright. He slid his hand to the back of the boy's neck and supported his weight with his other. His torso vibrated as Collin's muffled wails reverberated through him.

And so Baze held him—and would continue to hold him until he'd released everything he needed to. He prayed for the boy's heart, that healing would begin to soften the ache of grief. He also prayed that God's protective hand would keep the enemy at bay until they finished.

Time stretched on. Collin eventually quieted, and his trembling stilled. When he heaved a shuddering sigh, Baze could almost feel the emotion draining from his body.

Finally, Collin found his footing and pulled back. He tucked his face inside his elbow and smeared the tears from his cheeks. When he took his arm away, his face shone bright red, eyes swollen and puffy. Unlike a few moments ago, the strife marring his brow had faded—at least for now.

"Grief is a process, Collin," Baze said gently. "This will not be the last time you feel overwhelmed by it, but next time, don't force it down. Understood?"

Collin nodded slowly and swallowed against another hiccup. He stood a little straighter, breathed a little calmer. Then his attention drifted to Baze's chest, and his expression scrunched. "Sorry about your shirt."

Baze looked down. A wide wet stain stretched across the fabric. He chuckled. "It will dry."

*Crack!* A bullet struck the edge of the building near their heads.

They ducked together and pressed side by side against the wall. Baze peered around the corner and then shot Collin a grave look. "The gate to Dublin Castle is dangerously close to the fighting. I think we'll need to run for it. Are you with me?"

Collin smacked a fist over his heart. "I'm with you, Mr. F—"

Baze raised an eyebrow.

Collin coughed. "I mean, Baze. I'm with you. I promise."

Baze patted the side of Collin's face, then readied for the charge. At his command, they bolted into the street. Baze locked eyes on the target and ignored the burst of pain in his leg. Shouts and gunfire droned in his ears. He gritted his teeth, pushing past the raucous melee, and managed to stumble up to the wrought iron gate intact.

A constable stood guard before it as Darragh had said—Constable James O'Brien.

Heaving in air, Baze tapped his hand on his chest. "I'm Detective Inspector Ford. Superintendent Moore sent us. He said you'd be waiting for us."

O'Brien nodded gravely and unhooked keys from his belt. "I wondered when you lads might be showin' up. Come. Quickly now."

Over the constable's shoulder, Baze noticed a few of the Volunteers break from the fighting and stagger in their direction, but before he could act, the constable wrenched the gate open and ushered them through.

Baze caught O'Brien's hand in a swift but firm handshake. "Thank you. Be careful."

O'Brien nodded. "Godspeed."

Putting a guiding hand on Collin's back, Baze turned and urged him on. They dashed through a grand stone archway and emerged into the large courtyard of Dublin Castle. Hope swelled. A few more steps would deliver them into the protection of the British Army.

*Pop-pop-pop!*

Alarmingly close gunshots nearly brought Baze to his knees. He whirled back toward the gate in time to see Constable O'Brien collapse. A yell wedged in Baze's throat.

Three Volunteers loped into view and discovered the unlocked gate. One rushed through, whipped up his rifle, and took aim.

Baze reeled as a bullet whizzed past his ear and another flew overhead. He pumped his legs to escape, but his calf spasmed and brought him crashing to the ground with a moan.

Collin gasped and spun.

"No!" Baze waved his hand. "Keep going."

But Collin disobeyed and sprinted back. He thrust his hands under Baze's arms and yanked him to his feet just as the soldier fired again.

# Chapter Thirty-Six

BECKONED BY THE KISS OF THE morning sun's rays, Emily slipped from bed and dressed for the day, leaving Adelynn sleeping soundly. The poor thing had fallen into peaceful slumber soon after her nightmare and would hopefully receive the restoration her body and soul required. Great evil had settled upon the cottage last night, and Emily shuddered to think what would have happened to Adelynn if she had allowed it to take root. However, she had proven resilient and faithful, conquering her demons and plunging back into the Almighty's cleansing light.

Emily crept into the main room of the home containing a simple kitchen, a small dining table, and a rustic sitting area. There, she found Basil Allan snoozing on the couch beside the fireplace and a note from Finn stating he had gone to buy some food. She snuck to the window near the table and gazed out, absently grasping Bennett's ring hanging from the chain about her neck.

Finn's cottage was nestled on a flat green stretch of land along a shoreline interspersed with flat rock formations and lined with a mossy stone fence. Leaning for a better view, she glimpsed a dilapidated castle ruin towering atop a gentle hill to the left. Waves rushed toward shore. Whitecaps winked on the cerulean water.

Emily closed her eyes and listened. The ocean's soothing crashes lulled her into a state of calm, and the impression of Bennett's ring in her hand tugged her out of the present and plopped her back in their London residence, back in Bennett's unwavering and tender embrace— back when she had thought nothing would ever separate them.

The door of the cottage creaked open, shattering the memory and dropping Emily back at the window, the peaceful Irish shoreline stretching before her. Gulping in a steadying breath, she turned to Finn.

The Irishman clomped through the doorway with an exhale of relief and dropped several paper bags onto the round table. Fresh scents of sea salt and fish filled the room. He shook his curls out of his eyes, and when his gaze landed upon Emily, an easy, natural smile brightened his face.

Her breath caught. Cheeks warming, she turned to the table and investigated the fare he'd acquired—a carton of eggs, a loaf of sourdough, a pound of bacon, and a block of fresh cheddar. Several spices, vegetables, and other sides rounded out the haul. With raised eyebrows, she plucked out the bread. "You have impeccable taste."

He tipped his head and gestured a small salute. "That's a huge compliment comin' from you." He scrounged in a nearby drawer, came up with matches, and lit the stove. Then he snatched a skillet from the rack on the wall and flipped it with a flourish and a goofy smile. "Shall we cook up some breakfast?"

Emily giggled and joined him. They worked in tandem, side by side, their partnership effortless as though it had been rehearsed, with Finn frying the eggs and bacon and Emily slicing the bread and cheese. Somehow, his salt-and-earth scent overpowered the aroma steaming up from the food and dizzied her thoughts.

As they prepared plates of the cooked food, Adelynn shuffled into the room. Her flaxen hair hung loose and trailed over her shoulders, and she wore a basic linen dress she had likely discovered in the chest of drawers. More forgiving than her usual formal wear, the gown's bodice accentuated the slight bump hiding beneath.

Adelynn scooped up a groggy Basil Allan on her way to the table and sank into one of the chairs. She planted the child on her lap as Finn and Emily finished preparing the meal.

After they broke their fast, Finn rose and pulled on a loose coat that looked like it had seen more years than he had. "I'm goin' for some air, and I'll check with the lads in town again to see if there's any news out of Dublin."

"No!" Basil Allan piped up with intensity in his voice.

Finn raised his eyebrows in mock astonishment. "No?"

"No." Basil Allan scrunched his nose and mouth, crawled from Adelynn's lap, and ran to Finn's legs. "I don't want you to go."

Finn bent and wound his arms around Basil Allan's waist, and when he straightened, he flipped Basil Allan upside down and held the child tight against his chest. With his arms dangling and blood rushing to his face, Basil Allan let all pretense fall and squealed with untainted glee.

The sight very nearly made Emily's heart burst.

"I'll only be a little while." Finn poked Basil Allan's exposed tummy, then spun him right-side up and plunked him on his feet. "Here. I'll give you somethin' to pass the time. You won't even miss me."

Finn pulled out a silver tin whistle and knelt before Basil Allan. With nimble, practiced fingers, he piped out a lighthearted jig, much to the delight of the toddler.

When he finished, he handed the whistle to Basil Allan. "You try."

Basil Allan put the whistle to his lips and blew. A sharp screech pierced Emily's ear drums, and Adelynn's wince suggested it pained her as well.

Emily squinted at Finn as Basil Allan toddled around, piping happily on the whistle. "Could you not have chosen something quieter?"

"It worked, didn't it?" Finn winked with a roguish grin. "I'll be back soon." He nodded to each of the women in turn before departing.

Sharp flute notes continued to fill the space as Adelynn leaned across the table and jerked her head toward the door. "What are you waiting for?"

Emily blinked. "What?"

"What do you mean, what?" Adelynn's blue eyes shone with intensity. "Go with him."

Emily's heart began to pound. "Oh, I don't know . . ."

"Emily Bennett, if you don't go after him, I shall drag you there."

Adelynn shifted in her seat, and Emily hustled toward the door if only to pacify her friend.

"All right, but don't let Basil Allan—"

"Go!" Adelynn insisted.

Her legs quivering, Emily wrapped a shawl about her shoulders and rushed out the door. Finn hadn't gotten too far. Whistling a low tune, his hands in his pockets, he lumbered along a dirt path that ran parallel to the stone fence guarding the shoreline.

Trepidation and excitement propelled her forward. "Finn, wait!"

He halted and half-turned, brows drawn in confusion.

She jogged to catch up. "May I accompany you? I think the fresh air would do me good."

A slow smile stretched his mouth. "Of course." He bowed and offered his elbow. "If I may." Though he appeared composed, the wind lifted his hair to reveal burning-red ears.

Withholding a giggle, Emily slipped her hand into the crook of his arm and reveled in the strength of his solid muscle.

As silence commanded their stroll, Emily surveyed the area if only to keep her mind off his closeness. The flat land stretched for what seemed like miles, with a bay of water to their right and green fields to their left. Out ahead, roof clusters marked the town of Liscannor. She tracked the path with her eyes and arrived at a leaning castle ruin on the top of a slight hill.

"I heard what you were sayin' to Adelynn last night," Finn's voice slipped gently into the silence. "Is it true?"

"Is what true?"

"That no matter how far we've strayed, the Almighty'll still save us?"

Her heart warmed. "Yes, it's true. His grace knows no limits."

"Then why . . ." Finn looked down at his feet, picking his way around small pebbles in the path. "When I confronted Shay, I think I heard the Almighty speakin' to me. I felt such peace and control for one of the first times in recent memory. But now that the moment has passed, I can feel the darkness of my past tuggin' at my heart, like I'm just moments away from losin' that control. If I am truly saved, then why do I still feel this way?" His biceps tightened, squeezing her hand beneath it. "Am I doin' somethin' wrong?"

"No, of course not." She clasped his forearm with her free hand. "We live in a fallen world filled with evil. It targets everyone—and especially those trying to walk in the light. Your life was fraught with strife and darkness before you turned to God, and the demons of your past want to keep you bound in those chains. But you have been given the power to break free—you have *already* broken free. So whenever you feel as though you are going to be overwhelmed, you need only call upon that power as you did with Shay, and you will prevail."

He clenched his jaw, then nodded and let his muscles relax. "Thank you, Emily. It seems I have much left to learn."

With a smile, she rested her head against his upper arm. "You'll get there. I have no doubt."

The path soon sloped into a gradual incline leading to the castle. At the base of the ruins, Finn pulled from her touch for the first time since they left the cottage. Hands on his hips, he planted a foot on a large rock and nodded to the crumbling fortress. "This is Liscannor Castle. I used to play here as a boy." Memories raced across his features, coaxing his mind far away.

As he studied the castle, Emily studied him. She traced his profile—his sloped nose with a slightly rounded tip, his slim and angular jaw, his kind and compassionate eyes—and felt a tug of yearning. She wanted to be with him. Now and for the rest of their lives.

Turmoil and excitement waged war within her. Huddling her shoulders to ward off the cold wind, she fingered the chain around her neck and slowly lifted it over her head. Tears prickled her eyes as she dropped Bennett's ring into her palm. She gazed at it for a moment, then closed her fingers over it, preparing a goodbye.

"What are you doin'?"

Finn's voice startled her head up. Expression puzzled, he crossed the distance between them and pried her hand open. "What's this?"

Guilt rose to the surface and clamped Emily's throat. "It's Bennett's ring. I just thought . . . I didn't want you to—"

"Emily." Finn's eyes softened as he plucked the ring and chain from her hand. "Bennett was your husband. He's the father of your child. I would never ask you to bury his memory." Unhooking the chain, Finn crossed behind her. He circled it around her neck and clasped it.

Speechless, she touched the ring where it rested above her heart.

He turned her to face him with a melancholy smile. "My fiancée, Maeve, died a lifetime ago, it seems, but she will always be a part of me—just as Bennett will always be a part of you." Taking a slow step closer, bringing their bodies barely a breath apart, Finn twirled one of Emily's curls between his fingertips. "Those we love have gone on before us, and I think it's time we also moved on . . . together." He tucked the curl behind her ear. "I love you, Emily."

Heart racing, Emily stared into his clear eyes—eyes the color of the wild and untamed ocean—and allowed his life-giving words to warm her body and soul. A flutter from deep within tickled her stomach. Was she nervous? Scared?

No. This was a flutter of anticipation.

Finn swallowed, his gaze darting to her lips before tugging back to her eyes. "I realize it may not be the most proper request for a woman of your class, but . . . may I kiss you?"

Emily's breath stole away on the wind, and the flutter turned into a cyclone. Her voice weakened in her throat, but somehow, she managed, "You may."

Eagerness brightened his eyes as they dropped back to her mouth. Tucking a knuckle under her chin, he lifted her face as he bent and pressed his lips to hers—gentle but strong.

Dormant longing snapped to life. Her last kiss had been what seemed like forever ago, and with the distractions of the past three years, she had almost forgotten what it was like to feel desired by a man—and to desire him in return.

It nearly consumed her.

Placing a halting hand on Finn's chest, Emily tipped her head down, breaking their chaste connection and pulling a soft exhale from Finn's lips. She closed her eyes, but tears managed to squeeze through. "I'm sorry."

"Don't be apologizin'." His large, warm hand slipped around the back of her neck. "Take as long as you need."

But Emily didn't need more time. She grasped Bennett's ring and, for the final time, acknowledged the brief but beautiful life they had shared. She allowed that chapter of her life to slip shut—and then opened her heart to a new one.

Excitement flooded her as she lifted to her tiptoes and cupped Finn's jaw in both hands. "I'm ready to move on with you," she murmured. "I want to spend the rest of my days with you." She angled her mouth to his, stopping just shy of touching. "I love you too."

He hesitated but a moment before closing the distance between them. With a shudder, he slid his hand around her waist and tugged her body against his, cradling her neck in his other hand. She all but went limp in his arms as he melded his lips to hers, relinquishing all restraint and carrying her away to a place of newfound fervor.

"I don't have a ring for you," he said huskily against her mouth.

She savored him again, slower, before parting to catch her breath. "I don't need a ring."

His lips skimmed her brow. "Then say you'll marry me."

"I'll marry you." Beaming ear to ear, she wrapped both arms about his neck.

He touched their noses together, his smile as wide and bright as the sun, then dipped his mouth to hers once more.

"Oi, Finn!"

A shout wrenched their lips apart. Emily spun in Finn's arm to see a man loping up the hill, panting and waving his hand. Quick Irish spilled from his mouth, and Finn's chest tightened against her back, his forearm clutching her closer.

Tingles of alarm doused the fire in her body as she swiveled her head and absorbed Finn's concerned expression. "What is it? What did he say?"

"It's the rebels." His smile vanished. "They're mustering nearby."

# Chapter Thirty-Seven

THE VOLUNTEER'S BULLET WENT WIDE TO the right. With Collin's hand still hooked under his arm, Baze scrambled to his feet. He locked his eyes on the white peninsular section of the building directly ahead—the entrance to the State Apartments.

Bullets shrieked by as they raced toward the door. It cracked open, and a man's head poked through. He held it just wide enough for them to burst inside. Baze stumbled to a halt, bent over with hands on his knees. He sucked in air and glanced about. Picturing the map in his head, he surmised they had entered the main antechamber of the apartments, and the door straight ahead would take them to the Lord Lieutenant.

Several uniformed members of the British Army surrounded them, most with weapons drawn. A few kept watch at the windows, peering into the courtyard. The soldier at the door slammed it shut and dropped a crossbar in place.

Still breathless, Baze nodded to the man. "Thank you."

"You're lucky to be alive, you know that?" The man grunted. "What's got into your head running out in the open like that?"

"We're with the Dublin Metropolitan Police," Collin spoke clearly as though the sprint had hardly winded him. "Constable Donoghue and Detective Inspector Ford. We're here to protect the Lord Lieutenant."

Eyeing their commoners' garb, the soldier squinted. "No need to worry. We've got him and his family under guard in his quarters until we can find a safe way out."

Baze straightened to his full height, bristling at the soldier's suspicion. Though, were Baze in the Army's shoes, he likely wouldn't trust them either. What could he say to make them believe they had honest intentions?

He firmed his voice. "We're here under orders from Superintendent Darragh Moore. Please. It's imperative that we reach the Lord Lieutenant."

"I know Darragh." The soldier's intense stare relaxed slightly. "Why would he send just the two of you—and not in uniform?"

With urgency quivering in Baze's muscles, he opted for the full truth. "This was the only way to sneak through the city unnoticed. There's been a threat upon the Lord Lieutenant's life. The attacker plans to use the chaos of the rebellion to strike. We need to reach him before the enemy does."

Stroking his mustache, the soldier finally nodded. "I'll take you." He barked some orders to his comrades, then hastened toward the south door and gestured for Baze and Collin to follow. As they passed from the room, distant shouts erupted: "The guard room! They're attacking the guard room!" Pounding boots echoed through the halls.

Pandemonium quickly took hold—and the fighting had only just begun. How much worse would it become? Could the Army hold off the attackers long enough to allow them to reach the Lord Lieutenant?

A grand staircase lined with a rich red carpet and a dark carved railing loomed before them. Baze loped up the steps behind Collin and the soldier. The higher they ascended, the lower the temperature dropped—and with it, Baze's stomach. Though adrenaline seemed to have numbed the pain for now, his calf muscle contracted and threatened to give out. He gritted his teeth and persevered. *A little longer. Hold on just a little longer.*

At the top, Baze glimpsed hospital beds and Red Cross nurses through the opening across the landing, but the soldier veered right into a long empty corridor with several doors on either side and a rounded ceiling with gold-inlaid arches. His gait faltered. "There should be men standing guard," he muttered, then rushed toward the door at the end of the hall on the right.

Ice in the air chilled Baze's skin and turned his short breaths into fog. He didn't have time to shout a warning before the soldier kicked the door open and surged inside. Baze and Collin rounded the corner after him—and nearly ran straight into him. He'd stopped dead in his tracks. It took several beats for Baze to absorb the full scope of what lay before them.

With a lavish bed, ornate fireplace, and large wardrobe, the space appeared to be a bedroom. The bodies of three soldiers littered the floor directly inside the door. A woman and three shaking children huddled in the far corner, the whites of their eyes flashing. Katherine Quinn stood before them, one arm held at an angle as though shielding them.

And near the fireplace, O'Sullivan and the Lord Lieutenant were linked in a struggle. O'Sullivan held the man's head clamped in his grasp, and a gun gleamed in his belt—the first time Baze had seen him carry one. The Lord Lieutenant flailed his arms and gaped his mouth. Darkness clouded his wide eyes.

"Stop! Hands up!" The soldier hefted his weapon and took aim.

A shadow crossed O'Sullivan's features, his eyes narrowing and locking on the soldier.

Recognition propelled Baze's legs. He lunged for the soldier and gave him a strong shove before O'Sullivan could take hold of his mind. Then Baze thrust the man toward the woman and children. "Get his family out of here," he commanded. "Hurry."

Finding his footing, the soldier frantically looked from O'Sullivan to Baze.

Baze saw the argument forming on the soldier's face and spoke first. "You've no idea what this man is capable of." A crack of desperation wavered his voice. "Please. For your own sake, take them and get to safety."

Whether swayed by the tone of Baze's voice or his cryptic words, the soldier jumped to action. He scooped up the littlest child and jerked his head at the mother and older children. They scrambled from the room—but Katherine stayed put, her body rigid and expression severe.

Now with the civilians out of the way, Baze turned to O'Sullivan and drew his pistol. He took a mental note of Katherine shifting in his periphery and Collin hovering just behind his right shoulder before focusing on the Irishman.

"I wondered if you'd be showin' up." O'Sullivan used the Lord Lieutenant's head to steer him into Baze's line of fire.

"Release him," Baze said, low and steady.

O'Sullivan's mouth twisted in a grim smirk. "You're too late. He's already mine."

Baze clicked back the hammer. "You can't control him if you're dead."

"True, but that's assumin' you can get a clear shot."

"Clear shot or not, you won't be leaving here al—"

Pain zapped through Baze's calf and buckled his knee. He flailed an arm as his body pitched, but he managed to steel his healthy leg and lean into it before he could fully collapse. Cheeks burning with frustration, he clenched his jaw and fixed his aim.

O'Sullivan raised his eyebrows in amusement. "Still haunted by the ghosts of the past, I see. What a pity. Perhaps someone should put you out of your misery." His eyes flicked to something behind Baze. "Collin, why don't you finish the job you started."

Baze inhaled and turned.

Collin's baton slammed down on Baze's wrists. The blow spasmed Baze's fingers and flung the gun from his grip. Collin kicked out his knee and then swept his legs out from under him. He crashed onto his side. The floor knocked the wind out of him.

Collin booted him onto his back and dove. In one motion, he pinned Baze's right arm and swung the baton at his head.

Jerking his neck, Baze managed to avoid getting his skull crushed, but Collin attacked again. Baze caught the boy's wrist with his free hand, stopping the blow. Their bodies shivered, locked in a stalemate.

Despite the violent nature of his actions, Collin's murky eyes filled with panic. "Mr. Ford," he rasped. "I'm sorry . . ."

Anger pumped hot through Baze. Letting out a yell, he channeled all of his strength into his upper body. In one motion, he surged upward, wrenched free his pinned wrist, and twisted Collin's baton-wielding arm. The momentum threw Collin off balance. Baze used the brief window of confusion to roll them over. Coming up to one knee, he hooked his arm around Collin's neck and pulled him against his chest.

"Is this what you want? To be a destroyer of families?" Baze snarled, and something flickered across O'Sullivan's face. "Collin was already an orphan before you murdered the only family he had left. And now you're torturing him? He's innocent!"

"Shut up." The Irishman scowled. He narrowed his eyes, and Collin bucked in Baze's grasp.

Grunting, Baze shifted his arm to compress the artery in Collin's neck and render him temporarily unconscious. As Collin's body sagged, Baze lowered him gently to the floor.

Then he looked up—and found himself staring straight down the barrel of a pistol.

O'Sullivan had dropped the Lord Lieutenant, who lay limp at his feet, and held the weapon aloft, expression stoic—though, judging from his imbalanced posture and loose fingers on the pistol grip, he wasn't accustomed to handling a firearm.

Slowly, Baze raised his hands. He mentally pictured where his own gun had landed—too far to reach, and he wouldn't be able to dive for it faster than O'Sullivan could shoot. He risked a glance at Katherine. She still lingered near the bed, turmoil twisting her features.

Baze grimaced. "Are you just going to stand there and let your husband do this?"

She flared her nostrils but kept her lips pursed shut.

"Leave her out of this," O'Sullivan snapped. "You have failed, Inspector. There is nothing more for you to do other than surrender."

Invisible needles pierced the base of Baze's skull, clouding his mind with darkness—the same darkness that had consumed him when Cornelius Marx had taken control of Baze's body for a short time.

*No, not again. Don't let me fall prey again.*

The defenses held, rendering O'Sullivan's mental attacks useless. Bolstered by the revelation of strength, Baze managed to rise and stand tall on both feet, palms still exposed in submission. "Marx got me once. You're a fool if you think I'll allow that to happen again."

Unperturbed, O'Sullivan directed the gun's barrel to the center of Baze's chest and clicked its hammer into place. "You have a choice to make, Inspector. If you wish to leave here alive, then you must give your mind to me. If you don't, you will die." His eyes glistened harshly. "Think very carefully about your answer, now. You've a wife and child to consider."

Collin moaned and shifted slightly at Baze's feet, but Baze kept his eyes trained on O'Sullivan as the man's words seeped through him. Morbid as it was, Adelynn's vision had shown Baze's death occurring from a fall, not a gunshot wound. Besides, O'Sullivan didn't like to get his hands dirty, not physically anyway. It was possible he wouldn't actually have the fortitude to shoot.

Growing weary, Baze's arms drooped a tick. Whether the supposition was true or not, giving his mind willingly to O'Sullivan to do with what he willed seemed a fate worse than death, but if there was another way out, Baze didn't see it. Perhaps he could keep the Irishman talking long enough for an escape to present itself.

"You also have a choice to make." Baze spoke evenly despite the firing of every nerve within him. "You can stop this. You don't have to—"

"I see what you're doin', but it's a pathetic attempt." O'Sullivan curled a finger about the trigger. "I'll make sure Adelynn knows you died a coward's death."

Baze stiffened.

The pistol discharged.

Collin vaulted to his feet—right in the bullet's path. He grunted and crumpled.

A cry ripped from Baze's lips. He lurched and caught Collin's fall.

Dropping to the floor with him, Baze pawed at Collin's stomach. Buttons popped and flew as he tore open Collin's shirt and searched for the wound. Blood spurted from a jagged hole above his right hip bone.

Fear stole Baze's breath. A memory flashed. Bennett's own fatal wound—a mirror image.

Katherine's distant, warbled voice pierced through the ringing in his ears. Baze glanced quickly enough to see her skirt around the bed and cling to O'Sullivan's arm. "He's just a boy, Sully. You've completely lost control!"

O'Sullivan stood paralyzed, the smoking gun trembling in his hand, eyes locked on Collin.

A gurgle in Collin's throat snatched the shock from Baze's mind and sharpened his determination. He hadn't been able to do anything to help Bennett—he'd already been dead when Baze arrived at the scene—but Collin was still alive. He could still be saved.

Baze stripped off his coat, balled it up, and shoved it against Collin's wound, leaning with his full weight. The boy gasped.

"Stay with me," Baze growled. "You're not allowed to die. Do you understand me? I order you not to die!"

Wet coughs grated in Collin's chest. "Mr. Ford?"

"Don't talk."

"Are you . . . hurt? Did I . . . stop him from—"

"I said not to talk."

Air siphoned through Collin's lips as his eyelids fluttered.

"No, stay awake." Baze took one hand away to smack Collin's cheek. "Keep your eyes open."

A suppressed sob tightening his throat, Baze looked around frantically, just in time to see O'Sullivan dart through the door. Katherine, however, remained behind. Tears stained her cheeks.

"Katherine," Baze shouted, making her flinch. "Get The Red Cross. They're just down the hall." His voice broke. "Please. Hurry."

She hesitated, watching Collin with reddened eyes. Then her features hardened with resolve, and she nodded and bolted away.

"Don't leave me . . ."

Collin's weak plea seized Baze's attention. He returned both hands to Collin's stomach and pressed, blood soaking through the coat and dampening Baze's palms. "I'm not going anywhere," he whispered firmly. "You're going to get through this. Do you hear me? You're going to live."

Collin's eyes settled on Baze's face, and Baze watched helplessly as they grew unfocused.

*Gunshots echoed from every direction as I stumbled from Dublin Castle. Shouts of Volunteers and shrieks of artillery created a cacophony of sound in my ears. I had just enough wits about me to keep my footing and stumble down the street, away from the crux of the fighting in front of City Hall—but I couldn't escape that boy's face.*

*The fool. Why would he leap into my shot? Why would he throw his life away? The blame for his death lay on him—not me.*

*Didn't it?*

Relinquish your curse. Repent of your crimes. Seek redemption.

*Sharp pain squeezed my chest, deep and suffocating. Clutching at my shirt, I tripped and caught myself against a lamp post. Those words—where had those words come from? The darkness within me writhed against them, binding further to my flesh, burrowing deeper into my soul.*

*It was a beautiful sentiment . . . but not something I was capable of accomplishing. Ciaran had proven that. We were too lost—fated to carry this dark gift to our very last breath.*

*Was I foolish to believe that I could use it for good when it had already yielded evil?*

*Collin's face burned brightly in my vision once again—but this time, it morphed into that of a young Finn right at the moment I entered his mind and broke him.*

You yet have time to turn from this.

*The pain in my chest intensified. I cried out, sinking to my knees and clawing at my chest. With sweat cascading down my face and back, I trembled. Volunteers and British troops stampeded all around me—but they either didn't care or didn't notice that I was there.*

*"Finn," I whispered. "Ciaran." Sobs constricted my throat. "Kate."*

*Finn was broken, Ciaran was dead, and Kate was sullied—all because of me. And not just them. So many others.*

*For what?*

It's not too late.

**Don't listen to Him. You're a lost cause.**

No. You are worthy of redemption.

*The bloody battle of convictions waged inside me, threatening to tear me apart. A groan slipped through my clenched teeth as I rocked forward and pressed my forehead against the crackled pavement. How could I make this torment end? How could I wash the innocent blood from my hands?*

*I dove deep into my mind, grasping desperately for a reprieve. I sifted through memories of our little makeshift family—happy memories, memories of peace—and they dumped me out at the Cliffs of Moher. Wind whipped as birds soared in and out of the rocky craigs. The great ocean below beckoned.*

*Though still racked with pain, I shifted upright, got my legs under me, and wobbled to a stand.*

*The cliffs. That's where this would end.*

## Chapter Thirty-Eight

Dozens OF SOLDIERS WOUNDED IN THE Great War filled the beds of The Red Cross's temporary hospital. Being that it occupied the throne room and portrait hall directly parallel to the Lord Lieutenant's living quarters, Katherine had quickly returned with two nurses on her tail. After assessing the situation, one of the nurses retreated to enlist more help in transporting both Collin and the Lord Lieutenant. Baze retrieved his gun and then assisted in moving Collin to an empty bed in the throne room, leaving behind a large stain of blood.

"Move aside, sir," a nurse instructed as she elbowed Baze away from the side of the cot.

Unsure where to stand but unwilling to stray too far, Baze shuffled to the end of the bed next to Katherine. They watched the nurses in silence.

With practiced hands, the women tore away the rest of Collin's shirt and focused on stopping the steady blood flow. Fortunately, he didn't seem to feel the procedure as he teetered on the edge of unconsciousness, his breathing weak and erratic.

Dizziness expanded in Baze's temples as pain began to awaken in his leg. He gritted his teeth and shook his head as though to shake sense back into himself. Not yet. He couldn't let the adrenaline come down yet. If he succumbed to fatigue now, there would be no recovering, and it was imperative he remained focused—for the fight was far from over.

"Maybe you should sit down, brown eyes," Katherine whispered. "You're white as a sheet."

"No." Baze grasped the metal bar of the bed frame. "I'm all right."

"He's a tough kid." Her nose scrunched as her eyes glinted.

"Someone with the mental fortitude to withstand attacks by both Ciaran and Sully is surely strong enough to survive this."

Baze grimaced. Mental fortitude could do nothing against the bite of cold lead. If it could, then Bennett would have still been alive.

As one of the nurses pressed deep into the wound, Collin moaned. His lips moved, and barely audible words leaked out with his shallow breaths. "*Ná fág mé, Deartháir . . . Deartháir.*"

Baze's stomach clenched. "What's he saying?"

"He's calling for his brother," Katherine said softly.

Collin's mumblings continued, foreign and weak, until he suddenly switched to English. "Mr. Ford," he croaked, his eyes rolling under heavy lids. "Mr. Ford . . . where are . . ."

Before he could get another word out, a nurse clapped a cloth of chloroform over his nose and mouth, and within seconds, his body went limp. A grave-faced doctor in a black suit pushed through the nurses. Armed with a long instrument and scalpel, he sliced further into Collin's flesh and began prodding inside the wound for the bullet.

Bile stung in Baze's throat as he watched more of Collin's blood leak from his body.

"Come on," Katherine whispered and gripped his arm. "Let's allow them to work."

He resisted her tug. "No. He needs me."

"There's nothing more you can do for him." She huffed. "He's in good hands."

One of the nurses broke from Collin's side and approached. "The lady is right," she said gently, encouraging him with sympathetic eyes. "I've seen soldiers survive who were far worse for the wear than your boy is. The road will not be easy, but he'll pull through if we have anything to say about it."

Hesitant hope blossomed inside Baze. "Thank you."

With the imminent threat to Collin's life temporarily relieved, he reluctantly allowed Katherine to pull him away from the bed and direct him through the archway and onto the wide landing at the top of the grand staircase. His adrenaline had continued to drop, but he yet retained enough sense to absorb the full implications of Katherine's presence in Dublin Castle. She had simply stood there and watched as her husband shot Collin.

"I think you should have a seat now." She pushed on his shoulder, angling him toward a chair.

He lashed out and seized her wrist. "What were you doing here with O'Sullivan?"

"Unhand me, Baze." Her eyes flashed as she curled her upraised hand into a fist and yanked—but he held fast and used her wrist to jerk her closer.

"Was it your plan all along to come here with your husband?"

"I said, unhand me."

"You know, I think you came to us the day of Basil Allan's abduction so you could learn all about the countermeasures we were planning to use against your husband, and that's why you abandoned us—to scurry back home to warn him." Disgust sharpened his tone. "Did he help you fake your death in Bath so you could run away together? Was your life ever in danger?"

"You're jumping to incredibly egregious conclusions." This time when she yanked, he let go and permitted her to step out of his shadow. "You know better than that, Mister Detective Inspector."

He jutted his chin. "Then enlighten me."

One of her shoulders came up in a slight shrug as she folded her arms and sighed. "After we retrieved Basil Allan, I chose to leave your company with the hope that I could convince Sully to stop all of this."

"Then why did you accompany him here? Did you fail to turn him and so chose to join him?"

"You're jumping again." She smiled mirthlessly. "While you're correct on the former, the reason I came here was to try to prevent needless casualties. He's only after the Lord Lieutenant."

"Prevent them? You stood by and let them happen!" New adrenaline cycling hot through his body, he jabbed a finger toward the hall of bedrooms. "What about those three soldiers? What about Collin? You did nothing!"

"What should I have done? Jump in front of the bullet myself?" Rare tears glittered in her eyes. "I like to believe I have everything figured out, but when we entered Dublin Castle, I realized just how lacking I truly am." Her voice trembled. "I was certain I would figure out a clever way to stop him, but as Sully began his rampage, I could only watch. I was petrified. I didn't know what else to do. I had tried everything I knew to try."

Baze dropped his arm and brushed his fingers over the cool metal of the pistol in his belt. His tone fell. "You didn't try everything."

Blinking away the moisture in her eyes, Katherine shook her head. "No. I could never raise my hand in violence against him. It's not who I am." She closed the gap between them and placed her palm directly over Baze's pounding heart. "However, if you confront him again and see no other way, know that I shall not hold any ill will toward you should you choose to dispatch him the way you did Ciaran."

Baze swallowed and released a deep sigh. "I don't like killing, but I took an oath to uphold the peace and protection of the innocent, and I intend to keep it."

"You've an honorable heart." She pressed harder on his chest, then cracked a faint smile. "And such disarming eyes. It's easy to see why Adelynn loves you so much." Her smile widened as she patted his cheek. "Now if only you could learn to be a little more trusting, but we can work on that later when all this is but a memory."

Relaxing at her soft jab, he caught up her hand and squeezed, then cleared his throat. "I should check on Collin."

As he limped toward the entrance to the throne room, another layer of his tension melted away. The end was closing in—he could feel it. O'Sullivan had fled, but they had the Lord Lieutenant. If they could keep the man suspended in unconsciousness for the time being to prevent him from falling under O'Sullivan's control, that would give them an opportunity to—

Katherine gasped. A muffled thud sounded.

Baze spun to see her sprawled on the floor. Alarm spiked as he sprinted back and skidded to his knees. He glanced about as he lifted her torso, cradling her head. There had been no gunshot. No signal of an attack. What had struck her?

However, as he examined her pale face, twitching limbs, and distant gaze, he suddenly realized the cause—for he had seen these signs displayed countless times on Adelynn.

A vision had snatched her mind far away.

He propped her upright in his arms and waited with bated breath. After several agonizing seconds, her eyes focused, her limbs moved with agency, and her breathing returned to normal.

"What did you see?" Baze asked, bracing.

"It was Sully. He's on his way to the Cliffs of Moher." She paused, closing her eyes and wetting her lips, before confirming Baze's worst fear. "He's going after Adelynn."

A prickle of unease agitated my stomach. I massaged it as I stared through the window at the seashore and the breaking waves. My mouth grew dry as the feeling increased, intensified. Something had happened in Dublin. I didn't know what—and I dared not let myself speculate—but I knew with certainty that something serious had occurred.

*Don't take Baze from me*, I prayed fervently. *Please. Protect him. And Collin. Bring them both home.*

"Ada, look!" Gentle but insistent tugs on my skirt drew my attention to Basil Allan.

Soon after Finn and Emily departed, he had grown tired of the tin whistle, giving my ears a merciful respite, and occupied himself with a little carved sheep on wheels that I'd found while rummaging in Finn's family chest—what had likely been his when he was a boy. Basil Allan had taken the wooden animal and placed it on the back of his airplane.

I plastered on a smile and bent to his level. "How very clever of you! Will you show me how it flies?"

Flashing a toothy grin, he spun and zoomed it through the air while creating exaggerated engine noises with his mouth.

I chuckled, thankful that despite all he endured at the hands of Shay's men, he hadn't let go of his innocence. Resiliency was innate in him, and I had no doubt that resiliency would shape him into a strong and honorable man—just as Bennett had been.

The door clicked open, startling me upright, and Emily came spilling through with a gust of wind. She exhaled in a rush as she latched it shut.

"Mama!" Basil Allan directed his airplane toward her and stood still long enough for her to plant a kiss to his forehead before he took off running again. As she watched him go, her amusement melted into somberness.

My stomach clenched. "Where's Finn?"

Picking at the tangled curls draped over her shoulder, she joined me at the window. "We were approached by a couple of his acquaintances while we were walking. They told us there are rebels gathering nearby, so he went with them into town to collect more information. He told me we should remain here until he learns more."

Though my skin chilled at the potential of danger, I couldn't keep from raising my eyebrows and asking, "How was the rest of your walk?"

Color tinged her cheeks as her expression loosened from concerned to content. The corners of her mouth tipped shyly. "He asked me to marry him."

I grasped her shoulders, gaze intense. "And?"

Her lips spread into a full, joyful smile. "And I said yes."

A laugh leaped from my mouth as I tugged her into a crushing embrace. "Of course you did. I am so, so happy for you, Emily. Come. You must tell me every last detail of what happened."

A couple hours passed before Finn returned. He entered quietly, without urgency in his step. His gaze went straight to Emily, and I suppressed a smile at the unspoken affection that passed between them.

"They spotted rebels near the River Shannon—about a hundred of them," he explained as he shrugged out of his coat and plunked it on a hook.

"Where's that?" I asked.

"It's far enough away that we're not concerned for the time bein'." He pulled off his cap to scratch his head, then replaced it. "The lads have eyes on 'em and will send a messenger if they make a move, but for now, they don't appear to be a threat."

Emily and I expelled breaths in unison, but my prickle of warning remained. "What about Dublin?" I ventured. "Did they have any news—"

Pain struck my head and punched a gasp from my chest. My knees buckled, but Finn lunged and caught my fall. Gooseflesh raised on my arms as he clutched me tight and lowered me onto his knee. The edges of my vision feathered and flashed.

*No, not this. Not now. Not Baze. Please don't be Baze.*

I clung to Finn's shirt, focusing on the fabric's rough fibers and the tense muscle beneath—anything to keep me grounded, but the pull proved too strong. It sucked my consciousness into darkness, my thoughts twisting in a dizzying vortex until the light rushed up to meet me and the world bled back into view.

The majestic and imposing Cliffs of Moher stretched before me, a round tower presiding over them to my right. I lined my toes up with the rocky edge and gazed down at the sharp rocks slicing through crashing waves hundreds of feet below. One mere step would deliver me to the depths and break my body apart. I lifted my head and stared at the vast sky, so blue and so clear.

Shay. This was Shay. He didn't speak, didn't move in an identifiable way, but I knew. I'd touched his mind enough times to recognize the telling aura of turbulence. His body shivered, whether from the cutting wind or building emotion, I couldn't guess.

Why was he there and not in Dublin? Had he succeeded in taking the Lord Lieutenant and retreated to the cliffs to revel in his victory? Or was he wallowing in torment for having endured a crushing defeat at Baze's and Collin's hands?

Though I tried pulling back, my mind lingered in the vision. Was I afraid to let go for fear of learning my husband's fate?

No, this wasn't my doing. Shay was clinging to me, prodding at me. He wanted me to find him. A call to engage in a final confrontation—or a cry for help?

I thought back to Cornelius's last moments long ago in the Empress Theatre, remembering my swell of hope being dashed to bits as he rejected the call of the light and chose to remain rooted in darkness.

No matter what Shay had done, no matter the hatred stored in my heart, if there was any chance at all that he might choose the opposite path, I couldn't forsake him.

I had to get to the cliffs.

# Chapter Thirty-Nine

A LONE FIGURE STOOD AT THE precipice of the Cliffs of Moher. O'Brien's Tower loomed on an outcrop of rock in the distance. Tumultuous clouds blotted out the midday sun. Wind raged around me, tugging at my arms and coiling my skirt about my legs as though to stop me from proceeding, but I pressed on.

Finn helped me climb over the flagstones that lined the path and served to keep people from wandering too close to the treacherous edge. As my toes landed on the semi-hard earth, I gasped and grazed my eyes over the ground.

Tiny deep-blue flowers popped out against the green grass, poignant and ominous. I stooped and caressed the five telltale petals, picturing the first time they caught my eye—at the Empress Theatre in Cornelius's quarters. It was the flower he had planted in Sergeant Peter Moseley's eye. The flower that had loomed over the investigations in both London and Bath. The flower that was said to promise death for anyone who picked it.

Finn dropped to my level and glanced about. "This is where I met Ciaran—where he fell and I pulled him to safety," he whispered, absently sweeping a hand over the blossoms. "It's where everythin' started."

Resolve shivered through me. "Then it's where everything must end."

With a nod, he extended a hand. I grasped it firmly, and we rose together. When we had drawn close enough to Shay that I could distinguish the crude stitching in his coat, we halted.

Facing the sea, Shay either didn't know or didn't care that we approached. He stood still as a statue with his hands resting in his trouser pockets. Insistent gales buffeted him. He wobbled slightly and slid a foot forward, his toes jutting over the cliff edge and sending pebbles plummeting.

Finn slanted toward him, muscles taut and twitching as though ready to lunge.

The unease of being one leap away from death froze my legs in place, but I plastered on a brave face and said firmly, "What are you doing here?"

Howling gusts seemed to answer for him until, finally, the wind carried his weary voice to our ears. "I was defeated."

Defeated? How could he have been defeated and yet live? I'd seen Baze use lethal force before, and even if he had chosen to spare the Irishman's life, why would he have allowed him to flee? Unless Shay had incapacitated Baze somehow . . .

"What happened?" I ventured.

"I found the Lord Lieutenant," he said, voice hollow, "and I took him under my control."

Shooting Finn a confused glance, I held my breath and waited for Shay to elaborate. When no such explanation came, I said, "Isn't that what you wanted?"

"I thought it was . . ." Shay extracted his hands and stared at his empty palms for a long while. "Haven't you always been tryin' to appeal to me humanity? Tryin' to trick me into surrenderin' by claimin' my true victims are innocent." His tone grew low and contemplative. "It appears your claims were true."

Alarm prickled at the base of my neck. "What did you do?"

"Don't be worryin'." Turning his head to peer over his shoulder, he flashed a brief melancholy smile. "Your husband is alive." He curled his hands into fists and lowered them as he rotated toward me fully. "The same can't rightly be said for the young Constable Donoghue."

A hand flew to cover my mouth as shock stole my breath. *No, not Collin.*

The harsh rigidity of Shay's expression cracked as he asked, "How old was he?"

Denial sealed my mouth shut, and I fought against a rising sob.

"He's nineteen," Finn answered in my stead, drawing Shay's stormy gaze and returning it with a look of atypical intensity. "The same age I was when you took my innocence."

Shay nodded, resigned. "It appears you were right about me, then. I believed me power to be a gift, but I was wrong." A wet gleam in his eye caught the light as he swallowed. "I'm cursed." He half-turned and tilted to peer into the great abyss below.

"Don't jump," I blurted, then gritted my teeth, both angry and dismayed by the conviction in my appeal to the man who may have murdered Collin.

"Why shouldn't I?" he said, not looking away. "I see no other escape."

I bit down hard on my tongue, considering my next words carefully. Why not let Shay throw himself over and be done with it? He more than deserved it. Yet, seeing him weigh the decision of whether to fight for life or give it up brought dormant memories to light, memories of my final struggle with Cornelius. He and Shay had been bestowed a terrible power at their lowest moments, one that masqueraded as a solution and promised peace—but instead, it had corroded their thoughts and directed them to violence. It *was* a curse.

However, as Finn had demonstrated, that curse could be broken.

"You don't see an escape, because the darkness doesn't want you to," I said, measured and calm. "It's clouded your eyes and blinded you to the truth." My throat tightened. "The truth is there waiting for you. Finn discovered it long ago in a London jail cell, and it set him free. It can do the same for you."

A shadowy grin twisted Shay's mouth, and I wrapped an instinctive hand over my stomach. He jerked his head toward Finn with raised eyebrows. "Really? You think he's free? You think he's escaped his demons?" Shay barked a bitter laugh. "Then you're the one who's blind. There is no deliverance for those of us who have been cursed or damaged by this power." He stalked toward Finn, hand open and taut. "I'll prove it to you."

A cry ripped from Finn's mouth. His spine arced, stretched, and extended as though an invisible force had him by the skull and meant to tear him apart. Thick haze devoured the blue of his eyes and turned them completely black. He grasped empty air with flexed fingers. Pained groans crackled in his throat.

"On your knees," Shay commanded.

Finn collapsed to one, then the other. Tears the color of pitch oozed from his eyes.

I rooted my feet to the ground as wind churned around us, only able to watch Finn's struggle. There was nothing else I *could* do. His fight existed purely in the mind.

*Please Lord,* I prayed. *Let him remember that Your power resides inside of him. Lend him Your strength. Help him vanquish this evil for good.*

The biting wind softened and raised gooseflesh on my arms. Warmth began to swirl among the gales. Finn's eyes slid shut as he clawed at the ground.

"Is that what you've been doin', *a mhic*?" Shay snarled. "Struttin' around. Believin' you're better than the rest of us. Pretendin' to be free. Well, you may have everyone else fooled, but I'm not. I see straight through your trick."

Pushing his trembling torso upright, Finn half-opened one eye. "It's not a trick . . . and I'm no better than anyone. That includes you." He clenched his teeth and shifted one leg until he managed to drag his foot under him. His black eyes lightened to gray. "The only difference between us is that I've acknowledged I can't save meself and surrendered to the One who can. Because you're right . . . I battle demons every day." Shoving off his thigh, Finn wobbled to his feet. "They're strong, sure, but with the Spirit of the Almighty livin' in me, I have the power to cast them out." Clear, pure tears streamed down his cheeks, all darkness now washed away. "You can have that power too. You can be free."

The intensity of the wind lessened as Shay gaped at Finn, his body motionless as though made of stone. Thousands of thoughts raced behind his murky eyes. Slowly, redness crept into his cheeks as he gave the slightest shake of his head. "I can't . . ."

"Balderdash!" I blurted, my sharp voice smacking shock onto both his face and Finn's. I was weary of this constant petition—weary of his infuriating obstinance—and I was through being diplomatic. "You summoned me here for a reason, Shay. You want help but don't want to admit it, and that's the kind of idiotic pride that condemned Cornelius to an eternity of darkness." Fervent tears blurred my vision as I took a confident step forward. "Stop being so bullheaded. I know you think yourself cursed, but believe me when I say the light is strong enough to strike down the deepest darkness and cleanse every part of you. If you want to be free, then all you have to do is ask. That's it."

Surprise fading, he regarded me with bent shoulders and arms limp at his sides. He opened his mouth, closed it, and worked his bottom lip in thought. "If I do what you say," he rasped. "If I entrust my soul to the Creator . . . He'll release me from this curse?"

I twisted my hands against my stomach. In truth, I didn't know what would happen to Shay's mind or to his power. Would he be stripped of it all, completely made anew, or would the gift remain as a lifelong compulsion and somber reminder of all that he had done?

"I'm afraid I don't have all the answers." Ever so slowly, I closed the gap between us and rested my hand on his sweat-soaked chest. His heart struck wildly against my palm. "I do know this though: Even if your power remains, you will receive a far greater power that will give you every bit of strength you need to say no when it tries to command you."

Shay covered my hand with his and squeezed, staring intently as though trying to peer straight into my soul. His dark blue eyes swam with turmoil. His jaw popped, shifted, and then relaxed, his mouth falling open. An answer perched on the edge of his tongue—hesitant and unsure.

"Adelynn!"

The sharp yell whirled me around. Beyond the flagstones, Baze raced in our direction with Katherine trailing behind. He vaulted over the stone barrier, stumbling a bit as he landed, but he recovered and aimed his gun.

I lifted both hands. "Baze, wait! Don't—"

Shay's arm coiled around my neck. I cried out as he dragged me backward and planted us near the cliff's edge. Both Finn and Baze rushed toward us—Finn with wide eyes and Baze with a poised but tense demeanor. He kept his pistol pointed straight for Shay.

"Put your weapon down," Shay ordered.

"Release my wife," Baze shouted back.

"I don't think so. The moment I release her, I'll get a bullet to me chest. Do as I say or she will suffer the consequences."

I squirmed as his forearm clamped over my throat and then wheezed, "You don't have to keep choosing this path."

He burrowed his face against my ear and growled, "All your pretty petitions won't do me any good if your husband shoots me dead, will they now?"

Indeed, the calculated fury in Baze's eyes signaled that he hadn't come to engage in dialogue. The moment a clear shot revealed itself, he would take it.

"I can talk to him," I murmured back. "I can reason with him if you let me go."

"How can I trust you? How do I know you won't turn on me?"

"Because I'm tired of bloodshed." Sudden emotion filled my chest. "I don't want anyone else to die—and that includes you."

Shay sucked in a breath. Time stretched on as he held us still, the wind nipping at our clothes and trying to nudge us off balance. Then his muscles relaxed, his arms opened, and he permitted me to walk freely from his hold.

Baze stiffened, ready to fire, and I threw out my hands as though to deflect the bullet. "Stop. Please." I took measured steps and made sure to keep my body between him and Shay.

Glaring, he removed his finger from the trigger. "Move, Adelynn."

With a shake of my head, I stopped a few paces away. "He wants to surrender peacefully. You can take him into custody, and then all of this will be over."

Confusion drew Baze's brows together. His arms fell a tick as he searched my face. Then he looked back to Shay. A tidal wave of emotion crashed over him, flushing his cheeks and filling his eyes, and just as swiftly, that emotion hardened into resolve.

I inhaled a sharp breath. "No, Baze, don't—"

He lunged, reaching me with a single bound. He swept me aside with one arm and extended his pistol with the other. *Bang!*

A scream stuck in my throat as I whirled to see that Shay had dived to the ground and scrambled on all fours—unharmed. Baze aimed again, but Shay charged upright, throwing his arms around Baze's middle, then lifting and slamming him to the ground. A groan punched from his lips. Shay jumped atop him, scattering the gun and pinning his arms.

"Stop! Don't do this! Stop fighting!" I shouted and sprinted toward them, but Katherine's arms came around me and yanked me to a standstill. I thrashed against her as Finn joined the fray, catching his arm around Shay's neck and pulling him off Baze.

I watched in outrage as the scuffle drew dangerously near the cliffside. "Stop it, you idiots! Just stop!" But my commands went unheeded.

Shay spun and swept a leg into Finn's ankles, crumpling him. Baze came at the man from behind, but Shay reeled around, clamping Baze's neck in his hand and stiff-arming him back, a mere step from the brink. Lifted to his toes, Baze grappled at Shay's hand around his throat and gasped for air.

No. No more. This needed to end. Now.

Channeling every strand of power into my mind, I focused solely on Shay. Could I do this? Was it possible? I pushed out gently, tentatively, and felt the air ripple.

*Yes.*

I attacked, plunging into his mind and subduing his willpower with a commanding, *Stop!*

Shay's body seized. His muscles twitched and trembled, but his bones stayed immobile. Gritting his teeth, he fought to turn his head and stare at me, his eyes plastered wide.

Finn scrambled to his feet and drew beside me. "How did you do that?" he breathed.

"I'm not entirely sure," I whispered back.

With Shay paralyzed, Baze pried at the Irishman's stiff fingers still strangling his neck. The nails scratched his skin as he squirmed and pulled.

Suddenly, Shay's fingers snapped open. Baze stumbled backward.

And his heel caught empty air.

He gasped, and my mouth opened in a silent cry.

For what seemed like an eternity, he hovered there. Suspended. His eyes darted to mine, locked in disbelief.

Then he disappeared over the edge.

# Chapter Forty

TIME GROUND TO A HALT AS Baze fell.

I fell with him, earth rising to collide with my knees. Ice chilled my veins. The world grew dark. Sounds faded behind a shrill ringing.

Baze was gone. Just . . . gone. Without a warning—and so easily. All of it exactly as I had seen, exactly as I had come to dread.

A muffled voice slogged through the noise.

Barely possessing strength enough to raise my head, I peered through my lashes. Everything had smudged and distorted through a cascade of tears.

The voice echoed again, fragmented but sharper.

With a sob of effort, I managed to lift my chin. My eyes drifted to a blurred figure lying horizontally on the ground along the cliff wall.

"I've got him." The words sounded distant and warped.

Intent on the figure, I shook my head and mashed a wrist against my eyes, then blinked rapidly. My heart pounded as the outline cleared into someone recognizable.

Finn.

He lay on his stomach, his upper body tilted slightly over the edge. Then something jerked him forward another foot until half of his torso dangled in the sky.

Katherine burst past me and fell atop his legs, leaning all of her weight onto his waist. "Help me, angel!" she yelled.

Numb, I could only gape—my heart aching to hope but submitting to a barrage of doubt.

"I've got him." Finn's strained mumble sliced through my shock and yanked me to my feet. "I've got him, Adelynn. I've got him."

Hope overpowered my doubt and threw my legs into motion. I sprinted and skidded to my knees at Finn's side, then pressed my hands between his shoulder blades. His muscles bulged and vibrated as though they might snap at any moment. Gathering courage, I shifted my weight and carefully leaned over the great expanse of nothingness—and a cry tore from my lips.

Baze. Alive. Dangling by one arm. His body bumped against the sharp wall, and his feet scraped against the rocks in search of a foothold. Finn had both of his hands fastened around Baze's wrist, and Baze had a vice grip around Finn's wrist in return.

"I don't think . . . I can pull him up," Finn heaved. "My arm . . ."

I glanced to Finn's shoulder and spotted a large protrusion at the socket. Dislocation.

Panic rising, I rolled off Finn, shimmied onto my stomach, and extended just far enough to drop an arm over the edge. "Give me your hand," I shouted as uncertainty engulfed me. If Finn—a fully grown man—couldn't lift him, how could I—a petite pregnant woman—hope to do so?

Baze's head whipped up, and his eyes sparked with alarm. "What are you doing? Get back!" The surging wind modulated the volume and clarity of his words.

I shook my head. "No, give me your hand."

His face twisted in exertion as he swung his hand up and found purchase on a jutting rock just below my outstretched fingers. "I don't doubt your fortitude, Al," he grunted, "but I'm too heavy for you."

"Not with Finn and I both. Please." Tears dripped from my eyes, some sinking into Baze's shoulder, some falling to the ocean below.

Teeth clenched, Baze leveraged the rock to haul himself upward one inch, then two, then—

The rock shifted and broke free. Baze dropped. Finn's body jerked forward with a shout of pain. I yelled and threw myself onto his back. Somehow, Katherine and I managed to pin him enough to stop him from being dragged over the edge.

Keeping my weight centered between his hips, I tilted just enough to glimpse Baze. He had relaxed his arm and simply hung there. He looked to me, then craned his neck to look at the churning waves and jagged rocks beneath his feet.

"Don't you dare let go," I growled, unsuccessfully trying to sound resolute. "I swear, Basil Ford, if you let go, I shall never forgive you."

He brought his eyes back to mine. A single wet trail glistened on his cheek.

"I love you, Al," he mouthed, his voice stolen away by the wind.

"Baze, no!" I cried, clambering toward him, throwing out a hand. "Move!"

No sooner had the shout registered than Shay came barreling into me. He shouldered me aside and thrust his arm over the edge. He seized Baze's forearm under Finn's hands and yanked. Together, he and Finn muscled upward, first struggling to their knees, then pushing to their feet. Momentum carried them backward and hoisted Baze up over the side and onto solid ground. They didn't stop backpedaling until the last of his toes had crossed the threshold.

Then the three of them collapsed, panting and moaning.

"Baze!" I scrambled toward him, half crawling, half running—my only thought being to reach him. Weary though he must have been, he struggled upright and opened his arms to me. I fell into him. Air wheezed in his lungs as he crushed me to his chest.

"I thought I'd lost you," I cried. "I thought—"

"Shh. I know, Al," he whispered through chattering teeth. "I know."

"Tell me it's over. Please." I clutched a fistful of his shirt. "I just want this to be over."

"It's over." His quivering torso sagged under me, then finally gave out, dropping him back into a prone position, his embrace somehow enduring and pulling me with him. Heaving a great sigh, he said once more, "It's over."

As I lay atop his chest, my ear pressed against his hammering heart, I allowed every drop of my surging adrenaline to drain away. When my tears ran dry, my throat grew raw, and both of our trembling subsided, I exhaled deeply and squeezed his shirt tighter, finally allowing my thoughts to wander away from him. "What happened to Collin?" I murmured.

"He's alive." Baze's voice sounded so, so tired. "He's at The Red Cross hospital."

"Thank God." I closed my eyes in relief—until indignation flared. Lifting my head, I glowered down at him. "Of all the foolish things you could have done, Basil Ford, why did you come here? I *told* you I saw you fall from a great height. What could be a greater height than *this*?"

A challenge lit in his eyes despite his exhaustion. He removed one arm from me and muscled himself up onto his elbow. "I wouldn't have had to come here, *Adelynn Ford*, if you would just learn to stay put. Katherine said you were in trouble, and you're daft if you think I wouldn't come to your aid."

"I was fine. Finn was here, and I had everything under—"

His lips on mine effectively silenced the rest of my argument.

When we'd had our fill of one another, I sat up fully and looked to where Katherine tended Finn several feet away. She had crafted a makeshift sling from a torn scrap of her skirt and was positioning his limp left arm into it. A doctor would have to set his shoulder back in place. How he even managed to grip as strongly as he had in that condition was a marvel—and a miracle.

Baze shifted, and I helped him rise. He slumped against me, all weight on his healthy leg, as we approached. He thrust a hand toward Finn, and Finn took it tentatively. "You saved my life." Baze shook firmly. "Thank you. I'm . . . sorry that I ever doubted your motives."

"You were right to." Finn shrugged, then winced and grabbed at his shoulder. "If I never have to pull another soul from these cliffs, I'll be a happy man."

Soft chuckles passed through us, but a prickle of insistence, the feeling of something yet unfinished, sent gooseflesh skittering across my arms. My gaze darted about until it landed on Shay. He knelt quietly, hands flat on his thighs, observing our exchange.

Baze must have seen where my attention had drifted, for his body tensed. "This doesn't change anything, O'Sullivan," he said, tone sharp as a knife. "You may spend your entire life trying to atone for the things you've done and never arrive."

I placed a staying hand on Baze's chest, urging him into silence with my eyes. He took the cue and pursed his lips. Then I pulled away from him and eased toward Shay.

The Irishman watched me intently, cautiously—like an animal deciding whether to fight or flee. "You have me where you want me, graveling at your feet," he murmured. "What happens now?"

"That's up to you. You know what you must do to be freed." I placed my hands on either side of his face. "You are worthy of freedom. You are worthy of redemption."

Like a creature starved of affection, he slanted his head into my palm and closed his eyes with a shiver. Air thickened and swirled around us. His brows twitched together, and then he whispered, "Take this curse away, *a dhia, mo dhia*. And take me soul. You can have it."

Warmth filled my core, a deep, all-encompassing warmth the likes of which I had only experienced a single time—when I had stood before Cornelius and rendered his powers utterly useless at the Empress. In the moment, I had thought I merely deflected him . . . but what if I had actually stripped him of his power? If I could do that for Cornelius, could I do that for Shay?

*If it be your will, Lord, give me the ability to do this.*

Once more, I pushed out with my mind and plunged into Shay's. Darkness swallowed me, but a light shining from my core illuminated the void—and I sank deeper than I had ever dared go. Pitch-black sinew had fused to every wall and crevice of his mind, holding his willpower captive. The fibers lashed out, binding to me, hindering me, but I stayed the course. Scorching heat exploded in my chest and spiraled through my torso, across my limbs, and into my hands. Shay winced as I dug my fingertips into his skin. He squeezed his eyes shut, grinding his teeth.

*Free him. Free us. Free everyone who has been crushed under this curse.*

Bright beams widened and shone from every pore. The violent forces bulged and fought back. They thrashed and writhed, but they were powerless—and growing weaker. Light surged into every opening. Strands snapped. Darkness dissolved. The shadows scattered and fled, but there was nowhere they could hide.

Vertical gales twirled around us. Shay's groans morphed into a yell and faded into the roar. My vision burst white. With each thread of darkness I severed, Shay's chest expanded and his shoulders rose as though someone were peeling weights from him one by one.

Just like that, the last remnant of darkness dissipated. Purified. Leaving only peace.

The light dimmed. The air calmed. Bright sounds of birds and waves and wind took my spirits and carried them away into the skies. Unfettered joy squeezed me like a friendly embrace and sent my pulse skipping through my veins. I drew in a breath and released it long and slow as the clouds parted and warm sunbeams kissed my face.

Shay's features had relaxed, his head supported fully in my hands as though he slept. Tears trickled from his eyes and over my fingers. I smiled and rubbed a thumb along his cheekbone.

Everything in my mind had gone silent. No whispers. No premonition of another vision to come. For the first time since I made acquaintances with Cornelius three years ago at my engagement gala— when he had touched my mind, awakened my mysterious gift, and set this harrowing journey into motion—my mind felt free. And, somehow, I knew.

My power. Katherine's power. Shay's power.

Was gone.

## Chapter Forty-One

THE DRIVE BACK TO FINN'S COTTAGE was surreal. I nestled against Baze as he drove, peering out the windscreen through heavy lids, thinking through the events of the past hour and knowing I was an entirely different woman than the one who had gone to the cliffs with Finn to confront the enemy. I was lighter, more optimistic, and finally at peace.

Neither was Shay the same man. His curse had lifted. He had been redeemed, and he would never harm a living soul again—I believed that with all of my heart.

However, though the blood of the Savior could provide complete atonement for the spirit, it couldn't offer earthly payment for sins against human laws.

While still kneeing on the cliffs in surrender, Shay had looked to me with calm conviction. "I once criticized your obstinance, Adelynn— but it is that obstinance that has saved my life." His voice hitched. "Thank you."

Then, resignation had shadowed his face as he addressed Baze slowly, deliberately. "When it is safe to return to Dublin, you must deliver me to the police. I will accept the punishment for my actions— no matter how severe it may be."

Every instinct in me had fired, urging me to rebuke his request, but I had found the divine sense to remain silent, instead casting a sullen look to my husband.

Baze had worked his jaw for a long moment before nodding to Shay. "May God have mercy on your soul."

The rebellion lasted nearly a week before the British Army

overwhelmed the rebels and forced a surrender on Saturday. Hundreds of casualties. Thousands of prisoners. Irreparable damage to the city. We stayed at Finn's for as long as Dublin remained under siege, and as soon as the city allowed civilians inside, we returned.

As Shay prepared to accompany Baze to the Dublin Metropolitan Police, he and Katherine came together for a last goodbye. She extended her hand, allowing him to slot her silver claddagh back into its rightful place on her left ring finger, and then they shared a slow, melancholy kiss.

My stomach turned as I watched their emotional farewell. Katherine's glistening eyes opened wide the window to her soul, exposing a lifetime of yearning tainted by the heartbreak of betrayal. He had tried to kill her, after all—but he was also her first love. Her only love. And his curse had infected them both. Though she would bear those scars long after he was gone, forgiveness had managed to glue some of the broken shards of her heart back together and make way for healing.

When they finally parted, Baze took the Shay into custody and delivered him to the Dublin Police where he was quickly locked behind bars to await trial.

With that difficult task behind us, Baze, Darragh, and I went to Collin.

The Red Cross had worked miracles. They had cleaned and repaired the wound to the best of their abilities, saving his organs and restoring his blood supply—meaning he was well on the mend.

"I'm sorry for bein' in dire straits, sir." Collin's voice sounded clear and bright despite his circumstance. "I'll take extra shifts to make up the time I've lost. I'll work extra hard."

"Don't be worryin' yourself, Donoghue." Darragh chuckled and ruffled his hair. "Just focus on healin' up and gettin' back on your feet. That's an order, you hear?"

Collin scrunched his nose and waved Darragh's hand away, then angled toward Baze. "I've been thinkin', Mr. Ford . . ." At Baze's raised eyebrows, Collin cleared his throat. "Sorry. I mean, um, Baze. After I recover and your wife has the baby and all that"—his cheeks reddened as he glanced my way—"I thought I might visit you in London. If you would have me."

The hesitant anticipation in his voice squeezed my heart.

Baze smiled. "Collin, you may visit whenever and as often as you like. Our home will always be open to you." He glanced my way, and unspoken resolution passed between us. Collin had Darragh watching out for him and his fellow policemen providing companionship, but now that he had lost the last of his blood relatives, we had determined to pour into him with all the love of a family.

"I have an idea," Baze mentioned as we returned to Father's home. "I've already cleared it with Darragh, but I need Whelan's approval before we can make it official."

In Father's study, Baze hopped on the telephone and connected to Whelan. I sat backward on the desk, silent and listening. If I leaned just so, I could pick up the muffled voice through the receiver—though, Whelan was anything but quiet.

"Foooord!" he bellowed as soon as he came on the line.

Baze yanked the receiver away with an amused grimace. I covered my mouth to silence a laugh.

"I'm not one to be too sentimental, but I can't tell you what sweet music your voice is to these old ears." He lowered his volume but still spoke loud enough that I could clearly hear every word. "Have you done what you set out to do?"

"Yes, sir." Baze met my eyes with a contented smile. "It's over."

A rush of air crackled in Whelan's mouthpiece. "I don't suppose you've given my offer any more thought?"

Baze's promotion. We hadn't yet discussed it, but I trusted him to do what he thought was right.

"I have, sir." Baze scooped up my hand. "I accept. I know I'm not much good in the field anymore, but I want to mentor our new recruits and train them to be respectable men and efficient policemen. So many people have spoken into my life. It's my turn to do the same."

"Aye, that it is. Bennett always told me he saw greatness in you, and he was right—as usual," Whelan mused, then cleared his throat. "I'll put in the recommendation straightaway, then. Congratulations, future Detective Chief Inspector Ford."

Baze's chest expanded as I leaned forward and kissed his temple. "Sir, I have one more request before you go."

"Don't even think about asking for more than the regular raise."

"We can discuss that later." Baze chuckled. "No, I wondered if it might be possible to transfer one Constable Collin Donoghue from the Dublin Metropolitan Police to London. I think he would be a great asset to our team. He's driven, hardworking, and he stays out of trouble. I would—"

"Done."

"Sir?"

Whelan chortled. "Darragh's been keeping me abreast of what you've been up to in Ireland. Tell the lad to recover quickly and that I'll be putting him to work the moment he sets foot in London. Make sure he knows I'm a tyrant to be feared. Got that?" The serious words conflicted with the superintendent's humorous tone.

Baze shook his head. "Duly noted, sir. Thank you."

When he had replaced the receiver and shoved the telephone aside, he tugged my hand and pulled me onto his lap. His lips promptly found mine as his hand cradled my cheek.

Eventually leaning back, I said, "I'm proud of you."

His tender gaze roamed my face. "And I'm proud of *you*."

I swept my hands across the rough tweed of his casual garb. "You know, I quite like this look on you." I ran my fingers over his jaw and delighted in the scratchy softness of his weeks-old growth. The dark whiskers had begun filling in and heightened his handsomeness tenfold. "Perhaps we should remain here and live out the rest of our days as working-class citizens."

"Please, Al. You wouldn't last a day without the fineries of upper-class society." His dimple emerged with a smirk. "Besides, you can't cook. We'd starve."

I balked and wiggled his head. "It has been weeks since I have had access to our fineries, thank you very much. I would do just fine."

"If you say so."

"I say so." I bolstered myself, intent to continue the banter, but a sudden nudge in my stomach snatched my attention. I sucked in a breath.

Baze stiffened and looked me over. "What? What is it?"

I grabbed his hand and pressed it hard against the side of my abdomen, waiting.

"What is it?" he whispered.

"Shh." I held him still, barely breathing. Seconds stretched by.

There. Another nudge—firmer than the last.

Lips parted, Baze lifted his bewildered eyes to mine. "Is that . . . ?"

"That's our baby." Giggles bubbled in my chest. "She's kicking."

Spreading his fingers over my belly and pushing slightly harder, he waited for another tap, then grinned. "She feels strong. Like her mother."

We beamed and laughed, delighting in our child's newfound prods and pokes, until the joy of the moment swept us into an impassioned kiss. Whether spurred by his beard tickling my skin or the wild emotions swirling from my condition, I positively burned with love and desire for him.

He dipped his chin just enough to free his bottom lip and whisper, "Let's go home."

"Soon," I whispered back with a final lingering kiss. "There's one thing yet to do."

The pulsing sound of the sea soared into the evening sky. Gulls swooped and let loose their ambient calls. A sunset painted the sky with warm golds, pinks, and reds and lit Liscannor Castle's crumbling parapet with a heartening glow.

As her loose curls drifted about her face, Emily inhaled the salty air. She didn't often wear her hair down—not especially when in the proper society of London—but with each day that she spent in Ireland, she found herself conforming more and more to its casual and carefree nature.

Finn's gentle voice interrupted her reverie. "Are you ready, Em?"

First, she glanced toward Adelynn and Baze. Keeping Basil Allan occupied, they had perched a little lower on the hill, close enough to watch but far enough that they allowed a sense of privacy. Then, with an easy smile, she turned toward Finn. "I'm ready."

He beamed and nodded to the reverend standing beside them—a scruffy thirty-something man with a five o'clock shadow, tattered flat cap, and suit that barely resembled proper wedding attire. Similarly, Finn had donned a basic coat with a plain waistcoat and trousers. Emily matched his formality, or lack thereof, with a modest blue dress and a circlet of white flowers crowning her head.

"Ye've chosen to be handfasted, so if ye please, take each other's right hands," the reverend instructed.

Finn took up her hand in his, and they cracked eager smiles.

The reverend wrapped a cord braided from strips of leather in a crisscrossing pattern, binding their hands together—tight and unyielding. "This cord be representin' the marriage bond and of the commitment yer makin' to one another. Have ye any vows to exchange?"

Eyes alight and sparkling in the golden sunset, Finn said, "I vow to cherish you and love you for all of me days, as many as the good Lord will give me."

Emily smiled. "And I vow to do the same."

The reverend paused a beat, then huffed. "Not folks of many words, are ye? Then I'll be addin' my own." He bowed his head and extended a hand over theirs. "May the blessing of light be on ye—light without and light within. May the blessed sunlight shine on ye and warm yer hearts till it glows like a great peat fire. May yer home be filled with laughter. May yer pockets be filled with gold. And may ye have all the happiness yer Irish—um, or English—heart can hold. May yer blessin's outnumber the shamrocks that grow, and may trouble avoid ye wherever ye go. May luck be a friend to ye and be with ye in all yer days, and may trouble be to ye a stranger, always."

The benediction concluded, the reverend cocked his head and looked between them, waiting. When they didn't move, he smacked Finn's arm with his Bible. "Go on then, you eejit. Give her a right *póg* before she gets bored with you."

Emily laughed as Finn's ears flushed red, but as he turned to her and tracked his gaze across her face and to her lips, the embarrassment melted from his features. He stepped close, tucked a solid hand behind her neck, and kissed her soundly, sending a warm burst of tingles to the crown of her head and the tips of her toes.

"Mama!" Basil Allan's cry startled them apart.

"Stop, get back here!" came Adelynn's exasperated shout, soon followed by an "I'm sorry, Emily, he's so fast!"

Basil Allan scrambled up the hill. Emily chuckled and stooped to receive him with her free arm, and when she shifted him onto her hip, Finn bent his face to hers with a murmur. "I wasn't finished."

"No!" Basil Allan scrunched his nose and pushed Finn's head away. "Only I get kisses."

Finn rolled his eyes Emily's way and then raised a brow. "Is that so? Well, be careful for what you be wishin'." Together, he and Emily leaned in and barraged the child's cheeks with myriad kisses. He squealed and giggled, trying his very best to twist and escape the onslaught. Soon, he gave up and slumped against Emily's shoulder, heaving a defeated sigh.

Emily tilted her head against his and met Finn's eyes—her husband's eyes—and basked in the love emanating from him. For so long, she had doubted she would ever love another man in the way she had loved Bennett. Yet, through every trial and every heartbreak, God had shown up in her life. If she hadn't trusted Him to pull her from the depths of grief, committing to put one foot in front of the other, she never would have been led to Finn.

Now she saw that it was true. She wouldn't ever love a man as she had loved Bennett, for the love she held for him was unique and could never be replicated.

Rather, she had learned to love anew, her love for Finn unique in its own way—and just as strong.

And it made her heart whole again.

# Epilogue



*Five months later . . .*

I REENTERED THE WORLD SLOWLY, TWITCHING my toes, then my fingers. Sensations crawled back. Grogginess. Cold. A growing ache. Finally, I fluttered my eyes open. I lay on my back, head propped on a pillow. The pain intensified, centering in my abdomen. A groan rose in my throat, and I clenched but couldn't gather enough strength to lift my hand to it.

The blurry light of a lamp sparkled in my vision across the room. A tall shadow blotted it out, then blotted it again, and I realized a person was pacing before it. I blinked faster to clear my eyes until Baze's image grew crystal clear. He cradled something in his arms—what appeared to be a tight ball of linens, and in my state of delirium, that's all I thought it was.

Until the linen cooed.

My heart nearly ripped from my chest. Mustering the strength this time, I jerked my hand to my stomach. It lay flat. Empty. Bandaged.

The gentle grunting continued, then heightened into a sound of distress. Had I enough energy, I would have leaped from the bed and taken the bundle from him.

Baze dipped his head and kissed it. "Shh. It's all right. No need to fuss. Papa's here." With each of his tender whispers, the cries eased into a gurgle, then silence. "That's it. Just sleep now." He smiled, and the sense of purpose blazing in his eyes and commanding his whole posture rivaled no other.

Joy for the beautiful picture before me clashed with the deepening pain in my abdomen. Spikes of pain flared with every pulse. A sob escaped my lips and attracted Baze's attention. He was at my side in a heartbeat, perching on the edge of the bed and smoothing one hand over my forehead.

"It hurts, Baze," I whimpered.

"I know. It's all right." He continued smoothing my hair, worry crinkling his brow. "Frederick said we can give you more morphine in a little while."

This didn't feel normal. Something was wrong. "What happened?"

"Do you not remember?"

I shook my head weakly, digging for a recollection but only unearthing blank memories.

"You gave birth, Al." His chest filled slowly. "You labored for nearly twelve hours at home, and when we brought you to hospital, it continued for well over a day. Frederick said things weren't progressing as they should, that your small frame may be impeding your ability to carry out a natural delivery."

"They did a caesarian." My breath hitched. That explained the pain.

He nodded, then hesitated. Color darkened his cheeks as his voice dropped to a whisper. "You hemorrhaged during the surgery. Frederick said there was a lot of blood." His expression clouded as he focused on the bundle in his arm. "They acted swiftly to stop the bleeding and get her out, but to do that . . ." He met my gaze. "There wasn't another way. They had to—"

"Don't." I gripped his arm. He didn't need to say it. The truth was etched in the knot of his lips and the glisten of his eyes.

As he slipped his firm, comforting fingers around my neck, he tipped his forehead against mine. We sat in silence. Absorbing. Mourning. "I'm sorry," he whispered.

Rather than allow the reality of my condition to summon demons of anger and self-pity, I directed my mind to the heavens and fixated on a single word. "Her?" I searched his face. "You said her?"

The fierce, protective demeanor I had seen him assume moments ago returned, overpowering the troubles on his features. "You were right all along, Al." He shifted and carefully laid the bundle atop my chest. "We have a daughter."

As her dense weight compressed my lungs and her sweet scent overwhelmed my senses, every dormant maternal instinct flared to life. Her fair wispy hair, her little button nose, her chubby cheeks and double chin—everything about her was perfect. "She's so beautiful," I breathed.

Baze's tender eyes drifted to me. "You both are."

I shot him a wry grin. "You're just saying that. I'm sure I look affright."

"No, I meant every word."

Cheeks warming, I returned my gaze to our child, unwilling to look away from her for any longer than I had to. "What should we do about her name?" Tilting my head, I stuck my finger into one of her curled hands, and she latched on with incredible strength for one so new to this world. "I know we wanted to wait to see what she looked like, but now that she's here, I haven't the faintest idea."

Baze stroked the baby's head thoughtfully. "I was thinking Evelyn."

"That could work." I squinted at her face, trying it out. "What prompted Evelyn?"

"It means 'desired child.' I want her to know now and forever how loved she is."

With a sharp inhale, I gaped at him. Considering how strongly he had petitioned against a child barely a year ago, seeing him so naturally and enthusiastically slide into his new role as a father weakened and warmed every part of me.

"What?" He returned my stare with an eyebrow perked in confusion. "Do you not like it?"

I exhaled a growl. "Basil Ford, you know exactly what you're doing, and if I could move right now, I would kiss you."

His puzzlement morphed into understanding as he grinned. "I can help with that." He leaned over, pressing our daughter between us, and took my lips in a tender kiss.

No sooner had we begun than Evelyn gurgled and kicked her legs in the swaddle. The hint of discomfort in her voice set me on alert.

I broke from Baze's kiss, drawing a sigh from his mouth, and examined her urgently. "She sounds unhappy. Do you think she's unhappy? I don't know how to do this. What should I do?"

"She can manage for a few moments more. I'm only concerned about her mother right now." He guided my lips back to his. Evelyn's contented grunts soon intermingled with our punctuated breaths.

I squeezed her tighter and murmured, "I love you, Baze."

He grazed my cheek with a knuckle, then cradled our daughter's head. "I love you too, Al."

With Adelynn relegated to bed rest until she healed, Baze helped fulfill Evelyn's needs as best as he was able. Beyond enduring crippling nightmares—of defending Evelyn from faceless attackers and of watching Adelynn slowly dying on the birthing table—he could hardly stand to be in a different room than his daughter, sometimes even stealing her away from the nanny they hired.

"Mrs. Spencer is here to see you, Mr. Ford," the butler announced as he entered the bedroom. "And another car is on its way up the drive."

With a grimace, Baze mentally prepared for the onslaught of guests and clutched Evelyn closer. He had managed to keep visitors away at the start, but after two weeks and dozens of calls, he couldn't hold them back any longer. "Thank you. I shall be there shortly."

Leaving Adelynn to rest, Baze slipped into the hall, then paused outside the closed door—alone with his thoughts and his daughter tucked in the crook of his arm. He had been carrying her in that position so often now that it felt bare without her there.

From the moment he first held her, he knew he would never love the same again. Emily had been right. Evelyn had shattered everything he had once known about love. What he harbored for her now was an intense, feral love that fired every nerve and muscle within him each time she made a sound or targeted him with her large disarming eyes.

God help anyone who ever tried to deal her harm.

Baze found Mrs. Spencer waiting in the sitting room. She brightened as he approached and extended one hand to cradle Evelyn's round head. "Oh, isn't she a dear." She glanced up at Baze, then back to Evelyn and tapped her little nose. "I do believe you have Papa's nose. Yes, you do."

Chest tightening, Baze examined his daughter's face. He didn't see much of him *or* Adelynn in her pudgy features. "You think so?"

"Very much so." Mrs. Spencer laughed, then patted Baze's cheek. "I am going to see to my own daughter now."

Baze frowned and hefted the baby higher. "You don't want to hold her?"

"There will be plenty of time for that. Infants receive far more attention than their mothers when they first arrive." Her eyes twinkled. "Besides, your brothers and their families were right behind me, so I believe you are about to have your hands full."

Just as she predicted, the moment she retreated to Adelynn's bedchamber, the butler delivered Percy, Frederick, and Aubrey and their wives—along with several of their daughters—into the sitting room. Blessed silence transformed into dizzying chaos as Baze's nieces gave exuberant squeals of glee and snatched Evelyn away from him.

Anxiety spiked as he watched them pass her around, cooing and babbling at her face. He nearly jumped in to take her back, but his brothers blocked his rescue attempt with firm handshakes and pats on the back.

"Congratulations," Percy said, beaming.

"Indeed." Aubrey snickered and wagged his eyebrows. "Hardheaded though you may be, I knew it was only a matter of time before Adelynn broke you down."

Frederick elbowed him. "Don't start that."

Aubrey lifted his hands. "I'm not starting anything. Only stating facts."

"Well, see that you keep those facts to yourself, then." Frederick turned to Baze. "How is Adelynn today?"

"She is in good spirits," Baze said, eyes still following Evelyn's flight from woman to woman.

Aubrey's wife secured the baby next and sidled up to her husband, face alight. "Isn't she a doll? I so miss having a baby in our home. Wouldn't it be grand if we had another?"

Neck reddening, Aubrey cleared his throat. "I think the time for that has long passed, darling, but I'm sure you would be welcome to visit as often as you like." He angled his head and examined the baby, then shot Baze a sympathetic grimace. "She looks like you. Poor thing."

"Oh, be nice." His wife rubbed his arm, then wandered back to the waiting throng of nieces.

When she'd traveled out of range, Aubrey's face twisted in mock concern. "I do hope she'll grow out of it. Can you imagine having to saunter around with your unsightly profile?" He snorted. "Well, I suppose you can."

Spurred by the challenge, Baze lashed an arm around Aubrey's neck and locked him in place. "If she takes after me, at least we know she won't lack in height." He dug his knuckles into Aubrey's head. "Not that you would know anything about that."

Snickering, Aubrey wrenched away and shoved Baze's shoulder, and as Baze swung around with a loose fist, Percy barreled in and pushed them apart. "Enough. It seems there are two children in this room, and the infant isn't one of them."

Baze and Aubrey regarded one another for a moment, then turned and unleashed a barrage upon their eldest brother, prompting Frederick to spring to his aid. What followed was a flurry of lively tussling, lighthearted banter, and spirited laughter. Sides aching, Baze couldn't remember the last time they had let all pretense fall and interacted simply as brothers—and it felt good.

Clipped shoes coming down the adjacent hallway broke the brothers apart and restored some semblance of decorum to the room. Baze gave one last playful swipe to Aubrey's face before they smoothed their suits and calmed—just in time for Alistair and Frances Ford to enter.

A hush fell over the room as the steadfast patriarch led his wife to where their sons stood. One of the nieces crossed to them obediently and delivered the baby into Frances's arms.

The older woman's eyes grew teary as she bounced Evelyn gently. "She is so beautiful, Basil." She traced the baby's face with her thin, weathered finger. "What did you call her?"

"Evelyn." His throat tightened. "Evelyn Frances Ford."

Mother released a dramatic little gasp and laughed. "Oh, you sweet boy. What have I done to deserve such kind sons?" She grasped Baze's chin, shook it gently, and coaxed out his shy smile.

Alistair peeked over her shoulder. "She is quite a handsome child. You should be proud."

"I am," Baze said warily, bracing for where he knew his father's thoughts would go.

The man sniffed. "The first child is often the most difficult as you learn how to be a parent, but I know you are capable. May you and Adelynn be blessed with a large and prosperous family."

There it was. Considering the man's obsession with succession and pedigree, Baze had known it would enter the discussion, but things were different now and, as a result, so was his response. Instead of anger, or annoyance even, it only fostered sadness. For even if he wanted to, he could no longer produce a broad and extensive lineage.

"She is going to be our only child," he said quietly, though he may as well have shouted for all the eyes that locked upon him.

Saying it aloud awakened some of the emotion he had tried to shove away in the days following the birth—the utter terror and uselessness that had gripped him as he paced in the waiting room while Adelynn bled out on the operating table. "There were complications."

Everyone glanced to Frederick as though for confirmation, and he nodded somberly.

Vision blurring, Baze stared at Evelyn. He couldn't look at his father, didn't want to see the judgment or the disappointment souring the man's face.

"Well," Alistair finally said—and Baze stiffened—but when the man continued, his voice had lightened. "You shall have to try not to spoil this poor thing to death then. It is a vice of parents of single children, and if I know you, you shall dote upon her until you are blue in the face."

Baze raised his head in surprise, mouth falling agape.

Though Alistair's features remained stiff and stoic, a twinkle had sprung to his eyes. Baze sucked in a breath as he searched for the hidden reprimand, the dormant resentment that had tainted his boyhood and adolescence—but he saw nothing of the sort.

Only warmth.

A slow heat rolled from the crown of Baze's head out to every limb as Alistair squeezed past his wife and stood chest to chest, their eyelines nearly level. Baze suddenly realized just how old and weary his father looked. The man had lost several inches of his tall and regal frame. His once tidy salt-and-pepper hair now rested in wayward white waves, and the paper-thin skin of his face had sagged and wrinkled.

Alistair pulled at his fingers and twisted his wedding band. "I have given much thought to what you said many months ago, and I . . . I'm sorry." His face flushed as he captured Baze in his soft but steely gaze. "I'm sorry, Basil."

Baze could only stare as his father's humble words swirled in his mind. He snatched them up and buried them deep in his heart. They took root, absorbing into his soul where they began to repair a lifetime of damage. Though he would suffer the scars for the rest of his life, the wounds could finally begin to heal.

"I forgive you, Father," Baze whispered, the words coming free and easy.

With a curt nod, his father extended an open hand. Though Baze's hopes fell a little, he accepted the firm gesture. His father held on for an extended beat, his grip growing stiffer, his mouth twisting flatter, before he finally squeezed and yanked on Baze's hand.

Baze stumbled forward into the man's crushing one-armed embrace. Tears came swift and thick as he clung to his father. Alistair held him still and resolute, his arm clutching tighter and tighter until Baze couldn't breathe.

Just as quickly as he initiated it, Alistair pushed back. He cleared his throat, tugged his suit coat, and angled his chin into a noble posture. Face red with emotion, he reached into his pocket and produced an envelope. "This is for you."

Head and heart whirling, Baze hurried to clear away his tears as he accepted the packet. "What is it?"

"It's a gift. I would like you to open it with your wife after we have all gone." Father placed his withering hand on the side of Baze's face, cradling it as he might do to a small child. Father's lips stretched into a rare smile. "I am proud of you, Basil."

Evelyn's famished cries reached my ears before Baze entered our bedchamber. Holding her upright with her head pressed against his shoulder, he tried to quell the squirming infant's protests by rocking and shushing her—then finally resorted to reasoning with her.

With an amused grin, I pulled myself into a half-sitting position against my fluffed pillows. "Here, bring her to me."

He tilted her away, a challenge in his eyes. "No, I can get her to stop. I just need a moment."

"Baze, she's hungry." I tugged at the front of my nightgown.

Clutching her tight, he gave me the most pitiful expression. "One more minute."

Sweet as his motives might have been, every motherly alarm sounded within me. "Basil Ford, if you don't let me feed our daughter, I am going to leap out of this bed and take her from you, and Frederick would have your head if I tore these stitches open."

With a groan, he relinquished our child and laid her on my chest. He dragged over a backward chair and settled onto it, arms crossed over the backrest, as I helped Evelyn latch, silencing her wails. She drank fast and deep, her clear blue eyes wide and inquisitive. I smiled, stroking her cheeks.

Baze dropped his chin onto his forearm as he watched with awe and a twinge of jealousy.

I chuckled. "There's no need for urgency, Baze. She's not going anywhere."

He grimaced. "But she's barely two weeks old and already so big."

"And this from the man who didn't want children in the first place."

"I can't help it. Just look at her face." He jutted a hand. "She has no business being that cute."

My grin widened. "I do believe she has you wrapped completely around her finger already."

He rolled his eyes, but his expression and posture all but screamed the truth. He sighed and watched her a few moments more, then brightened and reached into his coat pocket and came out with a folded envelope. "Father gave me this. He told me to open it when everyone had gone."

Curiosity piqued, I tipped my chin. "Go on then."

After tearing into it, he pulled out two slips of paper and read the first silently, his eyes widening with each line. When he finished, he yanked out the bottom paper and scanned it. "It's the deed to your father's property in Ireland." He flashed the official document toward me. "He purchased it from your mother. He's giving it to us."

I gasped. After several months of no interest in the estate, I had hoped it wouldn't sell and that Mother would reconsider her venture. Then a buyer had come forward and dashed all of those hopes to bits. Little did we know, apparently, that buyer had been one Alistair Ford.

"Why would he do that for us?" I asked, skeptical.

Pride flickered in Baze's eyes. "I think he's trying to make things right. He's changing, Al."

Compassion warmed my heart toward Mr. Ford. Baze had explained the final call he made to his father before the rebellion, confronting him with the truth and offering reconciliation. His father had caused us so much strife that I doubted he would ever see the wrong in his actions, but it appeared that even a heart as cold as his could soften with forgiveness.

I smiled with a contented sigh. "I'm so glad."

With a great smack, Evelyn finished her meal and grunted happily. As I pulled my robe into a decent state, Baze perked up and set the papers on the end of the bed. "Can I take her now?"

"No!" I draped her across my shoulder, then patted her back. "You've had her long enough."

His face fell, but before he could speak, there came a knock at the door. He hopped up from the chair and answered it. "Yes, do you need something?"

"There are more visitors to see you, Mr. Ford," the butler responded.

I groaned, noting the lateness of the hour. "Send them away," I whisper-shouted.

He waved a dismissive hand at me and shook his head at the butler. "We have retired for the evening. Please tell them to return tomorrow."

"I'm sorry, sir, they insisted. They are quite adamant that you would like to see them."

A great rustle erupted on the other side of the door, and then a flurry of activity swept Baze aside—and when I caught the light of the beaming faces of Finn, Emily, and Basil Allan, I let out a loud exclamation and nearly jumped up to intercept them.

Emily leaped at Baze, squishing him in a small but mighty embrace, and then made straight for me. She climbed onto the bed and burrowed in beside me as our husbands exchanged a hearty handshake. Scratching light fingers over Evelyn's back, she caught her breath and shook her head. "I'm so sorry we missed the birth. Your call announcing her arrival took us by surprise."

"She surprised us too." I laughed. "I'm so delighted you've come. How long will you be in London?"

"Indefinitely, actually." She traded an excited, knowing smile with Finn. "We've decided that it would be best to raise Basil Allan here, in a familiar place and close to family."

As though hearing his name, Basil Allan clambered over my legs and crawled to his mother. He plopped onto her lap and stared at Evelyn with a suspicious scrunch of his nose. "What's that?"

Stifling a laugh, I positioned her faceup in my arms so he could see. "She's a baby."

He shook his head and pointed at himself. "No, I'm a baby."

"You're too old to be a baby, my love." Emily brushed his tousled brown curls out of his eyes and nodded at Evelyn. "There, now. How do you like her?"

His wary eyes roamed her face, and then he shrugged. "I like her just fine."

We laughed, and Emily poked his cheek. "You say that now, but wait a decade or two and I'm sure you'll be smitten."

Baze made a strangled, slightly incredulous noise. "Really, Emily? He may be my best mate's son, but you're daft if you think I'll ever let my daughter—"

"She was joking," I crooned but shot Emily a deliberate smirk.

Subdued for now, Baze turned to Finn. "Have you received any news from Katherine?"

The room grew quiet as the solemn meaning behind Baze's words hovered over us.

Finn swallowed, then nodded. "Kate sent me a letter a few weeks ago. Shay finally stood trial for the crimes police could provide evidence for, and the court found him guilty, as we expected. They sentenced him to hang . . . he probably already has." Finn's jaw pulsed. "Kate was plannin' to travel to the States once it was over."

Sorrow pinched my chest. Not only would we likely never see Katherine again, but I mourned that Shay's life had to end in that way. Not that he shouldn't pay the price for all the misdeeds he committed—the people he terrorized deserved justice—but I regretted that his choices had made that the only path forward.

Even so, I took heart in the fact that his soul had been freed from the shackles of darkness and was now basking fully in the light.

Thoughts of Katherine and Shay snatched my mind back to when this all started, back to my first innocent interaction with Cornelius Marx. A lifetime ago, it seemed. His clever stage tricks and deceitful charm had mesmerized me, awakening my unique gift—and thus began this extraordinary journey.

I had witnessed the future. Said goodbye to dear friends. Petitioned for lost souls. Clung to feeble hope. And in the face of incredible darkness, redemption had proven the strongest magic of all.

Lively banter tugged me back to the present. Finn, Emily, and Baze had entered into rousing conversation about their new home, when they might go back to visit Ireland, and what Finn would do for work—taking up residence as the Dubliner Magician once again.

Evelyn soon dozed off, and I stroked her tiny, curled fist as I listened quietly to the people whom I treasured. My eyes roamed across Emily, then to Finn. Finally, they locked on Baze.

Somewhere in the middle of his dialogue, he noticed me and smiled a deep and dazzling smile that awakened feelings and flutters just as strong and profound as the first time we had kissed so many years ago in the hedge between our homes.

Breathing a contented sigh, I returned his smile with one of peace and adoration and squeezed our daughter tight to my heart.

# Author's Note

On the morning of Monday, April 24, 1916, the day after Easter, a peaceful Dublin rustled to life, unaware that the course of Irish history was about to change in what would be called the Easter Rising. Armed rebels began gathering in the streets, comprised of several factions—the Irish Volunteers, the Irish Citizen Army, and the all-woman Cumann na mBan. Their objective? To overthrow what had been more than 700 years of British rule.

The rebels set up a perimeter around the center of the city, erecting barricades and posting troops at important government buildings—Dublin Castle included (more on that in a second).

Another of those buildings was the General Post Office. Side note: When I visited Dublin in 2012, I touched one of the many bullet holes that had damaged the Post Office's façade in the battle (though, there's controversy today over whether the holes were actually caused by bullets).

In my book, the combat first broke out in the morning, but it actually didn't begin until around midday. With Baze's strategic mind urging them to rise early to try to beat the fighting, I moved the conflict up a little in order to place more obstacles in their path.

Despite the raging battle, Baze and Collin arrived safely at Dublin Castle to meet Constable James O'Brien stationed at Cork Hill Gate. Constable O'Brien was a real person—he had been with the Dublin Metropolitan Police for twenty-one years—and he was reported to be the first casualty of the Rising, killed while trying to stop Volunteers from entering the gate. As fate would have it, the man who shot him, Seán Connolly, was the first rebel to die not too long after.

The rebels had the upper hand at the start, but the British Army was quick to bring in reinforcements and take control. The conflict ended less than a week later on Saturday, April 29, with nearly 500 casualties and thousands injured.

Though a failure on the rebels' part, the Rising made way for the fight to continue. The Irish War of Independence broke out in 1919, lasted for three years, and led to the Anglo-Irish Treaty establishing the Irish Free State as part of the British Commonwealth. Northern Ireland removed itself from the treaty, choosing to remain part of Britain, and the people of Ireland split again with some wanting *full* independence. This led to civil war. In 1937, Ireland adopted a new constitution, and they finally achieved their goal of independence in 1949.

**Dublin Castle**

At the start of the Rising, rebels tried to take control of Dublin Castle, but resistance from the British Army caused them to retreat. Ironically, had the rebels pushed harder, they likely would have taken it, because unbeknownst to them, the occupation of British troops was incredibly light.

The appearance of The Red Cross there was true. They set up beds in Dublin Castle when the Great War broke out and were mainly responsible for tending to troops injured in the fighting, which worked in my favor after our courageous Collin sustained his injury nearby.

It's also true that the Lord Lieutenants of Ireland lived in the Viceregal Apartments in Dublin Castle. However, halfway through the nineteenth century, that changed to a more temporary arrangement. They would split their time between Dublin Castle and a residence in Phoenix Park (where my heroes stayed for the duration of their time in Ireland). The Lord Lieutenants were typically only in Dublin Castle from January through March.

You might already see the discrepancy—because the Easter Rising took place in April. Knowing Dublin Castle was a central focus during the Rising, and because of the convenient presence of The Red Cross, I decided to extend the Lord Lieutenant's occupancy by a month so that the Castle could remain a featured setting in the final confrontation.

**Miscellaneous Facts**

The Dublin Metropolitan Police were in charge of policing the city and surrounding parts of the county, with the Royal Irish Constabulary responsible for the rest of Ireland. Collin's refusing of the gun from Baze was a nod to the DMP being an unarmed force.

The Irish blessing spoken over Finn and Emily's marriage was a real Irish blessing. It was a blessing of light, which I felt was appropriate to signify the overcoming of the darkness they faced.

I have stood in the small chapel at Glendalough where Emily sings "Amazing Grace." I went with a group in college, and we all squeezed inside and sang our own rendition of "Amazing Grace," complete with a cappella harmonies and beautiful acoustics.

The cross at the Rock of Cashel upon which Finn sees the face of Jesus Christ is called St. Patrick's Cross. Typical high crosses in Ireland use a circle to support the arms, but this unique cross displays the Latin design of two vertical supports on each side (representing the two criminals crucified with Jesus). Today, one of those arms has been lost to time, and the real cross sits inside the nearby museum, replaced by a concrete replica in its original location.

If you're interested in learning more fun history tidbits and about the book-writing process, follow me on Instagram or Facebook at @jessicaslyauthor or sign up for my newsletter at jessicasly.com.

# Acknowledgements

The creation of this series was an incredible journey that spanned just over 10 years—from when I first got the spark of an idea to when the third and final installment was delivered into your hands, dear reader. I didn't even originally intend it to be a trilogy, but the grace of God and the provision of my publisher made a way for these characters to learn, explore, and grow across three manuscripts—and me right along with them.

First, to my family, thank you for encouraging me to follow this lofty dream of publishing a book and standing by my side while I did it. You listened intently when I would talk about the complicated process or complain about writer's block or gush about my favorite characters. And when each book released, you shouted it to the world. Your love and support mean so much to me.

Miralee Ferrell, Kristen Johnson, and the entire team at Mountain Brook Ink, you came around me like a family and gave a home to these stories. You treated them with care and gave me the encouragement and teaching I needed as I navigated my first venture into publishing. I'm so thankful for you!

My friends and leaders, you showed me an outpouring of support, feedback, direction, encouragement, and prayer. Humans are not meant to do life alone—and the same goes for writing, as solitary as it can be. Thank you for giving me a community where I could go to fill my cup with wisdom and rest.

My readers, the enthusiasm you've shown for these books has floored me. Thank you for the time you've spent reading my books and sending me kind words! I'm so glad you resonated with these characters and have been touched by these stories.

And finally, my savior Jesus Christ, thank you for putting this drive in me—the drive to write, to tell stories, to explore Your love through my characters. You walked next to me through every emotional up and down of this journey and helped me pour wisdom into these books that I wouldn't have been able to come up with on my own.

*Soli deo gloria.*